The Wind Weeps

The Wind Weeps

Anneli Purchase

ACQUILINE

Copyright © 2012 by Anneli Purchase

Manufactured in the United States of America

Published in 2012 by Acquiline

Library and Archives Canada Cataloguing in Publication

Purchase, Anneli, 1947-
    The wind weeps / Anneli Purchase.

ISBN 978-0-9878089-0-5

    I. Title.

PS8631.U73W55 2012   C813'.6   C2011-907905-4

For Gary

Acknowledgements

My husband's expertise and reliable input on commercial fishing and navigating the coast have probably spared me from making some embarrassing mistakes in my writing. Any errors that remain are mine alone.

For their patience in reading my rough drafts, I thank Sonja, Hanna, Maggie, Dawn, Myrtle, Ursula, Lois, and Susan. Thanks to my brother Waldemar for insisting that I get out of my comfort zone to write my story.

Special thanks to two friends:

Darlene Jones, for critiquing, editing, and reading many versions of the manuscript. Thank you for the pep talks when I've felt defeated.

And Kathleen Price, for reading, editing, critiquing, converting files, and guiding me through the process of getting this work published. Your friendship and support mean a lot to me.

The wild winds weep,
And the night is a-cold;
Come hither, Sleep,
And my griefs unfold.

~ From *Mad Song* by William Blake

PART ONE

The Fledgling

Bored, the nestling looks about,
Adventure calls, and she leaps out.
On untrained wings she flutters down,
A spastic fledgling, faltering.
Too far from home, and on foul ground,
She shrinks from shadows all around.
Oh woe, the hasty choice she's made.
Too late, she is awakening.
A shocking truth, Reality,
She fights to keep her dignity.

~ Anneli Purchase

Chapter 1

I knew I must have the wrong address. He was absolutely stunning. My heart fluttered and thudded frantically. Heat rose to my face. I ducked my head in embarrassment, but couldn't keep my eyes off him.

I glanced at the scrap of paper in my hand—Single girl looking for roommate to share expenses. Call Monique. 604-483-5866

The guy who opened the door to the ground level basement suite was serious model material. Lean, broad shoulders, tight jeans, red plaid shirt—the healthy, outdoorsy type. His dark brown hair stuck up in spiky tufts when he took off his cap to greet me.

"Hello. Ah … er … Is Monique here?" I rechecked the address I had scribbled down when I talked to Monique on the phone. "Maybe I have the wrong place?" I backed up a step or two, looking for the house number again, unsure what to do next.

"Andrea?" he asked.

I nodded. "Do you live here?"

"Of course." He looked puzzled by my question.

Three's Company? What was I getting myself into? "Monique didn't say there was another person sharing the suite."

"No, dere isn't. It will be just de two of us."

"I don't think so." No matter how good looking he was, no matter how tempting he was, I wasn't about to move in with a man I'd never met before. I turned to leave.

He reached for my hand and pumped it up and down. "I'm Monique."

"You're Monique?" I stood there with my mouth hanging open as a second surge of warmth crept up my neck to the roots of my hair.

"Don't worry. It 'appen to me all de time. People t'ink I am a boy because of my short 'air and de way I dress."

"I—I'm sorry. How stupid of me." Relief—and disappointment—washed over me.

"Come in. 'Ave a look around and see if you like de place. You say you from Ontario?" I nodded. "*Eh bien*, we are almost neighbours den. I am from Québec."

"Have you been in B.C. long?" I scanned the room behind her as we talked. The place looked clean and bright.

"About a year."

"So what brought you here?"

"Why did you come 'ere?" She smiled as she threw the question back at me. "Probably de same reasons, eh? To be by de sea, to get away from de crowd, to be independent, to find romance, adventure? Am I close?"

"You're right on." We'd get along very well. "I like the place and if you like me, I like you."

Monique smiled broadly displaying beautiful white teeth.

"So you would like to move in?"

"I think so. Yes. But, Monique, if I don't find a job. You know ... I explained on the phone that I can only pay for a month or two if I don't find work soon."

"Dat's no problem," she said. "Dere is always work around 'ere in de tourist season and den after dat, we see."

She sounded so sure of herself. I wished I had her confidence. It had taken every bit of courage I could muster to come out here by myself.

"It's too far. Won't you change your mind?" My mother had clung to me, her face wet with tears. I almost changed my mind right then.

My dad shook his head. "I don't suppose there's any way we can convince you to stay? I hope you won't regret it. You're too stubborn for your own good."

I had put on a brave face and said something clichéd, like "I'll email you," but I had no idea if I'd even have access to a computer in Lund. It looked like a small place when I had chosen it at random on the map. As it turned out, I was right. It was a very small hamlet over four thousand kilometers from home.

No job, only $800 in my purse, no family, no friends— and now this gorgeous hunk of a man turns out to be a woman.

Chapter 2

All right then, little lady," the wharfinger said, "let's go down to the floats. I'll show you how to tie up boats that come in." Bert's huge pot-belly seemed to be a perfect match for his jolly disposition. He was always smiling. "Look here, Andrea. See how this boat is tied up here? We're going to untie it and then I'll retie it and you can watch me." He grunted as he bent over towards the knot. "On second thought," he said, as he straightened up again, "you could use the practice. Just hang onto the end of that line. The boat's still tied at the other end, but we don't want it swinging out and getting away from us."

"Okay, I've got it." How hard could it be?

"You want to make sure the line goes through the metal chock on the boat so it doesn't chafe or you'll have some mighty pissed-off skippers. Most guys'll tie up their own boats, but sometimes you'll have to move a boat to make more room. Or sometimes the inside guy wants to get out. You'll have to retie it, and these are things you want to be careful of."

I listened to everything Bert had to say and watched how he tied the knots. I wanted to show him I could do this job. I needed the money to pay my share of the rent. "You'll do fine," he said after we did a tour of the wharf. I grinned at his compliment. "And with new arrivals, don't forget to get their information. Remind them to check in and pay their moorage. Get their name, address, and boat name and number just in case they try to skip."

Bert pointed to the far side of the dock. "We tie sailboats on that finger over there. Commercial boats on this side."

"Why's that?"

"A heavy commercial fishing boat could damage a flimsy sailboat if the wind or wake knocked them about. Besides, the sailing customers don't like to get grease or fish slime on their fine designer clothes. Some of them fishboats stink and it's just a bit too real for the sailing types."

"Yeah, I got a whiff of one of them back there." I scrunched up my nose and made a face.

Bert laughed. "You're a real city slicker! We'll have to change that." He shook his head, amused. "But you're right. That shrimp boat's a real stinker. They aren't all like that. It's like housekeeping—some are sparkling clean and others ... well ... you'll see."

"It's too bad that shrimp boat is right next to the wharf where everyone has to smell it when they walk past," I said. "If it was on the outside of some of the other boats maybe it wouldn't be as noticeable."

Bert stopped short. "That's not a bad idea." He looked around. Then he pointed. "That's where she could go. We'll untie her and slide her back alongside the Raider. Good practice for you."

"Which end should I untie first?"

"You get the stern line and I'll untie the bow." I did as Bert said. "Hang onto that line, and kick her stern out."

"Kick it out?"

"Yeah, put your foot on the cap railing and push so the back end swings out. We need it to clear the Raider's bow and then we can slide her back. But hang onto that line."

I pushed with one leg on the boat and nothing happened.

"You gotta lean into it. Give it a good shove with all your weight," Bert said. I leaned into it and the boat began to move. "That's it. Now she's starting to swing." Bert smiled and gave me a thumbs-up. "Okay, that's enough pushing."

I tried to pull my leg back but I had too much weight leaning into the boat and not enough left on the wharf. I thought of jumping onto the boat, but I had no leverage and my feet were saying goodbye to each other.

My yell and the splash must have been heard all over the wharf. I sank under the scum-coated surface, closing my mouth just in time. I grasped at the grungy edge of the floating dock. *Damn! It's too high.* Fortunately, Bert's hand was there to haul me out. The ballast of his belly came in handy as a counterweight.

"Oh-h-h-h, yuck!" I was coated in scum and could only imagine what my hair looked like as Bert picked something green out of it.

"Sea lettuce," he said.

"Here's the rope." The sodden line was still clutched in my hand.

Bert's eyeballs nearly popped out of his head.

"Good girl." He quickly tied a couple of loops of the shrimp boat's bow line to the dock.

Two fishermen ran over to help. "There's showers beside the office at the top of the wharf. You go on. We'll tie up," one of them said. He looked down to hide a smile.

I was happy to get away from their stares, but the one who had spoken came running after me.

"Wait a minute," he said. "You'll need a change of clothes. I have some sweats you can put on and a towel you can borrow."

"That would be great. Thanks." My sodden T-shirt clung to me and there was no way I could hide my hard nipples.

I was too cold and embarrassed to be flattered by his gaze, but to his credit he seemed to be making an effort to keep his eyes focused above my neck. I was grateful for that small consideration.

"My boat's right over here—the Serenity. Wait here while I get the stuff. Oh, my name's Jim."

"Andrea," I said, through chattering teeth, arms clasped across my breasts.

That night Monique and I lounged on the threadbare sofa sharing a bag of potato chips and watching a rerun of an old sitcom.

"For sure t'ing you made de impression today, eh?" Monique punched me playfully in the upper arm and edged a bit closer to me. "I wish I could be dere to see you fall in. Den I be de 'ero and pull you out. Save you, no?"

"Just as well you didn't see it. I think I looked pretty bad. And I felt so stupid!" I shuddered, remembering the splash of that bracing cold water. "Not a great start to my plan of becoming a capable independent woman."

"Oh for sure t'ing, it will 'appen," Monique said. "So tell me, what make you come to dis rough tough province?"

She crowded closer and turned to look into my eyes for an answer. I squirmed to the corner of the sofa and propped a pillow on my lap.

"My parents had my life all planned out for me," I said. "Secretary in an office somewhere. Maybe a government job since I knew enough French. I'd be set for the rest of my life. I tried it for a couple of years, but, you know, the same old thing every day ... I was going nowhere fast."

"Sound like my parents too, except dey say 'learn English so you can get a government job.' Bor-r-ring!"

"Exactly! After a while I'd want to kill myself. Well, not really, but you know what I mean."

"Sure, I know exactly."

We munched on chips absentmindedly. The sitcom was pretty lame and my thoughts drifted home.

"Andrea," I could hear my mother saying, "you want a nice house and car someday, don't you? If you want the life, you need a job with security and benefits. It's the only way to go."

Yeah, and end up like you. Lower middle class dull suburbia. Mediocre house, mediocre car, mediocre life. And for that you're running yourselves ragged in your hamster-wheel existence, going round and round, getting nowhere fast. I wanted out of the cage.

"Have you heard the saying, 'Go West, young man'?" I asked Monique.

She shook her head. "Maybe an English saying?"

"Maybe. No matter. I think it's wrong. It should be, 'Go West, young woman.' Out West is where the men are. The fishing and logging jobs are filled with big, strong men.

Back in Ontario, because of the government offices, we've got women galore, but not so many men."

"So maybe it should be 'Go East, young man,'" Monique suggested.

"Yeah, well that hasn't happened yet. Seems like we have three women to every man in Ontario. I don't mean I was coming to B.C. just to find a man, but I want some adventure in my life—and okay, maybe a man. Don't you?" I looked to Monique for agreement, but she had a funny look on her face, as if she'd swallowed a bitter pill.

The wharf was a buzz of activity. Two old-timers argued the merits of fiberglass over wood as a third fellow chiseled out a piece of rot from the stern of a troller. The skipper of a gillnetter worked on a tear in a net that was stretched out partway over the float. Yet another fisherman sat on the edge of his boat, talking to a friend about grouse hunting spots for the fall.

Ah, there he was! Jim crouched on the dock moving a sander along the Serenity's cap railing. Even through his coveralls, I could tell he was in good shape. Slim, but not skinny.

"Good morning," I called. He gave no indication of having heard me over the noise of the sander. I moved closer to the boat and bent forward to look up at his face. "Jim?"

"Oh!" He turned with a jump and the sander whined into silence.

"Sorry. I didn't mean to startle you." I handed him a plastic bag. "Thanks for lending me the soap and shampoo, and all that stuff yesterday. I brought your towel and your clothes back, laundered and dried."

"You look a lot drier today too." Jim smiled warmly.

Friendly guy. Handsome, even coated in sanding dust. His hair and eyebrows were powdered beige with it. He removed his glasses and reached into his coveralls pocket.

"Huh. Thought I had a Kleenex."

I dug into my own pocket and pulled out a crumpled tissue.

"Here. Pretty sure it's clean."

"Hope so." He smirked as he gave his glasses a quick wipe and put them back on. "That's better. Now I can see you. That dust was getting pretty thick." He seemed awkward making small talk, looking at the boards on the dock and at his boat, as if he found it hard to maintain eye contact. So much for "Now I can see you."

"Good thing you wear glasses or you'd have that stuff caked in your eyes." Cool blue eyes, that I'd love to gaze into, if he ever looked at me long enough to give me a chance.

"Aw, it gets into every pore, but I'm used to it. Same thing every year, getting the boat ready."

"Ready for...?" Maybe he was going on a trip?

"Fishing. Salmon fishing." His brow furrowed. "You were kidding, right?"

"No, I'm from Ontario. I don't know much about the West Coast—yet." I hated to admit it. "But I want to learn," I added quickly. An awkward moment of silence followed. *Probably thinks I'm an idiot.*

"Well, I'd better get back to work. I have the ways booked for this afternoon."

Now I knew he was trying to get rid of me, but I couldn't stop myself from asking, "Ways? What's that?"

"Over there, near the hotel." He pointed towards the beach. "They haul the boat out of the water and you work on the bottom."

"The bottom?" Dammit. I had to stop parroting what he said. I sounded so stupid.

"Of the boat. You know, power wash the hull. Repaint it with copper paint."

"Do you need any help with that? I'm always looking for work. Gotta pay the rent."

He hesitated. It took so long before he answered that I wished I hadn't asked.

"I've put you in an awkward position. I know you're thinking I don't know anything about boats, but I'm a fast learner and a hard worker." I put on my most hopeful and eager expression.

"I suppose I could use a hand to copper paint. I should be ready to do that about four this afternoon. If you're interested that's where I'll be." He pointed again. "Wear your worst clothes."

I grinned and nodded. "All right! See you there."

"And a cap."

"A cap?" *Oh, no. Did it again.*

"Wear a cap." It was an order. "You don't want to get copper paint in that beautiful hair. Maybe tie it up somehow in a pony tail or something." His hands went over his head making "hairdoing" motions.

"Sure thing." He thought I had beautiful hair. So maybe I didn't blow it altogether. The day was turning out fine. I'd just landed another bit of a job, and working around a handsome guy, too. I tried not to gloat as I sashayed away smiling to myself.

Chapter 3

After working my hours at the wharf—it was only part time so far—I hurried home. I pulled open my dresser drawers and rummaged for shabby clothes. Naturally, I hadn't left Ontario with a bag of rags. But I did find one pair of jeans that were beaters. They would have to do.

I heard the key turn in the lock. Monique pushed open the door, kicked off her boots, and hung up her floater coat on a hook behind the door.

"Andrea," she called into the bedroom, "you won't believe it. Skipper George let me drive de water taxi partway over to Savary Island. 'E say soon I be able to do de trip by myself."

"That's wonderful, Monique." I came out to the living room, ready to go. "I wish I knew how to do things like that. But maybe I'll learn yet. What a great job you have. Traveling all the time."

Monique chuckled. "Yeah, back and fort', back and fort' all de time between Lund and Savary Island. But sometime dere will be odder trips, George say. Maybe Squirrel Cove, if de wedder is good." She stared at my stained jeans. "Are you going out? ... Like dat?"

"Helping Jim. He's having the Serenity hauled out and I got a job helping copper paint the hull. He said to wear my worst clothes, so that's what I'm doing."

"Aw, no. You 'ave to t'row dose clothes away when you finish. Maybe 'e got some coveralls for you. And what about your 'air? Your beautiful long brown 'air—" She took a tress of my hair and let it trail through her fingers.

"Oh! Thanks for reminding me. I'm supposed to wear a cap. But I don't even have one. I guess I should go buy one."

"No way! You can't go and buy a cap in dat tourist shop. You pay way too much. I give you a cap to wear."

"But it'll get ruined. I can't do that."

"No matter. Is an old one. Really old. You can 'ave it." She ran to her bedroom and I heard the closet door slide open. She came back with a weathered blue cap. "Ere," she said, "let me do your 'air for you and put it under de cap."

Her touch was gentle as she brushed up my hair and fastened it with an elastic. I closed my eyes and thought of the handsome young man who had first opened the door. Little bubbles of excitement danced in the pit of my stomach. My eyes snapped open. *Oh God! Am I enjoying this too much?* Then Monique put the cap on my head and stood back to admire her work.

"*Charmante!*" she said, and gave me a lingering kiss on the cheek. I picked up my bag and hurried out the door.

Chapter 4

I walked briskly to Stan's Marine Ways. Monique's kiss still burned. There was nothing wrong with a kiss on the cheek, was there? That was the French way. Right. They were always kissing. Even the men. You saw it on TV all the time. Presidents and such. It was nothing. I was making too much of it. *Just forget it.*

Jim and another man were slowly hauling the Serenity towards the beach in a cradle rolling on railway tracks that stretched out into the water. A cable winch powered by a motor higher up on land towed the cradle. When the boat was nearly out of the water, the winch stopped. The Serenity, leaning towards one side of the cradle, had been loosely tied to scaffolding that ran along both sides of the boat. Once the towing was finished, Jim tightened the tie-up ropes and the other man propped up the boat with thick timbers.

"That should do it." The man wiped his hands on his coveralls. "I'll leave you to it."

"Okay. Thanks, Stan," Jim said. "She should be ready to go back in the water by tomorrow evening."

"Right. See you then."

Jim looked me over and scowled as I approached.

"What?" I asked. "Something wrong?"

"Yeah. I thought you were going to wear your worst clothes."

"These are them." I raised my arms up and dropped them limply at my sides.

"You have no idea, do you?"

I felt my face heating up. He shook his head and climbed up the ladder that was tied to the side of the hull. Above me, in the wheelhouse of the Serenity, I heard him moving things around, and moments later he came back down the ladder. "Here." He tossed me a bundle of clothes. "Put these on."

The coveralls were way too big and I had to roll up the cuffs of the legs and arms. They covered me completely, but the crotch was down by my knees. They made these things to fit giants. Oh well, it wasn't a fashion show.

Jim looked at me and laughed. He climbed the ladder again. This time he brought a pair of gum boots down from the boat. "You'll have to put these on," he said. "Those dainty runners just won't cut it. We need to work on the bottom as soon as the tide goes out far enough to expose the hull and that often means standing in a bit of water. Anyway, even at dead low tide, it's mucky down there."

I was embarrassed to think how unprepared I was. I stuck my feet into the boots and put the runners on the cement retaining wall beside the boat. The boots were huge. I clomped around in them struggling to lift them with each step, hampered always by the low crotch of the coveralls. I felt hobbled. I took a deep breath to renew my determination. "So what would you like me to do first?"

"You can do the power washing of the hull. Have you used a power washer before?" At my shake of the head, Jim sighed. "No, of course not."

He went up to the shop at the top of the beach and got a coil of hose. He tossed it over towards me.

"Go attach the end of the hose to that tap over there." He dragged the power washer to the side of the boat, attached the other end of the hose to it, and set the machine on the retaining wall.

"Turn on the tap," he said. "Now watch carefully." He started the gas engine on the power washer and showed me how to run the wand back and forth to clean the boat.

"Okay, I think I've got it." I reached for the wand. "It looks pretty simple."

But Jim didn't hand it over. He picked up a block of wood. "Watch." He held the nozzle of the wand a couple of inches from the wood and squeezed the trigger to start the spray. Seconds later he stopped. "Now, see that?"

I nodded and tried to remember to keep my mouth closed. "Wow! It sure chewed a hole in that wood."

"That is what I do NOT want happening to my boat."

"For sure. I'll be really careful."

"Stay a good distance away from the wood and don't stop and spray one spot for too long."

"Got it." I reached for the wand again, but Jim pulled it away out of my reach.

"And another thing. Don't ever forget that the pressure in that spray is strong enough to chew up your toes right through your boots if you're careless about where you point the nozzle. Think of it as a loaded gun. And don't ever point it at a person—or yourself."

I gulped and finally took the wand from him. I'd come to help and it seemed all I was doing was making more work and worry for Jim.

The power washing turned out to be fun though. I loved the way the gunk flew off the hull with the powerful water spray, leaving the wood so clean. Green sludge and hairy seaweed were forced to loosen their grip on the wooden planks. I got all the higher parts done first, and as the tide ebbed, I was able to crawl under the boat's big belly where a few barnacles clung stubbornly to the underneath parts. I stepped back to admire the clean surface from bow to stern. The rusty burgundy of the previous year's copper paint had soaked right into the wood.

"It hardly seems to need painting," I said. "It looks so pretty the way it is."

Jim crawled out from the cramped space where he was working near the bottom of the hull on the other side. "It's cleaner now, but without a new coat of anti-fouling paint, it would be covered in weeds and barnacles in no time. Can't afford to have any teredos latch on and start digging into the wood."

"What's a teredo?"

"It's actually a kind of clam but looks more like a worm. They call them shipworms. If they get into the wood, it's bad. Like getting termites in a house."

"Oh, no wonder you have to do this copper painting then." Now it was starting to make sense to me.

Jim nodded. "I've got the zincs replaced on the far side. I'll trade you sides."

"Yeah, okay. Why do you have to put zincs on?" I know I sounded like a complete idiot, but I wouldn't learn if I didn't ask.

"Electrolysis would eat away the metal parts of the boat, like the propeller, the rudder, and the nails that hold the boat together. I put zinc bars on for it to eat instead." My face must have had a blank look as I tried to understand what he was talking about. He waved me off. "Never mind. Too complicated to explain. Trust me. They're needed."

I made a mental note to look up electrolysis. "Wow! You sure have to know a lot of stuff to run a boat. I used to think you just had to get aboard and steer."

"Yeah, I can see how you'd think that." He shook his head as if he was barely able to tolerate having me around.

"Guess I left myself open for that one. But you know, we have things back East that maybe you don't know everything about."

"I'm sure," he said, rolling his eyes and turning away.

I picked up the power washer wand to get back to work. I could see Jim was running out of patience with all my questions. *Way to go, Andrea. You're too stupid for words.* I would just have to show him I could do a good job and impress him that way.

I held the nozzle at the distance he had shown me and began to wash the far side of the hull. Sticky, stinky copper spray flew everywhere. As I glanced down and saw the condition of the coveralls, I realized what Monique was talking about when she told me I'd have to throw away my clothes after doing this job. I concentrated on the planks and cleaned them one by one. I felt all-powerful. Barnacles, mussels, and green slime—gone with one pass of my magic wand.

A long lump was sticking out between two of the planks, so I held the nozzle a little closer to get it out. Just a quick zap. The lump was a bit stubborn so I gave it another quick zap. And another, and another. At last it was starting to come off. God! It was a long one. Must be one of those teredos Jim was talking about. Well, he'd be glad I found it and got it out of there. I blasted it the whole length of the plank until a long piece of it plopped onto the ground. I laid down the wand.

"Jim! Come see this. Get a load of this teredo I found." Since I had gloves on I didn't mind picking it up to show him. When he came around to my side, I held it up and he looked shocked, just like I figured he would.

He turned pale and stammered. "Wh-where'd you get that?"

"Right here." I pointed to the space between two planks.

"Jesus Christ!" he yelled. "Didn't I tell you not to get that nozzle in there so close?"

"B-b-but I had to get it out of there." A stab of fear went through me.

"God dammit! You are the stupidest broad I've ever met!"

"I don't understand." I could feel tears welling up. I blinked hard so they wouldn't spill, but it was useless.

"This is the caulking between the planks. It stops the water from getting in. Oh, Jeezus!" He threw down his wrench and stomped off in the direction of the shop.

I sat down on the retaining wall and stared at my boots. No, not my boots—Jim's. My chin quavered as I fought to hold back more tears. I clasped my hands together between my knees and wondered what to do next. Should I get out of these coveralls and go home? No. I wasn't a quitter. I had really messed up, but I had to make it better or I'd never live it down.

When I discovered the "teredo," the job was nearly finished. I picked up the wand and washed everywhere except near the plank seam. In a short time, I had the last bit of the hull clean. I coiled up the hose and took the power washer up to the shop. I met Jim coming out with an armful of white fuzzy stuff and a couple of tools. He walked past me without a word and started working on the open seam. He stuffed an end of the wooly rope into the space between the planks and tapped it in with a little tool and a mallet. It didn't take him long to refill the seam.

Then he smeared some stuff that looked like putty over it. I kept out of his way, but watched him as he worked.

When he finished, I went over to him. "Jim?... I'm really sorry I made extra work for you. You don't have to pay me. I figure if you count the work I did and the work I caused, that makes us about even."

Jim sighed and looked at the ground. Then he looked at me. The corners of his mouth twitched. "I'm sorry I yelled." He tried to stifle a laugh.

"What's so funny?"

"You should see your face."

"Well, I can't very well see it, can I?" A sharp sigh of frustration escaped me. First he yelled at me; then he laughed at me.

"Trust me. You're a sight." His tone was lighthearted and his face softened. A smile continued to twitch around the corners of his mouth. "Look, let's call it a day. We'll copper paint tomorrow."

"We? You mean me too? You still want me to work for you tomorrow?" I crossed my fingers behind my back and hoped for the right answer.

"Yeah, I don't think there's any more harm you can do."

Chapter 5

Monique stirred hamburger bits in the frying pan. It didn't look all that good, but smelled wonderful. "'Ow did it go today?" I sputtered out a big sigh and stripped off my clothes in the entrance.

"Dat bad, eh?"

"Tell you all about it after I shower off this crap." I stomped down the hall to the bathroom. The hot water felt good as it pummeled my skin, washing away the scum that had transferred from the boat's hull to me. The coveralls hadn't protected my hands, face, neck, and hair, nor could they stop the odour from penetrating my skin. The iodine smell of decayed sea creatures had mingled with the copper and creosote of old "anti-fouling paint" as I'd heard Jim call it. I had to shampoo twice to loosen the sticky hunks of paint and god-knows-what-all from my hair. Bundled in my bathrobe and a towel on my head, turban-style, I padded back into the kitchen and slumped down on a chair.

"*Eh bien*?" Monique gestured with the wooden spoon. "Not a good day?"

Again, I blew out a big sigh. "I learned a lot, but I sure screwed up."

"What 'appened? I mean you just went to scrub de boat, right?"

"Yeah, that's what I thought. Like 'how hard can it be?' But apparently there was more to it than I expected."

"Well, don't keep me in suspense." She strained the macaroni that had been boiling on the stove.

I told her an abbreviated version of how I thought I was cleaning a teredo off and blew the caulking out of the boat. "Not my finest hour." I fought back tears.

"'Ey, don't look so glum. Is not de end of de worl'." She put an arm around my back and rubbed my shoulder. "We all make mistakes."

Somehow, all my resolve to be tough in spite of my bad day weakened at the touch of Monique's hands. "I guess so." I sniffed and wiped my dripping nose with the back of my hand. "It's just that ... I kind of like Jim, but the more I tried to impress him, the worse things got. I totally screwed up, but after he got mad at me—okay, which I deserved—he turned around and laughed at me. He said I was a sight. And I don't think he meant that in a good way." I didn't tell Monique that Jim seemed to be so disgusted with me that I thought he'd never want me to work on his boat again.

"Well, when you came in de door first, you would not win a beauty contest." She stood back smiling at me with her hands on her hips. "But maybe now dat you 'ave showered, you might."

"Oh, Monique." I waved away her compliment. I smiled and swallowed the lump in my throat. "Let's eat. What kind of dogfood have you got for us today?"

"'Ey! You just wait. It might look like dogfood, but it will taste delicious." She loaded up two plates and brought them to the table.

"Thanks, Monique. I'll deal with my hair later." I picked up my knife and fork. "You don't mind, do you?"

"Not at all. I t'ink de turban is perfect wit' de curry in de 'amburger."

Chapter 6

The next morning, I got up early to report to Bert at the wharf. "I just need a few hours to help with the copper painting of the Serenity today. I can make up the time by working on the dock here over the weekend."

"Okay," Bert said. "It's not very busy during the week right now. Just be sure you show up Saturday morning."

"Thanks, Bert." I patted his hand and gave him a quick smile. I grabbed my bundle of work clothes—the cap and an extra old shirt—and headed to the haulout yard a short distance from the government wharf.

Jim was already working. He had a small propane tank set up with a torch heating what looked like a giant soup ladle. In it, a lump of metal was slowly melting into silvery liquid. I didn't bother to yell "Good morning" to Jim over the blowing roar of the torch. I gave him a wave and he nodded back to me. He motioned for me to keep back from the melting metal, and climbed the ladder to the wheelhouse. He tossed me the coveralls and boots. By the time I was dressed, he had poured copper paint into a tray and placed a roller and a brush nearby.

"Take this masking tape and go all around the boat, taping it above the water line so the copper paint won't get on the white paint of the upper part of the boat."

"Sure. Just like taping the woodwork when you paint the walls of a house." I'd helped Mom do that back home.

"Exactly. Then, once you get it all taped, you can start painting. Use the roller on the big spaces and the brush on the parts near the keel that are harder to reach."

"Got it."

"And keep away from the torch. Molten zinc is a hell of a lot hotter than boiling water."

"What's it for?"

"That gets poured into the tin can I fitted over the wheel nut—" My brows furrowed in confusion. "Back there, by the propeller—to protect it from electrolysis. Same way the zinc bars work."

"I remember. The zinc gets 'eaten away' instead of the metal parts of the boat."

Jim looked surprised. "That's right."

"But why a tin can?"

"It's like a mold. When the zinc hardens, I knock off the tin can."

"I'm really impressed. I had no idea."

"Just be sure to keep out of the way till I get it poured."

I got busy with the taping and then dipped into the copper paint. The first roller pass I made coloured the boards a beautiful rusty red. Jim jumped up and took the roller from me. Now what was wrong? I stood there and watched, dumbfounded, as he reworked the patch I had just done. He spread out the paint until he'd covered a much larger area and the coat was quite a bit thinner. "I forgot to tell you. Treat this stuff as if it's liquid gold."

"Why?"

"Because that's almost how much it costs. So put on the least amount you can get away with and still cover the area."

After a while I started to get the hang of it. *Don't press hard with the roller after first dipping it, and then press harder as the paint is used up.* I chuckled to myself as I imagined my mom's face if she could only see me now. She wouldn't recognize the daughter who grumbled about having to help paint the bedrooms at home.

In my mind I saw her all dressed up in her tan linen skirt and blazer, matching beige pumps, watching me work. Her jaw would drop in horror to see me in these coveralls with the crotch just at the top of Jim's size 10 gumboots. She'd look at me with disdain if she saw the crud in my hair and the gobs of paint that were already sticking to my cheeks and neck from absentminded touching. I heard her shriek at the sight of me.

Wait a minute. Mom's not here. I heard a shout followed by two short low-pitched cries. I dropped the roller and ran toward the noise. A splash of silvery metal solidifying on the gravel caught my eye. *What the...?* Jim slumped against the rudder of the boat. He reached for his face with shaking hands.

"No, don't!" I called. "Don't touch it. Let me look."

One eye was closed. The skin around it was already bright red. I tore off my gloves and flicked bits of molten zinc from his cheeks and temple. Again he reached for the closed eye. "I—I—think ...," he said in a feeble, jittery voice.

"Oh, my God, Jim. We've got to get you to a hospital." The hand he raised to his eye had no skin on part of his wrist. "You've got a bad burn on your wrist."

He held his wrist out in front and tried to look at it with his good eye. "Oh, Jesus," he moaned.

"Don't touch anything. You have to keep it clean. And we have to get some help."

"Is the torch off?"

"Yes, you must have turned it off before you tried to pour the zinc."

"It was all going fine and all of a sudden it bubbled and splattered."

"Yeah, I see it burned a hole in your shirt too." I unbuttoned the shirt and carefully pulled it away from his stomach. "Lucky the cloth took up a lot of the heat. You should have been wearing coveralls." He winced as I pulled specks of zinc off his skin. "Hang on. I'll go for help."

I ran up to the shop. "Hello?" I yelled. "Anybody here?"

I followed the sound of an electric tool to the far end of the shop. Stan looked up from his grindstone and shut the machine off. "Come quick," I blurted out. "Jim's hurt."

He dropped what he was doing and ran for the Serenity. "Jim? What's up?" As Stan got closer, he grimaced. "Oh, Jeezus!" he whispered as he saw Jim splashed with zinc, trembling and moaning. "Nearest hospital's in Powell River," he said to me.

"But that's seventeen miles away."

"Best we can do. Let's get going. My truck's parked out back."

We took Jim by the elbows and led him through the shop to the parking lot. While Stan helped Jim into the truck I whipped off my coveralls and threw them into the back. Then I hopped in beside Jim.

Stan drove as if the back of the truck was on fire. "How're you doing, Jim?" he asked after a while.

"Good enough. I just hope my eye will be okay."

"Turn towards me," I told Jim. "Can you open it at all?"

"It is open, but I can't see anything."

"It may feel like it's open but the area around it is quite swollen. That's probably why you can't see. With any luck your reflexes saved your eye." I sent a desperate prayer to the heavens and thought how odd it was that believer and non-believer alike sent up prayers in times of need. "Here, let me hold that wrist so you don't rub it on anything and get dirt in it. There's a little patch that looks quite raw." I lifted Jim's hand and gently cradled it in mine. I felt it trembling ever so slightly and my heart went out to him for his pain and the shock he had suffered. "We should be there soon. Right, Stan?"

"Not too much longer."

A short time later Stan screeched to a stop at the hospital's Emergency entrance.

Stan took Jim's wallet out of his back pocket for him, riffled through it and handed over his medical card. The receptionist typed and asked questions related to the injury. She didn't seem to be overly concerned about Jim's condition. Maybe she saw too much of this kind of thing and for her it was "business as usual." Still, it always annoyed me how all this administrative processing took precedence over helping a patient.

I leaned over the counter. "Couldn't you do this later? Can't you see he needs a doctor. Now!"

Jim put his hand on my arm. "Andrea ... it's okay."

"No, it's not okay. They're supposed to be helping you." I turned to the receptionist. "Have you called for a doctor yet?"

"Yes, I have, Miss," she said through tight lips. "We do have other patients here."

I let out a loud sigh and sank back from the counter. "Okay," I said quietly. "But could you try to hurry? Please?"

After what seemed forever, a doctor appeared and led Jim to a cubicle to tend to his injuries.

Out in the waiting room, Stan and I sat down. I clasped and unclasped my hands, finally clamping them between my knees.

"Worrying isn't going to help, you know," Stan said.

"I know. Can't help it though. I feel like it's my fault."

"Oh, how's that?" Stan tilted his head at me.

I looked up at his grease-smudged face. "We didn't have a good day yesterday. I did so many things wrong. Jim was frustrated with me."

"Yeah. I know about the caulking. But that was yesterday."

Oh, no! Everybody knows. I'll never live it down.

"I think Jim was worrying about me doing things wrong, and so maybe he wasn't concentrating on what he was doing when he poured the zinc."

"Oh, I don't think so." Stan waved away the idea of my guilt.

"He was about to start on the zinc when I picked up the roller and had too much paint on it. He came running over to show me how to do it without wasting so much paint. See what I mean? He wasn't thinking about what he was doing."

"Now, don't you go beating yourself up over this." He patted my knee sympathetically. "Jim's got to take responsibility for it."

"I feel so bad that he's hurt." I blinked back the tears that prickled in my eyes, and swallowed to regain my composure.

"I know. It's a tough break, but he should've known better." Stan shook his head. "He's been doing this for years. He should've been wearing a leather apron. He should've been wearing goggles. I got 'em up in the shop for him to use. He knows that."

"I hadn't even thought of that. At least his glasses saved him from the bigger splashes, but they're just those narrow fashionable ones."

"And he should've had leather gloves on." Stan clicked his tongue. "Using a rag to hold the ladle. Damn stupid, if you ask me."

I helped myself to a tissue from the box on the waiting room table and blew my nose. "Still, I feel bad for him."

"Aw, me too. I've known that kid for years. He used to fish with his dad and they'd come in to Lund every spring to get the boat ready. Said they liked the quiet pace."

"He's been fishing for a while then?"

"Oh, hell yes! Been on his own boat for ten years."

"It didn't work out? Fishing with his dad?"

"Sure it did. His dad taught him everything he knows about fishing and running a boat. But the old man had a heart attack out on the fishing grounds one year. Jim had to bring the boat home by himself. He was only about seventeen."

"What about his dad? Was he dead on the boat all that time?" I shuddered. "That would have been horrible."

"No, no, no. The Coast Guard sent a chopper to medevac him, even though he was a goner by the time they got there, but then Jim was alone on the boat. They offered to bring someone to help him get the boat to port but he said no thanks, he could do it."

"Wow! That would have taken some guts."

"Yup! Brought it all the way in to Masset from the west coast of the Charlottes. He called me from there. I flew up and helped him get the boat home to Comox."

"Was that the Serenity?"

"No, he bought that the next year. He couldn't fish his dad's boat. Sold it. Be like fishing with a ghost."

That must have been so hard for him, to carry on by himself. Everything would be a reminder. "What about his mother?"

"Long gone."

"Dead too?"

"No. Long gone. Took off. Moved to Alberta. Couldn't handle all those summers alone. Happens to a lot of fishermen's wives. Too lonely, too long. Can't blame 'em."

"I wouldn't want that kind of life, staying home alone for the whole summer while my husband was away. I think I'd rather fish with him." *What an adventure that would be. I wouldn't mind that at all—with Jim.*

"It's a tough life. Hard, hard work. And then there're the ones that don't mind the work but they can't get over being seasick. That always does them in. Nothing worse than nausea. You just wish you could die."

"You sound like you know how it is. Do you get seasick then?" *I wondered how I would manage with the heaving ocean. Would I heave too?*

"No, but my wife did. And rather than have her take off on me like so many others I'd seen, I quit fishing."

"That must have been a tough decision."

"Yeah, but I like being around boats so I got this haulout shop going. Almost as good as being out there. I still do some sport fishing and I deckhand for some of the old-timers now and then. At least I still have a wife."

I could do it though. Marry a fisherman. I know I could. But what if I got seasick too? "A girl should probably think twice before marrying a fisherman."

"For sure. But on the plus side, there's never a shortage of good fishing yarns, and there's never a dull moment living with a fisherman—so my wife says, anyway."

When we got back to the Serenity, Stan and I insisted that Jim climb the ladder and lie down in his bunk.

"Look here, Jim," Stan said. "I've been working around boats my whole life. I think I can finish this here job without screwing up." The tools lay on the ground just as we'd left them when we took off to the hospital a few hours earlier. Jim headed for the propane torch.

"Don't do that, Jim. You'll get your bandages dirty. I can give Stan a hand and then tidy up." I took Jim's arm on one side and tried to lead him to the ladder.

"But I feel so useless." He gestured at all the tools lying around.

"Come on, Jim," Stan said. "There's a time to buck up and be a man, and then there's a time to use common sense. You get infection in that burn, you'll be paying for it later."

"I can't afford to miss out on the season." Jim's tone was less insistent.

"That's right. You're damn lucky your eye's going to be okay, but you'd better take care of that wrist or it can still turn bad. Andrea and I can handle this." Jim's good eye flicked over to me. He took a deep breath and let it out slowly. He was giving in.

"Yes, go lie down. I can finish the copper painting. Stan can supervise and pour your zinc. I know what to do. I'll go easy on the paint and still make sure everything is coated."

"We'll have it all done in plenty of time to put you back in the water tonight ... if we stop flapping our gums and get to work, that is. So go on. Get out of our hair and let us get on with it."

Under Stan's guidance I managed to do a pretty good job of the copper painting. He melted the zinc and poured it into the tin can form around the wheel nut. We fastened the cooling pipes back on the hull and made sure every last thing was tidied up as the tide began to trickle in under the boat.

After a two-hour nap, Jim emerged from the wheelhouse and climbed down the ladder using only his good hand for support. One eye was covered by a patch and his burnt wrist was wrapped and the arm tied in a sling. "You look like Captain Hook." That got a little half-smile out of him. "Feeling better?"

"Yeah, that painkiller they gave me at the hospital sure knocked me out. What time is it anyway?"

"Nearly four. Stan poured the zinc, and the copper painting is finished. Your tools are all up on the deck, and everything is done." I hoped he would be impressed. "The paint roller and brush are still out. I thought you might want to check things over before I put them away."

Jim nodded. "Looks really good. Where's Stan?"

"Up in the shop. He said to call him when you're up."

"Okay, I'll do that." Jim walked around the boat, looked at the wheel nut and the newly poured zinc. He checked out the hull from bow to stern. "Nice paint job, Andrea. Very good." I glowed inside with his praise. "You were right."

"About what?"

"When you said you're a quick learner."

"Thanks." So, I wasn't hopeless around boats after all. "It's been fun." Jim's eyebrows rose. "In a back-breaking way."

"It *is* hard work, isn't it? I wish the general public was more aware of that. Most people think all we do is sit back and swill our beer while we wait for the fish to bite, and that we rape the ocean. Like we eat all the fish ourselves."

"I know. I'm ashamed to admit I used to think that, before I came to work at the wharf."

"Speaking of eating, what do you say to a bit of supper at the hotel? My treat. A special thanks for playing nurse today."

After yesterday's teredo incident, I was tickled to think he still wanted my company.

"But don't you have to stay and get put back in the water now?"

"In a few hours, when the tide is high. We'll be right next door. We can see what the tide's doing. If you want you can come with me when I get put down—the boat, I mean. You can be my eyes and guide me back to the wharf."

"Sure! That reminds me, what about your glasses? You can't really wear them with that big patch on your eye, I guess."

"Not really, but I can manage without them. Just can't see faraway things very clearly."

"Well, I'll be your eyes for the trip around the corner." I'd love to go for a ride in the boat, even if it was only about a quarter of a mile. Too bad there wouldn't be much chance to tidy up before that. I'd rather look and smell nice, but I'd have to settle for a quick wash in the bathroom of the haulout shop. At least I could get some of the copper paint off my hands before we went for supper.

When we arrived at the government wharf, the sun was low in the sky. I jumped out and tied us to the wharf just as Bert had shown me.

"Thanks for hiring me, Jim. Hope you're feeling better soon." I hesitated, hoping he'd say—I don't know what. But then I realized that was silly and I turned to leave.

"Andrea, wait." Jim chewed his lip and studied the boards of the dock. "I feel really bad about yesterday."

"Why?" I waved him off. "Nothing to feel bad about."

"Yes, there is." He took a deep breath and continued. "I'm not usually such a jerk. I don't blow my cool that easily, especially not with women."

"Aw, that's okay. I did everything wrong." I didn't even like to think about it.

"Well, maybe a few things, but still, it was new to you and you really came through for me. Getting me to the hospital, and finishing up the boat. I was sure I wouldn't be able to get put down till tomorrow at the earliest, and here we are, all finished. Thanks to you."

"My pleasure." I felt I had passed some initiation test and, emboldened, said, "If you know any other fishermen who need their bottoms cleaned ..." I clapped my hands over my mouth, but couldn't stop the laughter from escaping. Jim grinned and immediately winced and reached for his eye. "I mean, if you know anyone needing ... you know ... just let me know, okay?" I shook my head and started to walk away, still giggling.

"As a matter of fact, I do," Jim called after me. "A guy I fish with is bringing his boat to Lund in a few weeks. He'll probably be looking for help when he hauls out. If you're interested, I'll let him know. His boat's the Hawkeye."

"Great! Thanks."

"Just ..."

"Yes?"

"Well, just ... be aware that he's different."

"That's okay. I need the money." I waved goodbye as I headed for home dancing on air.

Chapter 7

"M*on Dieu!*" Monique shouted as I came through the door. "Go look in de mirror." She laughed and jumped up to take my hand in both of hers.

"What's wrong?" I let Monique, still laughing, drag me into the tiny bathroom. I gasped. My face was splattered with copper paint speckles, the bigger patches wrinkled like prune skins. "Oh my God!"

"'Ere." She put the toilet lid down. "Sit, please." Monique ran hot water over a face cloth and put soap on it. I reached for the cloth. "No-no-no, is okay. Let me." She gently rubbed my forehead, cheeks and chin. "Is coming off a little bit, but I t'ink maybe try some face cream. I 'ave some cold cream. Works fine."

As soon as Monique put the face cloth down, I grabbed it to take over the job. "Those spots are really stubborn, aren't they?" I scrubbed and in seconds had several red blotches.

"'Ere, let me do it—please, sit down—wit' de cream first. Nice and soft so we don't wreck your beautiful skin." She must have felt me relax as she massaged my face. "Dat's better. Just enjoy it. I do."

My brow furrowed and she was quick to notice. "Don't worry. Is it not nice for a woman to 'ave someone do somet'ing for 'er once in a while? We don't 'ave to be always de one doing for de odders." She creamed my face gently as a mother with a newborn and rinsed the cloth to wash off the copper paint. I felt tears prickling as I thought of my mother so far away.

"Don't do that anymore, Monique."

"Why not?" She took a step back. "Somet'ing wrong?"

"It reminds me of my mother. Makes me homesick." *And I'm enjoying your touch too much ... but at the same time it creeps me out.*

"Okay. Not a big deal." She left me alone in the bathroom. Oh great! Now I felt really dumb. Did she think I was rude, pushing her away after she'd been so nice to me? Or that I thought she was coming on to me? Of course she wasn't. Was she? What was I trying to tell her? That it made me squirm to be touched by a woman? I couldn't tell her that. She'd think I was accusing her of being a lesbian. I knew better than that. But what if she was one? Well, so what if she was? I argued with myself until my head whirled with questions. I was glad she couldn't read my mind. I liked Monique—a lot—and I wouldn't hurt her feelings for the world.

"So tell me about your day," she called from the living room. Whew! She wasn't mad. "'Ow did Jim like your freckled face?"

"Oh no! I forgot all about that. The whole time we sat in the hotel for supper, I had splatters of copper paint on my face. I mean, I washed my hands. But I used the bathroom in the haulout shop. There's no mirror on the wall in there." That meant that all evening Jim was looking at this speckled face. And so was everyone else in the restaurant. "Oh God," I groaned.

Monique rolled her eyes and shrugged her shoulders. "'E is just a man. What's de big deal?"

I frowned and gave her a questioning look, but she waved it aside. "Never mind," she said.

Then I told her about Jim's accident.

"Dat must 'ave been a shock for you."

"Shock for *him*!" I thought of Jim standing by the boat, pale and traumatized. "But anyway, he's going to be okay. Bad burn on his wrist though. He was lucky the burn around his eye didn't touch the eye itself." What a day it had been. But it had ended well, and with the prospect of another job.

"Say, Monique? You've lived here for quite a while now, haven't you?"

"'Bout a year. Why?"

"Do you know a boat named the Hawkeye?"

"Sure! 'E comes 'ere every few months. Does 'is boat work in de spring and den goes fishing for salmon up nort'. Friendly wit' Jim."

"What's he like?" I wondered if, like Jim, Monique would think he was "different."

"'Andsome guy. Very smart. Can do lots of t'ings—very 'andy man, you know? Can fix anyt'ing. Maybe little bit strange, but good-looking guy."

"Strange?"

"Well, yes. I don't know 'ow exactly. 'E can be talking about one t'ing and den all of a sudden 'e stop and talk about somet'ing completely different. I don't t'ink 'e 'as many friends, dat I know of. Funny t'ing too, when 'e look so good." Monique shrugged her shoulders. "Why you ask?"

"Jim said the guy on the Hawkeye might be looking for help with the haulout. Might not be for a few weeks yet, but I'd get some extra pay if he'll hire me."

"Yeah, for sure t'ing. Go for it. Is a job."

Chapter 8

How's that eye today?" I was doing my rounds on the dock and saw Jim through the Serenity's wheelhouse window.

"Son of a bitch! Aw, shit!"

"Does the sight of me upset you that much?" I stepped on board. "What happened?" The countertop by his sink was full of water. I pointed at his shirt. "How'd you get so wet?"

"Trying to fill the kettle. Misjudged lining up the spout with the faucet." He wiped his hand on his shirt.

"Oh, no." I looked around. "Do you have a rag?"

He pointed. "But hey, I don't expect you to do that."

I quickly sopped up the water from the counter. "Won't take me a minute. So, how's the eye?"

"Not too bad. A bit tender." He reached for his eye patch gingerly. "Damn patch is a nuisance. I'll be glad when I can take it off and get my depth perception back."

"I hadn't thought about that. I guess it would make a difference with only one eye."

"Yeah, I just proved that." He chuckled and looked embarrassed. Again he tried to maneuver the kettle under the sink using his left hand; the right still thickly bandaged.

I couldn't stand to watch. "Here, let me do that for you." I filled the kettle and put it on the boat stove. "There you go. Tea coming up in no time." I turned and nearly bumped into him.

He put his good hand on my shoulder to stop me from connecting with his bandaged hand and sore eye. Gently, he let the hand trail down my arm. Tingles rushed through me. "Sure glad you stopped in. Thanks a lot." He gave me a quick peck on the cheek, but let it linger. My stomach fluttered. Did it mean anything? Or was it just a peck?

"This water should be boiling in about twenty minutes," he said. "Would you like to come have a cup of tea with me then? I'm assuming they give you a break from work."

"Sure, okay. See you shortly."

I hustled around the two fingers of the dock checking all the lines and making sure none of the boats were rubbing against each other. By the time I had finished my lap, Jim called out to me, "Tea time."

He had set up a feast on the small table in the wheelhouse—bagels, cold-smoked sockeye, and red onion. "It should have cream cheese to spread on the bagel first, but without a fridge it doesn't keep."

"Boy, this is pretty nice! So how did you keep the fish and the bagel if you don't have a fridge?" He might have got the bagels from the bakery here in Lund, but I wasn't sure if they made them.

"I have a little freezer. Top of the wheelhouse—only place there's room for it. Did you notice that plywood box up there?" I nodded. "Well, it's in there." Jim smirked and looked pleased with himself. "Do you mind pouring the tea?" He put two cups in front of me.

"Happy to. A bit cool out today, isn't it?"

Jim nodded over his mug of tea. "Nice in here though." Did he feel like I did, that the coziness wasn't all to do with the heat from the boat stove?

It was heartwarming to feel so at home. No formal handing the platter around and putting bits of food on side dishes with napkins. Jim loaded a bagel with smoked salmon and red onion and passed it over to me.

"Try this," he said. "I smoked it myself. Turned out good this time, I think." Our fingers brushed. I resisted the urge to let my hand linger.

"You mean it doesn't always?"

"I wish! But no. It's a real crap shoot. Sometimes it's fantastic; other times it's not good enough to feed a dog."

"Do you have a dog?" I knew so little about him. Did he like animals?

"No. I'd like to but it wouldn't be fair to the dog. I'm away fishing so much of the time. Couldn't really give a dog a home."

"Where is home?" Stan had told me when we were at the hospital, but it was a way of making conversation.

"Comox."

"What's it like there?" I wondered why he would choose to spend his time in Lund if he'd decided to live in Comox.

"Quiet. Clean. Nice." Jim handed me another piece of bagel and smoked salmon. "Don't be shy. Help yourself. There's plenty."

"Thanks. But why do you come over here to do your haulout if Comox is so nice?"

"Comox doesn't really have much of a haulout facility. They've got a grid at the marina where you can set your boat. You can work on it when the tide's out, but sometimes that's not enough time. Stan's is better—you're farther out of the water—and ..."

"And?"

"And my dad and I had been coming here for years before he died. So it's kind of a tradition." He sipped his tea and watched me over the rim of his mug. "Say, would you consider coming over to Comox to visit for a couple of days? I could show you around."

"Sure, I'd love to." Maybe I shouldn't have sounded so eager. "That is ... I'd have to think about it.... How would I get there?"

"You could take the ferry over from Powell River and I'd pick you up on the other side." He looked at me with a raised eyebrow, as if hoping for a nod.

"But where would I stay?" I knew this wouldn't work. I didn't know anyone over there. Or was I reading more into his invitation than he intended?

"At my place. I know that sounds like I'm trying to move fast, but you'd have your own bedroom and bathroom. For that matter, if it makes you more comfortable, bring Monique along. I have a few French-Canadian friends she'd probably enjoy meeting."

So he is interested. He'd been so much fun to be with when we had dinner last night. Lots of laughs and great conversation, not to mention his sexy build. I felt like I couldn't get enough of him. I buzzed with excitement at the thought of spending time alone with him. Monique would see to it that we had time alone. I took a breath to calm myself and be cool. "Well, that sounds like it could be fun. Can I think it over? And of course I have to ask Monique." I wanted a backup friend just in case. I didn't really know that much about Jim yet, but I wanted to know more, a lot more.

"I won't be going till I can use my hand and the bandage comes off my eye. Too hard to get the boat home otherwise."

A thought hit me. I took a sudden breath and raised a finger. "Or how about—just an idea—if Monique and I come over on the boat with you to help you out, and then we can take the ferry back another day?" Now that made sense to me. It would be fun and an adventure too.

"Hey! Now you're talking."

A bunch of guys had stopped what they were doing to watch us untie and pull away from the dock. They were nudging each other and shaking their heads. I heard one fellow say, "Lucky bugger."

"Happy to have you girls aboard." Jim grinned. "I'm sure I'm the envy of all the guys in Lund."

"Not if they had to get burned to qualify," I said. "But really, we want to be useful—be your eyes. We can help you watch for logs."

"And odder boats," Monique added.

"Great. I'll just sit back and enjoy the ride." I'd never seen Jim smile so much. It made me feel good to know he enjoyed my company.

Motoring along near the shelter of Lund's harbour, the Serenity cut through the small waves like a hot knife through butter, but as we got out into the open, farther away from land, that smooth action changed to a lumpier ride as the wind picked up. My hair whipped around my face as I stood on deck watching Lund recede into the background. Monique was in the wheelhouse, steering the boat, so Jim came out on deck too. He pulled one of the bumpers aboard and laid it on the side of the deck.

"Why don't you leave them out?"

"Because they drag as the waves hit them and slow us down."

"Oh. Makes sense. Should I pull up the ones on the other side?"

"Yeah, sure. Just make sure you hang onto something." The boat had begun to pitch around. While I pulled up the rubber bumpers that had kept other boats from smashing into the Serenity's wooden sides at the dock, Jim hooked a chain from one post to another along the side of the boat, like a waist-high guard rail. "To stop you from going over if you lose your balance."

Sure enough the waves were bigger already. I was unsteady on my feet and felt a bit queasy.

"You're looking a wee bit green there, Andrea. I think I'll drop the poles. Smoother ride. If that's not enough, we can still throw out the stabilizers." He saw my puzzled look and pointed to the two weighted stainless steel fins that were attached by cables, one to each of the trolling poles.

He began to loosen some lines that kept the poles upright. Holding the lines, he leaned back to counterbalance the weight of the poles and fed the lines out slowly, lowering the trolling pole until it was at a 45-degree angle. He fastened the loose end of the lines with a couple of wraps around a peg. Then he bit his lower lip, pulled his burned arm close to his body, and curled over it.

"Here, Jim. Let me help you with the other pole. Just tell me what to do."

"Yeah, okay," he said, sucking in air through his teeth.

"Let me untie the line and then when it's time for muscle, you can do that with your good arm." I looked for his nod and began unwrapping the coiled lines. As they loosened Jim reached over my shoulder to get a good grip on them with one arm. I held on with both of mine and we fed the line out slowly, lowering the second trolling pole. He still had to use his burned arm, but I hoped that I had been able to ease the strain on it.

I was aware of Jim's body against my back. Very aware. A stab of heat flashed through me. I fastened the lines on the peg and turned, right into his open arms. He kissed me then, tenderly. The blood rushed to my head and I thought I must have steam rising from my hair.

"Thanks for your help, Andrea," he breathed.

"Oh, any time. Call me when it's time to raise the poles again, won't you?" We grinned at each other. He still held me close and I thought he must feel my heart beating right through my shirt.

"Ah, dat's better," Monique called from the skipper's seat in the wheelhouse. "Much calmer ride now."

I had to snicker. "I don't know about feeling calmer," I whispered to Jim.

He laughed and took my hand, pulling me into the wheelhouse. "All right, ladies. What would you like for breakfast? I'll cook if you two want to keep an eye out for logs and boats. I'm suddenly feeling very hungry." He looked into my eyes and couldn't quite hide a mischievous smile.

"Can you see them?" Jim asked us as we neared Vancouver Island. He pointed in the general direction. "They're visible on the monitor but I like to make sure I can see the actual markers. Just a safety precaution."

"Dere is one." Monique pointed at a speck in the distance. She'd stayed in the captain's seat for the whole crossing, and Jim hadn't objected. He stayed close to me, talking about anything and everything, about our lives and our childhoods, about our likes and dislikes. Meanwhile, Monique seemed to thrive on following Jim's instructions as she manned the helm.

"Good. We're on course then. Make sure we keep on the outside of it and start looking for the marker that's beyond that one. It should be visible to the right." Jim pulled the patch off his eye. "Damn thing. I can't operate like this." He tossed it onto the table and looked in the small mirror above the counter. Carefully, he pulled at the bandage over his eye.

"Let me help you with that. Wait till I wash my hands, and don't do anything till I'm ready. Burns get infected really easily." I soaped up my hands and washed. Then I looked up at Jim's bandaged face. Gently, ever so gently, I peeled away the gauze bandage. "You're lucky the skin isn't coming off onto the bandage. It should heal better that way." I winced when I saw the crescent moon-shaped burn at the top of his cheekbone. Several smaller flecks of the hot zinc had left reddish brown marks on his cheeks and temple. "The eyelid is still quite puffy and red, but it doesn't have any bad burns. They're mostly on your cheek under your eye." That splattering molten metal must have hurt like hell. I pushed the hair off his forehead to check for more burns, and patted the good side of his face. "Poor baby. But don't worry. You'll be good as new in a few days."

Jim stood still bending forward slightly as I finished taking the bandage off. His face was so close to mine, I could feel his breath on my ear. Goosebumps rushed over me and I shuddered.

"What's wrong?" His brow wrinkled.

"Nothing," I whispered. "I just got shivers from your breath on my neck.... Good shivers." I smiled.

Jim's face broke out in a big grin. "I'll have to remember that. So there is something to that saying, 'Blow in my ear and I'll follow you anywhere.'"

"Well, I wouldn't go quite that far. After all, it was just ordinary goosebumps." I tried, unsuccessfully, not to return his grin. I peeled off the last bit of tape and stood back. "Now, how's that?"

Jim looked around the wheelhouse, then out the window. "Oh, this is much better. Even if I can't see much through that eye yet, I can see better with both eyes open."

"Coming up on de next marker," Monique announced as we entered the calmer waters near Comox Bay.

"Can you keep us on course, to the port side of the markers, while I raise the trolling poles?"

"For sure t'ing, cap'n." She gave Jim a smart salute and grinned widely. Like a kid with a new toy.

"I'd better come help you," I said to Jim.

Pulling the poles upright required strength, but it was easier than letting them out slowly when we had first lowered them. I coiled the lines and tied them onto the peg according to Jim's instructions. When the job was done, Jim took me in his arms—part of the ritual now— out of Monique's line of vision through the wheelhouse door. His body was lean and hard. No fat on him. He was muscular without being bulky. My heart pounded double time, or was it his heart I felt pounding? We were pressed so close together it was hard to tell.

"Careful of your burns." I kissed his cheek and eye on the unscathed side of his face. "You were lucky you didn't hurt your eye." Those clear blue eyes. Like the sea on a sunny day.

"I'm lucky I found you." He brushed his good hand through my hair, then pulled my head closer for another kiss. His tongue played around my teeth and lips. The warmth of his body filtered through his shirt, his jeans, and into mine, warming me until I thought I would melt.

"I'm glad you did." I let my hand slide down the firm muscles of his back.

"You have the most beautiful hair, you know?" He reached for it again. He leaned the good side of his face in it. "Smells great. Like fresh salty sea air in a forest."

Keep talking. I love it. I caressed the back of his head and kept him pulled close to me. His easy charm had disarmed me completely. I basked in his adoring words, loving every syllable. It was almost too good to be true. A painful thought flashed through me. What if it really was too good to be true?

Chapter 9

Jim closed his cell phone. "We're all set. Giselle and Simone will be waiting for us when we get in. They'll give us a ride to my place. They asked if Monique might like to stay with them."

"*Eh, bien.* Whatever is good for you." Monique winked at me. "Might be nice to visit wit' dem. *Parler le francais.*"

"They're excited to meet you. They're having a French-Canadian party tonight. Andrea and I will come too, and you can decide how you feel about staying with them or coming back to my place."

"Sound good to me."

"You okay with that, Andrea?" Jim asked.

"Sure. It'll be fun." I hoped Monique would want to stay with the girls. And me? Alone with Jim in his house tonight? Tickles of excitement fluttered in my stomach. I wasn't sure what I should expect. After all, I'd only met him a short time ago. Still, I felt like we had a connection from the start. He had been very friendly at the wharf, the whole time he was in Lund—friendlier than the other fishermen. I would like to have spent every day sitting on his boat chatting with him. And now, here we were. I had him all to myself. I had tingles just thinking about it. And yet, I hadn't planned on any major developments and wasn't taking birth control pills. But why was I even thinking about this? Sexy as he was, I didn't want him to think I was an easy lay. Jim was special and I'd lose him for sure if I gave in too easily.

Giselle and Simone dropped us off at Jim's house and said something to Monique, who shrugged and looked around at us for help.

Monique took a step away from the girls and whispered to us, "Dey want to know if I want to go wit' dem and 'elp get t'ings ready, and you can come later. What do you t'ink?" She stood back then, waiting for Jim's opinion. Smart girl. No way she was going to get stuck in an awkward situation where she was without options.

"You can trust them," Jim said quietly. "They're good people."

"All right den." Monique gave the girls a nod. "*Allons-y.*"

That evening I drove and Jim gave directions to Giselle's. He reached for me with his bandaged wrist. His fingers were exposed, so I held them gently while I steered with one hand. I had seen him pull his hand towards his body several times since raising and lowering the trolling poles.

"Does your wrist hurt a lot?"

"Feels a lot better since you doctored me up." He curled his fingers around mine and raised them to his lips. A zing of pleasure surged from my fingers straight down to my toes. I wanted to pull the truck over to the side of the road right there. *Get a grip. Take a breath.* I had to force myself to try to make sensible conversation.

"The Neosporin will help. But make sure you keep it wrapped to keep it clean." I knew I must sound like a mother hen, but seeing Jim hurt brought out the tenderness in me.

"I hope I won't have too many scars on my face."

"I don't think so, but even if you do, you'll still be handsome." If he only knew how good he looked to me. His light brown hair had enough curl in it to look like it was ruffled up even when he tried to tame it. His glasses gave him a quietly fashionable appearance and set off his fine straight nose.

"Aw, you're sweet!" He looked down and smiled to himself.

"Is it far to Giselle's place?" Not that it mattered now. I was relaxed and feeling more comfortable driving Jim's truck.

"Not too far. It's in Courtenay, about seven minutes from Comox." We drove along a road beside an estuary.

"Beautiful drive! You've got everything here—ocean, mountains, forest."

"Don't forget the glacier." He pointed ahead where the sun was setting near a flat snow-covered mountain. "The natives called it Queneesh, the great white whale. Some myth like the Noah's Ark story. After the rains, the glacier broke through the flood waters, like a great white whale breeching."

"Interesting. I didn't know Comox is such a scenic and peaceful place. You're so lucky to live here." I decided right then that someday I would live in Comox.

A few minutes later, Jim pointed to a typical boxy subdivision house, very plain compared to his modern home overlooking the bay.

"Here we are." Jim jumped out of the truck and came around to open the door for me.

Hmm. Nice manners. I hadn't had anyone do that for me in a long time. As I stepped down from the truck, he kissed my cheek. "When you want to leave, just give me a sign and we'll go."

He reached across the truck seat for the brown paper bag. "Can't forget the wine. Do you mind carrying it?" Then he took my hand and we headed for the house. It felt natural to hold Jim's hand, as if we'd known each other forever.

The sound of singing greeted us as Giselle opened the door.

"Hi. Come on in and meet everybody."

Several people worked in the kitchen, all of them singing in French. Monique raised a hand to us and kept on singing. Simone and another woman checked the oven.

"Smells delicious," I said as the song ended.

Giselle made the introductions: Simone, Maxine, Michel, and Jacques. True to French-Canadian tradition they all shook hands with us. Jim waved off the handshakes with apologies, pointing to his bandage, and immediately had to answer the obvious question—what happened to you?

The wine flowed. "It's help yourself tonight," Simone said as she put a platter with meat pies between two cheese plates on the dining room table. Jim poured us each a glass of wine.

Jacques brought out a guitar and the music went on all evening with little breaks for laughter and conversation. They were an easy group to be with.

I laughed. "I don't know what I just sang there. I don't think those were French words."

"Could have fooled me. But I think if I have another glass of wine I'll soon be fluent."

What do you think?" I asked Monique later when we were alone in the kitchen. "Do you like these people?" I hoped she would like them well enough to stay at Giselle's overnight.

"Dey are wonderful. And yes," she said, as if reading my mind, "I will stay tonight and tomorrow night. Dey already ask me to stay bot' nights. Dey are so nice, so French. Make me miss 'ome a little bit." I could see tears welling in her eyes.

"But isn't it nice to speak French and sing and think of old times?" I put my arm around her back and rubbed her shoulder blades.

"*Oui*," she sniffed. "Is very nice." She put her arms around me and hugged me. "You are a good friend to understand 'ow I feel." She clung to me so tightly and for so long that I had to extricate myself from her arms. I thought she might have had a bit too much wine.

"Of course, I know. I'm away from home too." I gave her hand a squeeze. "I think Jim and I will be leaving soon. So tomorrow, will you be doing French-Canadian things? Or should we come get you?" *Please say you'll stay.*

"I can stay here till day after tomorrow when you pick me up." She took a step back to look me over, giving me a knowing smirk. "And not too much 'anky-panky tonight, eh?"

"No. Not too much." I wasn't at all sure how or why I was going to keep Jim at arm's length tonight when every cell in my body was begging for sex.

I drove along the deserted main street of Comox. "There's not a soul around and it's only ... what? Ten o'clock?"

"They roll up the streets about seven in Comox. No rowdies here."

"Nice! No wonder you like living here." Although Giselle had brought us out there earlier, in the dark I would never have found my way back to Jim's house without help. "So which street is yours?"

"Just keep going. I don't actually live in Comox. I live outside of it on the other side."

Following Jim's directions, taking many turns along country lanes, I managed to get us home, and parked the truck in his driveway. Upstairs we stood in his living room.

"Wow! What a view. You can see the city lights, and even the lights way across the bay." I wondered how someone who was not yet thirty could afford a place like that.

"My dad loved it here. He built this house. When he died, I found myself alone and owning a big house."

"You could have moved, I suppose."

"No, I couldn't. Too many good memories here." He let out a big sigh. "I miss Dad ... but we can never go back. Only forward." He shook his head as if to shake off melancholy memories and forced a smile. "Would you like a brandy?" He turned the lights low. Soft music came from well-hidden speakers. We sat on the rich brown leather loveseat and looked out over the bay. Jim clinked his brandy glass lightly on mine. "To us." The clear "ting" of the crystal was like a seal of approval on the toast.

A small sip of the liquid sent a trickle of warmth flowing through me. Jim wrapped an arm around me. I rested my head on his shoulder. The loveseat was cozy, and I felt warm and comfortable. I imagined myself as

Mrs. Jim McIntyre, living here in this lovely house with this wonderful man. "I'm so glad I came over here."

"Me too." He turned his head slightly to kiss me on the lips.

Heat rushed to all parts of my body, but mostly to parts below my belly button. My panties were wet and I knew I wouldn't be able to say no if Jim continued.

I turned my head away and gasped. "Oh God, Jim. It's hot in here."

"Should we take some clothes off then?"

"NO!" I was surprised by my outburst, and laughed. "I mean, yes, I want to, but no, I really shouldn't. And I don't want to be persuaded." I pulled away from Jim. I didn't want him to think I was cheap. I wanted more than a tumble in bed. Something more long term. I didn't want to risk losing him.

His brow furrowed and he looked confused. "I don't understand. I thought you liked me. Maybe I haven't been reading things right."

"Yes. Yes, I do like you, a lot, but.... Oh, damn." How could I make him understand? "I do like you, but that's the problem. I like you an awful lot, Jim, and if I let down all the barriers, we'd make beautiful love, but then tomorrow you'd be glad I was leaving and you'd never ask me to come back."

"No, I—"

"Trust me, Jim. That's how it works between men and women 99% of the time." He stared at me, speechless. "And I'm not talking from personal experience here. It's not like I go to bed with everyone I've just met."

I had ruined the cozy ambience of the evening. *Oh damn. Me and my big mouth.* "Look, Jim, I—"

"No, you don't need to say anything. I understand. Really I do." He had turned sideways on the loveseat to face me. "I invited you over and I had no right to assume

that you would jump right into bed with me. I hoped
that you would, but I...." He stopped as if gathering his
thoughts. "Listen. Let's start over, and I'll try not to be so
... aggressive."

"That's kind of funny, you saying you're aggressive.
When I first met you, you were so shy you wouldn't even
look me in the eye."

"I know. But I feel like I know you a lot better now.
I'm really comfortable with you—almost like a sister. No!
I take that back. If I had a sister I wouldn't be wanting to
sleep with her. You're not like a sister. Not at all."

"Well, I'm relieved to hear that." We laughed, trying
to shake off some of the sexual tension. "Do you really
feel like that with me? Comfortable?" He nodded and I
was encouraged. "Because I do. I feel like I've known you
forever. I trust you."

"Great," he said, moving closer again.

I put my hand up quickly. "That doesn't change what
I said before. I don't want you to think I'm a flirt and a
tease. It's just that ... I can't go to bed with you. Not yet.
Much as I'd like to. I have a five-date rule about that."

He grinned. "So, okay, this is date two—dinner at the
hotel in Lund was one—tomorrow is three. That leaves
two to go." He kissed me again. "I'll just go take a cold
shower."

"And me? What am I supposed to do?"

"You can shower with me if you want. There's room for
two." He gave his eyebrows two quick lifts and grinned.

I punched his arm playfully. "Maybe another time."
My mind was running away with me again, fantasizing
about the two of us in the shower. My pulse quickened
as I imagined myself naked in Jim's arms feeling his
nude body against mine, the only thing separating us, a
film of soapy water.

He reached for my neck and put his fingers gently around the leather thong that held my amulet. "That's a beautiful piece of artwork. What is it?"

"Lapis lazuli. It's supposed to foretell faithful love if you dream of lapis lazuli. They say it offers protection—against what, I don't know." I shrugged. "I'm not superstitious, but I like the stone."

"It's a very unique deep blue. Wonder where they find these stones?"

"Mostly Afghanistan." I pulled the gemstone away from my chest and looked down at it. "My mom bought it for me before I left home so I wouldn't forget her and Dad. As if I would."

"Must have cost a small fortune with that silver design it's embedded in. Almost looks like a face and the drips of silver all around it are the woman's hair hanging down. Beautiful piece." He took my hand and bent to look at the blue gemstone more closely. The freshly shampooed smell of his hair, the nearness of his body.... I let my face drop into the top of his head.

He turned so his lips met mine and the heat was back on again. A moment later we were both gasping for air.

"Let's go out on the deck," Jim suggested. "If nothing else, it's cooler out there."

We stood in the dark, sipping the last of our brandy. The moon was hidden behind the tall fir trees, but its reflected light shimmered on the bay.

"It's so quiet out here," I whispered.

"I know. That's why I love living out here. It's peaceful. Out of town, but close to town at the same time."

A night bird called from the nearby firs. "What's that?"

"Great horned owl. He's there almost every night. Calls about every fifteen to thirty seconds. Sometimes he goes on for hours. Drives me nuts when I'm trying to fall asleep."

"But it's so neat to hear him ... or her."

The soft hooting sound came again. Sure enough, it was repeated at least every thirty seconds. Such a lonely sound. Maybe it was calling for a mate? I wondered, could Jim be mine? I snuggled closer to him. He put his bandaged arm around me and pulled me close.

God, I wish I could stay here with you forever.

Chapter 10

At the ferry terminal, Monique walked a short distance away so I could say goodbye to Andrea.

"Thanks for everything, Andrea. It was great having you over here." I put my arms around her, being careful not to press too hard on my wrist, which still hurt like hell. But, somehow, I didn't mind the pain while I was holding Andrea.

I buried my head in her hair. Fresh as a herb garden. I pulled back slightly to give her a kiss and her lips were already on mine. Our body language clicked perfectly. No awkward bumping of noses or clashing of teeth. It was all so easy and natural.

I trusted her and felt I could relax around her. She would never make me feel stupid if I said or did the wrong thing. She bolstered my self-confidence. No more shy guy. This girl was good for me.

"I've really enjoyed this weekend," she said. "Thanks for having us over." She lifted my bandaged wrist tenderly. "Be sure to look after this, won't you? That was a nasty burn."

"Don't worry. I'll take care of it. I need it healed for fishing time. Maybe I'll see you when I stop in at Lund on my way north in a few weeks?" I watched her expression carefully. She seemed to light up as if she liked the idea. Good. I'd hoped she would. "I'll call you, okay?"

"Okay. You've got Monique's number, right?" She gave me a light kiss on the cheek. "I'd better run." She looked over her shoulder. "The foot passengers are already boarding. Take care of yourself." She picked up her overnight bag and hurried after Monique.

Turn around and let me get one more look at you. I watched as she crossed the parking lot towards the ferry. Almost there, she turned to give me one more wave. Her smile was genuine, natural, beautiful.

Driving home from the ferry terminal, her smile hovered in the front of my mind. She had me chuckling to myself, as I replayed so many of our moments together. There was something easy and comfortable about being around Andrea. I didn't feel I had to role-play and try to impress her or be on my guard about what I said or did. I could just be me. She had an innocent way about her, didn't want or need impressing. I loved that about her.

So unlike Sarah. Most of that woman's sentences started with "I." When I went out with Sarah a couple of years ago, I thought she was pretty in an earthy way—the artsy type. But what a left-wing greenie. Nothing wrong with wanting what's best for the earth, but most of her beliefs involved way too much theory. Great ideas, but in practice, forget it. They just didn't work.

"Everybody has a right to have enough food," she said.

"Well, of course, everyone has a right to it," I agreed, "but sometimes circumstances prevent that from happening, and it doesn't matter if you have a 'right' to it or not. If food's not available, you don't get it."

"How can you be so hard-hearted?"

"I feel bad for starving people, but the reality is we can't save everyone."

Then she rolled her eyes and shook her head as if she couldn't believe my lack of understanding. She walked away muttering something about the bigger picture.

I could have just snapped her up and married her. She'd look good on my arm. But how would we pass the time when we weren't having sex? Yes, sex. It was just that. It wasn't making love with her—you need more emotion for that. But suppose we'd married and had the rest of our lives to spend together? I had a little taste of what that could be like when she deckhanded with me. Sometimes, when the fishing was slow, time dragged and it would have been nice to have a conversation.

"What do you think is going to happen with this new Euro coin they're trying to get all of Europe to use?" I asked her one day after hearing about it on the radio.

"I don't know." She shrugged. "Who cares anyway? That's way over in Europe. It's got nothing to do with us."

"Well, sure it does. It's going to affect the whole world economy. It'll probably have a trickle-down effect on the price of my fish."

"Is that all you can think of? Money?! You're just like all the rest of those capitalists."

"How can you say that? It's what feeds me and pays my bills. What's wrong with that? And believe me, what happens in European markets will affect all of us here."

"Oh, I sincerely doubt it," she said. She blew out an exasperated sigh and picked up one of her paperbacks with the picture of lovers on the cover.

Not a deep thinker. I was disappointed in her. She looked good, worked hard when we were into fish, and was pleasant enough to be around, but something was definitely missing with her. She was all about herself in the here and now. Her only thoughts about the world at large echoed the ravings of her left-wing friends. The only original ideas she had were in her artwork; never about practical things.

It just didn't work for me. Fishing was a hands-on job. About as real as you could get. There was no room for a lot of idealism on a fishboat. If you had a tangle in the lines, you had to get it out fast and get that line fishing again. You couldn't stand there and philosophize about how many chemicals went into making all that perlon and how it was ruining the environment. Sure I cared about the environment, but this was not the time to get out the placards and protest the use of polyester products in fishing lines.

"Did you know that wearing polyester underwear lowers your sperm count?" she said.

God, she was way out in left field.

"Mine's cotton." So there. For once I got the last word.

And now, a couple of years later, in spite of all Sarah's earlier left-wing green talk, she'd turned into quite the little capitalist after all with her gift shop in Lund.

I pulled into my driveway, shaking off thoughts of Sarah and wondering why I ever had anything to do with her when I could have someone like Andrea. Couldn't let this one slip away. I would call tonight. Or at least tomorrow—I'd forgotten that she needed a couple of hours of ferry time to get home and then she'd have to arrange a ride from Powell River to Lund. Either way, I'd definitely call her. Andrea was a keeper.

I ran for the phone. It had been ringing the whole time I fumbled with the key in the lock. I needn't have run. This caller wasn't hanging up.

"Hello?" I panted into the phone.

"Jimmy? Are you okay? You sound out of breath."

"Colleen? Is that you?"

"Of course it's me. How many half-sisters do you have?"

That was odd. Colleen rarely called. "Something wrong?" I held my breath.

"Well, yeah! Mom's Alzheimer's is bad. I can't deal with it anymore. I got the kids and I can't go running after her all the time. She's getting really bad."

"How bad? What happened?" I hadn't seen my mother or Colleen in a while. But Mom seemed okay last year.

"She wandered away from her apartment and I couldn't go looking for her. I got the kids, don't forget." How could I forget? I heard them screaming in the background. "Stop that, Charlie!" I held the phone away from my ear. "You just can't imagine what I have to go through. You got off easy. I'm dealing with her every day, and I'm working part time and I got these two toddlers. It's not the first time she's wandered off. She's getting worse fast."

"Is that it then? She just wandered off?"

"No. I told you, you can't imagine."

"Well, of course not. So you'll have to tell me, won't you." Why did women always have to beat around the bush? "Just spit it out."

"All right. Well, Mom is getting so forgetful, she left the stove on one day. Thank God for smoke alarms or she might have burned the building down."

"Jeezus. That's not good."

"No, and the apartment manager as much as told me to get her out of there before he has to evict her."

"Well, I guess I can't blame him."

"So I've given notice and I need you to help out."

"Where's Patrick? Isn't he helping?"

"That no-good lout? I kicked him out. Tossed his bottles out on the lawn after him. And can you believe he sat on the grass finishing off the dregs before taking off in my car? Oh, Jimmy, I can't do it anymore." She sniffed and I heard her blowing her nose.

"What can I do?" I dreaded hearing the answer.

"Come out and help me."

Oh shit. I suppose she thinks I can just drop everything. "When?" *Please not now, just before the fishing season.*

"Yesterday. I really need you to take over with Mom. I just can't do it all." Her quiet sniffling was nearly drowned out by the squabbling of her toddlers in the background.

I never could stand to hear a woman cry. "I'll be on the plane this afternoon or tonight if I can get a ticket. I'll call you as soon as I book it."

"Oh, thank you, Jimmy. I'll phone Patrick. Tell him I have to have the car back to pick you up. He won't dare say no if he knows you're coming. So call me when you're booked."

At the far end of the long hallway I saw Colleen bouncing up on her toes, waving to me above the heads of the crowd of passengers in the Arrivals section. After her phone call, I booked a ticket to Calgary, threw together a bag of clothes and toiletries, locked up the house, arranged for neighbours to keep an eye on things, and raced to catch the plane—all after a weekend of late nights with Andrea. The trip from Comox had only taken a little over an hour, but it was late in the day and I was burned out.

Colleen hugged me hard. "I'm so glad you're here," she said, "but you look like hell."

"That about sums up how I feel."

Colleen took a second look at my face. "What happened to your eye?"

"It's okay. Just a zinc burn from working on the boat. It's fine, really. Just looks bad."

"No kidding." Her brow wrinkled as she studied my face. "Well, if you're sure you're okay…. Do you have any baggage?"

"Just my carry-on. Ready when you are."

In Colleen's mud-splattered Honda, I pushed aside a plastic Etch-a-Sketch and a newspaper and settled into the passenger seat. "Where're the kids?"

"Patrick is back. He's looking after them." She shrugged. "He's promised to mend his ways, and I need some help, so ..."

"Hope it works out."

"You can stay with us tonight if you don't mind sleeping on the couch. Mom has more room for you, but I wanted to talk to you about her first and maybe get some plans in place."

Half an hour later we pulled into an older subdivision. Several of the yards were littered with toys. Most had tired, neglected lawns. Colleen's house was like all the rest. I didn't know how she could tell which one was hers.

I set my carry-on by the door. Patrick pushed himself off the couch and reached over to shake my hand. "How's it goin', eh? Like a beer?"

"Ah, thanks, but ... you got any coffee, Colleen?" She nodded and disappeared into the kitchen. "I feel like I've been dragged through a knothole backwards," I said to Patrick. "You don't mind if I pass on the beer for now? It'd just put me to sleep and Colleen said she wanted to get me up to speed on what's happening with Mom."

I went over to the boys and tousled their heads. "Hi guys."

"Hi," they said, totally involved in their TV show. Just as well. I was too tired for horseplay.

"Mom's getting pretty forgetful," Patrick said. "It's tough on us trying to juggle dealing with her and working and looking after the kids. I guess Colleen told you we've been under some stress lately."

"Yeah, she sounded pretty frazzled when she called."

"Well, I'm going to help out more. I know I kinda let her down, but I'm gonna fix that." He took another swig of his beer. "No more hard liquor for starters."

"Sounds good." I didn't want to get involved, but if they were working things out, all the better. "Well, I'll go talk shop with Colleen in the kitchen then and let you get back to the kids and your show."

"Lion King. Great stuff!" He sat back down on the couch and the two boys snuggled up to him without taking their eyes off the TV.

Colleen put down two mugs. She gave the kitchen table a quick wipe to get rid of blobs of spaghetti.

"So what's happening with Mom?" I braced myself for a litany of complaints, but Colleen surprised me.

"I'm sorry I called you when I was upset. I should have waited an hour or so, but it seemed like I was living Murphy's Law. Anything that could go wrong, did."

"No, don't worry about that. You have all the responsibility. I was out of touch for so long after Mom left. I didn't have the same bonding with her that you did. At least you've had a mother. I didn't – well, only for a little while. But still, I should do more now that she needs help."

"I'm really glad you're here. Patrick says he'll help more with the kids and the house—we had a big talk today— but I don't expect him to be much help with Mom."

"That's good. Some help is better than none."

"Yeah. Anyway, you'll be happy to hear that I've already taken some steps to make plans. I told you she left the stove on the other day."

"Yes, you said you'd given notice. Where's she supposed to go now?"

"I did a lot of phoning around and checking out different care facilities. It's not so easy to find one that will take her on short notice, but because she's an emergency case and can't be left alone, they've agreed to take her at Happy Trails Care Home. She can move in as soon as she's ready."

I wondered who was going to pay for this. I sure didn't have any extra money. "How much is that going to cost?"

"Luckily, Mom has always taken care of her money. She has a good financial advisor who has handled her investments for years. Mom gave me Power of Attorney before she got sick, and I've learned a lot from listening to the financial advisor. But don't worry, I leave it up to him. Her savings are looked after. She'll be able to pay for her stay at Happy Trails for as long as she needs to be there."

"Sounds like you've got it all covered. So you don't really need me then." I could get back to Comox, call Andrea, hear her sweet voice.

"Not completely. Here's where you come in. Right now I'm—well, she's—paying for a 'companion' to stay with her until I could make arrangements for her move. Now you're here, we can let that person go. You can help Mom pack the stuff she wants to take with her. You can sort and pack what's left and arrange to have it moved—to here, I guess—and we can have a garage sale. You'll have to arrange for the apartment to be cleaned and then get her deposit back and hand in her key."

I sipped my coffee and tried to digest what Colleen was saying. "Oh..." was all I could come up with. The weeks of chores and headaches loomed. I had work to do at home to get ready for fishing. I felt my world closing in. My chest tightened. "Oh..."

"I know it's a lot, but I can't do all this stuff and work and look after the kids too. Patrick is working all day too. I don't know how I could manage it all if you hadn't come."

I'd have to put my life on hold at least till the end of the month. But then I'd get back to my Andrea. *I should phone and let her know I'm in Calgary.* I dug around in my wallet.

"Looking for something?" Colleen asked.

"I had a phone number in my wallet. Someone I was going to call. Let them know I'd be gone for a while." I riffled through all the little compartments, dumped the cards and bills onto the table and spread them out. Put them back one by one. Nothing. I closed my eyes and leaned back in the chair to think. I saw Andrea giving me the number on a slip of paper, saw myself putting it beside the phone in the bedroom, knowing I'd be looking for it there. "Shit!"

Chapter 11

The Queen of Burnaby's lounge was less than half filled with passengers. Monique and I chose seats near the huge windows at the back of the boat. Slouched in the wide, comfortable chairs we closed our eyes and let the ferry take us home.

"Dis is much easier dan crossing in de fish boat."

"Takes less than half the time and we don't have to watch for logs. And it's not as rough." I was surprised that I'd felt queasy on the Serenity, but I was sure I would have gotten used to it in time.

"Don't have to lower de poles for stability eider."

I sighed, remembering the closeness of Jim's body then. A twinge of latent desire tickled my insides. "But no Jim to keep us company." I'd had two beautiful days with him. Now an empty life loomed.

"You like 'im a lot, eh?" She gave me a searching look.

"Yeah, a lot. We got along really well. He's easy to be with." I wished I was still with him.

"So did you ... you know?" Monique poked a finger in and out of a circle she made with her other hand.

I slapped at her gesture lightly and laughed. "Sorry to disappoint you." *Oh what would it have been like? Heaven!*

"I bet Jim was disappointed even more."

"For sure he was, but I didn't want to be too easy. He said he'd call me." But didn't they always say that? "He sounded sincere, but who knows?"

"A guy like dat must have a lot of girlfriend." Monique clapped her hand over her mouth and grabbed my arm. "Oh, I'm sorry. Dat was stupid of me. I only meant—"

"I know. Don't worry about it. But see? That's exactly why I didn't sleep with him. If he has lots of girlfriends, I'd be just another one who was quick to jump into bed with him. I want to get to know him. I want him to know who I am. I don't want to be another notch in his bedpost." I let out a big sigh and slumped back into the chair. "Maybe I should have put out. Maybe he thinks I'm a cold fish. Oh shit. I probably blew it. And I like him so much." I blinked back tears, took a big breath and shook my head hard to rid myself of the depressing thoughts that were crowding in. It had been such a fabulous weekend.

"I t'ink you were right to 'old off." Monique patted my hand. "I know everybody is doing it, but dat's de problem. Nobody take de time to get to know de person dey make love wit' and den, many time, it does not work out. 'Aven't you notice 'ow some women 'ave so many relationship? One after de odder? Dat's why. Too fast to 'ave sex first and get to know you later."

"Well, I hope you're right. I gave him your phone number. Hope you don't mind." And I hoped he'd use the number. All those hopes, and yet, a feeling of hopelessness was pressing in on me.

"Of course I do not mind."

Vancouver Island's mountains faded to a paler blue-green as the ferry put distance between us. I was suddenly filled with a longing, wishing I could have stayed in Comox with Jim. I'd never met anyone I liked so much. I sighed again and took out my book. Monique picked up her boating magazine.

I hope he calls. And soon.

Chapter 12

"T*abarnac!*" Monique stood over me with her hands on her hips. "When are you going to come back to join de living?"

I slouched with my legs tucked under me on the armchair, looking out the sliding glass door at the rain. Tears, rain, more tears, more rain. It was raining in my heart and raining outside our door. The downpour could go on all day and all night. Forever. I didn't care.

"Andrea!" Monique gave my shoulder a shake. "When are you going to stop feeling sorry for yourself and get on wit' life?"

"Sorry." I sniffed and reached for another Kleenex. "I just don't feel like doing anything. What's the point?" I ignored Monique's exasperated sigh. I hadn't heard from Jim since Monique and I had been to Comox three weeks earlier. Not a phone call, not a letter, not a peep. I got the message. *It was fun. But, baby, I've moved on.*

"What you are doing is not fair to yourself and is not fair to me eider. Now you listen to me. Put on dis jacket and come wit' me. We go for a walk in de rain if you like it or not." She threw my hooded rain jacket onto my lap and stood in front of me, poking the tip of a big umbrella into the floor. When I made no move to get up, she pulled me by the hand and yanked me out of the chair. "Put on de jacket!"

I stuck a listless arm through one sleeve and Monique grabbed the other sleeve and stuffed my arm into it. Then she dragged me to the door and pointed to my boots.

She reminded me of a mother dressing a sulky child. *Is that how I'm behaving? Like a sulky child? Oh, Lord, what must she think of me?* Did I care? Not really.

Outside, Monique popped up the umbrella. She hooked her free arm through mine and pulled me close. "To be under de umbrella," she explained in answer to my questioning look. "Now we walk." She set a brisk pace. Gradually, I could feel my sludgy blood begin to thin and flow to my lungs and my brain again. I took a deep breath of the fresh rain-washed air.

"Is good to be outside, eh?" Monique was grinning as she looked at my miserable expression. I couldn't stop the beginnings of a smile.

"Okay," I said grudgingly. "Is good."

"Now you listen to Dr. Fournier." She kept walking at a good clip as she talked. "I am sorry about Jim. But dis is not de end of de worl'. You 'ave to forget about 'im if 'e does not call. Dere are millions of odder people in de worl'. For de next few weeks you need to t'ink about Andrea only—and a little bit of me too. You are not what odder people make you. You are what you make yourself. I want you to snap out of dat funk you are enjoying so much, and t'ink of what is good for you—and me."

The rain eased up and Monique folded up the umbrella. I gave her a hug. "Thanks Monique. I'll try to pull myself together." It was time. I knew that.

As we headed home, Monique didn't release her hold on my arm. She was smiling so much, I didn't have the heart to pull away. And besides, it felt good.

Chapter 13

One of the perks of my wharf job was that I met everyone who came in. Sailors from all over, mostly the States, and quite a few fishermen on their way to or from the fishing grounds, pulled into the Lund wharf to have a quiet break in a safe harbour.

The Hawkeye was a pretty little troller, about thirty-seven feet long according to the wharf information its skipper gave me. He said his name was Robert Bolton.

"My name's Andrea. Jim, on the Serenity, told me you might be doing a haulout here." It hurt me even to say Jim's name, but I set aside the pain. I had to move on.

"That's right. He said he had a good helper lined up for me."

"That would be me." I found his bold stare unnerving, but I wanted the job, so I pushed on. "If you need someone to help power wash or paint, I can do that." He continued to stare at my face intently. "Is everything okay?"

"Of course," he said quietly. "Why wouldn't it be?"

"It's just ... you were ... staring at me." Intense dark brown eyes.

"Hard to look away from such a pretty face."

Oh my. Wasn't he the smooth one? I gave my head a shake and attached the pen to my clipboard. "Well, you know where to find me if you want to hire me for the haulout work. Have a nice day, Mr. Bolton."

"I will. And call me Robert." He smiled. Nice teeth.

Chapter 14

Monique and I arranged a ride to Powell River with Sarah who had lived in Lund forever. She ran a small artisan's consignment gift shop in Lund about a block up the road from the wharf.

"Where and when will we meet you?" I asked Sarah when we arrived at the mall.

"Couple of hours? I get everything I need right here, so how about we meet here at the car at noon?"

"Sound fine wit' me," Monique said. "We need mainly to get groceries."

"And I need to find some coveralls, or some old clothes."

"Thrift shop at the end of the mall," Sarah said. "I'll be at the Dollar Store and then the grocery store. Probably see you there."

Two hours later we loaded our bags into the back of Sarah's old Buick and headed back to Lund.

"Sarah, what's the attraction at the Dollar Store?" I'd seen her come out of there loaded down with bags of merchandise.

"It's amazing the things people will buy. I pick up Dollar Store items and put them out for resale mixed in with the local artwork."

"No kidding? Don't the customers know the difference?"

"A lot of them don't know and most don't care. You'd be shocked at the money they pay for the trinkets. Some people have no sense of good taste at all. Besides, they're on holiday. Anything goes, eh?"

"Don't you feel guilty selling them that cheap stuff for a big price?"

"Why should I? Buyer beware, eh?"

"Dat's right," Monique said. "Nobody is forcing dem."

"One guy bought a beautiful driftwood carving of a sandpiper. Paid big bucks for it. Then he bought a one-dollar keychain for ten bucks." Sarah smiled smugly.

"Why would he buy good art and junk at the same time?"

"Said he needed a keychain. His old one broke." Sarah shrugged. "See, that nine dollars I made on the keychain pays for my gas." Apparently her conscience didn't bother her.

As we pulled up to our house, Monique dug in her pocket. "Speaking of gas money, 'ere is five bucks for de ride today. T'anks, Sarah. Next week again?"

"Right on."

We unloaded our groceries, and I took my thrift store purchases into the bedroom. "Sorry to leave you with the groceries to put away, Monique, but I'm running late for my haulout job. The tide waits for no man, right? I don't suppose it waits for a woman either." I pulled on the baggy pants I'd bought and threw a big work shirt over top. Monique's cap was crusty with dried copper paint, but it would do for a few more jobs before I had to throw it away.

"Dat's right. You go on. You want stir fry for supper?"

"Great. But I'm not sure what time I'll be finished."

"No matter. I make de veggies and we t'row it all in de pan when you get 'ome, eh?"

"You're sweet, Monique. See you later." I picked up a couple of granola bars and my new used boots, blew her a kiss, and hurried to my job.

Chapter 15

Robert stopped working to stare at me when I arrived a bit out of breath.

"Thought you said you'd be here at noon." He looked at his watch. "It's 12:30 already."

I winced. "I had to get some old clothes from town, and my ride ... well, I wasn't driving." This was not the way to build a good reputation with the fishermen, being late for the job on the first day. I'd have to do better than that.

"Let's get busy then." His tone was abrupt and cold.

Never mind, I told myself. I wasn't here to be his good buddy. Might as well get down to business. The retaining wall had been swept clean and Robert had his tools all neatly laid out on it. The power washer was set up.

"Do you have a scraper for me?"

"You know where the tools are." Still cold. Reminded me of a kid, pouting and nursing a grudge. He pointed to the retaining wall. Sure enough, all the painting supplies, including the scraper, were meticulously lined up with the rest of the tools.

"Wow! You sure are organized." Maybe some flattery will get him into a better mood.

"That's how I like it." He looked right into my eyes when he spoke. I was beginning to think of him, rather than his boat, as Hawkeye.

Although it was early May, the air was cool the next morning. A low cloud ceiling covered Lund like a soft gray blanket, and a fine mist coated every surface. My face felt fresh as if it were bathed in a moisture cream.

The Hawkeye was secured to the scaffolding and looked helplessly stranded, literally high and dry. I smiled at Robert who stood on its deck watching my approach.

"You're looking chipper this morning," he said.

"I thought I'd make up for yesterday and be here early."
I noticed a smug smile playing around Robert's lips. *So,
he likes to be kowtowed to.* "What would you like me to do
this morning, sir?" I gave a smart little salute. *Oh, Master.*

"We won't copper paint until later in the day, just
before I get put back in the water, so why don't you be my
gopher? You know 'Go fer this. Go fer that.'" His eyebrows
went up as he waited for me to acknowledge the worn out
cliché.

I gave him another salute. "Aye, aye, sir. At your
disposal, cap'n." Might as well play the role.

I spent the morning hustling to fetch tools, plug in
cords, unplug them again, and coil them up. Robert
liked things to be orderly and tidy. I soon got used to the
routine, and although it was not as relaxed an atmosphere
as when I worked with Jim, there was some satisfaction
in knowing exactly where to find things.

Monique was right. Robert was handsome, but he was
certainly different. His habit of staring and his abruptness
at times were disconcerting. But it seemed that Monique
wasn't affected by his good looks, and maybe that's
why she zeroed in on his odd habits. As for me, I could
think of little else but his ruggedly sculpted face and his
muscles. If Robert's body got my insides tickling and my
hormones raging, all the better to help me forget Jim. He
had dumped me weeks ago and I wasn't going to slide
back into the depression I'd suffered afterwards.

"Are you going to melt zinc?" I was trying to show him
that I knew all about that stuff. He gave me a sharp look
and didn't answer. *Humph!* That was rude.

Once the tiger torch was set up with the flame roaring
under the melting pot, he said, "I have to concentrate on
what I'm doing." Okay. A bit strange, but it made sense
that he had to pay attention to what he was doing. I'd

seen what happened to Jim when he was melting zinc and not paying attention. I soon found it was better not to interrupt Robert with questions.

"Prop up this end of the cooling pipes while I unbolt the other end." The pipes were attached to the hull way under the boat, near the keel. We had to crouch down awkwardly in the cramped space and turn sideways while holding up the set of four copper pipes that ran parallel in one twelve-foot length. My job was to hold the pipes to keep them from bending too much once they were unfastened. It was heavy enough work for me but even heavier for Robert who had to unfasten the bolts while holding the weight of the pipes as they came loose from the hull. I heard him grunt with the effort. In that cramped space there was nothing to do but apply muscle and hope it didn't take too long. My arms were on fire with the strain. Robert had long, well-muscled arms and heavy wrists. He wasn't fat, but he was big, and could probably hold the cooling pipes by himself in one hand except for their awkward length. His thighs, too, were heavy. The hard bulges of muscles strained against the legs of the coveralls as he crouched. A strong man. I fantasized about touching those muscles.

"Okay, let 'em down easy now and set 'em on the ground."

What a relief to put the cooling pipes down and stand up to stretch my cramped muscles.

"You okay?" he asked.

"Yup. No sweat." Not much sweat, but my arms and legs were shaking from the effort.

"We'll lay them on those blocks of wood over there. Then you can gather up all the nuts and bolts. Make sure you count them and don't lose any. We'll need those when we put the pipes back on." Put them back on? I groaned inwardly. I'd been so relieved to put down the weight,

I couldn't bear to think about having to go through it all again. But no way would I let on how hard it was. I wanted this job and I was determined to handle it—even if it nearly killed me. With the pay from the two haulouts, I'd have enough for my half of another month's rent.

"Take the wire brush and clean off the cooling pipes, then take the Turk's head brush—" He stopped when I furrowed my brow. "The long-handled brush with the round head—to clean the hull under the pipes. Then you can start taping and painting."

Two hours later, the job was nearly done. "Here, I'll do the hard to reach parts under the keel before that tide reaches it." He took the brush from me. "You do the last bit of the stern with the roller." We both dipped into the tray for what remained of the copper paint. "You know, you look kind of pretty with all those paint freckles." He winked at me and I felt heat rising to my face. His compliments came unexpectedly. From machine-like orders and a no-nonsense work regimen, to a relaxed, light-hearted attitude—he was unpredictable. He had me completely off balance.

We put the last touches on the hull and put away the tools up on the deck. "That'll be it for today, Andrea." Robert reached into his wallet and peeled off four fifties. "Thanks a lot."

"Wow! Thanks. That's really generous of you."

"You earned it." He was staring at me intently again. "After I get the boat tied up and get cleaned up, would you like to have a beer with me?"

I didn't like beer that much, but a cool one sounded great after all that work. "Okay. What did you have in mind?" It would be interesting to see what he was really like when he didn't have to concentrate on his work. I wondered if he'd still be "different."

"I have to wait a while for the tide before I can get off the ways here. How about if you come down to the boat after I bring it around? It's turned into a nice evening and we can sit on the deck. I should be back at the wharf all tied up by about eight."

"Okay, see you then." I'd have time for a good long shower. I wondered if Robert would still think I looked pretty once I scrubbed off the paint freckles.

The evening was lovely. All day the weather had continued to improve. The morning's cloud cover lifted by noon and a light breeze blew away the last wisps of white clouds. The afternoon sun steamed off any remaining moisture. Now, low in the sky, it continued to send us warming rays. Robert put two lawn chairs on his deck and handed me a beer. He set out a bowl of potato chips on the hatch cover between us.

"I'll have to thank Jim for giving me your name. That worked out well."

My heart clenched at the mention of Jim's name, but I tried to pretend it didn't matter.

"Do you see him much?" How did I dare to ask? Could I keep a neutral face as I listened to Robert's answers?

"No, not really. We talk to each other on the radio mostly, especially during fishing season, telling each other where the fish are ... or aren't."

"When does the fishing season start?"

"For us? For salmon? Another three or four weeks maybe. DFO doesn't let us know for sure until the last minute." He snorted. "Afraid we might have time to get to the fishing grounds and be ready to fish when it opens."

"Really?" I thought he was having me on. "Why would they do that?"

"Power." Robert took a long draw on his beer. "They like to show us that they can make or break us." He sounded bitter, and a bit extreme, but maybe I would be too, in his place.

"Doesn't seem right."

"Course it's not right. But that's how it is. If Fisheries says it opens two weeks from now and everyone hustles to the fishing grounds, there's nothing to say they can't change their minds at the last minute and say it won't open for another week after that. Or the reverse, they'll tell you it opens in three weeks and then suddenly they'll change their minds and it'll open in three days. And nobody will be ready.

"It's hard for fishermen who have farther to go. Take Jim, for instance. He has to get all his groceries and clothes and things loaded. Then he has to secure his house for the summer."

"Do you have to do that too?" At the mention of Jim's house, I was back in his dimly lit living room again. What if I had slept with him? Would I be with him now? I shook off the image.

"Sure, but I live in Hope Bay, just around the corner a few hours up the coast. It's kind of on the way north so I don't have to be in quite the same hurry. I'll load my stuff in a few weeks and be ready to go. As long as the haulout is done, that's the main thing."

"So you have a house in Hope Bay?"

"Well, I'm renting a place. I'm on my boat so much of the time. Doesn't seem to be much point in buying. Besides, I'm not sure yet where I want to live for the long term." He stared at me again and pulled on his chin as he drifted into thought. It almost seemed as if he'd forgotten I was there. A few seconds later, he gave his head a little shake and spoke again. "And what about you, Andrea?

Where are you from? How'd you end up in a little place
like Lund?"

What's a nice girl like me doing in a place like this?
Sometimes men could be so predictable, but it was the
last thing I expected Robert to be. Oh well, I played along
making the traditional small talk and eventually it led to
more interesting conversation.

We ended up talking for a long time. Robert was
charming. He was knowledgeable about every topic we
touched on. I had thought I was well read, but Robert
seemed to have read everything in print.

I did think he'd been too regimented while we worked,
but I had to admit he was organized. And now that the
work was over, he seemed relaxed and easy to talk to.
His dark brown hair was thick and a bit curly. The slight
hook on his almost straight nose suggested a hint of
Arab influence, but with a name like Bolton, I decided
it had to be from way back if there was any Arab in him
at all. He certainly had all the handsomeness of Arab
features. Those nearly black, brown eyes. Good-looking
and educated, strong and well muscled, capable and
self-assured. A girl wouldn't have to worry about anything
if she were under his protection. What more could I ask
for in a man? If I couldn't have Jim, that is. I worked
harder to shut Jim out of my mind. After the second beer
I almost had myself convinced that Robert was the best
thing that had happened to me since coming to B.C.

Chapter 16

What do you t'ink about Robert now?" Monique lay on
the couch, head propped up with her elbow.

I sat on the armchair facing her. "Mmm ... he's pretty nice. Very handsome."

"What do you like about 'im? I want to 'ear it all, in detail." Her eyes were dark and big and her short spiky hair stuck out in all directions. Messy, but cute.

"Well, let's see. He's got muscles. Strong muscles. And there's a look about him that's fascinating. Maybe ... intense? Yeah, that's the word. It feels like his eyes are going to bore right into my head."

Monique scrunched up her nose. "And dat's good?"

"I didn't like it at first, but then I noticed that whenever he looked at me like that—really intensely—he always said something nice right afterwards. I got so I didn't mind it."

"Sound creepy to me. But never mind. What else?"

"You know I like to read."

"No kidding. You got more books dan clothes in your suitcase when you arrive."

"Well, Robert has read way more. Stuff I thought I should read but haven't gotten around to yet. He's read all the old classics and tons of technical stuff. He said he likes to read books that tell how to do things." Monique started to yawn as I talked. "Okay, I know it sounds boring, but maybe that's why he knows how to do so many things."

"'Ow do you know what 'e can do?"

"Just from watching him work on the boat, and from things he told me about his place. I think I'd like to see where he lives in Hope Bay."

"Uh-oh. Sound like 'e got 'is 'ooks into you."

Did she think I was a pushover? Or easy? I couldn't believe she would think me that stupid, to fall for him so fast, even if he was smart and good looking.

"Of course not, Monique. How can you say that? I hardly know him." But I needed a way to forget about Jim.

"Dat's my point exactly. Just be careful." She flopped her head back into the cushion and let out a long sigh.

Chapter 17

Robert stayed on at the Lund wharf after his haulout, sanding and painting the top side of the Hawkeye's hull. On Tuesday, as I did a lap of the wharf to check all the boats' tie-up lines, he called me over.

"I've been thinking, Andrea." He stared intensely, as usual, but by now I was used to it. "Would you like to go for a day picnic to the Copeland Islands just across the way? It's not far."

"How would we get there?" I wouldn't mind a change of scene. I never got to go anywhere. Might be fun. Who knew what might develop? Just the two of us, on an island.

He pointed to his freshly painted orange boat. "The Hawkeye, of course."

"I have to work today and Thursday, but I have tomorrow off."

"Tomorrow's perfect. Weather's supposed to be fine."

"What do I need to bring?" My camera for sure.

"Nothing. Just your personal things. Bathing suit if you like. Too chilly for swimming, but we might get some sun on the beach."

"Should I bring food?"

"I have the food and anything we might need. Everything is on board—sink, stove, toilet, beds."

Beds? "Just for the day, right?" I had no intention of staying overnight. Maybe things were moving a bit too fast here. If I was going to sleep with anyone, I should have done that with Jim. Missed my chance. But I couldn't think about that now. "I have to work on Thursday."

"Yes, you said that." He pressed his lips together as if he was irritated. I'd blown it now. He was probably wishing he hadn't asked me.

I was babbling the same thing over and over. Nerves. "Sorry, but I had to be sure we were clear on that." I wasn't ready for any big romantic moves just yet, but maybe I'd misjudged and that wasn't his intention at all.

"We're clear." Now he sounded pissed off. He turned his back to me and busied himself with a rope, laying the coils in a perfectly round circle neatly on top of each other. I wasn't sure if I'd been dismissed or if the picnic was on or off. I realized I'd been holding my breath and let it out in a whoosh.

Robert turned back to look at me with a little "oh" as if he'd forgotten all about me. "So?" he said, with a hopeful look.

I almost told him to piss off, but then I remembered Monique saying he's different. What if I'd been too quick to assume that all he wanted was to get me into bed? Maybe I had it all wrong. And he was a real hunk. Might not be so bad if he did want to get me into bed. I hadn't figured that all out yet. I wasn't even sure what I wanted, never mind what he wanted.

"Okay then." I slapped the outside of my legs nervously. "So what time tomorrow?"

"We'll leave at 9:00 a.m."

Wednesday morning, I untied the lines in the order that Robert directed and kicked out the Hawkeye's stern. This time I remembered to keep my weight on the wharf and to pull my leg back in time. As the bow inched away from the dock too, I was about to hop onto the boat. Robert's hand was there to pull me aboard. His tug on my arm had me flying through the air as lightly as a feather. Man, he was strong.

He ducked into the wheelhouse to steer us clear of the other boats and, at a snail's pace, backed the Hawkeye out of the congested harbour. Once we were underway, he explained the compass, the steering wheel, and the dial that showed which way the rudder was pointing. "You should know the basics for managing the boat by yourself."

"Me? Why?" It wasn't my boat. No way I was taking over that job.

"What if I fell overboard and disappeared? How would you get back to Lund?"

"Oh ... I hadn't thought of that." Now he had me worried. "Do people really fall overboard?"

"You bet they do. One summer during fishing season, a fisherman had his boat anchored safely in a little bay. He was a drinker. Got into his cups one night. Went out on deck for a piss—pardon my being so blunt—lost his balance and fell overboard."

"But the boat was anchored, so he was okay, right?"

"'Fraid not. That night it was pitch black and stormy. By the time the deckhand figured out where the yelling was coming from, the skipper was pretty far gone."

Oh my God. How horrible. "Couldn't he pull him aboard?" I shivered imagining that black water closing over his head.

"Well, as I said, the skipper was drunk, and the water is cold up north, even in the summertime. He would have been hypothermic in a few minutes. His clothes would have been waterlogged, maybe boots full of water too. He was like a dead weight. The deckhand didn't have the strength to haul him aboard."

"Helps to be strong, I guess." Robert wouldn't have any trouble pulling me out of the water. It was good to know I was safe with him.

"Maybe if the skipper had been able to grab the cap railing and hang on while the deckhand got a rope around him, he might have made it. But imagine trying to haul two hundred pounds of slippery weight straight up. And the waterline is already several feet below you. Physics was against him. The deckhand lost his grip and the skipper disappeared."

This fishing business was pretty grim stuff. "Did they ever find him?" I shivered again.

"Nope. Gone forever."

"So the deckhand was left alone on the boat?" I was pretty sure I would have freaked out completely if it had been me.

"Yup. They were anchored up, but imagine if they'd been underway when it happened and the deckhand couldn't run the boat?"

I was determined to learn what I could. "I can see that you'd have to know what to do." I pictured that poor deckhand, all upset, and then having to get himself together to run the boat. "Fishing sounds dangerous."

"Especially if you get drunk. Stupid guy. I don't allow hard liquor on board during a trip." Robert's tone was unforgiving and self-righteous.

"You don't drink?"

"Oh sure, I like a drink of Scotch just like the next guy, but not while I'm out on a fishing trip." He snorted with disdain. "The guy asked for trouble and he got it." Robert had no sympathy for someone else's imperfection. A bit hard, I thought. Would he be as unforgiving with me if I did something wrong?

"So what do you recommend for a quick lesson? For emergencies?"

"All right. Here's how you start the engine. You push this button. You'd have the throttle lever about here and the gear lever in neutral like this." He took it out of gear and showed me how to put it in neutral. "Then you ease the gear lever forward to go forward and back to go in reverse. Simple. Then push the throttle ahead." He pointed at the gauge on the wall behind the skipper's bench. "I don't like to run at more than 1800 RPM when we're going full out, but 1500 is better for fuel economy. That's enough for a first lesson."

I laughed nervously. "For sure. I think I'll need some time to absorb all that." I was glad I had learned something practical. What an opportunity. Hands on lessons. I glanced up at Robert. He looked pleased with himself. "Thanks for showing me all that stuff."

"Here. Sit behind the wheel and you can steer for a while. Just keep the compass heading on 303 degrees." Robert slid out of the bench seat and put an arm around my back to guide me onto the bench in front of him. His hand lingered on my shoulder and I didn't mind.

"I'll show you how to run on autopilot. You turn this knob here." He reached across in front of me. Our faces were close. An ever-so-faint lime scent emanated from him. Nice cologne. "And if you see a log in the water or another boat coming along, you can push either of these buttons here."

"The ones that say 'Dodge Left' or 'Dodge Right'?" At least those labels made sense to a landlubber like me.

"That's right. Hold the button down for a few seconds till the boat has turned enough to avoid whatever it is you want to avoid. When you let the button go, the autopilot will reset itself to the previous course. You don't have to do anything. Just keep an eye on it and make sure it's behaving itself."

"What if it's not?"

"Then you turn the button off Auto Pilot and go to Power Steer and you use the steering wheel to go where you want to go."

Robert went out on deck and I watched him through the open wheelhouse door. He unfastened the skiff's line that was tied to a metal pipe framework at the back of the Hawkeye. He hauled the small aluminum boat in closer and retied it.

"Why did you do that?"

"When we slow down to anchor, the line from the skiff will go slack and sag in water. If it's too long it could get wrapped in the prop and then we'd be in real trouble. Your boat is powerless if the propeller can't turn."

He busied himself in the galley then, until my curiosity got the better of me. "What are you doing?"

"Getting our picnic lunch together." He took bread and tomatoes out of a corner cupboard, stepped out on deck and brought in an armful of things—lettuce, mayo, cheese—and began making sandwiches.

I wondered where he kept the mayo on a warm May day. "Do you have a fridge out there on the deck?"

"Cooler with a block of ice."

"Is that what you do for a fridge in the fishing season?" Seemed a bit inadequate.

"Good Lord, no!" He laughed good-naturedly. "When it's fishing season, we're out for a week at a time or longer. All those compartments in the hold are filled with a couple of tons of ice chips. The fish are packed with ice and stored in the bottom of the hold. I use the shelves at the top—just under the hatch cover—as my fridge.

"Oh, Robert! A log! Right in front of us. What do I do?" He straightened up from his sandwich making and stepped forward to stand beside me.

"You know what to do."

How could he be so calm? "Dodge left?" My voice was an octave higher than usual.

"Yup. Just hold down that Dodge button." He wasn't at all concerned. I pressed the button and the boat steered towards the left, avoiding the log. When I let go of the button, it went back to the same steady course of 303 degrees.

"Whew!" I laughed with relief, and clapped my hands soundlessly.

"You could finish making the sandwiches. We're getting close to the anchorage so I'll need to take over the wheel anyway."

I was happy to be relieved of watch duty. As I slid down from the skipper's bench, Robert took my shoulders and gave me a quick peck on the forehead. "You did good."

I glowed with the praise and the kiss. The sandwiches were the finest I'd ever made. Every bit of lettuce and cheese and tomato I put on them was placed with care as I relived the moment. Sandwiches made in dreamboat heaven. I was in another zone—Cloud Nine, my girlfriends back home would say. He was such a good looking guy; so capable and smart. Jim had been great too, but that was over. Water under the bridge. I had to forget about him. Robert was a hunk and he seemed to like having me around. Sure, he had his moods, but didn't we all?

I wrapped up the sandwiches and put them into a bigger plastic bag along with two apples. Robert stuck his head around the corner. "Out on deck in the cooler—grab a couple of beers and put them in the backpack with the rest of the lunch." I wrapped some paper towel around the bottles of imported beer and put them into the bag.

Robert slowed the boat down and did a circle tour of the inside of the small bay, watching the depth sounder the whole time.

"You take the wheel now," he said. "You're in neutral. Just keep us aimed towards the center of the beach. I'm going to get the anchor ready to toss out. When I give you the signal, put the lever in reverse and give it a shot of fuel to set the hook. Then I'll give you a signal to put the throttle back and put the lever in neutral again."

I hoped I could do this. I really wanted to learn how to be useful and practical around boats. Okay, if I was honest, it was partly to impress Robert, but I wanted to be independent and capable too. I told myself I would do it right. No mistakes. Prove myself.

Behind the wheelhouse, Robert hauled a lot of chain off the anchor winch and let it collect on the deck. Then he went up to the bow and kicked the anchor off the boat. The chain rattled and clanked over the bow. Robert waved at me to put it in reverse. I did. Then he jabbed his thumb upwards several times for the throttle, then downwards to relax the throttle, and finally an umpire's "safe" signal to put the gear in neutral. He smiled at me and gave me a thumbs-up. I had passed the test.

"Great job, Andrea. You'll make a good deckhand."

I was hugely pleased with myself. I gathered up my backpack and the shore picnic bag while I watched Robert shut down the boat. The silence was fresh and beautiful. I stood on the deck and listened to the beach gravel burbling as our wake reached the shore. Seagulls shrieked overhead complaining at our intrusion.

We put the shore baggage into the skiff, and climbed in. Robert started up the outboard and in a few moments we were ashore on one of the Copeland Islands. The tide was out and much of the lower beach was wet. I handed our packs up to Robert.

"Hang onto that bow line till I come back to tie up the skiff," Robert called over his shoulder. He was packing all our things to higher ground.

"I can do it. I know how to tie it up." I grabbed a line from the bow and slipped it around a sturdy log before scampering after Robert.

The Copelands were a group of several large islands with many smaller islets sprinkled around them. I followed Robert up the trail that led from the bay where we anchored. A mere twenty steps later, the trail led us down to the shore on the other side. This part of the island was narrow as a wasp's waist.

Desolate and pristine, the natural beauty of the islands filled me with awe. No sign of human life anywhere. No garbage, no toilet paper, no bottle caps, tins, or plastic. We put our blanket down on the beach that faced southwest towards Vancouver Island.

Robert weighted down the four corners of the blanket with our bags to prevent the light breeze from lifting it up. "Want to take a walk around the island?" he asked.

"Yeah, hang on a sec'." I rummaged in my bag of spare clothes and held up my camera. "It's such a beautiful place. I want pictures to remember it." We picked our way over rocks along the beach. "Mom would never believe this. I'll have to send her photos to back up my letters. She'll be blown away by how untouched it looks here."

"It'll get busier later on. Sailors, kayakers, day picnickers from Lund."

"Sure is quiet now. Nice!" All I could hear was the repetitive swish and gurgle of waves mixing with the gravel at the water's edge.

"You like being in remote places?" Robert squinted at me. I wasn't sure if his face was scrunched up in disbelief or because of the sun in his eyes.

"Yeah, I do." His eyebrows went up. "What? Are you surprised?" I asked.

"Yes, to be honest, I am." He stared at me. "Most people, especially city women, don't like being alone. They'd rather be around other people most of the time. Groupies!" He scoffed.

"I like both. I like people, but I like my quiet time too. Not sure I'd want a lifetime of remoteness though." I stood on a log and looked all around. Nature's own rock gardens, arbutus trees, logs, grasses, tiny pink wildflowers. I lifted my arms as if presiding over the land. "This is so beautiful. I love it. I feel like it's all mine. Like I'm a rich landlord surveying my domain."

Robert looked pleased that I was enjoying his treat. His smile faded as he pointed to four seals sunbathing on a rocky ledge. "You'll have to share it with them."

I got my camera ready and zoomed in on them. "Don't they look sweet with those big eyes? Like black labs."

A scowl crept over Robert's face. "Sweet? Maybe if they didn't eat fish," he said. "They're bad at the river mouths, waiting for the young salmon to swim down to the ocean."

"They gotta eat."

"Sea lions are worse."

"Why's that?"

"They're smart, and lazy. They'll follow your fishboat around, and snatch the salmon right off the line. Bastards."

I thought a fisherman would love all the outdoors and its creatures. Robert's attitude disappointed me. "Whoa, you sure don't like them, do you?"

"They usually rip off gear along with the fish. Gets expensive."

I hadn't imagined they would be so brazen. "Could be a problem after a while if they're competing for your fish, huh?"

"No kidding. Especially if you're having a good day, into fish. They'll never leave you then." Robert smiled wryly and shook his head.

It seemed like an impossible problem to me. "So what do you do?"

He shrugged his shoulders. "Shoot'em." He said it so matter-of-factly.

"You don't!" I must have sounded naïve, but I couldn't believe anyone would do that. Had he really shot them? Robert rolled his eyes. Probably thought I was a real city slicker.

"Well, there is one other way of getting rid of them—I mean besides giving up for the day and going in to anchor up."

"What's that?" Maybe I was jumping to conclusions, thinking he was mean enough to actually shoot them.

"The sea lions follow your trolling lines, so you go really close to another fishboat, and then turn suddenly so your gear swishes close to the other boat. You hope the other guy has fish on his lines and the sea lions will find them attractive."

"How does that help?"

"While the sea lions go over to eat the fish on the other guy's lines, you gun it out of there fast as you can and leave them to their feast."

Seemed unethical to me. How could he do that to another fisherman? "Does it work?"

"Quite often, yeah." He had a smug look on his face.

"You could run out of friends that way." Didn't he care what they thought of him if he did that?

"Hmm." He had a blank faraway look. Lonely, I thought. Fishing was a solitary business to begin with and he probably didn't have a lot of friends if he pulled that kind of stunt. But, maybe this was where I came in. Maybe I could be the friend he needed.

"This is such a beautiful island. I'm glad you brought me over here."

"I hoped you'd like it." Robert jumped up on a huge rock that blocked off the end of the beach. He reached down a hand to me and pulled me up beside him easily, just as he had done earlier when he pulled me aboard the Hawkeye at the wharf. I felt weightless as I landed on the rock. I tried to find my footing, but lost my balance.

"Oops!" he said. He was quick to put an arm around my waist. The next thing I knew he was kissing me. He was surprisingly gentle and my knees felt like putty. "M-m-m. That was good," he mumbled. Then he kissed my nose and, all smiles, pulled back to look at me.

I had to agree it was good. Felt warm and inviting. I thought of Jim's tender kisses and a heat rose to my head, followed by the anguish of being dumped without a word. My face must have clouded over.

"Something wrong?"

I shook my head. "No, I just remembered something. Sorry. Nothing to do with us." I gave Robert a quick kiss to prove it and took his hand. "We'd best get on with our walk or we'll never get back to our picnic." We had the rest of the day to spend together and I didn't want things to move too fast.

A smile played at the edges of his mouth. "Right." He kept hold of my hand. He could certainly be charming. I liked that he didn't crowd me and make me feel uncomfortable about being here alone with him. Somehow I had thought there would be other people on the islands, and now I wondered how it would play out—us being all alone here—but so far, he was a gentleman. So far ...

For the next hour or so, Robert showed me many types of marine life near the shore: pink and creamy beige anemones that looked like dahlias perched on top of mushroom stems; purple sea urchins clinging to the rocks below the surface of the water, slowly waving their spines; oysters stuck together in clusters at the tide line; and dozens of other bits of sea life that I had only seen in picture books. It was magical. I set my digital camera on macro and took some great close-up shots.

We wandered back to our picnic spot, had a sandwich and a beer, chatted lazily and then dozed a bit in the sun. It was a perfect day. Robert got up at one point and walked to the rise of the trail to check on the Hawkeye.

"She's fine," he called. "Where did you tie up the skiff?"

"Right at the bottom of the trail." Why couldn't he see it? He must be looking right at it.

"No. Are you sure?" He started to walk down the trail. I got up to run after him and show him the spot.

"I tied it to a log right ... there." I pointed to the beach.

"Holy shit!" Robert yelled. "You tied it up?!" He flung his arm out towards the end of the bay. "What the hell's it doing out there?"

"I don't know. I did tie it. To a log." That was when I saw the log floating near the Hawkeye. The tide had come in and my log was afloat and the skiff was skimming away towards the main channel. "Oh, no. I'm sorry!"

Robert was already stripping down to his underwear.

"What are you doing?" I was worried now. The seriousness of the situation was sinking in at last.

"I'll have to swim to the boat and use it to go after the skiff. God dammit. I thought you said you knew how to tie up boats." He flung his jeans to the dry part of the beach. "Stay here. The portable VHF is in the pack. Put it on channel 6." He took off into the water and I could hear his gasps and some choice swear words as he dealt with the shock of the cold. He only had about 100 yards to swim to the Hawkeye, but even though he was a strong swimmer, the water temperature must have presented a challenge. Halfway out to the boat, he disappeared. My stomach tightened into a knot. I needed him to get me back to Lund. I couldn't let him drown. I struggled out of my sneakers and jeans, whipped off my shirt, leaving my tank top on. I ran into the water just as Robert's head bobbed up again, much closer to the boat. *Oh there he is. Thank God.*

He reached up for a bumper tire and pulled himself higher out of the water. Grabbing the rope, he put one foot in the bottom of the tire and swung himself up onto the Hawkeye. I heard the engine start up. Moments later, Robert appeared on deck in a change of clothes and hauled the anchor aboard. I saw him reaching up onto the wheelhouse roof for a long pike pole which he set on deck ready to use when he caught up to the skiff. He headed in the direction that the skiff had gone without so much as a glance back in my direction.

As the Hawkeye motored out of sight, I was overwhelmed by a feeling of abandonment. I took a deep breath. *Don't cry. Don't cry.* My mouth was dry. I'd never seen Robert so angry. Would he come back for me? Of course he would. But what if he didn't? Monique would come looking for me. But would I die of thirst first? What if he was fed up with me and made up some story about me changing my mind about the picnic. Would those tourists he talked about find me long after I starved to death, nothing left but a skeleton and scraps of my clothes? Why had I come here? Mom was right. I should have stayed home and taken that office job.

Damn! I was so stupid. Tying the skiff to a log that would float away? Even a city slicker should know better. Can't believe the grief I caused Robert. There went any good chemistry we might have had.

He'd been fun to be with all day. That kiss was delicious. Soft, warm lips that sent tingles through me and left me wanting more. Still, he allowed me space. He'd been friendly, but not pushy. For hours, we had lain on the blanket, chatting. I loved the feeling of closeness when his fingers traced paths along my arms and shoulders. Little rushes of excitement buzzed down to my abdomen and I wanted nothing more than to roll onto my back and clutch Robert tightly to me, feeling his weight on top of my body. I sighed. A perfect day. Perfect until I ruined everything with my carelessness.

I put my jeans and sneakers back on and sat on a log with my elbows propped on my legs, head slumped forward staring down at the wet gravel. Tiny beach crabs scurried along and dug under small rocks for safety. I imagined them terrified by the giant who hovered over them staring down hungrily. Seagulls squealed warnings. A tiny shorebird alternately hopped and ran in and out playing tag with the waves, picking at things in the sandier part of the beach. I wondered if I would still be sitting here a week from now, watching—and waiting to be rescued.

After the dull hum of the Hawkeye's engine faded, the eerie silence emphasized the fact that I was completely alone, and wave after wave of fear passed through me, tightening my insides. I wasn't sure what to do, but I couldn't just sit here. Sure I was stuck on an island, but I had to get moving. An island! Water on all sides. I should be able to see the channel if I scrambled up the hill. Maybe I'd catch a glimpse of the Hawkeye and be able to watch its progress. Inspired, I leaped up and strode along the flat beach around to the other side of the bay. On the far side, I climbed up a small hill towards the east shore of the island. I felt some of the worry leave me as I sprang into action. I could probably yell out to Robert from the top. Yell? That would be stupid when I had a radio. I'd forgotten all about it. I retraced my path, hopping over boulders and logs, back down to the bay and then along the trail to our picnic blanket. One of those bags holding down the blanket had to have the radio in it.

I clawed my way through the contents of Robert's backpack. There it was in a plastic Ziploc bag. Trust Robert to make sure the VHF radio was kept waterproof. All I had to do was tune it to channel six as he had told me, and I would be in business. I turned the "on" button until it clicked, and then looked for the number on the tiny dial beside it. I turned the dial so the six showed in the indicator slot. *Okay, all set.* I guessed that the lever on the side controlled the mike. Press and talk. I was feeling better already.

"Hawkeye. Hawkeye. Are you on here?" I waited and heard nothing. "Hawkeye. Hawkeye. Can you hear me, Robert?" Nothing. My shoulders sagged as my hope for contact was dashed.

I clambered back to the east side of the island that overlooked the main channel between the Copelands and Lund to the south. Holding onto the barkless trunk of an arbutus tree, I leaned out to look up the channel. There she was! Hallelujah! Oh thank God! Weak with relief, I sank to my knees on the moss-covered rocks. Everything would be all right now.

The Hawkeye chugged along on the far side of the channel. The skiff bobbed spastically in the slop of the waves close to the steep sides of the mainland. As the troller edged closer to it, Robert appeared on deck. Hope came flooding back through me. I wasn't alone. Robert grabbed the pike pole and reached to hook the skiff. It seemed he was leaning out too far and for too long. I held my breath. After what seemed an eternity, he popped up, but he had missed the skiff. *You can do it. You can.*

I chanted the words under my breath as if my good intentions could make it happen. Robert tried twice more before finally connecting with the skiff. He must have twisted the pike pole around the skiff's line to retrieve it. He fastened the skiff with a couple of quick wraps around one of the Hawkeye's trolling poles. When he straightened up, he instantly lurched forward and leaped into the wheelhouse. As the fish boat disappeared from sight behind the farther islands, a huge thick black cloud belched from its smokestack. Oh, my God! The Hawkeye was on fire.

Half an hour later, I was still watching the channel for the troller to reappear. I gulped. The boat couldn't be on fire. I'd see more smoke behind the outcropping of rocks. Wouldn't I? I took a deep breath. *Get a grip, girl.* It couldn't be anything as drastic as that. Could it? Surely he only had to give it a burst of speed to clear a tight spot and then he would turn around to come back to me. But then where *was* he? What if he'd gone up on the rocks? What if he'd sunk? I pressed my clenched fists to my temples and tried to keep myself from falling apart.

What if he wasn't coming back? Robert's home was only an hour or two to the north. He'd been so angry with me. What if he kept going just to get away from me? Oh, dear God. I could be stuck here forever. I'd die here. The birds would pick at my bones. No one would ever know. My stomach flip-flopped and I swallowed hard. Tears stung my eyes.

Slowly I worked my way back, craning my neck every few steps to catch the first possible glimpse of the bay, wishing, hoping I would see a troller anchored there. Nothing. Only the flat expanse of water. Water I couldn't even drink to stay alive.

I called him on the VHF again. "Hawkeye. Hawkeye. Are you okay, Robert?" I turned up the volume. Nothing.

He did have an accident. We'd both die out here. No, he was experienced. He went home. He left me to die here. He did. Tears flowed down my cheeks. Waves lapped at the shore relentlessly. Those same waves that I once found so soothing now kept me prisoner on this island.

I dragged myself up the path to the other side of the island and slumped on the blanket, stunned and at a loss for what to do. I had a sip from my water bottle. No, that might not be smart. I should be rationing my water. I had no matches to build a fire, no emergency flare to signal passing boats. Did boats even pass this way? They must. This was a fairly populated area. Wasn't it? I rifled through the cooler. Half a sandwich. A boiled egg. Two oranges and an apple. Three bottles of water—small ones. Enough for a couple of days. What if I was here longer than that? All I could do was wait. I laid my head down on my knees and let the sun warm me. Not that it made me feel any better.

I flinched and shrieked when something touched my shoulder. "Robert! Oh, thank God. You're here!" I jumped up and threw my arms around him. I was grinning with joy but my eyes were filling with tears.

"Miss me?" He sounded pleased that I was so happy to see him.

"How'd you get here? I watched so long. Finally gave up. Didn't hear you come up behind me." I craned my neck to look towards the bay but couldn't see it for the trees and the rise of land. "The Hawkeye okay?"

"Of course. Why wouldn't it be?" He pushed me away to study me at arm's length. "Hey, girl. What's wrong?"

"Last thing I saw was a big puff of black smoke. I thought you were on fire. I thought ..." I hastily wiped at my eyes.

"Hey, hey," he crooned, as he pulled me close again. "Don't cry. I'm here now."

I felt safe, enveloped in his embrace. I sniffed and tried to get a grip on my blubbering. "But what happened? The smoke...."

"Oh that!" He chuckled. "By the time I got the skiff tied on, I was pretty close to the rocks. I had to give the engine a quick shot of fuel to get back into deeper water. There's always a big cloud of black smoke when you do that." He hugged me again. "I'm sorry you were so worried." Then his brow furrowed and he looked serious. "But why didn't you answer when I talked to you on the VHF?"

"I called you but you didn't say anything." *If he says he talked to me I'll know he's lying.*

"Yes, I did. I answered you every time you called and then you didn't say anything more. You must've heard me. Did you have the volume turned up?"

"I had it way up, but I didn't hear you." He wasn't going to turn this around on me.

"Let's see the radio. Maybe the battery's gone."

"Maybe." I hadn't thought of that. I handed over the VHF.

He turned a button and loud static hissed and then stopped. "You had the squelch turned up too much."

"Squelch?" What the hell was squelch?

"This button here, by the volume button, has to be turned just until you hear all that static, and then you turn it back a tiny bit till the noise stops."

"And then what?"

"And then you'll be able to hear someone talking when they call you."

"Oh." I felt really stupid now. "Okay, now I know. Won't happen again."

"So you didn't hear me at all, I guess." Robert shook his head. "Did you think I'd gone and left you?" He was grinning, as if it was a big joke. How could he make light of it when I was so scared?

My jaw clenched in anger. "No," I ground out. "I didn't know what to think. Maybe you'd hit some rocks and sunk, or maybe you were on fire. I didn't know." My voice rose. I shrugged my shoulders and tossed my hands in the air helplessly. "I was worried, okay?" His eyebrows lifted and he looked pleased and puzzled at the same time, as if he wasn't used to someone worrying about him.

"Aw ... that's sweet of you." He put an arm around me and tried to pull me close again, but I stepped back. I needed answers first.

"Where were you anyway? I watched for a long time and you didn't come back down the channel." Seemed to me he could have come back a lot quicker and saved me the agony.

"I went around the outside of the islands."

"Oh." I hadn't even considered that possibility. He seemed to have sensible answers for everything. Maybe it was me. There was so much I didn't know about boating yet.

"It was easier than trying to make a tight turn. And anyway, it was less boring than coming back the same way. I kept going and made a loop and nipped back into the bay from the south instead. I didn't worry 'cause I thought you would've seen me."

Less boring! I'm all alone here on this deserted little speck of land and you're worried about being bored. "I was watching for you on the channel side." I spoke through gritted teeth. "I thought maybe something terrible had happened to you." Tears welled up in spite of my efforts to stay composed.

"Come here," Robert said quietly, and pulled me closer. "Everything's okay now." I wanted to stay angry, but when he stroked my hair and rubbed my back, all my worry and anger melted away. I felt safe and protected in the warmth of his arms. My tears soaked into his shoulder and he swayed back and forth as he held me. "Let's pack up these things and go back to the Hawkeye and I'll make us a nice hot toddy."

"That sounds good." I sniffed and fumbled around looking for a tissue.

Robert handed me one from his pocket. "Only used once." He smiled.

Exhausted by the stress of the day and relaxed by the rum and hot apple juice Robert had made, I struggled to stay awake. I couldn't stifle a yawn and quickly covered my mouth. "'Scuse me." I shook my head and laughed an embarrassed yawning laugh.

"Lie down if you want. We can stay here a while yet before we go back. I wouldn't mind a little nap myself."

"I suppose I could lie down for a few minutes."

"In the fo'c'sle. Sure." Robert pointed to the bunk that was down a small set of stairs.

"What did you call it?"

"The fo'c'sle. Short for forecastle. 'Cause it's in the front."

I was so tired I could hardly keep my eyes open. I wasn't used to that much alcohol. It was only two beers and one hot rum, but so much sunshine and stress, and the warm boat ... I was asleep in a minute.

Next thing I knew, I had company in the bed. "Rob—"

"Sh-h-h ..." he whispered. "Don't worry. I won't do anything you don't want me to." Where had I heard that before? Every date I'd ever been on.

He put an arm over my shoulder and stroked my hair. "You have beautiful hair. Rich deep brown and so thick. Smells like flowers."

"That's the shampoo."

"You know, Andrea, I really like you a lot."

"Yeah? That's nice. I like you a lot too Robert. But don't go getting any ideas." I started to get up, but Robert pulled my arm back down. It was a gentle pull, but insistent.

"Wait," he said. "Please?" Then he kissed me and I felt warm all over. I wanted him and I wanted him to want me. I felt myself relax and sink into the kiss. Heat flushed through my whole body.

"M-mph. Just a minute," I said. "Robert. Wait. Stop." I sat up in the bunk. "Listen to me. I like you a lot, and I like what you're doing. But if we don't stop now, the next time you see me at the wharf, you'll think of me as that girl that was an easy lay, and I don't want to be that girl." I hadn't put out for Jim right away, and I sure wasn't about to for Robert. Sexy as he was, I hardly knew him.

"Okay." He took a deep breath. "All right. I can appreciate that." He rolled out of the bunk and offered me his hand to help me out of the cramped quarters. "Does that mean if I asked you out to dinner some time you'd say yes?"

I smiled. "Yes, I would definitely say yes."

Chapter 18

Oh, Monique, Robert is so-o-o-o charming." I hugged myself and danced around the room. Monique looked at me as if I was crazy so I grabbed her and spun her around too. "He's been so good to me!" Yesterday's outing was one of many that Robert had taken me on since the Copelands disaster. I was still glowing with happy memories as I relived the latest trip. Monique grimaced and rolled her eyes. "Sorry. I guess I've been going on and on about him, but he's so handsome and charming."

"Never mind. Dat's okay. So long you 'ad a good time."
She stopped, then looked at me. "And he wasn't ... you
know ... strange?" She crinkled her nose and waggled her
fingers.

"No!" I put my hands on my hips. "And I wish you
would stop saying he's strange, he's different, he's—"

"Weird?"

"Monique!"

"Okay. Sorry. But I see 'im at de wharf many time
when 'e and odder guys were talking. All of a sudden 'e
start yelling and pointing 'is finger in deir faces. Real mad.
And so loud too. Was embarrassing for everybody."

"And then what happened?" I could hardly believe
Monique.

"De same like always when 'e gets mad. 'E 'as to go lie
down. Bad 'eadache."

I frowned. Why would Monique say that? "Well, he's
never done that to me. We had a beautiful day at Galley
Bay. He anchored the Hawkeye and put a lounge chair
on the deck for me. And oh, the most amazing thing
happened. He put a bunch of grapes on the hatch cover
beside me and said to relax and enjoy the sunshine while
he got a few things ready in the kitchen."

"De galley."

"Pardon?"

"De galley. De boat kitchen."

"Oh, okay. Yeah, in the galley. Anyway, I lay back in
the lounge chair and closed my eyes. The sun felt so good.
Then I heard a whirring sound and opened my eyes. A
hummingbird was hovering right by my face. It poked a
hole in one of the grapes and was drinking its juice."

"Dat must 'ave been somet'ing."

"I'll never be that close to a hummingbird again."

"Nature can be a beautiful t'ing."

"And Robert came out on deck just then and saw the hummingbird too."

"Did 'e even notice it? Men can be so stupid sometime."

"As a matter of fact, he did. I was surprised too, but he stood really still and whispered, 'Wow!'" I hadn't expected a man to care about a hummingbird. "It was a great trip. We saw otters on the rocks, and all kinds of seabirds, and seals, and—"

"Yeah, yeah, I get de picture." She turned her back to me and straightened the cushions on the couch.

"And the barbecued steaks were perfect."

"So 'e's a good cook den?"

"Yup. I won't have to worry about doing all the cooking."

"What are you talking about?"

"I wanted to surprise you so I've saved the best for last." I pulled a little blue velour box out of my pocket and opened it. I slipped on the ring and pushed my hand in front of Monique's eyes. "Robert asked me to marry him."

"Oh, my God!" Monique's jaw dropped and her eyes grew round. "Oh, my God! You didn't say yes?" She clapped her hand over her mouth and stared at me.

"But ... I thought you'd be happy for me." I covered the ring on my left hand with my right. I didn't know what else to say. I swallowed a lump of disappointment.

Monique's brow wrinkled as if she was fighting tears. "Oh, Andrea, come 'ere." She reached for me and hugged me long and close. "I was shocked at first." She smiled and I knew it was forced. "Really, I'm 'appy for you. But I 'ope Robert be'aves 'imself, dat's all." She rushed to the bedroom, and glanced back at me over her shoulder. She wiped at her eyes as she closed the door.

God! I was such a dummy. Monique must have wanted Robert for herself. No wonder she was so impatient when I went on and on about Robert. No wonder she was upset about the ring. I knocked on her door. A muffled voice invited me in.

"Monique, I'm sorry. I didn't realize you had a thing for Robert."

"Robert?" She laughed a humourless laugh. "No." She sniffed and wiped her nose with a tissue. "Oh, Andrea." She looked at me with a pained expression. "You are so naïve." She shook her head sadly.

"I don't understand."

Monique's eyes brimmed with tears. "It's you."

"Me? ... Me what?"

"It's *you* I 'ave a t'ing for."

Chapter 19

The Victoria Day weekend was a busy one at the wharf. Travelers from as far away as California stopped for groceries, showers, and fuel, loading up on last minute supplies for their trips to Alaska or to the marine parks of Desolation Sound famous for their natural beauty. Visiting boaters met fellow travelers and socialized. Many took advantage of the swimming in the pristine saltwater bays or in freshwater lakes at the end of a short trail hike. Happy hour get-togethers followed by barbecues on the back of a sailboat or on the beaches were a great way for boaters to get to know each other. Someday I'd do those things too. I just had to make it happen. And someday I would.

"Help tie up those two sailboats coming in," Bert said. "Get that guy on the yacht to pay before he leaves. Snug up those little sailboats and make room for one more on the end. And hose that goddamn dog shit off the end of the wharf. Bloody irresponsible jerks."

I was running all day. I might have resented Bert for bossing me around so much, except for two things: he *was* the boss, and in between telling me what to do, he often had praise for me. "You look right smart today, girl," he'd say. "Those sailboaters will remember Lund." Or, "Good work on those knots, Andrea. Nice snug tie-up jobs."

I dressed "flashy-practical" with my red shorts and black tank top. I kept my hair out of the way in a ponytail that came out through the back of my red ball cap. But more than looking good, I wanted to be good—at my job, at life. I came out here, an inexperienced city girl. I planned to change that and learn to survive in rural surroundings.

The wharf job was perfect for learning about boating life on the West Coast. I met people from everywhere. One fellow had just sailed in from Oregon. He was telling me about a beautiful day when he found himself among a pod of gray whales heading north. The story was cut short.

"Hey, Andrea." Robert jumped off his boat onto the dock and hurried over. He moved in front of the American and gave me a peck on the cheek. Keeping his back to the young man, he stood between us like a guard dog. "How's it going?"

"Good. Busy, but good." I leaned around Robert and spoke to the fellow from Oregon. "Very nice to meet you. Enjoy your stay in Lund." He nodded and gave me a smile before moving on. As he walked away I saw him turn and scowl at Robert over his shoulder.

I was shocked at Robert's rudeness. "Why did you do that?"

"What?"

"I was having a conversation and you barged right in."

"Just protecting what's mine," he said. "I'm leaving in a couple of weeks so I wondered if you wanted to take a trip up to see our house in Hope Bay."

I was still dumbfounded by the way he brushed it off so casually. He didn't seem to think it was any big deal. "Don't do that again!"

"Do what?"

"That ... that ... possessive thing. I'm not your property."

He waved away my protests. "So what do you say? Come with me to see the house?"

"Robert?" I waited till I had his full attention.

"What?" He looked at the sky.

"Don't do it again."

His mouth was closed, but his lips were working. "Fine," he said through his teeth. "Fine. Are you happy now?" His eyes were narrowed and I sensed he was still angry, but it was time to let this go. I had made my point.

"The house? Would you like to see the house I'm renting in Hope Bay?"

"Sure. That would be nice. It's near Desolation Sound, isn't it?" He nodded. "Must be nice," I added, "or all these boaters wouldn't be going there."

"Yeah, it is nice. That's why I chose to live there."

"Hope Bay, you said?"

"Yup. Very tiny little bay. Besides a few houses, it has a restaurant, and general store with a post office, liquor outlet, and clinic. Not much there, but it's a good place."

"When do you want to go?" I was curious to see where I would be living at the end of the summer. It would be interesting to see how Robert lived as a bachelor.

"Next week? Middle of the week is best for you, right?" Robert took my hand. "You can have a look and make a list of things you think you might need when we get married." He lifted my fingers to his lips. "Hey!" His face clouded over into a frown and his brow furrowed. "Why aren't you wearing my ring?"

"Robert." I gave him a "be sensible" look, but he shrugged and opened his palms in front of me. Obviously, he still thought it was a valid question.

"It's way too precious to wear on the job. It could snag on the lines when I'm tying up boats or it could slip off and fall into the water. You wouldn't want me to lose it, would you?"

The cloud moved on and his face became smooth again. "Yeah, you're right. I hadn't thought of that. But you wear it after work, right?"

"Of course I do." It sure seemed to mean a lot to him to show the world I was his. Well, maybe it was a good thing. He would certainly be looking out for me.

"Okay, so how about if we go to Hope Bay on Tuesday and come back Thursday. I have to load a bunch of supplies from home to take fishing when I go north."

"Do you have a date set yet for when you're leaving?"

"Couple of weeks. Jim's going to meet me here and we'll travel north together."

Jim. I had put him out of my mind. Most of the time, that is. But now his image floated in front of my mind's eye. I had liked him—a lot. Good looking guy. Quiet. A bit shy. Not so possessive. Maybe I had rushed things a bit by accepting Robert's marriage proposal. But Jim had dumped me. I shouldn't forget how much he hurt me.

"Andrea?"

"Huh?" I jumped. Probably the guilt. Thinking about Jim that way.

"What's wrong?" he asked.

"What do you mean?"

"You were like in a trance there."

"Oh no, I was just thinking about when I first moved here. Seems so long ago but it's only been two months." God, I hoped I wasn't making a big mistake.

Bert was happy to give me a couple of days off. "No problem," he said. "You've been a great help over the long weekend. Worked circles around Joe." Joe had to be part tortoise. It took him forever to do anything, but I accepted the compliment. "This will be good for Joe, to work your shifts for two days."

"Thanks, Bert. I'll be back in time for work on Friday."

He hooked his thumbs inside the suspenders on either side of his belly. "Not my business, Andrea, but you sure you know what you're doing?"

"What do you mean?"

Bert gave a subtle toss of his head in Robert's direction. "Quite a temper, that one."

I frowned at Bert. "Of course I know what I'm doing."

"I'm just saying—"

"Bert! I'll be fine. Don't worry." I shook my head and headed down the float to the Hawkeye.

"Well, have a good time," he called after me.

I didn't know why he was picking on Robert. It wasn't fair. I raised my hand to Bert without looking back.

I tossed my duffel bag onto the Hawkeye. Robert seemed anxious to get going. He untied the last line and pushed off as soon as I hopped aboard.

The route was familiar to me now after several outings and I felt comfortable taking the wheel to spell Robert— as long as nothing drastic came up, like several boats to maneuver around, or too many kelp beds or logs in the water. While I sat in the captain's seat and steered, Robert was free to do other things. I put the boat on autopilot for the long straight stretches. Bert's warning echoed in my head. Dammit! I wasn't going to let him wreck this trip. He didn't know Robert like I did.

"Keep an eye on that sounder. Your plotter will keep you on course, but it's always good to be aware of your depth." Robert was so capable and sensible. He was good with the boat and he was good to me, teaching me things. Bert was wrong.

On the way to Hope Bay we had time to talk about future plans. I felt comfortable with Robert most of the time. He still had an unnerving habit of staring at me intensely, but his facial expressions were easy to read. Most of the time his stares were accompanied by a not quite hidden smile. If I asked what he was thinking just then, he'd usually say, "How pretty you are," or "I was noticing how your eyes aren't blue; they're violet," or "What I'd like to do to you." They were flattering comments, but often the stares followed by the compliments left me confused and I wasn't sure what to say. I found that it was easier to ignore the intense looks than to probe into their meaning.

In a little over two hours, we turned into a tiny bay. A small float with a ramp led up to a fairly large building.

"That's the restaurant. Probably not open yet. It's mainly for tourists who come in to get a break. They can stock up at the general store too, if they want to pay the prices."

Robert angled the boat to the right to another float that didn't connect to the restaurant and store. "And this is the one the locals use for access to their houses. We can get to the store and restaurant by the trail."

It was an unpresuming dock. Six other boats occupied every foot of dockside space, leaving us no choice but to tie alongside one of them.

"God damn them. Just because I've been away, they think they can take my dockside space. Assholes. They're gonna hear about this. Fuckers!" I gasped at the vehemence of his words. Such a small thing. He was blowing it way out of proportion. His face was red, his eyes narrowed, and his jaw worked furiously.

He must have seen the shocked look on my face because he took a deep breath and in a calmer tone added, "Sorry. Don't worry about it. It's okay. Grab your duffel bag. I'll get the rest of the stuff."

It's okay? How could this kind of behaviour be okay?

"What just happened there?" I hadn't moved from the spot. "Are you feeling all right?"

"Course I'm all right. Why wouldn't I be?" His words came out tightly controlled.

"You were so angry."

"Don't worry about it. It just pissed me off because they're always doing that to me—taking my spot. Forget about it. I'm over it. Didn't mean to upset you."

"Okay." I picked up my duffel bag. "Here, I can take another bag in my free hand." Robert handed me a plastic bag of his clothes and gave me a tentative smile. Stepping over ropes and clutter on the deck of the boat we had tied onto, we made our way across it to the dock and up the ramp to the wharf head. I turned and waited for Robert to show the way, although I was sure we would be going up the only road there was. Robert pointed for me to go ahead and I was soon at the end of the track. From the top, a path went parallel to the beach in both directions.

"Left," he called. He was lagging behind, carrying the heavy picnic cooler.

Four houses stood on the hillside to the left, all small and all decorated with found items. Net floats, fancy bottles, washed-up boat parts, pieces of driftwood, and shells were arranged to make designs. One creation, with some imagination, resembled an otter; another made an original archway over a garden gate; yet another design went on and on to fence the yard.

"That's the one," Robert said. "The one with the fence." He set the heavy cooler down and reached inside the gate to unlatch it. The yard was neat and uncluttered. Weathered silver gray shakes covered the outside walls. Wood laths divided the old-fashioned windows into four smaller panes. Planter boxes fastened under each window held leafy geraniums with promising buds.

Inside, Robert set the cooler down on the rough hardwood floor and stood up arching his back as he took a big breath and blew it out again. "Whew! I'd forgotten it's a bit of a climb up the path."

We took our shoes off. His other boots and shoes sat in a straight row on the mat beside the door. I wasn't surprised that everything in the house was extremely tidy and clean. Every item had its place. No dishes cluttered the kitchen counter. Jars of herbs and spices stood on a rack each with the label looking straight ahead. Orderly. It reminded me of how he had the tools lined up neatly when he had the boat hauled out. He liked to be organized and that wasn't a bad thing. I liked things to be tidy myself.

I wandered around the country kitchen in my sock feet and pointed at the stove. "Wood?" I was incredulous. "People still use these for cooking?" The name Findlay was proudly embossed on a gleaming clean cook stove in the middle of the room.

"It keeps the whole place toasty warm in the winter." Robert was smiling as he noted my amazement.

"Oh, and look at this rug. Is it from India?" The red wool rug had an intricate mosaic pattern. "I love these rugs on a hardwood floor. And the coffee table and couch— did you make those?" Someone did. They were obviously handmade. Beautifully finished. The sofa with its wood frame and cushions reminded me of Ikea furniture, only more solid.

Robert nodded and glowed with pride. "Come see the bedroom." He took my hand and swept aside a curtain in the doorway. The bed was immaculately made up with extra pillows at the headboard. Night tables of the same style as the couch and coffee table stood at each side of the bed.

"Nice. And the bathroom?" I asked.

Robert's face dropped. "Inconveniently located through the door at the other side of the living room. Come I'll show you." He hesitated. "Might as well leave your duffel bag here. You can have this bed. I'll bunk on the couch."

I was disappointed that Robert was being so noble now.

"Are you sure you want to sleep out there?" I raised my eyebrows and gave him a teasing smile. After our engagement I'd made a point of taking birth control pills, just in case. I wasn't ready for babies yet, but I didn't want to play the prude either.

His head snapped up and a smile spread across his face. Without a word he brought his bag over and dropped it on the far side of the bed.

He gave me a wink and lifted my hand to his lips for a kiss. "Let's see how things go then."

We unloaded the cooler and made up sandwiches together. Fortunately Robert had a two-burner propane camp stove for those very hot days and we were able to boil water for tea without lighting the big woodstove.

As we strolled along the trail that afternoon, Robert showed me the other five houses and the general store. "It's also the post office and medical clinic."

"They have a doctor?"

"More like First Aid. Steve and Mary are the first responders in an emergency. You'll meet them later. If you ever needed help, they'd be the ones to call. We'll go have a look at the groceries and supplies in their store. Give you an idea of what's available and what's not."

"Do they live in the same building?"

"Yup. Living space at the back of the store; bedrooms and storage rooms upstairs."

Inside the store we found canned and dry packaged food, and the basic dry goods that were necessities for remote living; the kind of medical supplies you might find in a first aid kit, survival items like matches, candles, camp dishes, a couple of hammers, saws, axes, and nails.

Robert picked up a pack of noodles and a can of tomatoes, some onions, and a handful of potatoes. At the counter, he smiled broadly as he introduced me to Steve and Mary. "This is my fiancée, Andrea." I was very aware of the ring on my left hand. It felt strange and new to me, but Robert behaved as if it was the most natural thing in the world for us to be together. It was flattering that he seemed to be proud of me.

"Very nice to meet you, Andrea." Mary's smile was wide. "It'll be good to have more female company around here."

"Hi, Steve. Hi, Mary. Not many women living here then?"

"There are eleven houses, including the restaurant and store, and three of the owners are single men. That leaves only eight women, including myself."

"Small place for sure!" I gulped and wondered how I would fit in here.

"It gets pretty busy in the summertime with people coming to the restaurant for meals or to the store here for their groceries and liquor. But the rest of the time, it can get a bit lonely." Mary was only slightly older than me. I hoped we would hit it off.

"I see you have a book exchange in the porch. I have a few books that I could bring along to trade."

"You like reading then?" Mary asked. "That's great. So do I."

"Yeah," Steve added, "that was Mary's idea, and in the summer it's amazing the turnover we get. Like a real library." He grinned and put his arms lovingly around his wife.

"Well, we've got a lot to do so can you add these items to my tab and we'll be going," Robert said rather abruptly. It was as if he resented the focus not being on himself and I squirmed at his rudeness.

"Speaking of that tab," Steve said, "when were you planning on paying some down on that?" He had lowered his voice, but Mary and I could still hear him.

"When fishing is over, like everyone else does." Robert's hands balled up into fists. "What's the problem? My credit no good here?" His voice was embarrassingly loud.

"It's fine," said Mary, "but the cost of bringing the goods in has really gone up this spring, and we're barely able to keep afloat here."

"You know I'm good for it. I have a right to credit just like anyone else."

I tugged at Robert's arm. "I have some money, Robert," I whispered.

The way he glared at me made me wish I hadn't interfered. "No bloody way." He turned to face Steve again. "You put those things down on my tab. It'll be cleared after fishing season and you damn well know it."

Steve raised his hands, palms facing Robert. "All right, all right. Don't get your knickers in a knot." He turned to Mary. "Put Robert down for another $10.50."

Mary's face was white as she scribbled the amount on a pad of paper.

Robert swept up the grocery bag. I waved a timid, embarrassed goodbye and followed him out the door. As I glanced over my shoulder, I saw Steve standing with his hands on his hips, his jaw set firmly, and Mary shaking her head slowly and sadly.

With giant strides Robert headed straight back to the cabin. I felt like a child hop-skipping two steps to his one, trying to keep up with him. Once in the house, he whirled and spoke angrily, pointing his finger at me. "Don't say anything. They owe me a line of credit. They give it to everyone else. Damn them. They can't show favouritism like that. It's not right." He dropped the bag of groceries on the counter. I hurried to put them away, anything to keep busy and out of his way. I had a sick feeling in my stomach as it dawned on me what he was capable of. How would I get through the next two days? These sudden outbursts of anger scared the hell out of me. And I had invited him to sleep with me.

I looked over at him. He was lying down on the couch with the back of his hand on his forehead. "Robert?" I said quietly. "Are you okay?"

"I have a terrible headache. But it'll go away in a few minutes. I just need to lie here for a bit. Shut those curtains, will you?"

I rushed over to close them. "I'll sit outside on the porch with my book till you're feeling better, okay?"

"Fine," he muttered.

I stared vacantly at the pages of the book unable to focus on the meaning of the words. I couldn't shut out the disturbing thoughts that bombarded me. Robert's outbursts were shocking; so unlike the behaviour I'd seen until now. How could this charming man be capable of these bizarre explosive outbursts? Monique had told me about his tirades on the dock and how he had to lie down afterwards. Jim had said he was—what did he say?—

different? I had downplayed those warnings; dismissed them completely. But I couldn't ignore them any longer. I'd seen displays of Robert's anger three times now. The first time was my fault, when I'd lost the skiff. Okay, so I didn't count that one. I'd be angry too. But the second time over something as insignificant as not having dockside space? How could I rationalize that outburst? And then there was the scene at the store. Shocking, and embarrassing. I'd wanted to crawl under the counter and hide.

What if we had children? How would he react if the child disobeyed? Oh my God! That would be impossible. Bad enough with a small child but how would that child cope during the teen years? Would he or she rebel? Run away from home? Drink and drive? And what if I did something he didn't like? The possibilities made me shudder with dread. My head throbbed.

When I thought about it, he was right. Not right to get mad like that, but right about the issue. Maybe he was embarrassed at not having enough money to pay the tab at the store, and I had made it worse by offering my money in front of Steve and Mary. It would probably never happen again.

I had already written to my parents to tell them I was engaged. They'd written back that they were delighted with my news and wished me well. They'd even sent me a nice fat cheque of $1000 towards whatever I might need for the wedding. "Buy yourself a nice dress or a wedding gift for the house," my mother had written.

They'd die of shock if I wrote and said, "Sorry to have to tell you ... returning your money ... sorry if I disappointed you." *No, I can't do that. I want this to work out.* But how? What kind of help did he need? Could I do it?

I was still staring at the same page when Robert appeared on the porch after an hour's nap. He sat on the other lawn chair and waited for me to notice him. I dreaded a confrontation. My hands were shaking so badly I put the book down on my lap and slid my hands under my legs to hold them still. "Feeling better?"

"Yeah," he said in a quiet voice. "Andrea, I'm really sorry. I—I must have embarrassed you back there in the store."

"Oh." I shrugged one shoulder. "I could see you felt strongly about it."

"I did."

"But yes, I was really embarrassed.

"I'm sorry. I'll try not to let that happen again." I wanted to believe him. Did I dare to trust him? He reached for my hand and took it in both of his. He kissed my fingers. "So are we okay then?"

"Of course. Sure we are." I stood up, my hand still in Robert's. At least by holding my hand, he stopped it from shaking. "Would you like to have a cup of tea?" That's what my parents always did when there were problems. They made a cup of tea and then the world was all better.

"Good idea." He stood up too, pulled me close, and hugged me. "I'm so glad you understand. We'll be good for each other." His kiss was warm and he was so gentle and caring. He held me tight as if he needed me. And yet, he was not the only one to take comfort from the embrace. I needed to know he cared about me and that there was a loving side to him. He was almost a foot taller than me and as he wrapped me up in his arms, I felt wanted, loved, and safe. Everything would be okay.

While Robert put the kettle on the propane stove, I got the teabags out and found the teapot. "How about a few crackers and cheese to go with the tea?" I asked. "Maybe sometime I'll figure out how to use the big stove and make some cookies, but for now we'll have to make do with what we have."

"You know how to make cookies?"

"Of course. Cookies, muffins, bread. My mom showed me how to make all those things. She's a great baker."

"I can hardly wait." Robert beamed at me. "That'll be a first for me, having someone make cookies for me."

I stared at him. "Your mother never made cookies?" He looked at the floor.

"No. She was very strict. Said it would spoil me to have treats all the time. I needed to be tough to be a man." He shook his head. "You might say she was not the cuddly type."

I felt so bad for him. I could picture him as a little boy watching all the other boys take cookies out of their lunch bags at school while he had none. "I'll bake you lots and lots of things."

"How about we get married as soon as I get home from fishing?" He studied my face as he waited for me to agree. "Not just because of your baking," he added with a grin.

"No? Why else?" He looked so sexy when he smiled. Hard to believe he'd ever been angry.

With one finger, he stroked my throat under my chin. "Why else? I could show you sometime, if you wanted. He pulled me closer and I could feel that he was hard and wanting me.

"Yes, you could do that sometime ... sometime soon if you want."

"I'll check my schedule and see what I can arrange. But you haven't answered my question. After fishing is over?"

"That sounds okay. Where would we get married?" For sure there was no minister here in Hope Bay.

"We'll go to Powell River in the boat and get married by the Justice of the Peace if that's okay with you. Sorry, but I'm not big on church stuff."

"Me either, so that suits me fine." At least we wouldn't argue over religion. "I believe in doing what is right and good. Having religion wouldn't make me a better person. I'm happy with who I am."

"I'm happy with who you are too," he said. "All right. Let's say we get married in the last week of August?" He nuzzled my neck and gave me goosebumps that went straight to my nipples.

"All right. Last week of August." I barely breathed the words, as I felt my body heating up.

"And Andrea?" He spoke very quietly.

"Yes?"

"I promise I'll be good to you. I ... I ... well ... I love you." *He does want me. He does.* "I love you too, Robert."

I was pretty sure that was true.

Chapter 20

Monique embraced me and gave me a kiss on the cheek. She had taken it well once we talked over why I couldn't be more than a friend to her. "'Ow was your trip?"

"Good. Mostly good."

"Mostly?" Her eyebrows went up as she waited for me to fill her in on the details.

"Hope Bay is a quiet place. The people there seem to care about blending in with nature. Very conscientious about 'doing the green thing' if you know what I mean. I met most of the neighbours. Nice people."

"But?" Monique drummed her fingers on the table.

"But I found out what you mean about Robert's angry outbursts."

Her eyes grew rounder. "What 'appened? Did 'e blow up?"

"Twice," I said bitterly.

"So tell me, tell me, tell me." She was bouncing up and down on the balls of her feet. I could see she was dying to say, "I told you so."

"Well, he was mad because someone took his dockside space on the float. And he got into an argument about when he should pay his bill at the general store." I sighed, possibly with the relief of having confided in someone at last.

"Oh, *mon Dieu*! Were you shocked? Embarrassed? Scared?"

"All of that, at first. But then he calmed down."

"Did 'e 'ave to go lie down?" She continued to press me for details. I felt like a traitor talking about Robert like that.

"Yeah, he did. It was as if he had a migraine. He wanted the curtains closed. I had a migraine once. It was terrible. I felt sorry for him."

"And den what 'appened?"

"After he slept for a while he felt better. He was really gentle, caring, and charming. He apologized. Said he loved me."

"Ah! So did you sleep in de same bed togedder?" She placed her palms together and shoved her hands between her knees.

"I thought you told me you were gay, so what do you care about what Robert did?"

"Well, yes I like women, but dat does not mean I cannot like men too. I like bot' kinds of sex. Bi-sexual, dey call it. So tell me, did you sleep togedder?"

"He said I could have the bed; he'd take the couch." Monique's head tipped to the side and she grimaced in disappointment. It seemed odd to me that Monique wanted to hear about sex so much, but maybe she didn't get to have sex as often as she'd like. "But then after a while I thought it was ridiculous for him to sleep on the couch in his own house. And we're going to be married in three months anyway."

"Oh!" She perked up. "And 'ow was it? Is 'e good in bed?"

"Monique! You shouldn't be asking things like that." I would never be so forward with personal questions, but to Monique it seemed like the most natural topic of conversation.

"Why not?" She shrugged. "Is just girl talk."

"Still ..."

"So give it up. 'Ow was 'e? Does he 'ave a big one?"

"Monique!"

"You 'ave to stop saying 'Monique' and tell me all about it. Come on. Girl talk. Just between two girls. And I see your face is getting red so it must be a big one."

"It's not bad." I laughed and turned my face away.

"Is dat all you 'ave to say? 'Not bad'?"

I took a deep breath. "All right ... yes, it's a big one. Are you happy now?" She nodded and smiled brightly. "He made love to me gently and fiercely all at the same time. He handled me as if I was made of fragile porcelain. And yet, he needed me so badly that all my porcelain threatened to break. It was like he could never get enough. Like he had to own all of me."

"*Mon Dieu. Mon Dieu!*" She grasped my arm and studied my face. "So what did you t'ink? What did you feel?"

I shrugged my shoulders and bit my lower lip. What did I feel? So many things. "I felt small. Helpless. Powerless." I hesitated. "But I was on fire too." Oh, I remembered feeling like I was burning up. I was so ... so moved by his power. But still, there was something not right.

"Sure sound like 'ot sex to me." Monique shook her head slowly. "What more could you want?"

"I've been thinking about that all day. The loving and the sex, that part was great. Sensual, full of emotion, everything a girl could want. He tried to make it good for me, to give me what he thought I wanted."

"What is wrong wit' dat?"

"Nothing. But he didn't let me give anything back. He just took what he needed. He had all the control."

Chapter 21

My heart pounded as the Serenity slid into the empty space at the dock. I caught the midship line thrown to me and did a quick wrap around the bull rail. Jim stepped onto the float—his jeans still fit perfectly—and tied up the bow line while I fastened the stern line.

"Andrea! Great to see you again." Jim wrapped me in a great bear hug and couldn't seem to stop smiling.

What the...? "Good to see you too, Jim." As if nothing happened between us. Those bright sparkly eyes sent a stab of pain through me. I could barely stand to look into them. My nerves quivered. Would I be able to keep smiling without breaking down into tears? How could he be so friendly and smiling, as if he hadn't dumped me? As if we were still in some sort of relationship.

"You look even better than I remember," Jim said.

"Stop! Don't say that." My hands flew to my hair. Did I look okay? I wasn't sure how to take his compliment.

"Why not? You do look good. And I've missed you."

He stepped back and his face grew serious. "I know you must be wondering what happened. I said I'd call and—"

"You don't have to explain." I couldn't bear to hear his excuses.

"But I want to—I have to." He reached for me again. "I've missed you so much."

"Oh, no you don't! I don't hear from you for a month and you come on as if we said goodbye at the ferry yesterday." I swallowed a painful lump in my throat and kept my head down, studying the wharf planks while I tried to compose myself.

"I was going to call but—".

"Well, you didn't. I'm not stupid. I know what that means." I wrenched my arm out of his hand. "Just leave me alone. You go on with your life. I'll go on with mine."

"No, you don't understand at all."

"What's to understand? When it's over, it's over." The finality of those words spoken out loud unleashed the tears I had tried to keep inside.

"Andrea, please." Jim put his arms around me and pulled me close.

I wanted to be angry and turn and run, but I wanted Jim near me even more. I fastened my arms around him and buried my face in his shirt. "I'm sorry," I sobbed. "I'll be okay in a minute and then I won't bother you anymore." *What did I do wrong? Why didn't you want me anymore?* But he did say he'd explain. I had to pull myself together until he told me what happened.

Jim stroked my neck. "I had to go to Calgary," he blurted out quickly. "Now let me explain what happened. Please?"

"Calgary?" I dug around for a Kleenex and dabbed at my eyes. "What were you doing in Calgary?"

"It's kind of a long story. How about if we go to the bake shop for coffee and a goodie? I can explain everything there."

He's asking me to spend time with him? In spite of having dumped me? I opened my mouth to say no. "I'd love to. My morning shift's about over anyway. I'll tell Bert I'm going and Joe can take over." *Oh God! I'm hopeless.*

He made small talk on the way to the bake shop.

"Robert called me. Said he wants to leave tomorrow. Wants us to travel north together. Safety in numbers," he added with an awkward chuckle.

"Robert's gone to Powell River for the day to 'grub up' as he puts it. Should be back tonight around five, he said."

"Well, then there's no rush. We can take our time at the bake shop. They make the best cinnamon buns."

I was surprised how powerfully my buried feelings re-surfaced. Jim wasn't handsome like Robert, but there was something disarming about him. I felt at ease around him. Maybe all he wanted was for us to be friends and nothing more. Oh, how I wanted it to be more. But what was I thinking? I had Robert now. *I shouldn't even be here with Jim.* And yet he already had me making excuses for being with him. How did he do that to me? It was like being pulled by a magnet. And I didn't even try to resist.

We sat at a patio table outside the bakery with our coffee and cinnamon buns. Jim took a deep breath and began.

"I had to go to Calgary the same day after I saw you last. My mother has advanced Alzheimer's and she'd wandered away from her apartment. I had to put her in a care facility and clear out her apartment. I wanted to call you but I had to leave in such a hurry and I forgot to bring your phone number. I didn't know Monique's last name."

"Oh!" My hands went up to my cheeks. "Oh, my God. And I thought—"

"You thought I didn't care?" He held my trembling hands. "Aw, Andrea. I'll always care about you."

Oh, what have I done? I've tied myself to Robert. What was I thinking? But Jim dumped me! I tried to concentrate on what Jim was saying, but a sick feeling crept over me as I remembered that Jim didn't know yet.

"The first time we sat at a table together, your face was freckled with copper paint." He smiled at the memory. "You were so new to all this boat stuff."

"I've had more practice since then, doing Robert's boat, for one." *Oh Lord, all this time I thought—*

"How'd that work out?" He leaned forward in his chair and crossed his arms over his chest.

"Oh, not bad, once I learned to stop asking so many questions. He's not as patient as you are."

"He sure has some strange ways. But anyway, he's okay to fish around most of the time. It's not like I have to live with him."

I chewed my lip and clasped my hands tightly in my lap.

"What? Did I say something wrong?"

"I ..." I didn't know how to tell Jim. Hadn't dared dream I might see him again or that he might be glad to see me. "Well, Robert ..."

"What about Robert?" he pressed.

"He asked me to marry him." I blurted it out fast. Jim's jaw dropped and his eyes widened. He took a big breath and sat up straighter.

"Please tell me you said no." Anguish was written all over his face.

I shook my head. In a pained sigh, he let out the breath he'd been holding. Elbows on the table, his head dropped into his hands.

"Oh, no. No, no, no." Then he jerked his head up to look at me. "Why, Andrea? Why would you do that? Don't you know what he's like?"

I swallowed a lump in my throat. "A little bit, yes." My voice came out barely more than a whisper.

"That bastard! Very slick of Robert to rush you like that. But how could you say yes? Don't you know how I feel about you?" He looked stricken.

"No! You never told me. You never called or said anything."

"Damn him! Now I know what he kept hinting at on the phone. He said he had a surprise for me. That prick!"

"I'm sorry." I didn't really know why I was apologizing, unless I was regretting that I agreed to marry Robert. *Was I?*

"It's not too late." He grabbed my arms and shook them. "You're rushing into this. You'd have so many more opportunities. Don't do it."

"Opportunities? Like what?"

"Like me?"

I wanted to cry, but I was so shocked. Everything I had wished for—evaporated. *Why now? When it's too late?* "I can't go back on my word." Robert would be so mad. "And anyway, I've already told my parents."

"Andrea, I know Robert. Please don't do it."

I shook my head and whispered, "Too late." The conversation had me emotionally drained, confused, and deflated. My hopes and dreams had just fallen into a bottomless black abyss. "Thanks for the coffee, Jim. I guess I'd better get going." I tried to smile and put on a brave face.

Jim looked pale. Frown wrinkles creased the bridge of his nose. "Is there somewhere you have to be?"

I shrugged. "Not really. But I don't want you to feel you have to spend the afternoon with me, especially since I've dropped that bombshell on you about Robert." I probably should have told him right away, but I'd been so happy to see him that I'd wanted some time with him. Now my head felt heavy, weighed down by guilt.

"After Robert gets here, I won't see you anymore—not for a long time. We're leaving first thing in the morning." His smile was lopsided. "Let's go for a walk up the road and later we can go down to my boat and wait for him to arrive."

"Okay. It's quiet down that road." I was happy to have more of Jim's company before I had to let him go forever. Now that I knew he cared, all I could think of was keeping him near me as long as possible one last time.

In a few minutes, we'd left all hint of town life behind; trees lined both sides of the narrow back road, not a soul in sight. Jim reached over and took my hand. Why didn't I pull away? I didn't understand the attraction between us; only knew it was there and had been from the start. If only Jim had not been so shy back then, and I had not been so naïve. Maybe if I had given in and we'd made love, things might have been different.

"I feel so comfortable with you," he said. "I can talk to you about anything. Some women are really limited in what they talk about."

"Hey, men are no different. I've dated some guys who could only talk about two things; sports or themselves."

"I'll be sure not to talk about either." He managed a little grin.

"Of course you can, silly." I nudged him with my elbow. "You know what I mean. If that's all they can talk about, it gets boring pretty fast. You must know guys like that." I glanced up and saw him nodding. We were both working hard to try to keep the conversation light. "You really know a lot about the ocean, and the coastal animals and birds. To me, that's so interesting. Different from Ontario." I could listen to him all day and never get bored. "And you don't go on and on, all preachy."

"You must have had some terrible dates. That's good."

"How can that be good?"

"Makes me look better."

Oh, if he only knew how good he looked to me. I bit my lip and looked at the ground. Jim stopped walking. He still held my hand. He put his fingers under my chin and tilted my head up. Then he gently brushed my upper lip with his finger. "You have some cinnamon there. It doesn't seem to want to come off that easily." Then he kissed me. "Yup, cinnamon, all right." Before I could decide how to react, he said, "There's a bit of brown sugar there too," and kissed me again. I melted into him and the kiss became more intense. I wrapped my arms around his shoulders and clung to him tightly. When we came up for air, I wailed, "I shouldn't be doing this. I'm a terrible person to do this."

"No, you're not. But you're engaged to the wrong guy."

I'd spent weeks getting to know Robert, smitten by his good looks and charm. I thought marrying him would make me feel safe and cared for. No more worries. Now I wasn't so sure. Jim's reappearance had stirred up old feelings in me, strong ones, unexpected ones. "I can't do this to Robert." I dropped my hands by my sides in resignation. "We'd better go back to the boat."

Jim took my hand as we walked and I didn't pull away. "Okay." He sighed. "Don't worry. I'll let go of your hand when we get to the main road."

On the Serenity, Jim brought out a snack of trail mix and two Sleeman's light ale. We talked as if our time was limited—like prisoners on death row.

"Here comes the Hawkeye," Jim said at last. "I'll ask you one more time. Please don't marry Robert."

"But I've promised him." I choked out the words through the catch in my throat. Tears threatened to spill. "I can't break that promise."

"That's one promise you shouldn't keep. Robert is a thug. If you don't know that already, you should."

"No, he can't be. He's so nice to me."

"I've seen how he can turn on the charm. Believe me. He has another side to him."

"I have to go through with it. I'm sorry. You'll never know how sorry I am." Sobs formed deep inside my heart.

"Aw, shit." He spun away from me and looked up at the sky. Then he let his head drop and he sighed. "You're too stubborn for your own good. You're making a huge mistake."

I shook my head in denial and kept shaking it while he spoke. "What's it to you anyway?" I blurted out. "You could have called when you got back to Comox, but you didn't, and now all of a sudden you pretend to care again."

"I didn't worry about calling then because I knew I'd see you in a day or two, when I came over to leave for fishing. But Jesus! I didn't think you'd be engaged so fast."

A twinge of shame snagged me. I had no answer for his implied insult. He was right. I had moved rather fast.

Finally he threw his hands in the air. "I hope you won't be sorry. But I have a terrible feeling about this." He dug out his wallet and pulled out a business card. "Here. Keep my phone number in a safe place. Call me if you ever need me."

"Yes, okay. Thanks."

"Promise?"

"I promise."

"All right. Look chipper. Here he is."

We stood side by side, waiting for Robert to bring the Hawkeye in to the dock. I had seen to it that his dockside spot wasn't taken. I didn't want a rerun of his rampage.

Chapter 22

July 15

Dear Mom and Dad,

How's it going? What's new at the office, Mom?
And how about you, Dad? Anything new in the
insurance business? Is that awful guy—what was
his name? Percy?—still getting under your skin
talking *all* the time. How does he get any work
done?

Speaking of work, I love my wharf job. I meet lots
of nice tourists on their way north. They rave
about the wonderful summer boating on the B.C.
coast. I hear some great stories.

Robert's been fishing near the Queen Charlotte
Islands for a month already. Six weeks to go. If
you look at a map, just follow the coast up from
Vancouver till you get to Prince Rupert and then
go straight across the water to the Charlottes.
Pretty far away, eh? As soon as Robert comes
back we'll get married. Then I'll send you my new
Hope Bay address.

For now I'm still living with Monique. She's gay
and we have different ideas about some things.
She's great though. Very caring, and fun to be
with. We've become the best of friends.

Are there ever some characters out here. One
old-timer, Edgar, is a beachcomber. Mostly does
log salvage. Lives all alone in a shack outside of
Lund. Just him and his cat, Spuzzum. Treats
that cat like a person. He told me that one day

he let Spuzzum drive the car on the logging road. Said he only had to reach over once or twice to help steer. Can you imagine? How crazy is that?

But don't get me wrong. They're not all weird here. Remember Jim? I told you about him. He's the first guy who hired me to help work on his boat when he did his haulout. Well, he's really nice. He came back for a visit—lives in Comox— and he's gone fishing with Robert. Jim has his own boat. They fish near each other. It was really sad to see them head off. I won't see either of them again for a long time. But my job keeps me busy, and I have Monique, so don't worry about me. I'll be fine.

That's all the news. I'll write again soon. You keep writing, too. Love getting your letters. Miss you.

Love you,

Andrea

P.S. Wish you could be here for my wedding.

Chapter 23

"This is fantastic, Monique. And perfect weather, too." We were buzzing along near the shore in an aluminum skiff she had borrowed from George, her boss at the water taxi service. "I love exploring the beaches. There's always something interesting washing up."

"For sure t'ing," she shouted over the noise of the outboard. "I found once a rubber boot, a rubber glove, and a white plastic 'elmet, all close togedder. Made me wonder where de fisherman was." Her handsome face lit up with a grin so I knew she was joking. "And den, nearby I found a bottle of Suntory whisky, so I t'ink 'e was a Japanese fisherman. One who liked too much de drink."

"His stuff must have come a long way, like those Japanese glass floats they sell in the tourist shops." I smiled as I put the scene together in my mind. "You could make up quite a story from what you find on the beach."

"Yes, but I wonder sometime, what is de real story. If we could know dese t'ings. Would be interesting, eh?"

I got out my notebook and put today's date in it. Monique tilted her head at me. "I like to keep a journal," I explained.

"Are you not afraid someone will read it?"

"No. I don't put in personal things. Mainly things I want to remember. Like if we do anything special."

"What will be somet'ing special about today?" She thought a moment. "I t'ink we could find a private little beach and 'ave a special time."

"No, not *that* kind of special. Not sex things. I'm talking about something ... oh anything. Anything noteworthy that happens."

"Maybe you would like to learn 'ow to run de outboard motor, eh?"

"I'd love to." I could surprise Robert with new-found expertise.

"I will take us to de Copelands. Lots of little bays to explore and you can practice around de islands."

"I never did see much of the Copelands after losing the skiff that time with Robert. Not my finest hour. But we'd better be really careful. I'd hate to be stranded again." I shuddered as I relived that desolate feeling of having been abandoned.

"Don't worry. I always 'ave de portable VHF and we 'ave de life jackets. We be fine." She waved away my concerns, smiling to dispel the anxieties I couldn't hide.

In the protected areas between the islets, the surface of the clear water was without a ripple. Weathered logs lay criss-crossed haphazardly, flung above the high tide line by winter storms.

"This place is so beautiful in a wild way," I said. "No sign of people having been here. No garbage."

"Dere are people here, many time in de summer. But dey keep it clean."

Monique showed me how to tilt the motor up in shallow water, and how to give it a little lift to unlock it and put it back down in deeper water. Other than that it was pretty basic; push or pull a lever for forward and reverse, push the handle back and forth to steer right and left, and turn the grip for more or less speed.

"This is really simple when you know how, isn't it?" I ventured farther out, ran some circles, then came back in and putted around the small islets.

Sitting in the front, Monique stretched her neck as she peered into the water. She pointed to the left frantically. "Go left!" Afterwards she pointed at the underwater rocks I hadn't seen. I broke out in a cold sweat. "You 'ave to watch for rocks and logs. You don't want to 'it de prop on dem."

"Yikes! That was close." I grimaced with embarrassment. "I think it's time for a break. You packed a couple of sandwiches, right?"

"For sure t'ing. Why don't you go 'round dat point?" Monique waved at the end of the big island. "Turn into de bay dere and we go to shore."

I tilted the motor partway up and putted through the shallow water until we were close enough to coast the rest of the way. I turned off the motor, tilted it up completely, and grinned at Monique.

I gave my shoulders a swaggery shake and tried to look smug. Monique raised her head and looked down her nose. We giggled, and enjoyed a moment of power and pride in our accomplishments.

"Who needs a man, eh?" she said. We slapped our palms together in a high-five.

Monique jumped out into the shallow water and pulled the skiff higher onto the beach. She tied the line onto a sturdy shrub well above the tide line. Carrying our sandwiches and water bottles, we picked our way between rocks and sticks up to a wide open picnic area. What I thought at first glance was grass, turned out to be dry moss, soft and clean. We spread out our jackets and sat side by side, marveling at the scenery. In my notebook, I jotted down things to remember.

The arbutus trees with their glossy leaves and reddish, barkless trunks reminded me of movies of Africa. I half expected a giraffe to stick its long neck around the treetops to peer at us. But the view towards the water was unmistakably West Coast. Shorebirds picked their way along the beach among rocks, driftwood, and waves. Limpets and urchins, anemones and starfish clung to the sides of the rocks just below the waterline.

"Have you ever seen anything so naturally beautiful?" I didn't expect an answer; certainly not the one I got.

"Yes, you." Monique was studying my face which I felt heating up.

"I'm flattered, Monique, but really, I'm not that special." I hoped she wasn't planning to take this too far.

"I t'ink you are naturally beautiful. Clear skin, rosy cheeks, violet eyes and dark lashes. Pearly teeth and...." She hesitated.

"Don't, Monique. You know this can't go anywhere." I looked around for an escape but didn't want to hurt her feelings.

"Lips dat want kissing," she said and leaned towards me.

I crammed a big bite of the cheese sandwich into my mouth. "Mmm. Yeah, tha's wha' Wobert said too," I mumbled as I chewed. Monique's perkiness deflated.

"Did 'e kiss you 'ere on dese islands?" she asked. I nodded. Monique's chin rose in challenge. "'Ow did 'e do it?"

"Aw, Monique. Here we go again." I shook my head. "Look, I don't want to talk about it. Anyway, you don't want to talk about Robert."

"You are right. I radder talk about you."

"Why don't we talk about both of us? I mean as friends. Just as long as you realize I can *only* be your friend and nothing closer."

"All right." She looked dejected. "I 'ad 'oped we could be more, but I understand."

"I know, and I'm sorry. I—"

"No problem. If you don't feel dat way, den dere is not'ing you can do. But I will miss you when you go to marry Robert." She chewed her lower lip and shook her head slowly. "You really should not do it, Andrea."

"Shouldn't do what?"

"Marry Robert. 'E is not good for you."

She was jealous, so I didn't take her comments too seriously. "But Monique, have you ever seen a more handsome guy? I mean, if I sent my parents a picture of him, they'd think it was of a movie star I ripped out of a magazine. He's so gorgeous."

"Well, for sure t'ing, 'e is a good looking guy, but 'e is not *dat* great." Monique made a sour face. I thought at first she was jealous, but she continued, "I am afraid for you if you marry 'im. 'E is very charming, but I t'ink dere is anodder side to 'im. What if 'e will 'it you?

"Don't be absurd. He wouldn't hit me. He loves me."

"Still, I t'ink you should be careful. Maybe marry somebody else. Or nobody. And just live wit' me. You should listen to me. Robert is bad news."

She didn't want to let up and I'd had enough. "I think we should drop this conversation or we won't be friends much longer."

"Eh?" Monique was quiet all of a sudden. "I only do not want to see you 'urt. But all right. I can see dat dis is a sore subject."

I was afraid we would both regret saying too much if we got riled up. "Yes. For the sake of our friendship, can we drop it? Please?"

"Fine."

"You'll have to find a new roommate when I move out at the end of August. Maybe you should advertise for someone who is ... you know ... has an alternate lifestyle." I had a hard time imagining Monique with a woman who would love her as a man would love me. A woman touching her lovingly, kissing her lips, her eyes, her neck. Putting her hands in Monique's most private places. The idea was so foreign to me that my mind refused to conjure up the image.

"Dat is a good idea. Save me from de 'eartbreak over and over." She pulled up her knees and laid her head on them. Any second she would break my heart too. I felt so bad for her.

I put my hand gently on the back of her head. "But Monique?"

"Mmm?" She glanced up at me, her eyes watery with tears.

"I want us always to be good friends."

"For sure t'ing." Her smile was warm. She put an arm around me, pulled me close, and leaned her head on my shoulders. "We be dere for each odder."

"For sure t'ing." I pulled her to me tightly.

Chapter 24

August 1

Dear Andrea,

I hope you got the CARE package. Be sure to use the glycerine cream. Your hands must be in terrible shape after handling ropes all day. And what about your face? You're not getting all wind burned and weather beaten, are you? You have to look after yourself if you want to keep a man interested.

Maybe Monique would like to share the cookies and the bridge mixture with you.

I wish we could afford to fly out for your wedding, dear, but even if we had the money to spare, your father and I could never get the time off work. You know how it is. You said you'll have a small wedding, just a couple of witnesses and the Justice of the Peace, but take lots of pictures to send us. What are you doing for a wedding dress? Do you want me to send Grandma's to you? Tell Robert we're sorry we haven't been able to come meet him. Maybe the two of you could come here for a late honeymoon. We hope you'll be very happy with Robert.

But who is this Jim fellow you're always talking
about? You talk about him more than Robert.
Now that you're engaged you should only be
thinking of Robert. Once you give your promise....
You're not getting married just because you're
lonely and far from home, are you? Be sure it's for
the right reasons.

Listen to me, lecturing like you're still a little kid.
I guess the mothering never stops.

Your dad and I are fine. You just take good care
of yourself.

Love and hugs,

Mom and Dad

P.S. Dad got himself some earplugs to wear in
the office when he needs to get some work done.
Percy doesn't even notice that nobody is listening
to him.

Chapter 25

Edgar's beat up log salvage boat, Prowler, sidled up to
an empty dock space, the engine roaring and spewing
blue smoke. Below the waterline, the exhaust sputtered
and rumbled. A rainbow film of gasoline crept over the
surface of the water. The floating wreck couldn't have seen
a coat of paint in years. Specks of white—all that was left
of the original paint—stuck to dented, scarred aluminum.
I assumed the jagged metal teeth attached to the bow like
pieces of a huge, big-toothed saw, were for pushing logs.

The open boat had a canopy over the bridge where the skipper and a deckhand might sit somewhat protected from the weather. But, exposed to the elements, the back was littered with coils of rope, peevee poles, power saws, axes, and piles of chains. Ugly, loud, and stinking of gas and oil, the Prowler's arrival could not be ignored.

One of the older boat owners and a permanent resident of Lund, Edgar was probably in his seventies, but he hopped out onto the float with the spryness of a much younger man. He was shadowed by an invisible pong of oil and garbage. I wrinkled my nose and reached for the stern line to help him tie up.

"Hi, Edgar. I'm surprised to see you here. Don't you usually tie up at the floats at Finn Bay?" I knew Bert wouldn't be pleased to have him tie up here.

"Hey there, Andrea. Yah, that's right. I won't be long. Just have to run up to the general store to git some more tobacco. I run out right in the middle of the job and it makes me right owly to be without it."

"Course it does," I said. He had the sallow, wrinkled skin of a seasoned smoker.

His grimy hand reached for the line I was about to tie. "Here, I'll do that. These lines is kinda dirty and I don't want ya gittin' yer hands fulla grease 'n' stuff." I gladly gave the line over to him.

"How's the log salvage business going?" I didn't really care, but it was a way to make conversation.

"Oh, terrible. Terrible business to be in. No money in it. More and more guys getting into log salvage. Harder 'n' harder to make a living. And them wood cops is all over me all the time. They figger I'm cutting these logs in the woods."

In the front of the boat, under the partial canopy, Spuzzum lay curled up on oil-stained gray Stanfields rumpled up on the passenger seat. "I see your deckhand's having a nap." I gestured towards the cat.

A grin spread across Edgar's face and I was treated to a good look at his gums. "Hee-hee-e-e," he wheezed and smacked his lips as if searching for his missing teeth. "Best deckhand I ever had. You shoulda seen 'im. He was steering the boat all by hisself whiles I had a nap." My jaw dropped. "I see ya don't believe me. I kin understand that. There ain't many cats like old Spuzzum around."

I loved dogs and cats. "Can I pet him? Will he let me?"

"Oh, sure he will. C'mon aboard. Just be careful not to git grease on ya."

I climbed aboard and picked my way to the front, being careful to avoid the wrenches and jugs of chainsaw oil. "Hey, Spuzzum," I said softly. He lifted his head and yawned widely, curling his raspy tongue. As soon as I touched him he began to purr. "Sounds like he's got a spare inboard motor."

Edgar had followed me back onto the boat and couldn't stop showing me his gums as he looked at Spuzzum fondly. "He likes ya. I kin tell."

I smiled at Edgar. "Purrs like a mini chainsaw."

"Good Lord, Andrea." He pointed at my hand as I petted Spuzzum. "Where'd ya git that rock?"

"Oops! I don't usually wear it at work. Forgot to take it off this morning."

"But it's an engagement ring, right?" His mouth was still agape. "Who's the lucky fella? Somebody I know?"

"Sure. You probably know Robert Bolton."

His brow furrowed. "Robert? Does he have a boat?" I nodded. "Don't know a lot of last names. What's his boat's name?"

"The Hawkeye."

"That guy?" His voice was considerably louder now. "That guy?" he bellowed. "Naw, that cain't be right."

I felt an alarming flutter in my stomach. "Why not? He's a nice guy."

"That Robert—that one from the Hawkeye—is a goddammed asshole, if you'll 'scuse my French."

I swallowed hard, shocked and barely able to resist clapping my hands over my ears.

"He's nothin' but a loudmouthed bully." He spat onto the float for emphasis.

"You can't be talking about the same guy. My Robert is really nice. You're probably thinking of another Robert." I couldn't understand it. Why did so many people dislike Robert? He was so charming.

"No way. I know the guy you mean. Sure he's good looking, but that's only on the outside." Edgar waved his hand dismissively. "He's a real shit." Neither of us said anything for a moment. "He was yelling at me just because I wanted to tie up beside him. There was no space at the float and I had to tie somewheres."

"Maybe he didn't want to get grease on his boat. Your boat is pretty dirty, don't you agree?" I tried to say it as gently as possible. Hoped he wouldn't take offense.

"Oh, sure it is, but I wasn't gonna git any on 'im. And anyhow, all's he had to do was say it nicely—don't tie here, I'm leaving soon—or some such thing. But no, he come flying outta his wheelhouse, fists up. I thought he was gonna deck me."

Echoes of the scene at the floats at Hope Bay flashed through my mind. My stomach turned over with a sick feeling. "I'm sure he wasn't going to do anything like that."

"Andrea, if you're engaged to that lunatic, you'd better think twice before tyin' the knot. He's got a lotta history, and it ain't good. That's all I got to say. Yer a nice girl and I think it'd be a cryin' shame if you married that hothead."

"Well, thanks for the advice, Edgar." I was too stunned to think of anything else to say. "You have a good day now." I climbed out of the Prowler and hurried to the other end of the floats. Useless to continue to defend Robert. Who knew what really happened? I wasn't there. Maybe it wasn't as bad as Edgar said. For sure, I wouldn't want him tying his stinking tub to my boat either.

But as I imagined my approaching wedding day, the little voice in my head whispered louder than before, *What if I'm making a big mistake?*

I knew it. Deep in my head, I knew there was something off about Robert. Those tantrums, the staring, the barely contained anger. And yet, I shut my ears. I wasn't ready to listen. He was beautiful to look at in a rugged way. Muscular and sexy. He was good to me, adored me, indulged me, wanted me.

Those people who said things about him were just jealous. Somebody had to be on Robert's side. It was my job to believe in him. After all, no one was perfect. And if he had some little imperfections, he would change in time. Everything would be all right. After all, I had made a promise to him and we were going to be married.

Chapter 26

"Wahoo! I love these downhill stretches." Monique and I had decided to bike to Finn Bay, or at least in that direction.

"Is good exercise for de lungs, eh? So nice to be out in de nature, too."

"I'm a bit worried I might see more of this nature than I want."

"You don't like it?"

"Didn't you notice the bear poop on the road? I wouldn't want to meet one of those guys." We had bears in Ontario and on one trip to the lake my dad had shown me bear droppings.

"I t'ink dey are too much afraid of us to come out in de daytime."

"I hope you're right." I was nervous about this bicycling idea but I didn't want to be the one to wimp out, so I worked the pedals harder and got out in front of Monique.

Second growth firs, about the height of a man, covered the slopes on either side of the road. I'd heard the locals refer to them as Christmas trees. The air smelled fresh and clean. Except for the creak of our pedals and the crunch of our tires on the gravel, it was peaceful and quiet. A movement in the trees caught my eye.

I put on my brakes and waited for Monique to pull up beside me. "You know, Monique, I think I'd like to head back now."

"So soon?"

I pointed to the trees. "Something was shaking one of the trees in there, and with all the bear sign we've seen ... well, I'd feel more comfortable if we were heading towards town."

"Aw, Andrea, dere is not'ing in dere. You see a little poop and you scare yourself."

"It's not that. But the trees were moving and it's not windy."

As we stood talking with our legs straddling our bikes, I saw one of the Christmas trees shaking way more than any small animal could have caused. My guts tightened as a surge of alarm passed through me. I jumped on my bike, turned it around and took off down the road. In spite of my trembling legs, I managed about twenty good pedal pushes before shame overcame me. I slammed on my brakes and turned to look for Monique. How could I have left her behind to be eaten by the bear?

Monique lurched around me. "Jeezus! What you stop for? I almost smash into you."

We laughed, first from relief, and then from embarrassment. "I realized what a coward I was leaving you to the bears. It's good to know you're no braver than I am."

As we pedaled homeward, side by side, I looked over my shoulder frequently to check for pursuing bears. Relief flooded through me when the first houses came in sight.

"See? We were not in danger," Monique said, "but I t'ink you will 'ave a sore neck tonight from looking over your shoulder."

Huge shaggy bears lumbered towards me in the darkness of my bedroom. *This is silly. Go to sleep.* I drifted off and dreamed about home and our cabin on the lake. I was hiking through the forest following a trail to the cabin. In the distance, a monstrous black bear shuffled down the hill. As it came closer I saw that the shaggy thing had Robert's face, his handsome features transformed; beady black eyes set in hairy cheeks, long teeth protruding from jaws dripping with saliva. We would surely meet beyond the bend in the path. No! I couldn't let that happen. I struggled out of the cobwebs of my dream and bolted up in bed gasping for breath.

In T-shirt and panties, I tiptoed into the living room and quietly settled on the couch. Some potato chips were left in the bowl on the coffee table so I turned on the TV with the volume very low and set the chip bowl between my legs. I didn't care what I watched so long as it wasn't a documentary on bears.

Monique stood in the living room doorway. "You are still up?" She sat down beside me and crossed her legs tucking her feet under herself. "You okay?" She reached for a chip.

"Oh yeah. Can't sleep for all the stupid bear dreams. Thought I'd try to think about something else before I go back to bed." I flipped through the program guide, finally deciding on a Meg Ryan love story from the 90s.

"She is very cute, eh? Don't you t'ink?"

"Who?"

"Meg Ryan. In dis show." She waved a chip towards the screen.

"I don't know. What do you like about her?"

"She 'as a sweet face. Not much of a body, but in a boyish way, still nice to look at." We were drawn into the developing love between Tom Hanks and Meg Ryan. Sometimes our hands reached into the chip bowl at the same time. Monique reached in, absentmindedly groping the edge of the bowl, sometimes missing and patting my thigh. At first I turned my head quickly to look at her but she was absorbed in the show. No, she wasn't trying to make a move on me. Moments later, her hand missed the bowl again and rested on my leg. Eyes still on the TV, she said, "Aw, dat is so sweet. Dat's de kind of love I want to find someday."

Her hand was burning a fiery patch on my thigh. I tried not to like her touch, but if I forgot the fact that she was a woman, it did feel good. Monique seemed in no hurry to withdraw her hand. She was completely wrapped up in the show. Lightly, her fingers moved towards the crotch of my panties. My body was aflame. Alarm bells jangled while hormones raced through my boiling blood spreading to the tips of my fingers and toes. Yes and no battled in my head. I was embarrassed to think that my panties might show a wet spot if I moved. Warm fingers slipped under the elastic seam. I felt them spreading through my pubic hair.

"Ah … er … Monique. Oh, God …" I moaned. Her fingers slipped down into the wetness. "Monique! No! I can't do this." I jumped up, spilling the bowl of chip crumbs on the floor. "I - I'm sorry," I whispered, and hurried to my room. From my doorway, I heard her sigh. I glanced over and saw her slump down on the couch. Then the TV clicked off and she padded back to her room.

I lay in bed less able to sleep than when I was fighting images of bears. Monique was gentle and caring. She was a good person. What was wrong with me? Well, I wasn't gay. That's what it was. And yet, I liked her touch. If I was honest, it wasn't her touching that bothered me; it was that I liked it. I flung back the covers and sat on the edge of my bed, thinking. At last, I took a deep breath and in the dark groped my way to Monique's bed. Lifting up her blanket I slipped in beside her.

Chapter 27

"Andrea, you've got a driver's licence, right?" Sarah asked as we entered Powell River on our weekly grocery shopping trip.

"Of course."

"Would you like a part time job? I need a driver to run errands in town and for buying trips, and someone to help mind the store. I can't do it all. It's peak tourist season." She waited. "So what do you think?"

"Sure. That would be great. As long as it doesn't interfere with my wharf job."

Monique reached up from the back seat to pat my shoulder quietly. She gave it a squeeze which I took to be approval of my new job.

"I'm sure we can work around Bert's schedule," Sarah said. "Could you start today? Help me pack my things to the car and save me some shopping time."

"I guess." I turned to look at Monique in the back seat and raised my eyebrows, silently asking her opinion.

"Sound good to me," she said. "I do de grocery shopping, no problem, and I meet you wherever."

"Great," Sarah said. "Andrea can come with me and we should get this town trip over in half the time. We'll meet here in the parking lot, say in an hour?"

"Sure you don't mind, Monique?" I hated to dump the chores all on her lap, but I could sure use a second job.

"Not at all." She gave me a big kiss on the forehead and headed for the Overwaitea store.

Sarah showed me how to place the price tags upside down after dusting the carvings. "If it's an expensive item, always have the tag face down. We don't want to scare the customer away."

"But they'll find out the price anyway. Why not be up front about it?"

"Of course they will, but first you want them to be very interested in the item. The longer you can get them to look at it before finding out the price, the more they will want it and the less the price will matter. That's how it works with art."

She knew all the tricks. "You have the perfect location, right in the path of tourists coming up the hill from the wharf. You live in the back part of the store, right?" I asked. "Very handy. How long have you had this shop?" It looked like it had been there forever. The floors were wide-planked wood. Walls, too, were finished in wood, but the boards had been painted a pale yellow so the room wasn't as dark as it might have been.

"I bought the house five years ago with the inheritance my dad left me, but I only decided to turn it into a shop last year. Flip that sign on the door. Let's close up for a half hour."

"Are you sure?" I thought it was odd for her to close in the middle of the day.

"There won't be any customers till this rain lets up. Let's take a load off." I flipped the sign and followed Sarah. She showed me to a canvas lawn chair on her covered porch.

"Oh, this is nice," I said. "Listen to that rain on the roof. What a perfect spot you have here. Gorgeous view of the ocean." Raindrops dimpled the smooth surface of the water.

"It's not bad. It's where I come for quiet time once in a while." She brought a pot of tea and poured us each a cup.

"Smells delicious. What is it?"

"Combination of things—peppermint, chamomile, a bit of fennel seed for that licorice flavour."

"Did you buy this in Powell River?"

"Good heavens, no. I picked the leaves and seeds from my herb garden out back."

I craned my neck as she pointed to a small square of garden surrounded by a high fence made of driftwood. "You're full of surprises, Sarah. So talented. You should sell this to the tourists."

"I'd have to check it out. See if it's allowed, being a food item, you know?"

Intriguing shapes of driftwood placed in the corners of her porch served as supports for many of her potted plants. "Everywhere I look, you've taken something from nature and turned it into art."

"I try to work with nature, rather than fight it," Sarah said, "but for the flowers, I broke down. Bought those petunias and snapdragons as bedding plants in Powell River. I love bright flowers."

"I guess you'd end up with mostly moss and ferns if you tried to stick to nature in the planters."

Sarah smiled. "No kidding."

I looked out over the water and the wharf. "Hey, you can see all the boats from here. You can probably watch me at work."

"It's handy to know when there are lots of sailboats coming in. I make sure the shop is open and looks inviting. I try to put some special items on the veranda to lure them closer and then reel them in. Like fishing."

"Have you ever gone fishing?"

"Yes, a season on a commercial boat as a deckhand. Thought I'd try it once." She had a sad smile, as if it was an uncomfortable memory.

"Didn't like it?"

"Didn't work out." She stopped talking and seemed to want to end that line of conversation, but I was dying to know more about commercial fishing.

"What happened? Did you get seasick?"

"No, nothing as simple as that." She hesitated again. "I'm a bit embarrassed to say it, but I kind of had a crush on the skipper. Young guy, nice looking, easy to be around."

"And?"

"I don't know. We'd gone out a few times. Hiked the Sunshine Coast Trail."

"That takes a few days, doesn't it?"

"Yes, it's a huge trail system but we just did a little loop south of town. Stayed overnight at one of the campsites in a pup tent."

"M-m-m, that must have been cozy."

"Yeah. It was wonderful. He was so sexy. Young and lean and hard ... everywhere." We laughed. "I was in heaven. All that fresh air went to my head, I guess."

"What went wrong?"

"What didn't?" Sarah shook her head. "I asked if I could deckhand for him that summer, and right from the beginning he was uncomfortable with the idea."

"Why?"

"He said, 'It's not a sailing trip, you know. It's rough and ugly and you never get enough sleep.' But I didn't care. I was crazy about him so I begged him to take me along." She snorted. "Big mistake. He was like a different person on the boat. He had no time for me and I felt like I was always in the way."

"Oh, poor you! You must have felt terrible."

"Well, to be fair, it's often very stressful because of the weather and you always have to watch what you're doing—there's no room for mistakes—but sometimes I felt like I was just a dog in the stern."

"A dog? What do you mean?"

"Some of the fishermen call their deckhands that. And it was, 'Do this. Do that.' And forget about romance while he was fishing. It was all about catching enough fish to pay the bills. At the end of the day—long days, sure, like eighteen hours—he was too tired to do anything except sleep."

"So was he no fun at all on the boat?"

"Oh sure, there were times when we could relax and there weren't huge waves, or major gear tangles, or tight situations, but by then, we'd had words so often that it was hard to stay friends."

"Why didn't you go home?"

"Well, it's pretty remote. It's more than a good day's run to get back to Masset to fly home and that would be lost fishing time. I suppose I could've left when we came to town to offload the fish, but I didn't think it was fair to leave him without a deckhand after I'd begged to come along."

"What about the harbour days? Were things better then?"

"The boat is small and we were always bumping into each other. I thought the sex was great, but maybe he didn't. I don't know. No point in asking. I don't think anyone ever got an honest answer to 'was it good for you too?' He was really shy, and that didn't help. I felt like I was always the one initiating sex and I wondered if he thought I was a slut. At the end of the season, Jim dropped me off in Lund and kept on going to Comox. Same day, tired as he was. He said he liked me, but he wasn't ready for a relationship."

Had she heard my sharp intake of breath at the mention of that name? My pulse was thumping at the base of my throat. "Jim?" *Jim kissing cinnamon and brown sugar off my lips on the logging road?* I gulped. "What boat was that?" Afraid I'd drop my teacup, I set it on the table. All my strength had drained out of me.

"The Serenity," she said.

A wrecking ball slammed into my stomach.

"You know the boat, right?" She looked at me for acknowledgement. "Are you okay, Andrea? You look white as a ghost. I hope it's not my tea."

"Oh, no. I'm fine. I was just remembering that awful time when I blasted the stuffing out of the Serenity's planks with the power washer—before I knew what I was doing." I couldn't let Sarah know I loved Jim. I was supposed to be over him. But maybe I didn't know the real Jim. He never said a thing about Sarah. Damn him! I was right not to do it with him. Another notch in the bedpost—that's all I would have been to him. Anyway, I was marrying Robert—and sleeping with Monique. Oh good grief. What was I doing?

I tried to pull myself together. "So how is it now between you two? Are you still seeing him?" I was afraid of Sarah's answer, but I had to know.

"We had some laughs and a few beers when he came over from Comox to work on his boat each spring, but nothing ever came of it. I still think he's adorable though. Wish he felt that way about me." Sarah slouched back in her lawn chair staring at the harbour.

Oh my God. Sarah and Jim! I had to get out of here before I got sick. "Well, the rain has stopped. Thanks for the tea. I should get going. Joe will be waiting to be relieved." And I had to go get my head together. I prayed she didn't see my hands shaking.

Chapter 28

An old Chrysler rolled down the road and lurched to a stop in front of the general store. Edgar got out of the passenger side of the car. I stood gaping, and nearly dropped my bag of junk food. I couldn't see anyone in the driver's seat.

"Hey, Andrea," Edgar called. "Did ya see that? See Spuzzum drive the car? Told ya he kin do it."

I found my voice at last. "Edgar! You can't keep doing that."

"Doing what?"

"Letting Spuzzum drive. That's dangerous. To you and everyone else." Of course the cat wasn't driving. Edgar drove from the passenger side reaching over to make adjustments as needed, but still....

"Aw, it's jest fer fun!"

"Well, be careful just the same. So what's new?"

"I hear they closed the salmon season up north a few days ago. Guess your man'll be comin' home. I hope you know he's had a brush with the law."

"No. What do you mean?"

"Oh, nuthin' too serious. Jest his temper got away on 'im an' he decked a guy. Police come and took him away for a few days to cool off."

"I'm sure there was some good reason."

"Well ... you jest remember what I said about that fella yer so damn set on marryin'. Think it over, my dear. Think it over. They say that's the longest sentence in the world."

"What is?"

"I do." He walked into the store shaking his head.

I didn't know whether to laugh at his joke, be mad at him for being so pessimistic, or be scared in case he was right. And what about this "brush with the law"? Edgar had stirred up doubts I'd tried to keep buried. As they resurfaced, my stomach churned and burned all over again.

Chapter 29

Andrea!" Monique waved wildly to get my attention. "Phone for you."

I left the weeding in the backyard, where I'd tried to plant a bit of a garden, and ran for the house. Who would be calling me here? My parents? But they didn't call in the middle of the day.

"Hello?"

"Andrea, sweetheart. How's it going?"

"Robert?" I couldn't keep the surprise out of my voice. "Robert? Is that you? Where are you?"

"I'm at Hope Bay. I should be in Lund in a few hours. Thought we'd go get married tomorrow."

My heart lurched and I felt faint. "Tomorrow? Oh. Oh, dear—."

"What's wrong?"

"Nothing's wrong, only someone told me you'd had a brush with the law, and it got me a bit worried."

"Aw, that was nothing. Don't worry about it. Some guy at the wharf had his rigging lowered over the back of the Hawkeye to work on it and we had words over it. The guy reached for something kind of fast and I thought he was going for a knife so I decked him. I explained it all to the police and that was the end of it. Nothing to worry about."

"Oh well, that's good then. I ... okay. I guess. See you soon ... in a while."

I put the phone down and started to shake. Tears welled and spilled. Monique came in, took one look at me and put her arms around me. "Sh-sh-shhh ... dere, dere, is gonna be okay." She stroked the back of my hair and I let myself cry into her neck.

"Oh-h-h-h, Monique. What am I going to do? I want to do the right thing, but I don't know. I just don't know." What if everyone was right and I was the only one who didn't see the disaster I was walking into? I felt like I was in way over my head. My life was heading in a direction I wasn't sure I wanted to go.

"I tell you what you do. You go 'ave a shower. Get all pretty so you feel good. Den you go all by yourself to de far side of de beach and you sit by de ocean and t'ink about it all. Nobody will bodder you and you can make up your mind what to do. Maybe you need more time. But you need to listen to your 'eart."

"Yeah." I sniffed and groped for a Kleenex. "Okay." I had to find a way to put Robert off and buy myself time to think.

Chapter 30

Monique was right. The lapping of waves on the shore was soothing. I sat on a log and looked out across the water. Way out there towards the west was Vancouver Island ... and Comox. I refocused on the shore farther up the beach. Couldn't think about Comox just now and that wonderful man who didn't want me until it was too late.

What a mess I was in. Robert was charming. No doubt about that. He was big. He was strong. But Jim was attractive too and he got my heart racing. Oh, why did my thoughts keep coming back to Jim? He dumped me—at least I'd thought he had. How could I forget that pain? That's how I ended up letting Robert into my life. I sighed and kicked at the pebbles under my feet. Yes, Robert. He's the one I'm supposed to marry. He was smart. He read a lot. He was capable. There was no practical problem he couldn't eventually solve. Robert had a lot going for him. But, I always felt like I was walking on eggs around him. Did I want to do that for the rest of my life? Even if I couldn't have Jim, I wasn't sure Robert was the one for me.

Monique said so from the start. Ah, Monique. She and I had been close this summer. No one knows how a woman feels but another woman. No one can know what a woman wants, like another woman. And Monique was good and kind. She was fine-looking too, model material if she'd been taller. I loved how her dark hair spiked up here and there, as if the wind was always messing with tufts of it. I admired her tolerance and patience. And she loved me. But, she didn't get my parts tingling like Jim or even Robert did. Was I prepared to live my life with another woman?

Now Robert was coming home. I could hardly remember what he looked like after three months. I remembered his dark brown hair that he let grow a little bit longer than most. It gave him a wild look, yet not unkempt. Wild, in the sense of adventure and daring. Very sexy too, I thought. How long would that last though? Was a wild hairdo enough reason to marry someone? Oh, boy! Whatever happened to my rational thinking skills?

And what about Jim? I was attracted to him, no question. Our bodies were like opposite poles of a magnet exerting an incredible pull on us. At least that's how it was, once. I wondered if I still had my magnetism. I didn't know much about Jim. Wished I did though. Stan had only praise and admiration for him when we talked in the hospital waiting room that day Jim had burned himself. It was his fun-loving ways that I found irresistible. His kiss on the logging road had been so tender and innocent. Robert's kisses were demanding. Jim's were giving and sharing. But what if he had a thoughtless side too, as Sarah said? What if he still carried a torch for Sarah like she did for him? What if I had met Jim before he met Sarah? What if I had gotten to know Jim better before I met Robert? What difference? It was too late for us. Why couldn't I get that through my head and forget about him?

My parents had tried to be supportive in their letters, but I could tell, reading between the lines, that Mom thought I had rushed into this engagement. I should call her. She'd know what to do. What was I thinking? Sure, she wanted what was best for me, but in her plastic world, appearances counted for a lot. She'd be horrified. I could hear her now. *What will I tell my friends?* She'd be mortified if she had to go back and tell them it was off. I was sure Dad felt the same. Dad would prefer I not marry at all, ever, and just stay his little girl, but of course that wasn't going to happen.

I should listen to my parents. I should listen to Monique. I should listen to Jim. I should listen to Bert and Edgar. I should listen to the people at Hope Bay. I should listen to my heart.

Okay! I had decided. I would tell Robert I had to put off the wedding. I needed more time. Then after a while I could say I didn't think it would work out and we could gently, mutually withdraw from our engagement. Yes! That's what I'd do. My mind was made up.

I inhaled the fresh sea air, feeling wonderful without this marriage burden weighing me down. I would be all right now. I strolled towards home, content with my decision.

Way down the beach, a man walked briskly towards me. As he approached, my heart began to race. What was he doing here? Already! In his hand, Robert held a huge bouquet.

Still holding the flowers, Robert flung his arms around me. "Andrea, darling. It's so good to see you. Even more beautiful than I remembered."

"It's nice to see you too," I blurted out. *Oh Jeezus! What am I going to do now?* I had to say something. Letting him down could come later. "But, we have to have a talk."

"We'll have lots of time to talk." He kissed me hungrily. The heat from his lips sent twinges to my core. I was still gasping for air when he pushed the bouquet in front of me. "Special delivery for my bride-to-be."

"Orchids? Wherever did you find them?" Not in Lund. Certainly not in Hope Bay. "They must have cost a fortune." I let my fingers trail lightly across one of the velvety white petals. So pure. Unlike me, these days. Monique's face flashed in front of me, kissing me. Then Jim kissing the cinnamon off my lips. *No, no, no! What's the matter with me?*

"I went past Lund and straight on to Powell River. They had them at the florist's there." He was beaming happiness and I stammered as I stalled, dreading having to tell him the wedding was off. And now he'd bought these expensive flowers. I didn't know how I'd find the courage to let him down gently. *Oh, bloody hell! I'm so screwed up.*

Jabs of panic churned at my insides. "You - you've been to Powell River already? T-today?"

"I had to take care of a few things." He counted off the tasks on his fingers, like a to-do list. "Got the Justice of the Peace all lined up for us for tomorrow at 4:00 p.m., hotel booked, dinner reservation at the best restaurant in town, flowers for my girl."

"You've already done it all?" *No! No! No! I need more time. I need more time.* Everything was happening too fast. I wished the gravel on the beach would open up and swallow me. My knees buckled as that sinking feeling became real and Robert was quick to catch me.

"Here. Lean on me." He put his arm around my waist and pulled me close to him. His big, warm body, so strong, made me feel safe. Robert's faint manly scent with a hint of lime aftershave drew me in. I reached up to touch his freshly shaved chin, meaning to push him away gently. I would take a moment, catch my breath, find a way to tell him I needed more time.

But Robert took my hand and placed a kiss on the inside of my palm. His lips continued to nibble feathery kisses up the inside of my wrist to my elbow.

"I ... ah ... Robert ... I ..." When his lips moved from inside my elbow to my neck, I knew I was in trouble. When he was this close to me, I wanted to believe in him and be his. If he had thrown me down on the beach right there, I would have helped him tear off my clothes.

"Come on down to the Hawkeye," he said, his voice husky and urgent. He grasped my hand and walked briskly to the wharf. "You can't imagine how good it is to see you. It's been a long three months."

Clutching the orchids in my free hand, and taking two steps for every one of his, I couldn't manage more than mumbled replies.

Inside the Hawkeye's wheelhouse, Robert closed the door behind us and latched it. He took the orchids from me and threw them into the sink. His hug almost crushed me, his kisses, as desperate as mine, engulfed me. He whipped my shorts off. His pants dropped and in a second we were in his bunk. He was hard and big. I was small and helpless. I was surprised to find myself so willing, and was ashamed at my weakness, wanting—no, needing—sex like that. *I'll tell him afterwards that I need more time.* The logic was so ridiculous, I burst out laughing. Robert stopped cold. "What are you laughing at?" His tone was harsh and accusing. He looked so stern, it scared me.

"I was thinking we're doing things backwards; first the honeymoon, then the wedding." He smiled with relief, but his face was the only part of him that was relaxed. His lovemaking was forceful and insistent, like a man who'd been lost in the wilderness for too long. I tried to give him what he wanted, but with Robert intent on taking, I had to be satisfied with being taken from.

PART TWO

The Captive

My life wastes away,
Water and woods, prison walls.
Tamer than my captor, wild animals prowl.
They alone hear my cries.

~ Anneli Purchase

Chapter 31

"Do I look okay?" I hated myself for asking. And where had that timid, mousy voice come from?

"You look great." Robert eyed me up and down. "Wanna have a quickie before we head out?" He raised his eyebrows meaningfully.

"I would but I don't want to have to do my hair and tidy my clothes all over again." The last few times he'd been so rough. I didn't want to go to the potluck dinner with a bruised wrist or a hickey on my neck. "And we'd be late getting to Steve and Mary's." I hoped that would be good enough to put him off till later.

"They'll wait." He grabbed my wrist and dragged me into the bedroom.

"Robert, I just finished doing my hair." But he wasn't listening to me. He was already unzipping my pants and tugging at them. "Here, wait. You'll tear them." I pulled off my pants. It was easier than having Robert yank them off. I had learned that resisting just made it worse. Not that I didn't like sex, but in the two weeks since we got married, I was liking it less and less with Robert.

He was finished before I could even get in the mood. "Okay, let's hurry. Gotta go or we'll be late." He ran into the bathroom. I heard the toilet flush and the water running. He came out looking refreshed, hair tidy. "Ready?"

"Can I have a minute to get my clothes on?" Selfish bastard. All he thinks about is himself. I grabbed my pants and pulled them on again, smoothing them out. My favourite lavender sweater was crumpled and pulled out of shape. I whipped it off and rummaged in the closet. The older red one would have to do. I wanted to make a good impression at Steve and Mary's potluck welcome dinner. Most of the residents of Hope Bay would be there.

"Did you put my smoked salmon on a platter?" Robert called from the porch.

"I thought you said you were taking care of that, since it's your home-smoked stuff? I got the crackers ready."

"Jesus, Andrea. That's the woman's job, putting the food together. Hurry it up, will ya? I've got my shoes on already." I heard more mutterings and the door opening. "I'll wait for you outside."

"Men!" I took a deep breath and counted to ten. Fortunately my hair was co-operating today. I twisted it up in a knot and stuck a wooden pin through to hold it in place. If it came apart later, I could live with it. I hurried to the fridge, took out the smoked salmon and quickly cut it into pieces, threw it onto a platter, and covered it with plastic wrap.

I was about to leave when I realized my hands smelled like smoked fish. Another quick hand washing and I was out the door.

"'Bout time," Robert said.

God! Surely the evening could only improve.

Carl's black lab, Wilbur, came bounding up the path from the store, barking fiercely, but I could see he was wagging his tail.

"Goddamn mutt," Robert snarled. "He knows better than to come near me."

I lifted the platters of food high up out of the dog's reach and looked to Robert for help as Wilbur made happy leaps towards the food. "He's not going to hurt us. He just wants the food." Robert snarled and lunged at him. He looked more savage than the dog, who ran off with his tail tucked in.

Carl appeared at Steve and Mary's door. "Oh hi, Robert. Have you seen Wilbur?"

"Yeah, he ran past us barking at something. Chased it behind the store," Robert said. I didn't dare look at Carl, afraid the guilt would show, although I hadn't done anything. I glanced up at Robert's face. He wore a benign, innocent expression.

"I tried to leave him home but he wouldn't stay. Every time I left the yard, he'd follow me, and then I thought, 'Aw, what the hell. He's not going to hurt anything as long as he stays outside.' Wouldn't have him near the food though."

Carl reached out to take the platter and then shook my hand. "Andrea, right? I'm Carl. Come on in and meet the rest of the folks." Carl put the platter on the table. "Listen up everybody! This here is Andrea, Robert's new bride." Hands went up and everyone called out "hi." Carl pointed at people around the room, naming them.

"I'm sure I've forgotten every name," I said, when he was finished, "but I'll work on it."

"Wine?" Robert appeared beside me with a glass. He had a scotch in his other hand.

Mary leaned towards me. "So nice to see you, Andrea. Let me take you over to meet Molly and Phillip." She took me by the elbow. I gave Robert a look to signal that I'd see him later and smiled at him over my shoulder.

Molly's brown pageboy style was generously streaked with gray, but her blue eyes were bright and sparkly. "Welcome to the boonies, Andrea." She reached out to take my hand and put her other hand on top adding warmth to the handshake.

"I'm Phillip." Her husband, a tall thin man, reached over to add his welcome. "What do you think of our little community so far?"

"I—"

"Before you say anything, I must warn you that we're writers and anything you say could be published in some form sooner or later."

"Seriously?" I wasn't quite sure how to take his comment.

Mary and Molly laughed as Phillip explained. "We keep busy with a local newsletter that we print ourselves and distribute at Steve and Mary's store and at the restaurant. Mostly for the benefit of the tourists passing through, but also for our own entertainment. Do you do any writing?"

"Only small stuff, like a journal for special outings. Nothing good enough to publish, although, I like the idea of it."

"If you ever want to try your hand at writing up one of your outings for our newsletter, it might be a breath of fresh air for us all," Molly said. "Sometime when you're bored enough, why don't you bring your journal over? It might be just the thing we're looking for."

"Well, I ..." I looked at Mary for her opinion, and saw her nod vigorously. "All right. Maybe I'll do that one day. Thanks."

"Andrea brought a big boxful of books for our shelf in the store," Mary told Molly and Phillip. "Good ones, too."

"That's great," said Phillip. "We can always use some new reading material. Now if you ladies will excuse me, I'll go join the men and find out who caught the biggest fish." He winked as he left us to go talk to the group gathered around the makeshift bar.

On the other side of the room, Robert had settled into an overstuffed armchair and was holding forth on the best way to hook up a water system to get creek water to the house. On the couch, Larry, the carver who lived next door to us, listened politely. Tom, sitting next to him, rolled his eyes and got up. I could just make out the comment he mumbled to his wife, Elizabeth. "Mr. Know-it-all's at it again."

"How are you getting on, ladies?" Carl asked as he joined us. Suede desert boots, khaki pants, blue plaid shirt, brown leather vest; that casual image must have cost a pretty penny to achieve. He had a masculine look despite the blond locks that curled into his neck.

"Fine," I said. "Thanks for introducing everyone. Hope I remember half their names." I shrugged a little apology. "Did you find Wilbur? Is he okay?"

"Oh yeah. He never goes far. That's the trouble with him. He always wants to be where I am, and most of the time that's great, but sometimes, like today, it would be nice to have some space."

"He's really friendly though."

"I'm kind of attached to him. I thought I'd lost him the other day."

"Oh? Did he take off after something?"

"No, I mean lost, like permanent. He was really sick. Took a bite of a poisonous mushroom."

"Did you see it? What do they look like?"

"It was an ammonita. You know, those red ones with the white dots? Luckily he threw it up."

"Pretty dangerous stuff. Are there lots of mushrooms around here?" Poor dog. I shuddered, remembering the savage look on Robert's face.

"Mushrooms? Loads of them. We pick them right up till the frost hits. But you have to know which ones are safe. Guess I'll have to watch Wilbur more closely." Carl shook his head slowly. "That was a close call."

Mary's face lit up. "Andrea, would you like to go mushroom picking sometime? Not the poisonous kind, of course."

"I'd love to, but I know less than nothing about it."

"No problem, I'll teach you. It's just the start of the chanterelle season. I'll ask Samantha if she wants to come. She loves picking too." Mary was almost bouncing with excitement. "We're going to have a great time." She craned her neck to look across the room, and waved at Samantha to come over. "The three of us can go. Day after tomorrow okay with you?"

Molly was invited but declined. "I'd rather not go bear watching."

"Bears?" I felt my eyes grow round. "Really? Bears?"

Samantha patted my hand. "Don't you worry. We all have bear spray, but we probably won't need it."

"I don't have any." Oh Lord! Images of bear poop and rustling Christmas trees flashed through my mind.

"You can get some at the store. We always have some on hand."

"If you're sure you want to take me along. I mean I really want to go, but I'm not kidding when I say I'm a city slicker." They both smiled forgivingly. "But I'm a fast learner." I knew I would dream about bears again.

"Now how about that wonderful food?" Mary said. "I think it's time to take up our supper and find a place to sit outside by the fire. Steve should have it going by now."

Planks had been set up on bolts of wood to make benches around a bonfire. Robert and I loaded our paper plates with crab, baked halibut, scalloped potatoes, and barbecued salmon. He sat on the end of a bench and I sat next to him. Carl came over to sit next to me on the other side.

"Wow! Look at that food!" I said.

"Yeah, great stuff," Robert said with his mouth full. He washed it down with another swig of scotch. His eyes were slightly bloodshot under droopy eyelids.

A glance at Carl's face told me he had noticed the same thing—Robert had been hitting the scotch pretty hard tonight and on an empty stomach too.

Wilbur came from behind the bench, nose up, sniffing the food. Robert raised an elbow at him and snarled, "Get outta here." He kicked at him and missed, and the jerky movement caused some of his scotch to slosh onto my sweater.

"Hey now, Robert." Carl jumped up. "I'll take care of Wilbur." He grabbed the dog's collar and led him away to the corner of the store where he tied him up.

"Robert," I hissed at him. "Be nice. You can't go kicking other people's dogs."

In a loud voice, Robert told me through gritted teeth, "Goddammed mutt's got no goddammed manners." I could feel all eyes on us. I wished I could crawl under the bench to hide.

"And neither have you," Carl said from behind him. He picked up the plate of food he had put on the bench and took it over to Wilbur. "Eat up, boy," he said.

I took my plate back into the house and sat in a corner picking at the delicious, now tasteless food. Carl came in and started to apologize.

"You didn't do anything wrong, Carl. I'm sorry though. I feel responsible, even if I didn't do anything either."

Carl took hold of my arm and looked into my eyes. "Jesus, Andrea. You seem like a nice girl. What the hell have you got yourself into?"

Just then Robert lurched into the room. "Take your paws off my wife." He sneered and swept a look over Carl from head to toe. "Mr. Fancypants. Think you're so cool."

Carl raised both hands in the air. "Ease up there, Robert. I was just telling Andrea not to feel bad. No harm done."

Robert took my arm much more roughly than Carl had just done. "We're goin'."

And without so much as a "Thank you" to our hosts, he steered me along the path to our house.

Behind us all conversation had stopped.

Chapter 32

Robert stormed up the path from Steve and Mary's. I followed him because I didn't dare not. Partway up the hill, I glanced over my shoulder. The neighbours who had gathered to welcome me to the community stood, frozen in mid-action, as if someone had hit the Pause button. Most eyes were looking our way. I read pity and disgust in their gazes. My face burned with shame and I quickly averted my eyes, staring instead at the ground. What must they be thinking of us? I had begun to make friends, and now Robert's boorish behaviour had put those friendships at risk, if it hadn't extinguished them altogether.

I dreaded going into the house. Robert's determined stride all the way home told me he was fuming mad. He pushed the door open so hard that it swung wide and slammed against the coat hooks on the wall behind it. I tried to ignore his tantrum and took off my shoes. I remembered Edgar's warning then, about Robert's brush with the law. I could see now that there might be more to it than Robert had led me to believe. His explanation on the phone had been too quick.

"Would you like a cup of tea?" I asked quietly. He didn't answer but went straight to the cupboard and poured himself a scotch, dashing it down his throat in one gulp, and immediately pouring another. I'd had no idea he could drink so much.

He glared at me through squinting red eyes. "Just shut up. Sit down and shut up." I wasn't about to argue. I sat down without a word and tried to make myself smaller. "Now, do you wanna tell me what's going on between you and Goldilocks?"

"What?" I had no idea where this was coming from. "What are you talking about?"

"You know damn well what I'm talking about. Carl! Carl and his fucking golden locks." He towered over me swaying slightly. An ugly sneer spread across his mouth. "And don't try to deny it. I saw his paws on you. You and him in a cozy corner, talking about me. You traitorous bitch." He grabbed my upper arm and yanked me off the couch. "I'll show you who you're married to." Robert pulled me close and kissed me hard. I tried to pull away but that only made him yank me back harder.

I turned my head away. "You stink of scotch." Too late, I thought—I shouldn't have said that. It might only make him madder.

He exhaled in my face. "Yea-a-ah. Learn to like it." Still gripping my arm he staggered through the bedroom doorway, but there wasn't quite room for both of us to pass. The whole side of my body scraped heavily along the doorframe. With a jerk from Robert, I went flying onto the bed. His big body collapsed on top of me. I expected the worst. It would be brutal sex for sure this time.

I lay still, tears spilling onto the pillow, waiting for the crazy, rough sex I had come to hate. But moments later, loud snoring filled the room. "There is a god," I breathed.

I woke to an empty bed. The events of the previous evening flashed before me and I groaned. Tears welled up. What would I be in for today? Was Robert going to be hung over and in a bad mood? I wiped my eyes and sat up. His side of the bed was tidy. I know he had fallen asleep practically on top of me. Passed out was more like it. Where was he anyway? Maybe he was in the bathroom.

I winced at the pain in my arm as I pulled on my jeans and a T-shirt. Seeing me standing in the doorway to the kitchen, Robert jumped up for the coffeepot and filled my mug. He had two place settings ready for breakfast.

"Good morning, sweetheart," he said with a big smile. "Feeling okay this morning?"

"Of course. Why wouldn't I be?" He was the one who'd had too much to drink. I wondered where all this was going. After last night's interrogation about "Goldilocks Carl" I was expecting more of the same. Maybe he was getting ready to launch into me again. My hands trembled as I reached for my coffee. I gripped the mug tightly to stop the shaking. Robert didn't notice and seemed cheerful.

"I just thought maybe after last night, you might be feeling a bit under the weather."

"Me?! I only had a glass of wine. It was you who got into the scotch rather heavily." What in the world was he trying to do? Turn it around so I was the one who drank too much? Unbelievable!

"I guess I did get into my cups a little. Must have been nerves. So you're feeling okay?"

I nodded. My arms were bruised from when he grabbed me and from scraping the doorway, but he probably didn't even remember that part. Should I remind him? No. That would be asking for trouble.

"Great. I thought I'd make breakfast for you. Sit down. Let me take your order, ma'am." He pulled the chair out for me and bowed like a waiter in a fancy restaurant.

"All right," I said. I'd play along. Safer that way. I sank weakly onto the chair. My hands shook as I expected the charade to blow up in my face any second. "I'll have eggs Benedict." I wondered how he would deal with that. Maybe I shouldn't have pushed my luck. His good mood might disappear at any time.

"Coming right up." He took a dozen eggs out of the fridge and set them on the counter. The frying pan was already on the propane camp stove. Robert stared at the carton of eggs for a moment. Then he spun around. "Ma'am, we seem to be all out of eggs Benedict. How about scrambled instead?"

"Fine. With toast please." I was still angry with him, but afraid of him at the same time. And yet, he was making a big effort. I relaxed as much as I dared.

Robert hustled to make breakfast. It was so typical. A woman would get up early to make breakfast for a man after a loving night together. Robert was up early to make breakfast for me because, it seemed, he felt guilty for screwing up.

We ate breakfast lost in our own thoughts. Robert had an expectant look on his face. I shook my head in disbelief as he refilled my coffee mug. What did he expect me to say after he was so horrible last night?

"Thanks for breakfast."

"You're welcome." Robert hesitated, looked at his empty plate and back up at me. He took a breath.

Okay, here it comes.

"Andrea, about last night ... I ... I think I was out of line."

"Yes, I think so too," I said carefully.

"I saw you talking to Carl, and I was double pissed off. His bloody dog is always in my face, shitting on the dock, right in front of my boat, right on the tie up line—always on the knot, of course—and he's into our garbage, and into our food at the party. It pisses me off. And then when Carl had his hands on you, I saw red." Robert was breathing faster and his face was flushed.

"Carl was apologizing about the dog. And the hand on my arm was a way of showing that he really felt sorry about it." Yeah, sorry for me for having married you.

"Well, anyway, I don't know what came over me. I got so mad. I couldn't stop the rage." He looked down at the table. He was always so good at staring me down. For once he couldn't hold my gaze. "I'm sorry. Sometimes I think there's something wrong with me. I feel like everything makes me mad. Steve and Mary asking to be paid, the dog shitting on the wharf, anybody looking at you, someone tying up in my spot at the dock. And then afterwards I get such a terrific headache." He stopped abruptly. "What happened to your arm?"

"You grabbed me rather hard last night," I said through gritted teeth.

"Oh, God, I'm sorry," he whispered. He came around to my side of the table and put his arms around my neck from behind, leaning his head beside mine. "Andrea, dear, I'm so sorry."

"Do you think maybe you should go talk to someone? I mean like a doctor or a counselor?"

"I don't know.... Maybe ... maybe next time we're in town. I guess I should.

"I think it would be a good idea."

Chapter 33

I was up early with my fanny pack loaded. Mary said she'd have bear spray for me and put it on our tab. She and Samantha had compasses. I'd stay close to them. I brought a small first aid package—a few band-aids, some tape and gauze, and my Swiss Army knife. Water bottle and sandwich, a couple of plastic bags for the mushrooms and I was ready.

The walkway to Samantha's door was bordered with driftwood. Like Sarah back in Lund, Samantha had an eye for art in nature. Macramé plant hangers decorated the covered veranda and more of them hung inside the windows of her house. Mary and Samantha were sitting on handcrafted wooden chairs on the veranda. Both women wore jeans and long-sleeved lightweight tops.

"Before we leave, tell me if I forgot anything." I opened the fanny pack so they could see. Samantha rummaged around in it, her long mousy-brown hair falling in her face. Then she went back in the house.

"Here," she said when she came out again. "Take this whistle, just in case. We each have one. Use it if we get separated so we can hear where you are. It carries better than our voices."

"And here's the bear spray," Mary said. "It's good for about fifteen feet. Don't bother to try to spray it farther than that. It won't be as effective."

"Does it really work?"

"Don't know. We've never had to use it. Here. Hook it into your belt so it's handy just the same."

"Okay, let's get going." Samantha took the lead and we followed a trail up the hill, leaving the houses behind. It was quiet in the woods. Calm and peaceful.

At the top of the rise, we stopped. Mary took out her compass. "Now look here, Andrea." She had flipped the compass open and turned herself until the red needle pointed to the north. She pointed with her arm. "There's north. So which direction is home?" I pointed to the west. "Right. We'll be heading inland, to the east, so when we want to come back home, what do we do?"

"We'll head west?"

"Right. We may not come out exactly at our houses, but it will take us to the water, and in a pinch we can always follow the shoreline. I brought some flagging tape that I'll tie to branches now and then. We can watch for the flags when we come back."

We spread out so we were about twenty feet from each other, and I did as they did, walked along watching the ground. "Here's a mushroom," I called.

Samantha came over to look. "No, that's the kind that Wilbur ate. Don't pick up the poisonous ones. You can get it on your hands and then touch a good one and contaminate it. I mean, it's a long shot but it's best to play it safe. There are a few types of mushrooms that are really quite poisonous."

Mary held up a mushroom. "Andrea. Come see. This is a chanterelle. The colour of peachy champagne. Check for ridges going up the stem and right under the cap. They don't stop suddenly. If they do, it's probably not a chanterelle. And here, I left some so you can see how they look before they're picked. See how some are covered by the moss? If you pull it back a bit, you can see the whole mushroom. Cut the stem way down like this." She took her knife and made a cut just below the ground and pulled up a firm sweet-smelling mushroom. "That's what you're looking for."

After a few false finds, I gradually got to know what chanterelles looked like in their various stages of growth. I'd forgotten all about bears and cougars and wolves and anything else that might get me. I was intent on watching the ground and filling my bag with chanterelles. The soft moss absorbed the sound of our footsteps. The forest was silent except for a few birds and the faraway scolding of a squirrel. Tree trunks lay crisscrossed all through the woods. A few looked recently fallen but most had thick blankets of moss covering them. Ferns too, some waist high, decorated the forest floor.

"I almost expect to see a stegosaurus wandering through the ferns," I said to Mary. She was busy in a patch of chanterelles she'd found.

"Beautiful isn't it? Here, come and help me pick these. There's plenty for us all."

On my way over to her, I stopped short. "Ah, er ... Mary?" I pointed at the ground. "Is this what I think it is?"

She stood up. "Yup. That's bear shit all right."

"Do I need to worry?"

"Stick your finger in it. If it's hot, get your bear spray out." She laughed. "I'm just kidding. No, you don't have to worry. If that bear was here even five minutes ago, it's long gone now." She took a stick and poked around in the pile. "See what it's been eating? It's got a lot of seeds and is a dark blue colour. Most likely it's been eating salal berries or blue huckleberries."

"What do salal berries look like?" I asked.

"I'll show you when we come across some." She tilted her head and looked at me with a puzzled expression. "You haven't been out in the woods much, have you?" I shook my head. "Well, never mind. You'll soon get used to it."

"I was worried about the bears, but I love it out in the woods. It's so fresh and everything is untouched and clean. No plastic or garbage. And it's quiet. I like that." Good for my nerves after being around Robert.

We picked mushrooms all morning and worked our way inland. Mary showed me salal berries and Samantha pointed out huckleberries. She broke off two branches of a huckleberry bush and handed me one. We ate the berries as we walked.

"This reminds me of stories of people lost in the forest surviving on nuts and berries," I said.

"Well, we're not lost, I hope," Samantha said, "and there are no nuts." Suddenly she laughed. "Except us!"

Our bags were nearly full of chanterelles when Mary suggested we stop to eat our sandwiches. We looked around for a place to sit. Samantha found an open spot and felt the ground. "M-m-m, a little bit damp, but not too bad." She opened her fanny pack and pulled out a big green garbage bag. Mary did the same. They put them side by side and three of us sat on them close together.

"Next time I'll know to bring one," I said.

"Very handy. You can use them as a ground sheet, or cut a hole in the top and on the sides and wear the plastic bag like a shirt to keep you warm and dry in an emergency. I always carry a couple of them. They roll up so small it's no trouble to have them along."

"You and Mary are such outdoors experts. I was lucky to meet you." I took out my sandwich and bit into it hungrily. "Boy, you sure work up an appetite out here, eh?" I smiled at my two new friends and realized I hadn't felt this happy in quite a while.

Chapter 34

October 10

Dear Mom and Dad,

Sorry I haven't written for so long. We've been
busy getting a few new things moved in. The
house is really nice but it needed a woman's
touch. We bought some cushions for the couch
and pictures for the walls, a couple of vases—that
kind of thing.

Getting to know the people who live there. Well,
Robert already knew them, but now I'm getting to
know them too.

Samantha and Mary have taken me mushroom
picking. They're really nice and I'm glad I have
two new friends. I'm learning so much about
outdoor survival. Can't quite make a fire by
rubbing two sticks together yet, but I'm working
on it. (Just kidding.) But still, you'd be amazed at
what I can do.

Now that I'm not working at the wharf in Lund
anymore, I'm doing a lot more reading, and
I'm even dabbling in some writing for our local
newsletter with an older couple who are both
writers. They're helping me learn to write better.
Who knows? I might even send some of my
adventure stories to a magazine someday.

I'm enclosing the newsletter so you can read
the piece I wrote about our mushroom-picking
adventures.

How are you guys doing? Can't wait to hear from you. Do you ever get out to the cabin? Those were fun days, eh?

Are you thinking about retiring yet, Mom? And how's your friend Percy doing, Dad? Still talking non-stop? Are you staying sane? Any trips planned for this winter? Maybe a week in Florida? Tell me everything.

My new address is easy:

Andrea Bolton
General Delivery
Hope Bay, B.C.
V0P 1S0

Love you and miss you,

Andrea

Chapter 35

I threw my clothes on and grabbed the backpack I had prepared the night before.

"Come down when you're ready," Robert said. "I'm going to get the engine warmed up."

"Be right behind you. Have to find my list." Squirrel Cove! Yes! I punched the air. I hadn't been out of Hope Bay since our wedding.

Robert had made the trip to Powell River a few times in the past weeks, to see a psychiatrist. He hadn't wanted me along on those trips. I hadn't pressured him. He probably wouldn't have been good company anyway, to judge by his withdrawal into sombre moods afterwards. He wouldn't talk about his sessions.

But today I was buzzing with the excitement of getting out for a while. I'd make sure I filled the boat with all the things on my list. I'd been adding items to it for weeks—baking and cooking ingredients I'd had to do without, supplies I missed when I wanted to sew. I'd bought a sewing machine at Sears to bring to Hope Bay, and then realized I had very little thread. I didn't know if they had what I needed at Squirrel Cove but I'd get what I could in the way of zippers and threads. Surely they'd have the basics.

From his Powell River trips, Robert had brought me a few items—a compass, a whistle, and a belt knife—to finish outfitting my fanny pack for mushroom excursions. My Swiss Army knife was fine with all its gadgets, but it was good to have a solid knife, heavy enough for tougher jobs. I'd noticed that Samantha and Mary carried these tools as casually as I used to carry a purse in the city.

I swung my backpack onto the Hawkeye's hatch cover. "Do you want me to untie the lines yet?"

"Yup, if you're ready to go," Robert called from inside the wheelhouse. "Do the bow first."

I had the lines untied in no time and, holding onto the sturdy pipe frame that held the spools for the trolling wires, I pushed the boat away from the dock before hopping aboard.

Robert put an arm around me as I stood beside him at the helm. He was often affectionate when he wasn't upset. More and more the gentle gestures were initiated by him and not by me. In a way, I liked his touch, but so often it led to that rough sex that satisfied only him. I became increasingly reluctant to encourage him. "Got your list?" he asked.

"Yeah, I found it. It reads more like a book though. So many things on it. Like a Christmas wish list."

"Let's have a look." He held out his hand for the list. His eyes scanned the paper. His eyebrows went up. "Hmm ..." He turned the paper over. "Lots of things. Sure you need it all?"

"Need? No. Want? Yes. I could live without all those things, sure, but life would be more fun and more comfortable with them—no doubt about it. But it's your money. What do you want me to do?" Might as well be clear about this right away. Why go to all the trouble of shopping if it was going to be vetoed at the cash register? I could spare myself that embarrassment.

"No, you go ahead and get the things on your list," he said, "if you can find them. Squirrel Cove doesn't have everything. It's just a little general store, you know."

"Well, maybe they can order things they don't have and send them on to us." It was a little closer to civilization than Hope Bay was. Why, it wasn't that far from Lund, really.

"Maybe," Robert said vaguely, as if he didn't think it would happen. "Here, you steer the boat for a while. Good practice for you."

"What are you going to do?" I hoped he wasn't going to be down in the hold rearranging things and leaving me to deal with the boat. I knew what to do, basically, but on the water you never knew what situation could arise with the changing tides and currents, the wind and floating debris or other boats, not to mention shoals that had to be avoided. For me it was always stressful to be in charge of steering the boat. It wasn't so much steering, as watching, anticipating trouble. I was getting to be an expert at the latter.

"I thought I'd make us some breakfast," Robert said. "An omelette? Toast? Coffee?"

"Sure. Or I could make breakfast and you could steer."
And I'd get back into my comfort zone.

"No, I think you need the practice. If we go fishing
together, you'll have to know what to do, right?" He
looked smug, as if he had it all figured out that we would
someday fish together.

Fishing? Trapped on the boat with Robert for weeks
and weeks? I hesitated and then said, "I'm not sure I want
to go fishing. But I guess it won't hurt to know how to run
the boat." There was a time when I thought the idea of us
fishing together was romantic. Not anymore.

When we got near the dock at Squirrel Cove, Robert
took over the wheel again while I went out on deck and
got the lines ready. As soon as I finished tying up the boat
and Robert had shut down the engine, we took our empty
backpacks and walked up the ramp to the wharf head.
The nearly full high tide had floated the dock higher,
making the incline of the ramp only slight. At low tide it
would have been a much steeper climb.

We followed the trail over to the general store. I
supposed, compared to city stores, it was sparsely stocked,
but I was amazed at all the items on the shelves. Besides
a huge array of dried and canned foods, the selection
of hardware was twice that of Steve and Mary's store at
Hope Bay. Robert checked out the fresh vegetables while
I went around the corner to a section with sundries. I was
looking at the sewing threads when I heard my name.

"Oh my God! Monique! What are you doing here?" I
squealed. We threw our arms around each other. "It's so
good to see you." And already the tears came. "I don't
know why I'm crying. So good to see you," I said between
sniffs.

"You look wonderful," Monique said. "I'm so 'appy to
see you too." Then she looked around and lowered her
voice. "So 'ow's it going? Be honest."

"Oh-h-h-h." I waggled my fingers. "Ups and downs." I rubbed my forehead and used my hand to hide my face in case Robert glanced over. "You were right," I whispered and swallowed a big lump in my throat. "Do you ever see Jim?" I felt I had limited time to talk to Monique. Might as well get the important things said first.

"Not for a long time." She looked disappointed that I'd mentioned him. Maybe she still hoped I'd come back to her.

"If you do, will you tell him I wish I'd taken his advice? Here. He gave me his phone number. Copy it down, just in case. I'd call him myself, but I never have a chance to do it without Robert finding out."

"In case? In case what?" Her brow furrowed. "Is it dat bad already?"

I sighed. "I don't know," I whispered. "I'm trying my best, but I think there's something wrong with him. And Jim has a boat, and well, just in case...."

"Now you are scaring me. Are you okay?"

"Yes." Tears started anew.

"Andrea, look at this. Oh! Hello, Monique." Robert's eyes widened. "What a surprise to see you here."

"Hi, Robert," Monique muttered.

"What's wrong?" he asked when he saw my tears.

"Oh, nothing. I was so happy to see Monique. That's all." I couldn't meet his intense scrutinizing gaze.

"Well, I'll let you two catch up, and then we should get our stuff together. I want to be out of here as soon as the tide changes, which will be pretty quick now." He wandered off to another part of the store.

"Monique, so quick, tell me. How come you're here?" I clung to her arm as if it were a life ring.

"I take de water taxi. Remember I told you sometime George will let me take de taxi to Squirrel Cove? Well, 'e let me drop off a customer today. Maybe anodder time 'e let me do it again. Do you come 'ere much?"

I shook my head tightly. "I wish! But no. This is the first time. Here it is November, and we've been in Hope Bay since late August. It's only because there's a break in the weather that we've been able to come."

"Same wit' me and dis customer today. Only because de wedder is good."

"Did you find another person to share the rent after I left? I felt so bad leaving you in a lurch like that."

"Oh, yeah. No problem." She waved her hand as if to brush away any concerns. "I'm living wit' Max now."

"Max? No kidding! So you've decided to go straight?" I knew my mouth must be hanging open.

She looked puzzled for a second and then laughed. "No, no, no! You got de wrong idea." She laughed again. "Max is ... well, Maxine! You remember Maxine from Comox?" She giggled some more. "Dat's too funny. Me going straight."

"Oh, of course. Maxine. I'm so glad you have someone to share the rent." I was unaccountably disappointed when I should have been happy for her. Don't be so selfish, I told myself. She deserves to have someone. And so do I, but I'm supposed to be happy with Robert.

"Andrea ... Jeezus, you look so miserable. I am worry for you."

I lowered my voice. "Monique, will you call Jim for me? I think I'm headed for trouble. Just a feeling I've got. I don't know what to do and I don't know what I want him to do, but I don't want him to forget me. He cared about me once."

She sighed. "I guess I can do dat. I wish you would come back and live wit' me. Max is nice, but she is not you."

"Oh, Monique. You know I love you too. But—"

"I know, I know. Don't worry about it." She hugged me close and patted me on the back until my face was a mess of tears.

"Andrea, come on. Hurry it up, will ya?" Robert called from the far side of the store.

"Coming." I gave Monique a big kiss on the cheek and held her close. "Bye," I whispered. When I turned for one last look I saw that she was blinking back tears.

Chapter 36

Samantha, Mary, and I went out picking mushrooms a couple of times a week, whenever the weather was tolerable. Steve called us The Three Mushketeers. When hunting season opened we started wearing red. We weren't about to take any chances.

"Our guys are busy doing other things today," Mary said, "but sometimes fellows come up from Comox or Powell River by boat to go hunting, so you never know. Could be other hunters out there."

"Well, I think we're fine." Samantha waved away any concerns. "Andrea's got her red cap, you've got your red windbreaker and I've got my surveyor's vest. And we don't need to go far to find mushrooms."

"For sure they can't mistake us for any furry animals." I took a deep breath and grinned. "Mm-m-m. The air smells so fresh and it's so quiet." A squirrel scolded us from a branch overhead.

"Yeah." Mary laughed. "So quiet."

"I mean the no-people-kind-of-quiet." I bent down to pick a chanterelle and saw three more off to the side. And many more beyond those. "Wow! Look at this! The mother lode! Mary, Samantha, come help pick these."

"Listen to you crowing. So much for the no-people-kind-of-quiet," Mary teased.

"I can't believe the size of them and they're everywhere. Pinch me. I think I'm dreaming." I was smiling so hard my cheeks hurt. I calmed down and stopped my "crowing" and concentrated on collecting the mushrooms. We were cutting like crazy and filling up our bags when the silence was shattered. Instinctively, we shrank together at the crack and zing of what had to be a rifle shot.

"Holy shit!" Mary muttered. "That sounded like it was near home."

"Stay down just in case," Samantha whispered, "and listen."

Another shot followed about twenty seconds later, this time accompanied by a drawn out high-pitched yelp of pain that went through my body like a jolt of electricity.

"W-what was that?" I stammered. Mary and Samantha looked at me with shocked expressions on blanched faces.

"Holy Mother of God," Mary whispered. "What on earth?"

"Not a deer." Samantha stood stock still, listening. "It sounded like a dog. Maybe someone shot a wolf?"

"Wolves?" I'd forgotten there were wolves around. I fumbled for my bear spray.

"I think we should go back," Samantha said. "Whatever it was, someone is out here with a gun and they might not realize we're in the area. Best to play it safe."

Another shot rang out. Then we heard him. "You fucker! That'll teach you not to shit on my ropes."

My eyes flashed open and I wiped frantically at the water splashing on my face. "There she is," Mary crooned. She put down her water bottle and patted my cheek softly. "Okay now?"

"What happened?"

"You fainted, but you're fine now."

I was confused for a moment. Then memory surged back and I was living the nightmare again. "Oh, no!" I wailed.

"Now, Andrea. We don't know what happened yet. Try to calm down. We'll find out soon enough when we get home." Samantha nodded at Mary and they put an arm under each of mine and lifted me up. I choked back the nausea that filled my throat. If I heard what I thought I'd heard ... if it was true what I thought happened ... oh, God. I cried silently.

As we emerged from the trail I could see a crowd gathered outside the store. Angry shouting. Fingers pointing accusingly. All directed at Robert.

Larry and Jared struggled to hold Carl back, gripping his arms and digging in their heels. Carl's face was almost purple with rage. "You mother fucking son-of-a bitch. When I get my hands on you, I'll kill you."

Robert stood alone several yards away from the group and beckoned to Carl with his fingers in a "come on" gesture. "Bring it on, Goldilocks," he snarled. "I can handle you. You're a useless piece of shit. Just like your fuckin' dog."

"Robert! Robert! What did you do?" I tugged on his arm to make him look at me. He flung me aside like garbage and sent me sprawling in the dirt. I didn't have the strength to get up. Deep raspy sobs tore out of my throat. Mary's arms went around me.

Behind her I saw Wilbur's bloodied body lying against the outside wall of the store. "Oh no! Wilbur!" I gasped for air and sobbed. "No-o-o...."

Carl lunged towards Robert. Larry and Jared tightened their grip. In the background I saw Phillip, Molly, Tom, and Elizabeth. Every face reflected fury or disgust. Steve took charge. He turned to them and raised his arms. "Now listen, everybody. Robert, you go home, right now. The rest of you come into the store and we'll figure this out."

Robert spat on the ground and stomped up the path to the house. Samantha came over to me. "Mary, let's take Andrea to my place. She can't go home right now. Let Robert calm down first."

"Good idea. We can have a cup of tea and get cleaned up a bit, eh? Come on, Andrea. Up you get."

I could hardly see where I was going, but my two angel friends guided me to Samantha's house. Mary helped me brush off my clothes and get washed up. She cleaned and bandaged the deep scrape on my arm.

"He didn't mean to hurt me. You know that, don't you?" What must they think? Now they've seen what he's like.

"Sh-sh-shhh. Of course he didn't."

We sat at Samantha's table sipping her herbal tea. I wiped at my eyes.

"This is a nightmare." My voice quavered. "What do you think will happen now?"

"I don't know," Mary said. "Robert has been pretty difficult to have around sometimes. I don't know how you manage to live with him."

I inhaled sharply. I wanted to lash out and say they were wrong, but I knew it looked bad. And yet it was my job to find the strength to defend him. "He's not like that all the time." They didn't know he could be charming and pleasant too.

"I don't see how they'll let him stay now. No one can trust him." Samantha shook her head sadly. "I feel so bad for you." She reached across the table and squeezed my hand.

"There's something wrong with him. He can't help it." My throat ached as I fought tears and tried to explain. "I don't know what it is, but it's getting worse. After a blow up, he has to lie down because his head hurts so much, and then everything's okay again until the next incident. But each time it gets worse. I don't know what to do."

Mary looked at Samantha and mumbled something I didn't catch. She clicked her tongue and Samantha shook her head ever so slightly, her mouth set firmly. "How about if I go down to the store and find out what's going on? I'll come back and let you know. Might be easier that way than you facing the whole crowd." Mary got up to leave and Samantha nodded her approval. I could only sit there with barely enough strength to lift my teacup.

Samantha suggested I lie down on her couch and close my eyes for a bit while she got cleaned up. I put my head down for a few minutes. If only I could make it all go away—shut out the world by shutting my eyes. As if it never happened.

When Mary came back her expression was grim. I braced myself for the worst. "I'm sorry, Andrea. They've decided that Robert has to go. We can't have him living here. We're afraid someone will get hurt if his rages escalate, and they're bound to. There's been too much trouble over the past months and it isn't getting better."

"But he's seeing a doctor. Maybe he will get better." They both looked at me blankly. I don't think they believed me.

Mary patted my hand. "Everyone feels terrible about it because we've all come to like you so much. But we just can't have Robert stay here anymore. He'll have to go just as soon as he can pack his things. Steve has gone to tell him now."

I felt like I'd been punched in the gut. I started crying again and both women hugged me tightly. "We're so sorry," they said. "We don't want to interfere, but if there's any way we can help you, just let us know."

I dug a Kleenex out of my pocket and blew my nose. "Thanks. I'd better go home now."

Chapter 37

With shaking hands I threw the last of our belongings into green garbage bags and tied the tops securely. Robert would be back shortly to carry them down to the wharf. With each load he collected he had snarled some reproach at me through clenched teeth. "If you'd kept your wandering eyes to yourself this wouldn't have happened. You and Goldilocks. Well, I got even with him. Hah! That bloody dog wasn't worth the bullets it took to bring him down."

What a jerk! Blaming me for his overactive imagination. Blaming me for getting us kicked out of Hope Bay. The only thing I was guilty of was staying with him longer than I should have. But where would I go? I had no place to go and no means to get there if I did. Stuck! I'd loved him, once. But now he terrified me. He'd probably kill me if I tried to leave him. I could only hope that he would be his old self again, friendly and charming, once we were away from people.

I brought the last of the bags down to the dock and watched him hurl them into the hold of the Hawkeye. Luckily it had plenty of room. We needed it today. Everything we owned had to be stored on the troller. It was to be our home until we could find another place to live. Someplace where there were no people for him to try to get along with. Someplace where we wouldn't be asked to leave.

Chapter 38

I had hoped that we might head south towards Powell River or maybe—that would be too much to hope for—to Comox, but when we pulled away from the dock at Hope Bay, Robert turned the Hawkeye north and my heart sank. The grayness of the dreary drizzle and low cloud ceiling insinuated itself into my mind. My throat knotted up and I swallowed hard to keep from falling apart. I sat quietly, hands clasped in my lap, in the passenger seat at the front of the wheelhouse, watching Robert covertly. When the whiteness of his knuckles receded, I spoke for the first time since leaving Hope Bay.

"I had hoped we might find a place to live in town."

"Nope. Can't do it."

My stomach knotted. "Because...?" *Please don't let him fly into a rage again.*

Robert let out a big sigh. He rubbed his brow with the back of his hand. "I don't handle town very well. I can manage it for short periods, but to live there, I can't deal with it."

I gulped, surprised at his honesty in sharing that self-realization. "Okay ... do you have another plan in mind?" Maybe I could work with him. Easier than fighting against his chaotic temperament. I didn't have any options anyway, so why not make the best of my situation? When the time was right I'd talk to him more about his problem, but I'd have to choose that time carefully.

"There's a cabin a bit farther up the coast, not too far from here; practically around the corner, in the next bay. Nobody has used it for quite a while. I thought I'd check it out."

"How do you know about it?"

"Well, you can see it from the water, and I've gone there a few times on deer hunting trips. The owner's got a little dock there. It's rickety, but good enough to tie up the Hawkeye. I've stayed in the cabin when I took the skiff there to hunt the area."

"Doesn't the guy care about people making themselves at home like that?"

"People who have cabins in remote places expect them to be used by anyone in need. It's almost like the law of the land. The rule is you leave it as you found it, or better. Leave firewood for the next guy. Maybe leave a tin of food."

"Do you know who owns it?"

"I've heard his name is Owens, but I'll find out for sure next time I go to Powell River. He's an old man and I think he wouldn't mind unloading it. Probably get it for a good price."

"Maybe I could come along to town?" And run away first chance I got.

"We'll see. Most likely I'll combine it with a doctor visit though, and in that case, I think it would best to go by myself."

I should have known better than to get my hopes up. We spoke very little. The Hawkeye's engine droned, carrying us ever farther up that desolate coast. I fought to beat back the fears that kept surfacing. Being stuck in a cabin so far from people; I wasn't sure I could handle it. Maybe we'd both end up crazy. Half an hour later Robert tapped me on the shoulder and pointed towards the shore. He handed me the binoculars. "There. That's the cabin."

It was hard to see through the wheelhouse windows, but Robert turned the wiper blades on and I was able to make out a small building set back from the beach in a clearing. All around the clearing were evergreens. Such a lonely, dark place. A shudder went through me.

"What?" Robert asked. "What's wrong?"

"Just got a shiver. Must be the rainy weather." He put an arm around me. He did feel warm and nice. But could I trust him to stay that way?

I looked at the tiny cabin as we came closer to its dock. Next summer, Robert would be away fishing for at least a couple of months. Maybe I could get him to let me go to live with Monique for the summer. I dreaded being in such a remote place, alone without him. But even more, I dreaded being there alone with him.

Chapter 39

The place was small. Two rooms. Only one exterior door, but the bedroom window was big enough to crawl through in case of emergency. A medium-size bunk without a mattress sat on one side of the bedroom wall, a kitchen table and two chairs the only furniture in the main room.

"No bathroom?"

"Outhouse." Robert pointed. "Up the trail and over."

God! An outhouse. And winter was coming. It was November already—wind and rain. Well, I would figure something out. Maybe a chamber pot. My grandmother had told me about them.

I was glad to have the propane cooktop. I supposed I could keep a fire going in the small woodstove and have a constant supply of hot water. That's what most fishermen did on their boat stove.

I ran my fingers over the wooden planks of the counter top. Dust so thick I could write my name in it. The floor was worse. The corn broom standing in the corner was well worn, but it would do for now. I started at the far end of the cabin and swept my way towards the door.

"What about the water supply?" I asked Robert as he dumped another bag of our belongings on the porch. I was going to need water for cleaning.

"Creek mouth is about 100 yards that way." He pointed out the grimy window.

"Maybe for now I'll just use a bucket of sea water for the first cleaning. Can you get us some drinking water?"

"Yup and I'll make a fire. That should help make things cozier. But I think we should sleep on the boat tonight."

"Suits me fine. It's going to take a few days to make this clean enough to live in." Filthy, filthy, filthy place. Thank goodness we had the boat to sleep in for now.

It took us a week to move everything from the boat. Space was limited. Robert built a small covered storage shed at the back of the cleared area for our tools and supplies that didn't have to be inside the cabin.

"I'll put up a bigger shop once we're settled. We'll be able to store canned food there too, so there's more room in the house." He seemed to be quite content with the way our home was shaping up. I cleaned, cleaned, cleaned, and organized the inside of the cabin. My sewing machine would come in handy for making curtains once Robert got the gas generator going. He seemed happy to be working on the heavier jobs, like patching a leak in the roof and laying a hose to the creek for a temporary water supply, things that would normally be considered men's work. I often heard him humming to himself as he worked.

"I've been making a list of things we need as I think of them," I said. "More matches, for sure. How about if I hang it here by the door and you can add to it if you come across anything we need?" It was a challenge, making do with the basics, and an interesting lesson on what we could manage to do without.

No store-bought bread? Bake my own. No fridge? Use the picnic cooler outside. Put a container of cold creek water in it to keep things cool longer. No clothes dryer? Make up a rack to place near the woodstove. No electric coffee maker? Boil water on the woodstove or propane burner and pour through a reusable cloth filter balanced on top of the pot. Keep it warm on the side of the stove. No cream for the coffee? Use canned milk.

"Good idea about the list. I'll be heading into town as soon as the weather breaks."

Yes! I could sure use a trip to town. See some people, stores, civilization. Yes, yes, yes!

"You'll be okay here for a couple of days, right?"

What? Oh no. Oh shit, shit, shit! I took a deep breath and silently counted to ten. He needed to hear me say yes in a confident way. For my safety, I couldn't chance upsetting his equilibrium. He'd been good to be around for several days now.

We had seen the occasional black bear on the beach nearby. "What should I do if a bear comes around?"

"Nothing. It'll go away again."

"Well, I suppose in a bad situation I have my bear spray." I didn't for a minute believe that would be all it took to be safe. Robert must have heard the doubt in my voice.

"Tell you what. While I'm gone, I'll leave my revolver here with you. It's registered and legal, but I can't be taking it to town anyway. Do you know how to shoot a revolver?"

"No." I shook my head and backed away a little. "Where would I have learned that?"

Robert took the gun out of a canvas duffel bag he had stashed in the bedroom. "Okay, look here. It's a .357 so it can do some damage but it's not so big that it's cumbersome to pack around. I like to have it handy just in case."

"In case what?" I was getting nervous looking at him with that gun. He wasn't above using it on a dog. I'd heard it said that kind of thing could escalate. I hoped he didn't fly into a rage. I didn't want to end up like Wilbur. But he seemed to be in a good mood. For now.

"In case there's a cougar that won't leave, or a wolf or a bear. Who knows? It's better to be armed than not. If you don't have to use the gun, you're no worse off, but if you needed it and didn't have it, that would be bad."

"So what do I do with it?" I could see I really should know how to use the revolver and not regard it as the enemy. It could save my life someday.

"First rule, never point the gun at anyone, even if you're sure it's not loaded. Second, always check to see if it is. Out here, I always keep it loaded. What the hell use is an empty gun?"

Robert showed me how to load it, how to make sure it was empty of bullets before cleaning it, and how to hold it to shoot. It was simple. I just had to remember not to shoot my foot off.

"I'll be very careful with it."

"Maybe tomorrow we can do some target shooting so you can get used to using it. For now, we'll keep it here in this little drawer by the door." Robert smiled. "I'm glad you weren't all freaked out by the sight of a gun. I hate it when people—especially women—overreact. 'Man with a

gun! Man with a gun!'" He flapped his arms and mimicked
a silly overzealous brainless woman. I smiled at his goofy
sense of humour. "You're okay," he said. He pulled me
close and kissed me tenderly, very tenderly. I couldn't
help feeling surprised.

"I like it when you're gentle like that." Maybe he would
change if I helped steer him the way I wanted him to go.

"Let's try out that bed in there," he said as he backed
me into the tiny room. He was pulling off my clothes as he
pushed me down on the bed, still gently.

"Robert, I like having sex. Would you like to know how
I like it?"

"For sure," he breathed into my ear.

"Well, for a start, you have to remember your size."

He laughed. "Okay, I think I can do that. Right now
it's size Extra Large."

"No kidding." I chuckled. "But I mean you have to
remember that you have a very big body and I'm quite
a bit smaller. I don't enjoy being crushed under your
weight."

"I can fix that," he said as he entered me. "You won't
feel crushed. But oh God, I need to scratch that itch."
He didn't know how to make love any other way than
intensely. He was definitely extra large and, inadvertently,
he more than satisfied my needs. But first, it was all
about satisfying himself. I sighed. Well, at least he kept
most of his considerable weight off me this time.

"Better?" he asked as he collapsed on top of me forcing
the air out of my lungs.

"Yup, better," I gasped, and squirmed out from under
him. I would have to work on this a bit at a time.

I rummaged through my cosmetics bag and discreetly
swallowed the birth control pill I had forgotten to take
that morning.

Chapter 40

Three days later, the weather broke. The wind died down and the skies cleared. At its peak, the sun was so low in the sky at this time of year that its rays were weak, but even in its meager light, the grass was greener and the water was bluer. The extra brightness lifted my spirits. They would have been lifted higher if I had been going to town, too.

But Robert had been adamant. "I've got a lot of things on my list and I can get more done if you stay here. Besides I might have to stay an extra night to get my appointment with Dr. Briscoll. It's just easier if I only have to think about myself in town."

"I could find things to do to amuse myself while I wait for you. I have a list of things I need for my sewing, and for baking. I could shop for some of the things we need." I felt like a kid pleading with my parents to be allowed to go to the movie.

I saw Robert's jaws working and realized I was pushing him towards another blowup. I was getting good at reading the signs that preceded an emotional explosion. Best to back off a bit.

"I need to do this trip alone. Give me your list. Maybe you can come along next time." He was all but gnashing his teeth, so I hung my head and gave in.

"Okay." I let out a big sigh. "Okay."

He took a backpack of toiletries and a change of socks and underwear. Everything else he needed was on the boat.

"Will you stop to check the mail at Hope Bay?" I hadn't heard from my parents in ages.

"No need. I told them to redirect everything to Squirrel Cove. I don't ever want to set foot in Hope Bay again." His brow furrowed and his expression darkened. He had been so good since we arrived at the cabin. I didn't want his mood to slide back to the way it was when we left Hope Bay; he'd been angry for hours.

"Okay," I said quickly. "Don't mail my letter till you get to Powell River though, will you? It'll be faster that way." The wrinkles on his forehead smoothed. I smiled brightly and reached to hug him. I wanted to keep him in a friendly mood as much as possible to avoid those outbursts.

"Take care of yourself," he said. "I should be back in a couple of days. Don't worry if it's three or four. If the weather changes I could be stuck till it blows over." He hugged me tightly. "I do love you. You know that don't you?"

I nodded. "Take care."

"If anything happened and you needed help, you know how to use the VHF, right?"

"Right." I waved goodbye as the Hawkeye pulled away from the dock. Then I trudged along the footpath back to the cabin. Now that Robert was gone, there was no reason to hold back my tears of frustration and fear.

Finally I realized my crying wasn't going to change anything. I made myself a pot of tea and brought a kitchen chair onto the front porch. With a sweater wrapped around my shoulders, I sat in the weak December sunshine, holding a cup of peppermint tea so it warmed my hands. Wherever I looked I saw only undisturbed nature. No manmade noises disrupted the tranquility. It was too damn much of a good thing. I craved contact with people. Robert didn't seem to be bothered by the lack of conversation with friends, but he also was able to get away to town once in a while. Beautiful as it was, I felt trapped here in this remote place.

He had to let me come to town with him next time or I would go stir crazy. Ha! Me going crazy. Wouldn't that be ironic? But he probably wouldn't be going to town again for another month. *Oh God. How am I going to make it that long?*

It seemed to me I had two choices. I could make the best of it and try to make a happy life for myself with Robert. That would involve a whole lot of giving on my part. Or, I could give up on this marriage. But if I did and managed to escape from here, what would my parents say? They'd be so shocked and disappointed at having to tell all their friends what a screw-up their daughter was. I couldn't bring myself to tell them I'd made a big mistake marrying Robert. And yet, eventually I knew they'd understand. The real problem was one I hadn't wanted to acknowledge. I was trapped here. If I tried to use the radio to call for help, on the remote chance that someone might be in range and might risk investigating my whereabouts, Robert would probably kill me—or them.

He did love me. And I loved him too in a way. But I knew it wasn't the big love that I had been looking for in my life. Still, if I resigned myself to staying, I would have Robert to take care of me. All I had to do was try to make the place homey and cook for him. I could make those cookies for him that he had said no one had ever baked for him. What kind of a mother did he have anyway? I'd have to use the oven on the Hawkeye for now, but he'd be happy about the cookies. I'd give in when he wanted sex, maybe gradually get him to think of how I felt and what I needed, and maybe, hopefully, add some variety to his one method of getting his rocks off so super intensely. And, most of all, I'd keep out of his way. What a bizarre goal for a newlywed—to try to keep out of her husband's way.

I was stuck here. I might as well do my best to make it work—look at the positive side. Maybe Robert would turn out to be okay after all. I could work on him gradually, talk to him about the things that bothered him, and maybe he would change. He was making an effort to go to his appointments. True, he didn't want to discuss them with me, but maybe in time he would.

He could be interesting and entertaining. I liked him when he was calm. He had a good sense of humour and could be fun to be with—as long as something in his brain didn't snap. Trouble was, I never knew when that might happen.

Knowing he could have a meltdown at any time was turning me into a nervous wreck. I needed a backup plan. What if he went really berserk some time and it was just the two of us here? What if he hit me? I'd have no one to help me.

That awful day at Hope Bay, he hadn't even realized that he'd thrown me into the dirt after he shot Wilbur. Didn't remember a thing about it. What if he used a knife or one of his many rifles? I wouldn't have a chance. Oh Jeezus! I hadn't even thought about all those rifles of his. I needed some escape options. But I wasn't in a hurry to run into the bush to get away, right into the jaws of cougars, bears, and wolves. I was definitely stuck here. There was nowhere to go for help. Not by land anyway. The only option was by boat, and Robert had full control of that. It was all too overwhelming. My best chance would be to try to please him and go along with him.

Might as well get started and transform this shack into a home I could stand to live in. I put my empty teacup down, picked up the axe and went out into the backyard. The whole world was my backyard now. At the end of the grassy area where the forest began, Robert had stacked some bolts of wood he had cut from a windfallen log. I don't know why he didn't think to leave me some firewood already cut. Maybe he thought sawing up the log was good enough, but for sure the pieces were too big to put in that little woodstove and expect the fire not to go out. Using one of the bigger bolts as a chopping block, I set a smaller round of wood on end and swung the axe to split it. The axe glanced off and went sideways barely missing my shin. *Holy shit! I'd better watch it. That's all I need when I'm out here by myself. Cut my leg off and bleed to death.*

I stepped back a pace, took careful aim and split the log. Better. I set the halves up again and split them one at a time. Now I was getting the hang of it. I had a couple more close calls that served as reminders to take more care, but after an hour I had a pile of wood split that would last me till Robert came back. *Pisses me off though. He'd better not try to pull that stunt again, leaving me without any firewood.*

I could hear him answer me, *Or what?*

I put the axe down and sat on the chopping block to catch my breath. The forest was dark and cool behind me. Out of the corner of my eye, I saw a shadowy figure streak up the slope into the trees. I whipped my head around to stare at the spot where the shape had disappeared. Nothing. I shrugged my shoulders. *Must have been my imagination.* I gathered up an armful of wood and headed for the cabin. Goosebumps prickled my neck and I turned to look for the shadow again. Then I saw it. A cougar, his back end still behind a tree, was crouched down watching me. I almost ran, but I'd heard that running would trigger the chase instinct. I hustled to the cabin, sent the armload of wood clattering on the porch. I yanked on the door, rushed through, closed it quickly behind me and slid the bolt into place. I leaned my back against the wall and heard nothing but the pounding of my heart.

I had enough wood for the night, but what about tomorrow? The last thing I wanted to do was go outside again. And yet, what if it rained and the rest of my wood got soaked? I really had to go bring it to the covered porch. My nerves were raw. I could bring the revolver outside with me, but then it would be awkward carrying the wood and what if I fumbled it and it went off? I buckled on the belt and carrying pouch for the bear spray instead.

I checked from the windows for any sign of the cougar. All clear. With the door open a crack I let my eyes scan the immediate area. So far, all looked serene and safe. Step by step I tiptoed out onto the porch, stopped to look around again, and then moved down the path to the wood pile. Hastily, I loaded an armful of wood. I was shaking so badly that I dropped pieces of wood all the way to the cabin. When I bent to pick them up, I remembered hearing stories of cougars jumping on people who were bent down. The cats must feel emboldened when the prey looks smaller, especially if the victim is looking away. I made sure to stand up quickly each time. I brought several more loads to the porch, looking over my shoulders as I hustled back and forth. At the edge of the trees I saw cougar shadows everywhere, although he was probably long gone. At least, I hoped he was.

I would have to be careful out here by myself. I had a five gallon container of drinking water in the kitchen so I should be fine even if I were confined to the cabin for any reason. I would never go out without my bear spray or the revolver again, as long as I was here by myself.

Night began to fall. I put a bucket in the corner of the bedroom for a chamber pot, and checked to make sure the door and all my windows were secured.

Day one of my plan to make a go of it, and all I wanted to do was run. I had thought I was tough enough to manage to live here. But, my God, how brave was a girl expected to be?

Chapter 41

Two days later the weather turned ugly. I had plenty of wood chopped and stacked beside the cabin door. I'd wrapped a plastic tarp over it and weighted it down with several chunks of wood. I didn't want the rain blowing in sideways, soaking my firewood. Keeping the fire going had become a priority.

I wondered if Robert would show up that evening in an effort to beat the coming storm, but by five o'clock, as darkness fell, he still hadn't returned. I opened a can of stew and poured it into the pot. I could have lit the propane cooktop, but I was in no hurry. I had nothing but time. Since the woodstove was going anyway I set the pot on it next to the kettle. I couldn't bake in this woodstove, but it had a flat top for cooking. And, it saved on propane. It was mid-December and I didn't want to run out of propane while Robert was away.

Hours later, the wind had risen from brisk to screaming and I knew that Robert wouldn't be back that night or possibly for several days to come. It would be suicide to go out in a boat in this storm. The waves crashed onto the shore, pounding the gravel beach relentlessly. Behind the cabin, the forest roared as the wind tore through it. I cowered at the sound of creaking and cracking branches, and the occasional dull thud of what had to be a falling tree. The wind buffeted the cabin mercilessly and I bolted from the chair each time flying branches clattered over the roof. Now I knew why the cabin was sited in a clearing. No tree would be landing on it. At least, I hoped not. Oh God, why did I think of that? How tall were the trees anyway? I peered out the window but couldn't see the tops, could barely see the trees. Were they tall enough to crash across the clearing and hit the cabin?

Wrapped in a blanket, I huddled in the chair by the stove trying to concentrate on reading by the light of the kerosene lantern I had set on the table nearby. I had no radio. No music. No one talking. And yet it was far from quiet. Until that moment I hadn't realized how noisy or terrifying a storm could be. I'd been sheltered from nature. At times like this I wished I had never left the city.

The storm continued for three more days. I tried to make good use of the short daylight hours. I had brought extra fabric remnants for sewing but I didn't have enough of any one colour to make curtains. I dumped the box of scrap material onto the table; a meter of something flowery, two meters of plain blue, and bits of leftover scraps of assorted patterns. If I didn't waste any fabric I could make curtains for the three small cabin windows. I decided on a patchwork trimmed with the blue. It was fun and challenging to find a pattern that was pleasing to the eye. When I had all the pieces measured, cut, and pinned, I started up the Honda generator on the porch to keep the fumes outside. I dragged the table closer to the door so the sewing machine cord would reach. In no time I had the panels sewn together and the curtains hemmed.

A couple of nails at each side of the top of the window, a piece of twine pulled through the top seam, and my curtains were hung. I stood back to survey my work and grinned. They were beautiful. Bright, creative, and pretty. I hoped Robert would be pleased.

The sewing job done, I looked around the small living space and wondered what to do with myself for the next hours, days, or who knew how long? I'd love to be able to phone my friends or family, but of course, there was no phone. I thought I could resort to the next best method of communication.

I got out some writing paper. Maybe it would feel like I was talking to Monique if I wrote to her.

Dear Monique,

Robert has gone to town. I wanted him to take me along but he wouldn't have any part of that. He said he'd be back in two days, but then this storm came up. I wonder if he's tied to the wharf in Powell River. I wonder if he even cares how I'm surviving this storm. He must care. He said he loved me before he left. You can't love a person one day and not the next. Can you? I wish he'd come back, but I know he can't until the weather breaks.

I know. I can hear you saying, "Are you nuts? Why do you want 'im to come back?"

Well, maybe I don't really love him, but I like him a lot when he isn't having a meltdown. See, I've spent intimate moments with him, talked with him about so many things, gotten to know him well. Sure, I don't like everything I learned about him, but he isn't all bad.

He has a bit of a neatness fetish that sometimes drives me crazy, but I can work with him on that. I like things neat too, although not to the point where all the tins in the cupboard have to be lined up so you can read the labels. Or the shoes! They have to be lined up properly. Left on the left, right on the right. Isn't that crazy? I'm sure he's got obsessive compulsive personality disorder. But there's a lot of good in him too. Did I already say that? Sounds like I'm trying to convince you … or myself.

I just wish he wasn't so unpredictable. He doesn't seem to be able to control his anger and I haven't figured out what sets it off or how to turn it off.

Sometimes I wonder if this is all that life has in store for me—living with a guy that I would have few complaints about if he could manage his anger.

Oh shit. I just remembered that when I saw you at Squirrel Cove, I asked you to phone Jim. That was stupid of me. I was desperate then. Fed up and disillusioned. Now? I feel more resigned. Maybe a bit defeated. Ready to settle for "like" over "love."

I felt more sparks and a magnetic pull with Jim (and you too) than I ever felt with Robert, but I have to try to forget about that.

Anyway, what could Jim do, supposing he wanted to do anything? I'm Robert's wife. It's not as if he can just breeze in here and take me away. Sail off into the sunset like in the romantic movies. It was a fantasy, nothing more.

Hope you're doing fine. Miss you.

Andrea

Oh crap! I couldn't just trot down to the mailbox and put this letter in. Did I trust Robert not to read it? No. There was a good chance he'd be the one to take it to Squirrel Cove to mail it. What if he opened it? I crunched up the letter and threw it into the woodstove. How stupid of me to think I could put any personal thoughts on paper.

It was mid-afternoon and the wind had died down considerably. The sun peeked out from between the clouds that were still scudding past. The ocean was a bit choppy, but the white caps were gone. That was a good sign. I searched the horizon for a mast. Nothing yet.

I looked for something to eat. Crackers. A few potatoes. A couple of onions. Half a cabbage. Some carrots. Not a lot to choose from, but I chopped up a bit of everything except the crackers, put it in the frying pan with some oil, and swept the cabin and porch one more time while the frying pan heated up. I must have cleaned everything three times today. I had one book left to read. After that I'd have to write my own. I chuckled at that idea. But why not? Didn't mean anyone would have to read it, but it would be something to do.

I stood on the porch, watching the last light dance on the water. It was that time of the evening when the sun's low-angled light painted everything gold. Beautiful! It was then I saw the mast. I jumped up and down and clapped my hands. Yes! Beautiful!

I grabbed my jacket and ran down to the dock. Robert was still a few minutes out, but I couldn't stay in the cabin waiting. I waved madly. And yes, madly was the word. I had learned all about cabin fever.

The Hawkeye pulled up to the dock. I grabbed the midship line and did a quick wrap around the big iron ring embedded in the dock plank. I jumped aboard and hugged Robert.

"Am I glad to see you."

"Same here," he said with a surprised look on his face. "So now I know what to do. I have to go away more often to make you glad to see me."

"No way!" I gave him a punch in the arm and another hug. It was like hugging a big warm teddy bear. The comfort I got from that hug was a direct reflection of the desperate loneliness I had felt this past week.

Robert gave me a kiss on the forehead. "Let's finish getting this boat tied up and shut 'er down. We've got a lot of stuff to unload."

"I'll soon have arms like a weightlifter," I said as Robert and I passed by each other yet again. We had boxes and boxes of supplies to bring from the boat to the cabin.

"Look pretty good to me." He gave me a wink.

I let Robert give directions for where he wanted things to go. Easier that way. I put cases of canned food at one end of the porch. Perishables like potatoes, carrots, turnips, and cabbage all went into a big box by the front door. It had a hinged cover and was probably meant to hold kindling.

"I'll have to build an enclosure for our food on the porch."

"Kind of like an outdoor pantry?"

"Yeah. This'll do for now, but we don't want to attract bears or raccoons."

"We've already attracted a cougar." I told Robert about my cougar sighting. "I never went outside without my bear spray after that."

He hugged me. "Oh you poor thing. I'm so glad you're okay. I think in future if you go any distance from the cabin it might be best to take the revolver with you."

I had expected Robert to downplay the cougar incident but he seemed to be taking it seriously. He must have believed the threat was real enough to cause concern. I'd heard of cougars attacking people and was glad to have Robert's support. I would be on my own out here from time to time and I had no choice but to learn to take care of myself. I knew I'd feel safer with a gun.

"Okay, maybe I'll put it in my fanny pack. Then it's always there if I go out for mushrooms or any other reason."

Robert packed the heavy things like the extra cans of gas and propane, while I brought in boxes of apples and oranges, rice, potatoes, oil, flour, jars for canning venison, and the tastiest treat of all—a big round of gouda cheese.

"I thought we'd eat well since it's nearly Christmas," Robert said. "And just before Christmas, we can take a run over to Squirrel Cove and pick up some more fresh fruit and vegetables."

"Sounds great. You did say we?" I watched his face carefully.

"That's right. We." He smiled. "But for now we'll have to make do with what I've brought."

"Seems like you cleaned out the Powell River stores."

"There's one more thing. I'll go get it. Meanwhile, why don't you go make us a pot of coffee?"

He had a funny smirk on his face that left me wondering, but I went into the cabin to make the coffee while he went to the boat to get whatever it was.

The cabin was cozy with the fire on. Robert came in and hung up his jacket. He went to the basin to wash his hands.

"Nice curtains." His eyebrows went up in surprise. "You made those?"

I beamed with pride in my accomplishment. "Yup. You like them?"

"Beautiful. I didn't know you were so talented." He pulled me close and planted a kiss on my forehead. "Coffee smells good. Now we need to have something to go with it." He pushed open the cabin door and reached for something he had apparently left outside on the porch. "For your coffee." He handed me a bag. "And I hope you'll share them with me."

I peeked into the bag and couldn't keep the smile off my face. "Oh my God! It's been so long since I've had a box of chocolates. But these are really fancy ones. Thank you, thank you, thank you." I wrapped my arms around him and stretched up for a kiss. "These are going to be so good."

And they were. I rationed myself to three for now. I savoured each one, taking tiny bites and letting every morsel melt in my mouth before taking another nibble. Robert ate his a little faster but smiled as they went down. Then he fidgeted and drummed his fingers.

"What's the matter? You look like you're on pins and needles. Help yourself."

"Oh, no. It's not that. You go ahead and enjoy them." He got up and left the cabin. Strange. Seconds later, he came back in carrying a big box that looked quite heavy. He plunked it down beside the table. "I hope there's something in there that you like."

I stared at him, puzzled, but opened the box. It was jammed full of books. Must have been at least fifty in there. "Wow! Oh my God. Wow!"

"Some are new; some used, but the woman in the bookstore guaranteed me they were good reading. I'd told her you were a discerning reader."

"Oh, Robert. That was so thoughtful of you. Thank you." Again I hugged him. "I think you did this just to get extra hugs."

"Maybe I felt I owed it to you. I haven't always been easy to be around."

"No, sometimes you haven't. But let's not go there now. This is so nice of you."

"I know you wanted to come to town, but I had to go by myself this time. Needed time to think. Needed to see the shrink." He pulled a crooked face. Embarrassed to talk about it, I guessed.

"How did that go? Okay? Did he help you?" Maybe I could get some pointers on how to help him.

"Yeah, I think so. He had some good ideas, but some were pretty stupid. He said to try to avoid stressful situations."

"That's a no-brainer."

"And if I felt like things were making me angry, to try to think of something that makes me happy or calm. Like close my eyes and think of this thing—whatever I choose—and then it's supposed to take the place of whatever makes me angry." He shrugged his shoulders. "I don't think that's gonna work. I mean can you picture it? I'm on the dock and somebody's just walked on my freshly oiled decks. Instead of confronting him, I'm supposed to close my eyes and think of—whatever—a bouquet of violets or something. Horseshit! That's not gonna work." His breathing sped up and his face reddened.

My stomach tightened. Oh, no. He's going to fly into a rage again. "Well, don't worry about it right now. I can see you have to find another way." His good mood couldn't be disappearing already. "Let's have a look at the books you brought, okay? Might be something in here for you too." I hoped to distract him. I could see that there was a lot of turmoil just below the surface. The cabin floor was covered with eggs that I needed to walk on very carefully.

"Oh, jeez!" Robert jumped up. "Be right back." I peeked through the window and saw him go out to the boat. When he came back he handed me an envelope. "Sorry I forgot. A letter from your parents."

Chapter 42

November 30

Dear Andrea,

It's been ages since we've heard from you. Is everything okay???

Our girl, mushroom picking? Dad says be careful. Lots of them are poisonous. Thanks for sending that newsletter. Loved your little article about mushrooming. Who knew you had such a talent for writing?!

You're ambitious, baking bread. I haven't made any for a long time. Too much work, but I remember how good my mom's homemade bread was. Remember when we baked cookies together when you were little? You had flour all over the place. What a mess, but what fun. I haven't baked cookies in ages. Maybe I'll do that today. Your dad would be pleased. You know what a sweet tooth he has.

Your dad and I are spending more weekends at the cabin. He has a great time fishing and barbecuing. His idea of roughing it is when we run out of propane for the barbecue and he has to cut kindling and make a real fire. But it's fun. We cooked some wieners on a stick (your dad didn't have any luck fishing). Haven't done that in years. Not since you were little and we camped out there. Those were fun times.

Hope you're having a fun time too. You need to write more letters. You never mention Robert. Is everything okay?

Wish you didn't live so far away.

Love,

Mom and Dad

Chapter 43

I folded the letter and tucked it away with all the others in the pages of A Fine Balance, my favourite book this year. I chuckled to myself, thinking how appropriate that title was for my situation. From time to time I liked to take out the letters and read them again, like talking to old friends. But while I waited for new words from home to cling to, life in the cabin went on, and we were usually busy with repairs and food preparation.

With the new supply of groceries we ate well, but we also canned deer meat using the pressure canner Robert carried on the Hawkeye, and so had a steady supply of venison.

I'd been nervous about going along with Robert on the first deer hunting trip, afraid I would make a noise at the wrong time and scare a deer away, but I needn't have worried. The rut was on and the bucks thought only about chasing does, all caution forgotten. How typically male.

A big buck stood sniffing the air and Robert signaled me to stop and be quiet. "Keep your eye on it," he whispered, "in case it runs after it's hit." He raised the gun to his shoulder and leaned against a tree for support. The shot rang out and the deer went down. So simple. But then it kicked and kicked and kicked. I watched, horrified until the last feeble jerks stopped. I looked at Robert. The pumped up excitement evident on his face was a stark contrast to my own feelings. So that's what the "thrill of the kill" looked like. I started to walk away, my face wet with tears.

"Here!" Robert called. "Get over here. Let's get a rope around it. I'll gut it. Then we'll drag it back home. It's mostly downhill."

Reluctantly I stood by while Robert gutted the deer. The smell of warm blood was nauseating to me, but he was into the cavity past his wrists, pulling out the innards. When he stood up to stretch his back, his hands were red with drying blood and his face had blood spatters everywhere except in his glassy eyes.

"At least there's no flies when it's this cold," he said.

"Yeah, at least there's that," I agreed distractedly. I shook my head to rid myself of the killer image.

Later, with the deer hanging upside down from a rope looped over a roof beam of the porch, Robert got out his skinning knife. A few little cuts into the thin membrane between the meat and the skin, and the hide peeled off as easily as taking off a sweater.

He sawed the carcass in half as it hung there and then brought one of the pieces to a makeshift bench of a couple of planks laid across bolts of wood. As Robert cut the meat away from the bone, I took large pieces of meat into the cabin and cut them into strips and chunks small enough to fit into quart-sized canning jars.

"Normally we'd hang it for a couple of days but since we're going to can it, we don't need to," he said.

The smell of the raw meat threatened to gag me at first, but I had to get used to it. This was no time to be squeamish. The water was already near boiling in the pressure canner. I put the clean lids and rings on each jar and stacked two layers in the huge pot. Once the canner lid was tightly sealed, I watched as the pressure went to ten pounds and then turned the heat down to keep it steady. Ninety minutes later, the first batch was done. A freezer would have been so much easier, but without electricity, canning was the next best thing.

"It's a lot of work to can this deer meat," I said a few days later, "but it sure makes an easy meal afterwards. Just dump it into a pot, thicken it for gravy and *voilá*, instant supper."

"Venison is fine, but I think it's time to put the crab rings out and have something different for a change. Want to take a run out with the skiff to throw them out?"

"Sure!" Looking at the four cabin walls all day and all night was more than enough quiet time for me. Anything for a chance to get out. "How many rings do you have? And where are they? I haven't seen anything like that around here."

"They're on the roof of the wheelhouse."

"Oh, you mean those big circles of re-bar frame with netting across?"

"That's them. I only have two but that'll be plenty for us."

We putted out a short distance with the skiff, the crab rings stacked on the bow. Robert had fastened a fish head to the center of each ring as bait. When he reached a spot that wasn't too deep he said, "Okay, throw one over." As it sank, and the line ran out of the skiff, Robert yelled, "Jesus! Get your feet out of the rope coils!" I jumped back and sat down with a plop. "You wanna to go for a swim in December? Christ, I thought you had more sense than to stick your feet in the rope." I detected a hint of fear under the anger. Maybe he worried about what might have happened if I'd gone over. Maybe he cared what happened to me after all.

"Okay, okay. I'm still here. I'll be careful." I wasn't sure what upset me more; the shock of being yelled at or the close call. Moments later, the adrenaline hit and my knees shook as I realized I might have been pulled under and drowned. In spite of the cold day, a faint coat of sweat covered my brow.

As soon as the ring settled on the bottom and the float on the end of the line bobbed at the surface, Robert gave the outboard a sudden burst of gas. I hadn't expected it and slid off the aluminum seat, landing at Robert's feet on the oar lying on the floor of the skiff. My tailbone hurt like crazy. Robert laughed. "You look so funny with your legs in the air."

He made no move to help me up. Seemed to enjoy watching me struggle. Fortunately I was facing away from him. He couldn't see my pain. I fought back the tears stinging behind my eyes. Goddamn him. Rather than slowing the motor so I could get back up, Robert sped up. The momentum of the boat made it impossible for me to get back on the seat and the water that inevitably collects in the bottom of the skiff all ran towards the stern. What the hell was wrong with him anyway? When we reached the next crabbing spot, the boat slowed suddenly. Robert put a hand under each of my armpits and none too gently gave me a boost to get up. I could hear him laughing behind me.

"What?" I asked angrily.

"You should see yourself. The seat of your pants is soaked with fishy water. Hurry up and throw out that other ring."

I was so hurt and angry that no words came to mind. I grabbed the crab ring and gave it a huge heave, being careful not to step in the line that was feeding out as the ring sank. Once the float on the end of the line hit the water, I settled myself on the bench and got a good grip on the sides of the skiff, ready for whatever surprises Robert might have in mind. Sadistic bastard. What had I let myself in for, living out here in the boonies with this lunatic?

He spun the boat around and sped back to the dock. After the sudden stop, the wake of our waves bounced us up and down, knocking the boat against the float again and again. "Jump out," Robert said. But I waited for the waves to calm before I tried standing up. One mishap was enough for me today.

Once my feet were on the shore, I rushed to the cabin. I poured water in the basin and took off my pants, washed myself with a facecloth, and then rinsed out the seat of the pants. I draped the jeans over a chair by the woodstove to dry.

Robert came in and slammed the cabin door. "You've got no sense of humour."

"You think that was funny?" The tears that came now were angry, not hurt.

"Well, ... yeah. You looked funny lying there with your feet sticking up in the air." His face twisted into a nasty smirk. "So what's the big deal?"

"The big deal is that my tailbone landed on the oar and it hurts." I pulled on a dry pair of pants. "And you did nothing to help me get up; like you were enjoying watching me struggle."

"So, you did look funny. God! No sense of humour at all. Well, fuck you then. Get out of my sight." He slammed his fist on the table.

I scurried into the bedroom and closed the door. *You get out of my sight. If only I could send him packing. I've got to get out of here. I have to escape. I need to plan.* I picked up a book from the big box and remembered how

Robert had brought them home from Powell River. He'd been so loving and kind that day. He changed so quickly it made my head spin.

I was still staring at the first page of the book, unable to think about reading, when the door flew open. "I've changed my mind. Before you get out of my sight, you can see to my needs." He took off his shirt and unzipped his jeans. I tried not to let my dread show, but I knew my eyes must be huge as I sucked in my breath and backed up into the pillow. He grabbed at my ankle and pulled me towards the foot of the bed. "I think a little submission is in order." He jammed my head down onto his erection. "Make it good," he said with a hint of "or else" in his tone.

Chapter 44

I'm going to pull the crab rings. You coming?" Robert was friendly. You'd think yesterday hadn't happened.

"No thanks. I don't think I'd be much help. I'd only be in the way." *And I have no desire to go out in the skiff with you again. Ever!*

"Well, at least put some water on to cook the crabs."

I slammed a big pot of water on the woodstove to heat up. I grabbed the binoculars and watched him. Maybe he'd get caught in the coils and fall overboard. He stopped the boat by the farthest marker, reached for the float and started pulling the line in, coiling it in the bottom of the skiff as it came over the side. When the ring came up, he set it on the seat in front of him and gingerly grasped the two crabs that were now trying to clamber out of the netting. He tossed them into a bucket in the front of the skiff. He repeated the process with the closer ring, this time pulling up three crabs. After tossing them into the bucket as well, he pried loose a starfish that had settled on the fish-head bait and chucked it back into the water. With the second ring securely on board, Robert scooted the boat over to the dock again. I threw down the binoculars and tried to look busy as he came in the door.

"Put that pot of water on the propane stove now. Set it up on the porch or it'll stink up the house. I'll have those crabs ready to throw into it in a few minutes. Lots of salt in the water?"

"A good handful," I said. "Is that enough?" He nodded and went back to the dock.

Once I had the water set up, I watched him tear the shells off the live crabs and crack their backs on the edge of the dock, breaking the bodies in two. Then he leaned over the float, swished out their guts in the water, and put the halved bodies in another pail.

"Get me another crab out of the bucket, will you?"

I reached in to pick one up, but it turned its beady black eyes on me and stood up on its back legs, front claws open, ready to do battle.

"Ah ... er ... how do I pick it up without losing a finger?"

"From behind. Like this." Robert reached in and picked it up. "Fingers on top, thumb underneath. That way they can't reach your fingers with their claws." He tossed it back into the bucket and said, "Okay, go ahead."

I started to reach in and again, the crab stood up tall on its back legs, holding its claws towards me. I turned my hand this way and that, trying to picture how to pick it up. *Thumb on top, fingers underneath. Or was it fingers on top and thumb underneath?* I made a move towards the crab and it went into action facing off with my hand whichever way I planned to grab it.

"Oh ..." I wailed. "I can't do it."

Robert easily picked up the crab. I thought now he'd be angry again but he was trying to hide a smile. I took that as my cue to get away while I could.

"I'll go check on that water."

It was a brutal business, boiling a potful of live crabs even in halves, but later, when I tasted them, I forgot all about that, and how intimidating they had been when still alive. We laid the cooked crab on old newspapers on the porch to let them get a good chill. That didn't take long in the December air.

"They're really meaty this time of year," Robert said, wiping at the crab juice that dripped down his chin.

"You mean they aren't always?" I picked at the meat of a claw using the small end of one of the crab's own legs.

"They stop eating when it's time to molt and grow new shells in summer and early fall. While the new shell is still soft, the crab hasn't grown enough to fit into it yet. They aren't as meaty then as they are later."

I let Robert tell me all about it. He liked showing off his knowledge. I had to feed that need for my own sake; keep him happy.

"I bet even millionaires don't get to eat this much crab at once."

"And for sure, not as fresh as these." Robert reached across and wiped my cheek. "You had a bit of crab flake there." He smiled.

"My wrists are dripping with crab juice." I dried my hands on some paper towel and picked up a piece of garlic bread.

"This is great bread," Robert said with his mouth full. "Really good. I didn't know you could bake bread."

I almost said, "Janine taught me," but swallowed the words quickly. Janine had baked goods for the restaurant at Hope Bay. I didn't want to turn our thoughts back to that time. "Yup. I can," I said lightly. "You like it?"

"Fantastic. Goes perfect with this gourmet crab feast."

After the last crab leg was picked clean we pushed away from the table, groaning.

"That was good," he said, "but I'm so stuffed, I never want to eat crab again."

"Yeah, me neither." I laughed. "Till next time."

Chapter 45

Two days before Christmas we took a run over to Squirrel Cove. I had a few things on my list, but mainly it was all about fresh fruit and vegetables. Those would always be in short supply. We bought things that kept a long time—cabbage, turnips, onions, potatoes, carrots, apples—but for the short term it was a luxury to bring home some lettuce, tomatoes, and bananas.

"Let's splurge and buy a frozen chicken. We can pretend it's turkey and cook it in the boat stove for Christmas dinner."

I looked at Robert hopefully and again hated myself for groveling and hated him for putting me in this position. He kept the finances completely under his control, and in any situation where money was needed I had to ask him for it. I didn't like it one bit. I was used to having my own money and being independent. How had this happened to me? I shouldn't let it go on. And yet, I was afraid to bring up the issue. Afraid of the backlash.

"Sure, if you really want that. Or we could have a salmon. I'll catch us a fresh one." He shrugged as if he didn't care what I made for Christmas dinner. He didn't seem all that keen on chicken.

"Okay, never mind. It was just a thought. Trying to make it traditional." But everything in my life was different now, so if Christmas was different I'd get over it. I was losing any enthusiasm I'd had for it anyway.

We loaded up on groceries and it occurred to me that I might phone Monique from the store. Robert would never approve, but maybe while he was taking the first load of food down to the boat, I could make a quick call.

As soon as he stepped outside with the first of the boxes, I said, "I'll be along in a minute. I want to have another look at the sewing things." Then quickly I looked for the storekeeper to get his attention.

"Excuse me?" I called across the room to him. "Do you have a—"

Robert stuck his head back in the door. He looked at me with a scowl and motioned with waves of his hand for me to continue the question.

"Ah, er, do you have a ... washroom I could use, please?"

"Sure, right back here, miss." He pointed down a dark hall. "On the right."

By the time I got into the washroom my impromptu need to pee became real. I had so nearly been caught. Robert would have been furious to catch me reaching out to someone—anyone but him. And worse yet, he didn't like Monique.

He always said, "What Monique needs is a man in her life to tell her what to do. Who does she think she is, doing whatever she pleases? I don't like you hanging out with her. She's a bad influence on you." Why would I want to phone her? he would want to know.

Arranging to run away? A shiver of fear went through me. Was I really contemplating running away? Was it what I wanted? Yes! Yes! Yes! Oh yes!

I flushed the toilet, gave my hands a rinse and hurried out.

"Thank you," I mumbled to the storekeeper. I picked up the remaining box of groceries and headed for the door. "Oh!" I stopped. "Is there any mail for me? Andrea Bolton?"

He shuffled through the letters he kept under the counter. "Yes, there is. It's been here a while, but I hang onto letters longer than the post office says. I know people live far out and don't get in here that often."

"Very nice of you to do that." I looked around the store. "Robert? Is he still here?"

"He's gone." I wondered later if he saw my shoulders sag with relief. I folded up the letter very small so it fit into my jacket pocket, out of sight.

"Oh, okay. Thanks. Well, Merry Christmas."

I was rewarded with a warm smile. "And merry Christmas to you too. I hope it's a good one for you." I nodded. *I hope so too. But chances are it'll be just another day ... if I'm lucky.*

With my hood up, I bent forward over the box of groceries to save it from the pelting rain and walked briskly across the wharf head, down the ramp, and along the float to the Hawkeye. My arms felt like they were breaking off by the time I handed the box to Robert who stood on deck waiting for me.

"Come on inside. We have some time before the tide turns." He helped me take off my jacket and hung it up on a nail near the stove. "Sit down on the bunk by the table. I have a little surprise for us."

I was on full alert. When Robert had a surprise for me, I could expect just about anything—good or bad. These days it was more often bad, with glares, orders, and sex on demand. But then sometimes it was something good.

He always kept me off balance. Maybe that was part of his game plan.

In the back of the dish cupboard, he dug around and found two small glasses. From another cupboard, he took a bottle of brandy. My eyebrows went up.

"Did you just buy that here? Now?"

"Yeah. That's what I came back in for, when you were asking about the bathroom." He looked pleased with himself. *If you knew that I had been about to ask to use the phone and plan my escape you wouldn't be smiling like that.* I hung my head. I felt like such a deceitful sneak. How could I have thought of doing that to him?

"You're not happy about this?" He poured us each a small glass of brandy.

"Oh sure! I'm ... surprised, that's all."

"Well, there's more." He went out and took something out of the picnic cooler. Keeping the object hidden, he got two spoons out of the cutlery drawer, and then put the treat between us on the table.

My eyes went wide and I shrieked. "Haagen Dazs!"

Chapter 46

December 5

Dear Andrea,

I'm surprised to hear that you've moved so soon after settling at Hope Bay. How great that Robert has bought a place. No more renting. But you say you have no neighbours? Do you think that's good? So remote and so isolated?

Of course you have Robert, but what about when he goes fishing? You'll be all alone in the wilderness. Why don't you ask him to reconsider and both of you move into town?

I know you, honey, and this is not for you. Come back to us or at the very least move to the nearest town.

We've tried not to interfere in your life, but I have a bad feeling about you living so far out. Your father and I are worried about you. Please move back to town. If you need us, we're here for you. No matter what, you know you can always come home.

Your dad and I hope you have a lovely Christmas. Wish you could be here with us. Wish you didn't live so far away.

Love,

Mom and Dad

XOXOXO

Chapter 47

I read the letter while Robert was talking to another fisherman out on the float. Then I tore it up into small pieces and stuffed it into my jacket pocket before he came back.

"The wind's picked up." Robert stepped aboard and immediately pushed the button to start the engine. "We'd better get a move on or we'll take a shit kicking on the way home."

"Should I untie us?"

"In a few minutes. The engine needs to warm up first."

In the meantime, with my hand buried deep inside my pocket, I gathered up all the little pieces of the letter in my fist so none would be missed. After a while he nodded "okay" to me. I jumped up, and stepped over the cap railing onto the float. Out of Robert's line of vision, I bent to untie the first line, and discreetly dropped my mother's letter into the water between the boat and the dock. I hated to part with her words to me, all love and caring, but I couldn't risk Robert finding the letter.

He had been right about the weather. We bucked into the tide with the wind at our back, which made for a rough ride. Almost home, we rounded the point at the entrance of our bay, just as the wind-driven drizzle turned into torrents of rain. We left white caps behind us in the open channel and were thankful for the protection of the headland.

"Ah, that's better." I was relieved that the rough part of the ride was over. I didn't know how much longer I could have held onto my breakfast.

"Half an hour later and we would've been rockin' and rollin' pretty good. Get that starboard midship line ready. When I pull up alongside the float, get a couple of wraps around the ring as fast as you can. I don't want to run aground in this wind."

"Got it." I had learned that one wrap of the rope didn't do much to hold a boat, but two always did the trick.

Holding the line, I hopped onto our float. As I bent to tie us up, the wind whipped my jacket over the back of my head. I resisted the urge to pull it down when I felt the rain pelting onto my back. Thank God, I ignored my jacket. It was all I could do to get that second wrap around the big iron ring before the Hawkeye could be pushed away from the dock by the rising wind.

Chapter 48

Christmas was a non-event. It was as if it didn't exist. Robert couldn't go out to catch a salmon because of the storm that had followed us from Squirrel Cove. It took another three days to blow itself out. As soon as the weather broke, I grabbed my jacket.

"I'm going for a walk. I have to get out for a while." I knew Robert wouldn't say I'll come with you. We were both sick of looking at each other. I grabbed the fanny pack and strapped it around my waist.

"You're not going far, are you?" He pointed at the fanny pack.

"No, but I wasn't far away when the cougar came around either. I just like to have the pack with me." It had the revolver and the bear spray. I felt safe from everything as long as I had the pack. Everything except Robert, that is.

"Okay, don't get lost."

"I've got a compass." I pushed open the door and took a deep breath of the fresh sea air. The tang of iodine told me it was low tide. It wasn't a bad smell, but it definitely belonged to the seashore. I pulled my toque over my ears against the chill and started up the trail behind the house. Immediately the iodine smell gave way to the aroma of moss and decay, and the scent of firs freshly washed with rain. The forest floor was soft with layers of organic material; fir needles, ferns, moss, and decayed fallen trees made the ground firm enough, yet spongy. I wondered for how many thousands, maybe hundreds of thousands, of years that had been going on. I filled my lungs with the wholesome earthy aroma. If I stayed here long enough, maybe I would die here and become part of this cycle. There were worse places to end up.

I took a compass reading. Our bay was to my northwest. I wanted to become familiar with the immediate area behind our cabin and orient myself. I decided I would make walking a regular thing whenever the weather was good. I was heading south, exploring. *Exploring escape possibilities?* Not for today, I told myself, but maybe for some other time.

"How was your walk?" Robert asked as I came out of the woods. He was chopping wood and put down the axe.

"Great. I'm going to do this every chance I get. It's so nice to get out in the fresh air." *And each day I'll go a little farther until I'm comfortable finding my way.*

He pointed at the woodpile. "You want to give your lungs a workout, you can help me bring some of this wood to the house."

"Sure. I'll just put the fanny pack away. Don't need it if I have you to protect me, do I?" I gave him a hopeful smile.

"That's right." He grinned broadly.

Throughout January, and into February, Robert was often out fishing with the skiff. His blowups were less frequent, but when they happened they were more intense. I had several bruises now and was doing my best to avoid getting any more, agreeing with him on everything. He hadn't been to his Powell River appointments since before Christmas but I wasn't about to bring that up and have him explode again.

"Almost Valentine's Day," I said. I winced as I set a cup of coffee in front of him. My wrist was red and sore from where he had twisted it last night.

"Soon be time to think about doing some boat maintenance." Robert dropped his head and ran his hands through his hair.

I brightened. "Are you taking the boat to Powell River? I could help you scrub the hull and paint." *Oh God! A chance to get out of here!*

"Yeah, I was thinking about it. I need to get a bit of gear too, and probably I should change that water pump. It's starting to make tired noises." He scowled. "More money down the drain. Fuck! It never ends. Seems like more money goes out than comes in."

"Well, we don't spend much out here," I offered, hoping to smooth things over and improve his mood.

"You complaining again? What do want from me? You want to go shopping? Don't I provide everything you need?" His voice got louder and louder as he worked himself into a rage.

"Robert! I wasn't saying anything like that." My heart thumped louder and my throat tightened, anticipating an explosion.

"No, but you were thinking it! Goddammit. Women! They're never satisfied." He slammed his fist on the table spilling his coffee. The hot liquid ran down onto his lap and he jumped up in a fury. "Now look what you made me do!" The expression on his face.... I thought I was going to pee myself. My knees quaked as I stood up. *Oh no! Here comes trouble!*

Robert grabbed my arm and threw me against the door. It hadn't been latched tightly and my weight flung it open. I landed on my backside on the porch and scrambled to get up. The Hawkeye bobbed gently at the dock. Could I hide in there? No way I was going back into the cabin now. I ran for the boat. The skiff was tied to the float. Even better! If I could undo the lines quickly enough, I could push off and be safe. Robert probably expected me to come back into the cabin and so turned his back long enough to give me the head start I needed. I untied the lines, tossed them into the skiff, jumped in, and pushed away from the float. Safe! When Robert got to the float I was out of his reach—just.

"You fucking bitch! Get back here, right now! What the fuck do you think you're doing? Crazy bitch. You get back here, or I'll fuckin' kill you." His words came out in a roaring scream. His face was contorted with rage as he shook his fists at me.

Now what? I was sure he really would kill me if I came ashore again. There was only one solution—make a break for it. I squeezed the rubber bulb in the fuel line to put some gas into the carburetor, pulled the cord and the motor came alive. I put it in gear and took off. A glance over my shoulder told me I had made the right decision— the only possible decision. Robert stood at the end of the float waving his arms wildly. His mouth was opening and closing, presumably shouting obscenities. I was glad I couldn't hear them above the roar of the outboard motor.

Buzzing with adrenaline, I crossed the bay towards the channel. The light chop on the water was enough to slam the skiff up and down repeatedly. *Okay, calm down now. Slow the motor down. No need to pound the waves so hard.* I cut back on the throttle and still cruised along at a good clip. On the other side of the bay now, entering the channel, I kept close enough to shore so I wouldn't be in the worst of the weather or the waves, but far enough from the beach so I didn't hit any hidden rocks.

Now that I was away from Robert, I started to shake. Some of the shaking was the terror catching up to me, some was from sheer cold. I'd had no time to grab a jacket—hadn't planned to be on the frigid gray sea in February. The icy wind cut through my sweat shirt and the chill of the aluminum seat seeped into my jeans as I motored along. I didn't allow myself to dwell on the cold. I only had to get to someplace where there were people. If I could get to Hope Bay, I'd be safe. Squirrel Cove might be closer, but I didn't want to risk crossing the open water in this little skiff. Better to hug the beach and make a beeline for Hope Bay. Later I'd find my way to Lund. *Oh Monique, it's going to be so good to see you. I can hardly wait.* Tears filled my eyes. I would be out of this nightmare at last. My chin quivered and I gulped back the tears of relief at having left Robert behind.

I glanced back to the point of land that marked our bay. "Oh NO!" I screamed into the wind. The Hawkeye! Black smoke poured out of its smokestack. Robert had it roaring at full throttle, like the maniac he was.

Still, I knew I could easily outrun him in the skiff. I opened it up and bounced along the choppy waves. My kidneys took a beating with every jolt. *Away! Away! Away from that crazy madman.*

I could see the entrance to Hope Bay ahead of me. Not far beyond that was freedom and safety. I was putting good distance between myself and the Hawkeye. Suddenly the skiff jerked and lurched and began to slow down. The motor sputtered. No. No. No.

I picked up the gas tank. It was disappointingly light. *Oh no! No, no it can't be!* I turned it on its side and tried to drain the last drops into the fuel line. The motor coughed and the boat lurched forward again. Just another half a mile and I could be safe. But it was not to be. The outboard gave one last sputter and died. Silence.... The waves lapped sadly against the sides of the skiff. I turned and saw the Hawkeye relentlessly belching out smoke, in dogged pursuit.

With trembling hands, I rammed the oars into the oarlocks and clambered into the middle seat to start rowing. Now, facing the back of the boat I watched in terror as the Hawkeye gained on me. I rowed furiously and fought the waves, but made no headway. I realized then that the tide was carrying me back two feet for every one I rowed forward. I thought of going ashore with the skiff, if the tide would allow it. The Hawkeye couldn't follow me there. But steep cliffs lined the shore all along. Not a hope of beaching the skiff. Still, I kept rowing. I couldn't give up now. I knew what awaited me.

I could see his face in the wheelhouse. His jaw was set in determination. When he pulled alongside he grinned.

"Hello, Andrea," he said pleasantly. "What brings you out here on a day like this? A bit chilly for a joyride, isn't it?"

I pulled on the oars desperately and as he reached down to grab the one closest to the boat I took it out of the oarlock and swung it at him, clipping him on the shoulder. He jumped back. I tried to row away from the Hawkeye but with one oar out of the oarlock I flailed uselessly.

Robert reached for the oar again, and again I swung it at him, but this time he caught it easily and kept a firm hold on it. I let it go and tried to row with my remaining oar, but I knew it was over. He held the skiff pinned down with the oar, reached down, and fished out the bow line. Then he let the skiff drift back and tied its line to the davit at the back of Hawkeye. He disappeared into the wheelhouse and gave the Hawkeye a burst of fuel, turning the boat back towards our isolated cabin in the bay. I sobbed and shivered in the skiff.

I thought about pulling the skiff closer to the Hawkeye, to come alongside and untie it, but with the skiff under tow, the strain on the rope was too much. *I'm such an idiot. I don't have to untie it where it's tied to the Hawkeye.*

I can untie it at the bow of the skiff. The knot was tight though, and I didn't have my knife. Still, I leaned forward and pulled hard on the tow line to gain a bit of slack. With my weight leaning so far forward in the skiff, each choppy wave sent a shower of freezing water over my shoulders. Holding the line in one hand, I worried the knot back and forth with the other hand until at last the skiff came untied. The Hawkeye kept going without me. I picked up the one oar I had left and paddled canoe style towards shore. It was much farther away now, but I had to try.

The tidal flow was strong and my efforts to fight it with one oar were futile. Exhausted and shivering with cold, I put the oar into the boat and dropped my head into my hands. Totally defeated, I cried out with great tearing sobs. By the time Robert caught up to me again, I was reduced to a compliant zombie. He pulled me up from the skiff like a rag doll. I barely felt his fist connect with my cheek before I fell onto the bunk.

Chapter 49

Somewhere far away in the thick fog of my mind, I heard soft crying, sniffling; the short, quick intakes of breath that come between spasms of suppressed sobs. I tried to open my eyes, but only one of them allowed any light to enter through nearly closed lids. Through that tiny window into my conscious world, I puzzled out my surroundings and recognized the bedroom walls of the cabin.

I lay still, trembling with cold, unable to think clearly. My last memory was of Robert lifting me easily from the skiff onto the Hawkeye. After that, blackness. A dull pain shrouded my body. Yet the crying sounds were not from me. Gradually, I became aware of Robert's body next to mine. He was naked and huddled close to me. I was thankful for his warmth.

His hand gently caressed my head and smoothed a tress of hair down my cheek and neck. He followed the contour of my body with his hand, touching my collar bone and shoulder. He nestled the side of his face under my chin.

"I'm so sorry," he whispered. "I didn't want to hurt you." Softly, he rubbed my shoulder. "You still feel so cold. Please don't die." He climbed over me to the other side. "You've just got to warm up." He pulled me close to his body, covering my cold legs with his warm ones. There was nothing sexual in his actions; only tender touching, as if he were trying to be my human blanket.

"I love you so much," he said, very quietly. "Why am I always hurting you?" The soft sobbing began again. "Oh God, what's wrong with me?" His voice was barely a whisper now. "No wonder you tried to run away."

I was too exhausted and defeated to try to respond, and something in the back of my clouded mind told me it was best to lie still right now. I closed the small slit of eye that I'd been able to open, and lay still, listening, shivering with the pain of being too cold.

Robert kept his body pressed close to mine, all the while talking to me as if he were talking to himself. "Andrea, I promise you, I'll be good to you from now on. Just please don't die."

I could feel his tears running down my jaw and throat to my collar bone. No matter how I might have hated him before, all I could think was how cold I was and how I craved the warmth that seeped from his body into mine. My steady shivering and trembling slowed and became intermittent shudders until at last, they quieted completely.

When I stopped shivering, and lay still, Robert raised his head and cried out, "Oh no." He felt for my heart. Then I heard him exhale and drop his head on my shoulder. "Oh thank God. You didn't die."

It was about that time I thought, *I wish I was dead.*

He fell asleep and I carefully eased my free arm out from under the quilt. I felt my face and understood then why I couldn't see well. My eyes were swollen. It hurt to touch my nose and lips. My fingers came away with dry crumbles. I brought them up to my face for a closer look and saw that it was blood. Tears began to leak out of my puffy eyes. I felt sorry for myself, but after listening to Robert I also felt sorry for him.

What I'd heard when he thought I was asleep was genuine remorse. He wasn't saying those things to gain my favour. He was well aware that he was carrying around a demon in his head—a demon he had no control over. He was to be pitied.

I must have drifted back to sleep. I woke when Robert lifted his head to look at me. I felt his hand smoothing my forehead.

"Andrea? Are you awake?"

"Mmm-hmm," I mumbled through thick lips. Inside I trembled a little, not from cold anymore, but fear, wondering what frame of mind he was in.

"What can I do for you?"

"Water," I whispered.

He got up and tucked the quilt all around me. For the next two days he tended to my every need, even helping me find my way to and from the outhouse.

On the third day I was ready to stay up. Every muscle in my body ached and I barely had the strength to get dressed. When I saw my face in the mirror I started to cry.

Robert was right there. "It'll get better. You'll be as pretty as you ever were. And don't worry. This will never happen again." He really seemed to believe what he was saying and his remorse sounded so sincere he almost had me believing it too. But my shoulders sagged, knowing it was only a matter of time. For now, I had to find the strength to keep Robert calm and avoid more trouble.

I pressed my bruised lips together and nodded.

Chapter 50

Robert took the Hawkeye to Powell River in May. He'd been careful to control his anger after beating me so badly in February—never laid a hand on me—but he still wouldn't take me to town.

"I'm really sorry," he said. "I know you want to go to town, but I can't risk you taking off on me again. I couldn't bear to lose you." He hung his head.

I raised my hands and dropped them again helplessly. "How long is this supposed to go on then?" I was almost in tears. "I feel like a prisoner." *If my parents could see me now. What would they think? Someday I'll get out of here, but until then I have to keep Robert from getting mad again.*

"I thought you loved me. If you did, you wouldn't argue. You'd do as I say. Can't you stay with me because you want to?" He sounded desperate.

"But I do love you, Robert. I care about you a lot. But I'm afraid of you when you lose it."

"I haven't lost it since ... you know ... since you took off."

"No. That's true. But you've come awfully close, and I'm afraid it's going to happen one day."

"If you'd do what I ask, we wouldn't have any problems. There'd be nothing to make me mad."

"I try, Robert. I really do. And I'll try harder, but I still worry that it won't be enough to keep the peace." *Nothing will ever be enough.*

"Well, there's nothing I can do or say then. If you're so convinced something is going to happen ... nobody can know something like that for sure." He shrugged his shoulders and shook his head in frustration.

But I do. I know for sure. As sure as the sun will rise tomorrow, you'll flip out again. And I'll pay. "What if I promised you I wouldn't try to take off? Couldn't I come along? Please?" I hated to beg, but I needed to get out of here so badly.

"If I didn't care about you, I'd say okay, but I can't lose you. I just can't." He looked totally frustrated and I could see it was no use. I slumped into a chair. I'd never convince him to let me come to town.

"I'll be back as soon as I can. Give me your list and I'll do my best to get everything on it. And I won't forget your birth control pills."

"Thanks," I muttered darkly.

"And Andrea? When I come back we'll get the house ready to lock up and the boat ready to go, and you'll come fishing with me."

"Sure, okay. Whatever you say." I could feel the walls closing in. Stuck on the boat would be even worse than being stuck out here. At least here I could leave the cabin and walk a bit. But on the fishboat ... tight quarters with nowhere to go. I was sure to get on his nerves in a hurry.

He left. I brooded. Being on the boat with him day after day would be hell. But then a little light came on in my brain. We would have to stop at places on the way north to fuel up and get groceries. I'd see people! And then once we reached the Charlottes, after each trip, we'd have to come into town, probably to Masset, to unload the fish. Every five days was the rule. This was starting to sound better all the time. Wait a minute! Jim and Robert fish together. Yes! I grinned and punched the air. Maybe this fishing wouldn't be so bad after all.

PART THREE

The Rose

O Rose, thou art sick!
The invisible worm,
That flies in the night,
In the howling storm,
Has found out thy bed
Of crimson joy;
And his dark secret love
Does thy life destroy.

~ William Blake

Chapter 51

Making preparations for the commercial fishing season was like getting ready to go on an extended camping trip. We loaded three months' worth of basic supplies. Groceries, water, and fuel could be replenished in Prince Rupert or in Masset on the Queen Charlotte Islands, but we brought what we could from home to keep expenses down.

I gave the Hawkeye a thorough cleaning from ceiling and walls to cupboards and floors. Dishes and cutlery were inventoried and topped up from the cabin's lot. Cleaning supplies, toiletries, first aid and sewing kits, bedding, towels, and linens; everything had to be checked and missing articles scrounged up.

Rice, pasta, beans, canned food, spices, tea, and coffee—the lists went on and on. We would be away a long time and these foods would provide some comfort. I would be cooking on the boat and so wouldn't have to work as hard to make a fire or fetch water. In a way it was exciting to be embarking on a different kind of adventure. At least it would be a change from the cabin and if there was a chance to see Jim—Oh, my God! Jim! To see him again. There was hope yet!

When the Hawkeye was loaded, we battened down the little cabin. I felt no regrets at seeing it closed up. All perishables were removed, valuables hidden or brought onto the boat. Certainly, no valuables like jewelry or money were left behind, but appliances that made life easier, such as the meat grinder and my sewing machine, were valuable to me. I put those under the counter, out of sight and, hopefully, out of mind of anyone who might break in.

Robert didn't want all his rifles and shotguns on the boat. "I can't leave them in the cabin. Someone could come along while we're gone and steal them."

I thought of my fanny pack loaded with carefully selected survival items. No way I was giving that up. While Robert dealt with his rifles, I brought the fanny pack out to the boat and stashed it in a cubbyhole at the foot of the fo'c'sle bunk.

Robert boarded up the windows and door. With any luck, the cabin would remain untouched while we were away. I didn't dare get my hopes too high that I might escape before I had to return here. The disappointment of another failure would be devastating.

We slept on the boat that night and, at first light the next morning, pulled away from the cabin's dock and turned the boat north. Robert sat in the captain's seat. For a while, I stood next to him looking at the big compass in the middle of the dash.

"What did you do with your guns?" I wondered if he had a secret hiding place for them.

"Buried them."

"Won't they rust?"

"I wrapped them in cloth and then in garbage bags and buried them in three different places in the yard. If anyone accidentally finds one, at least I'll still have the others."

"That's good thinking." Not that there was much chance of anyone coming along to dig in that yard, but I didn't mind knowing where they were in case I ever needed them.

"Where's the revolver?"

Damn! Damn! Damn! I'd hoped he'd forgotten about it. "It's in my fanny pack, down below." No point in lying about it.

"Okay. That's fine. Just keep it out of sight. We're not supposed to be taking it from home without a permit."

"But this is home. For three months." Three long months!

"Yes. That's right." He reached to put an arm around me and before I could stop the reflex, I flinched as he raised his hand. He was concentrating on the water and hadn't noticed. Whew!

"Jim's going to meet us tonight at Sointula."

Butterflies tickled my insides. He had my full attention. "How do you know that? When did you talk to Jim?"

"I called him on the sideband. It has a long range."

"But you must have arranged this days ago. Right?" How had I missed all this?

"Yeah. Didn't I tell you I saw him at Lund when I did the haulout?"

"No. You didn't tell me much of anything about your trip."

Robert made a face and shrugged. Easy for him to be nonchalant about a trip to town. For me it would have meant a lot to hear about it, especially since I couldn't be there.

"Well, what did he say? What's he been doing? How is he?" I stopped. Too late. Robert's face clouded with suspicion.

"What do you care what he's up to?" The conversation stopped abruptly. After a long pause, Robert added, "And anyway, he's been spending most of his time at the gift shop. With Sarah." He watched my face carefully as he spoke.

I forced a smile. "That's great. I know Sarah really likes him." My chest felt too tight and I thought I would faint. *I'm lost now. Lost forever.*

Chapter 52

When we pulled into Sointula's harbour, the Serenity was already there. Robert brought the Hawkeye around so we could tie next to her. I thought I would melt when I saw Jim standing on deck. Kindness and thoughtful caring were written all over his face. Robert was drop dead gorgeous, but it was Jim who looked beautiful to me. My pulse raced and I couldn't look at Robert lest my face betray every emotion I was feeling about Jim.

"Tie our midship line to the Serenity's pole," Robert called out.

"Okay!" I gladly stepped over the sill of the wheelhouse door and out onto the deck where Robert couldn't see me. I unwrapped the line and Jim reached for it as the boat closed the gap between us. His hand lingered on mine. Such a gentle touch. I had to fight the urge to grasp it tightly. His hand was a lifeline I dared not cling to. Not yet.

"Hello, Andrea," he said very softly. "How are you doing? Okay?"

I swallowed hard. I knew Robert might be watching my every move. I could only nod and fight back the tears. "Yup," I whispered, and turned my head.

Jim looked up as Robert came out of the wheelhouse. "Well, you made it. Let's get you tied up and then why don't you come over and have a beer."

"Sounds good. Andrea can make us some sandwiches. Eh, Andrea?" Robert looked to me for agreement. He flicked his head to signal me to go into the wheelhouse.

"Sure." I hurried inside.

But Jim said, "Wait a minute. I've got some stew on the stove. Just bring the bread."

Robert shrugged. "Great." He called to me, "Bring over one of those fine loaves of bread you've been baking."

God! Mr. Big Shot! I hated his bragging.

We sat on the Serenity's deck with a beer and it almost felt like days gone by when Jim and I had sat on this same hatch cover waiting for Robert to come back from Powell River. Was that only a year ago? Oh, if only I could go back and do it over. Differently. If only I had listened to Jim.

"How do you like living in the cabin way up there, Andrea?" Jim asked.

"Oh, she's getting used to it fine," Robert said. "Aren't you, dear?"

I nodded and hid behind another sip of beer.

"Not worried about the bears?"

"No, she's getting to be pretty tough."

Yeah, I was getting tough all right, but it wasn't from fighting off bears.

Once or twice, Jim caught my eye when Robert wasn't looking and I knew that he knew how things stood. I shrugged, a mere twitch of my shoulder that Robert didn't catch. I could feel tears forming at the corners of my eyes and my throat tightened. Jim nodded so slowly it was imperceptible unless you were looking for it. There was no need for more. We had communicated all that was necessary.

"Well, I'll dish us up some of that stew. Andrea, would you like to give me a hand and slice the bread? Robert you just relax on the deck. You've had a long run. Here."

He handed Robert a can. "Have another beer." I went into the wheelhouse and started cutting the bread. When Jim walked past me to get the bowls from the cupboard, he brushed close by me and quickly squeezed my shoulder. "Hang in there," he whispered.

"I can't go back there," I said under my breath. I was terrified that Robert would see us. All he had to do was move his head a bit and he could look right into the wheelhouse. "Can you help me?"

"Yessiree!" Jim said loudly, nodding at me. "A doozer of a stew we have here."

I wanted to explore the town of Sointula. Robert was too tired. The short walk over to the showers at the marina was all he would agree to, and there was no question of me going alone. Robert watched every move I made, paranoid I might make a run for it. And I would, too, first chance I got.

It wouldn't be here in Sointula though. A small town on a small island meant small chance for me. I wouldn't risk another failure. Sometime the opportunity would come, and I'd be gone. For now I had to watch and be careful, try to look and act normal.

With towels and toiletries in our backpacks, we walked to the marina. The quaint homes and the laid back atmosphere of the community charmed me.

"Aren't these houses clean and tidy? And look at the gardens people have here."

"It was settled by Finns and many of their descendants still live here." He sounded like a tour guide.

"This would be a great place to go for a bike ride. Hardly any traffic. Country style roads, but paved."

"Well, enjoy it because there aren't many places like this."

"It's not typical? What are other towns like?" I hadn't seen much of B.C. yet and had no idea. If I could get him talking about the different places maybe I could get an idea which ones were best for making a run for it.

"Rougher." One corner of his upper lip fletched in disdain. "We'll see them soon enough. Better get to bed right after our shower. We're leaving at first light for Port Hardy and then across to the mainland side."

Like most trollers, the Hawkeye had single bunks meant for the skipper and deckhands. Since we needed our rest, I was thankful to have my own space in the fo'c'sle bunk.

We ran all the next day, taking turns at the wheel while the other napped. At last we pulled into Safety Cove and dropped the hook. Serenity anchored nearby. Although we were separate floating islands in our boats, I felt safer because of Jim's proximity. Robert wouldn't risk making a big scene or beating on me with any witnesses nearby.

And so it went, day after day, from one scenic anchorage to the next. This part of the B.C. coast was almost without human habitation except for a few small Indian villages along the way.

Robert pointed out the old fish cannery at Butedale. "The whole thing is gradually falling into the water. All the dock and pilings."

History in decay. "Can we go have a look at it?" It looked like it was quite the going concern in its day.

"Not safe. A few years ago some guy tied his sailboat to the dock and climbed up the stairs to the landing. One of the boards gave way and he fell back to the dock and broke his neck."

"Good Lord! That must have been horrible. And way out here so far from anywhere."

"They would have radioed for a chopper."

"Yeah, but still...." I shuddered. It would be best to be careful out here. Help was far away. And who knew that better than me?

The long corridor of sheltered water known as the Inside Passage, or Grenville Channel, was breathtakingly beautiful. If I were a painter I would only need cool colours to depict it. Shades of blue, green, and gray. Dabs of white for the mountain tops. Grenville Channel was like a wide river so deep the sounder didn't even register in places. Mountains on either side rose steeply out of the water. I imagined myself with X-ray vision looking into the depths but not seeing the bottom. I felt very tiny in this massive landscape.

On a log floating near shore a Bonaparte's gull rested for a moment. When it flew, one of its wings drooped. Its flight was short. Again and again it flew a short distance with its hurt wing. I empathized. I knew just how that injured seabird felt.

Robert pointed. "Up ahead! See that thing that looks like a deadhead?"

"Yeah." I took the binoculars he handed me. "It's got eyes! And ... oh, my Lord, it looks like a walrus without tusks. But look at that long floppy nose!" I handed the glasses back to Robert.

"He's gone. That was an elephant seal. You hardly ever see them. They often feed at depths of more than a thousand feet." Robert was like a walking library. He seemed to know a bit of everything. "Gives you an idea how deep the water must be here. Amazing, eh?"

"No kidding. And yet we're so close to land. Not that we could go ashore." That got me thinking. "So what do we do when it's time to anchor up? We can't toss out the anchor in a thousand feet of water."

"There are a couple of places along here where a river comes out and we can duck into its estuary."

That night, anchored in Lowe Inlet, I marveled at the perfection of nature. A waterfall at the river mouth rushed and splashed. Everything else in the inlet was calm; a glassy pond protected from the wind. Serenity. And there she was, the Serenity, anchored nearby.

Chapter 53

Robert opened his notebook and started a list. "When we get to Rupert, we'll get more fuel and then give the boat a good cleaning."

"Looks pretty good to me now. What did you have in mind?"

"We'll get the seaweed washed off the anchor, and wash the mud off the deck under it. Hose everything down so it looks fresh."

"I can do that." Our stop would give me a chance to talk to Jim and it would be easier if Robert was in a good mood.

"Then tonight we can relax a bit and take it easy. We'll stay in Rupert for a couple of days and wait for this wind to go down before crossing Hecate Strait over to the Charlottes."

"Are we going to get groceries before we cross?" I was craving an orange or a salad. "Fresh fruit and vegetables?"

"Yup. That's why I got this list going. If there's anything you think we need from Safeway, jot it down. Tomorrow is shopping day."

I could hardly contain my excitement. Going to town! Any town! Rows and rows of things on the shelves. People everywhere. People to talk to. So what if it was the cashier or the kid who stocked the shelves, or another shopper?

There would be people to talk to and they would talk back to me. I thought I would throw up from all the excitement. Like a kid who had too much cake at her own birthday party. How pathetic was I to have come to this?

The next morning, Robert arranged with Jim to share a ride to Safeway. I was buzzing with excitement when the taxi arrived. The three of us sat in the back. The cab smelled like it had chauffeured many a drunk home from the bar. Even the whiff of vomit couldn't ruin this adventure for me. I hadn't been in a car since ... I couldn't remember when. I left the seating arrangements to Robert, and I could see he would have liked to sit between Jim and me, but etiquette demanded that the woman sit in the middle. Robert clamped a hand on my right thigh. But it was my left thigh that was on fire and I made no move to ease the pressure from Jim's leg.

In Safeway, we pushed our shopping carts towards the produce section. Robert chose a cabbage and placed it in the cart.

"You know, Robert, I've done grocery shopping before. If you have things to get at the hardware store, I can do this. Just make sure to get back in time to pay for the groceries."

He looked around uncertainly. "I suppose I could do that." Then he reached for his wallet. "Here. If I'm not back when you finish shopping, here's some money for the groceries. Just wait out front for me and we'll get a taxi back. I should be back before you're done though."

"Okay." I stuffed the money into my jeans pocket. It had been over a year since I'd needed a purse. "I'll be right here when you get back."

"You'd better be," he growled. But then he chucked me under the chin and gave me a quick kiss before leaving. Apparently, his emotions were as conflicted as mine, but with a different game plan. While he showed increasing desperation to control me and make me love him, I tried not to show my increasing desperation to escape. I had to lull him into letting his guard down, and watch for my opportunity.

Robert wasn't out the door for a second when Jim wheeled his cart over beside mine. "So talk fast," he said. "What's been going on?"

"You were right. I should have listened to you. But it's been way worse than I imagined. Way worse!" I forced back the tears. I couldn't cry here in the store. And what if Robert came back suddenly? I looked over my shoulder for him. He had a habit of popping up unexpectedly; he was so paranoid. And I was beginning to get the same way. I took a deep breath to calm myself. "He hits."

Jim's hand went out to my arm automatically. "Oh, Andrea. No! I'm so sorry."

"I made a run for it with the skiff back in February." I grimaced, embarrassed. "I ran out of gas. He followed me in the troller and finally caught up to me. He nearly killed me."

"That bastard!" Jim said under his breath through clenched teeth.

"I think it scared him when he realized how badly he'd hurt me, and he's been pretty much hands off since then, but I can see it building again, just under the surface. I've got to get away."

"Andrea, you know I've loved you all this time, don't you?"

"You have?" I blinked back the tears. "Oh, Jim. I wished it and dreamed it. But I.... No—"

"What's wrong?"

"Robert told me that when he was in Lund a couple of weeks ago, he saw you there."

"Yeah? And?"

"Well, he said you and Sarah were an item."

"What?!" Jim's voice rose. Then he caught himself and said more quietly, "That's complete bullshit. I saw Sarah a few times a couple of years ago and there's nothing there. He's saying that to make sure you're not interested in me. Just to hurt you."

I breathed a sigh of relief. "Oh, thank God for that."

"Listen. You and I are going to be together. But he's a loose cannon and we have to plan this out carefully. We both need this fishing season, so if I stay around nearby, do you think you can manage to fish with him till the season is nearly over. I mean assuming he doesn't beat on you again. If he does, you just get on the radio and scream it to the world and I'll be right over."

"Yes, I can hang in there a while longer. I can do it if I know there's hope at the end." A lump of emotion knotted my throat. I would be saved. I blinked hard as tears began to well, and smiled.

"We'll be in Masset often to unload our fish. One of those times near the end of the season, you can literally jump ship and come home with me. If you want, that is."

"If I want? If I want? I've never wanted anything more in my life."

"Meanwhile, just remember I love you, okay." His clear blue eyes looked straight into mine and I knew he meant what he said.

"I love you too," I whispered.

A chubby woman bumped into my cart. "You two hot peppers mind moving away from the turnips so a person can get their shopping done?"

Jim turned his cart and headed for the other side of the store. I threw vegetables and fruit into my cart double time. Robert could be back any minute and would wonder why there was nothing in my cart. The cart may have been empty but my heart was full of joy and hope.

Chapter 54

The stiff breeze that had been blowing since we arrived in Prince Rupert eased up at last and we decided to go as far as Qlawdzeet, a sheltered anchorage tucked in at the end of Stephen's Island. The locals referred to it as Squatteree. It was the last point before the eleven-hour crossing—for Hawkeye—of open water to Masset, in the Queen Charlotte Islands. We wanted to be sure of the weather and this was a safe place to wait.

"It's not a big deal crossing to the Charlottes," Robert said, "but it never hurts to have someone nearby in case you run into trouble. That's why Jim and I fish together."

"I think it's smart. You can watch out for each other." And Jim will watch out for me.

On arriving at Squatteree, we did a bit of jigging near the rocks. The clarity of the water allowed a rare view into the undersea world. Possibly the visibility was enhanced by the rocks. Smoothed from eons of washing by the waves, they were a pale gray-green and reflected the sunlight down into the depths. While Robert jogged with the Hawkeye, keeping us off the rocks and standing relatively still, I dropped a line with a jigger over the side. It was a heavy chromed weight and hook with a red plastic lure on the end. As it dropped, I unwound the 200-pound-test fishing line from around a small board, like unwinding a kite string. When the jigger hit the bottom and the line went slack, I rewound it a few feet so it wouldn't get snagged. Following Robert's instructions, I yanked the line up and let it sink again, repeating the action every few seconds. Moments later I felt a strong tug on the line.

"Keep tension on it and wind it in," Robert called. "Don't give it any slack."

I wrapped the line around the piece of board, but Robert yelled at me not to bother with the board. While I stopped winding to look at him, I felt the line go slack and the fish was gone.

"Aw!" I dropped my arms limply by my side.

"D'you lose it?" he shouted. I nodded. "Jeezus! You stupid cow. I told you not to give it any slack. Can't you fuckin' do anything right?"

My eyes went wide with surprise. Robert had been so controlled until now. "What's it to you?" I asked. "It's my fish and if I lost it, I'm the one who should feel bad. What are you all upset for?" And now I'm a stupid cow and we're into name-calling. Oh God! What next? How will I get through two more months of this?

He pointed at the water, still furious. "Throw that jigger back in there and get that fish back." I knew how sound carries across water. Jim must be hearing every word. And thinking how stupid I am for putting up with it. Every time Robert yelled at me, I hated him more. I hated myself more too, for putting up with it, but what choice did I have?

I tossed the jigger into the water, but it tangled and I had to pull it back in. I was sitting on the hatch cover, untangling the knot with trembling hands when Robert came up behind me and slapped the side of my head— hard. I fussed with the knot faster and by some miracle it came undone. I tossed the jigger into the water and stood up to let it sink.

Robert had to run into the wheelhouse to keep us off the rocks. I glanced over my shoulder to look at the Serenity, anchored a few hundred yards away, and saw Jim standing on deck shaking his head. I knew he'd heard every word and seen it all. I lowered my head quickly and brushed at the tears of shame that crept into my eyes.

I yanked the line up and down as I had done before. It wasn't long before I caught another fish, or perhaps the same one. This time I brought the line in hand over hand allowing no slack. As the struggling fish came nearer to the surface, Robert stood nearby with the gaff. He reached down to take the line in his left hand, gaffing the fish with the other.

"Wow!" I tried to pretend I was excited about my catch. "What is it?" The fish was huge and orangey red. "It's not a salmon, but what is it? Is it any good to eat?"

"You bet it is. It's a red snapper. The best." The pride in his voice told me I had, at last, done something right. Well, thank God for that.

We crossed the small sheltered area and anchored near the Serenity. Once Robert had set the hook and shut down the engine, he called across to Jim, "Come join us for supper. Andrea caught a huge red snapper."

"Sounds great," he called back. "I'll bring some scalloped potatoes."

Robert rummaged in the cutlery drawer for the filleting knife. "I'll clean the fish and you get it into the oven right away. You don't mind, right?"

As if I had a choice to mind. "Sure. I don't care. Plenty of fish for us all." I don't care. Not much. If there was anything I cared more about than having Jim's company, I didn't know what it was. But I had to work hard to play the game right. I had to fool Robert into thinking all was well. What was a little slap upside the head? I had to keep things together or my plan to escape with Jim later in the summer would fail.

An hour later, Jim rowed his skiff over and tied to the back of Hawkeye. He handed up the potato dish and then climbed aboard. I took the casserole into the wheelhouse while Robert and Jim talked fishing on the deck. I was so happy to have Jim near. I stayed out of sight at first, lest my roller-coasting emotions give me away. I tried to calm myself. Forget about the slap and the embarrassment of that scene. Put aside the love I feel for Jim. If I don't look him in the eyes I'll be okay. Otherwise, Robert might notice the sparks. I dished up three plates of food and took them out onto the deck. The baked snapper made a delicious dinner with the scalloped potatoes and salad. Afterwards I busied myself cleaning up the wheelhouse.

I heard them talking about all sorts of things. When their conversation turned to life in the remote cabin, I held my breath.

"Must be a pretty lonely life out there by yourself," I heard Jim say.

Robert forced a laugh. "Oh, I don't mind it. Keeps me out of trouble."

"How about Andrea? Doesn't she miss seeing people?"

"Oh, sure, but she'll get used to it. Anyway we've got each other for company."

"I guess." Jim sounded doubtful.

"Works out pretty well. Long as she does what she's told. She knows better now, but at first there were times.... Well, anyway, you know how women can be. Even now, sometimes when she won't agree with me, it pisses me off. Once in a while I have to deck her one just to keep her in line."

"You don't!"

"If she doesn't do as she's told. Honour and obey, right?"

"It's not right to hit a woman." Jim's quiet voice seemed to keep Robert calm.

"Oh sure, but that's the quickest way to have them do what you want."

"I think a lot of that talk about 'decking' a woman is just that—talk."

"Not for me. I want results, and if a little smack now and then will get them, why not?"

"It's not right. I wouldn't do that to another person, especially a woman."

"That may be okay for you, but it's not how I operate. I'm no namby-pamby. I like to be in control. No woman's gonna henpeck me."

"Well, let's hope it works out well, you two fishing together." Jim stood up to leave and stuck his head through the wheelhouse doorway. "Thanks for a great meal, Andrea. I'd better get going. We're getting an early start in the morning."

I thanked him and handed him his casserole dish. He rolled his eyes at me and shook his head slightly, and left. I knew he'd done his best to give Robert a message. I doubted it would do much good.

Chapter 55

The weather outlook was promising for crossing to the Charlottes and we were making good time. I could already see the trees on the north end of Graham Island.

"Why didn't you go straight across to the top corner of the island?" We had angled quite far north of it. "Couldn't we have saved some time?"

Robert tapped his finger on the map. "Rose Spit. Here's the spit on the northeast corner. It looks like you can go straight along, but if you check out the depths you'll see the sandbar goes a long way out. We had to give that a wide berth."

"Anybody ever run aground there?"

"Oh shit, yeah! Lots of boats. Even if they know to go around, boats have been caught in the weather and got too close."

"What happens to them? It's so far from anywhere."

"Usually another fishboat comes along to help out, or sometimes the Coast Guard. If the boat's salvageable they'll tow it to Rupert; if it's a goner they try to pick up the crew. The sand soon swallows up the boat."

"Serious?"

"About what?"

"The sand. Swallowing the boat."

"Sure. I saw a guy once—years ago—drove his truck on the beach along the top end there. See that long beautiful empty beach?"

I took the binoculars and scanned the north shore of Graham Island. I marveled at the pristine lonely sandy beach. "Paradise—if it was warmer."

"Well, this guy drove on the beach—hard-packed sand, and he had four-wheel drive—to get to where the good digging was for razor clams. But he got stuck. By the time he got a tow truck there, his cab doors were sunk into the sand. No way the tow truck could get near enough to pull him out. And anyway, it was sinking into the sand by the minute—you know, from the wave action around the tires. A couple of weeks later you could hardly see the top of the cab anymore."

"Very expensive lesson."

Robert laughed. "Not really. He came out of the whole thing with a new truck. Insurance paid for everything."

"Oh, that's good. I bet everyone was more careful after hearing that story."

"Are you kidding? There was a rash of trucks stuck and sinking in the sand. Guys wanted a new truck and drove their old one on the beach."

"That doesn't seem right. Isn't that illegal?"

"Sure it is. But prove it wasn't an accident." Robert chuckled as if he approved. "Course it wasn't long before the insurance stopped covering beach mishaps."

"You sure know a lot about what goes on around here. Guess you've spent a lot of time up this way, huh?" Stroke the ego. Keep him calm. And, the more I can keep him talking, the more I'll find out. Maybe it will come in handy someday.

A few hours later, as we approached the entrance to Masset Inlet, Robert pointed out a small settlement.

"That's the old town of Masset, the original native settlement of the Haidas. They call it Haida. Farther into the inlet is the newer town of Masset. That's where we're going to fuel up between trips, sell our fish, get groceries, do laundry, all that town stuff."

Oh, to be on land again, and do "land" things. "We have a couple of days before it opens for spring salmon so we can stay in town for a while, right?"

"Not really. We'll grub up and then we need to get out to the west coast of the Charlottes and be on the spot when it opens."

"How far is that?"

"Another five hours across the top end and then a couple of hours south."

"Long way." I groaned inwardly. I was so tired of the boat already and we hadn't even started fishing. "Well, at least we can stretch our legs a bit in Masset and explore the town." And I could find out how to get out of Masset. Although, being on an island, most likely by boat or by plane would be the only options, and I had no money for a plane ride.

"I can guarantee you won't be wanting to do much exploring."

"Why not?"

"You'll soon see."

Chapter 56

Robert was right about one thing. It didn't take long to finish exploring Masset. Besides fish plants, there were the Co-op, the hardware store, the liquor store, and the local pub.

Later that first evening in Masset, we went for a walk and peeked into the beer hall, a concrete block structure with cafeteria-style chairs and tables.

"Sure is shabby, isn't it?"

"No place for a woman." For once I had to agree with Robert. I couldn't imagine being a female alone inside or walking home alone from a place like that.

A drunk came towards us. I hadn't even seen him lurking in the dark.

"Hey pard," he slurred. "You got a loonie for a beer, eh?" The sound of wretching, swearing, and bottles breaking came from somewhere farther along the dark outer walls of the beer hall.

Robert growled at him, "Piss off, asshole." He pulled me closer and walked a bit faster. "So much for stretching our legs. Seen enough?"

I shuddered and it wasn't from the cold drizzle we'd been exposed to since arriving. "Remind me not to take any late night strolls up this way—not that I have any intention of doing that." I stayed close to Robert and felt safe enough. His big frame came in handy at times like this.

The next day I walked up to the Co-op. Robert had given me a list and money.

"Take a taxi back with the groceries," he said. "I have to do an oil change while you're gone."

In the daytime Masset was quiet, gray, and dreary—far from intimidating. Dandelions thrived in the cracks of the sidewalk in front of the town's small high school. Empty chips bags and cigarette packages lifted by a gust of wind resettled in new resting places farther along the gutter. I crossed the street, stepping aside to avoid a shard of broken beer bottle.

At first glance it seemed like a forgotten derelict town, but beyond many of the picket fences, I could see that the locals took meticulous care of their yards. Rhodos flourished and grew as large as trees. Flowerbeds and window boxes decorated modest but well kept-up homes. People waved and called friendly greetings as I passed by.

On the cement steps in front of the Co-op, a scruffy, unshaven old man sat playing with two ball bearings on a string, watching in fascination as they clinked together over and over. He stopped their action, leaned forward and put his head between his knees. With a filthy gnarled finger pressing one nostril closed, he blew through the other. He pinched off the snot with his thumb and forefinger and flung it onto the sidewalk. Thank God, I had already given him plenty of space. I hurried into the store. Behind me, the old man took out his ball bearings and resumed his hypnotic pursuit.

I pushed my cart along the produce section. Tired vegetables lay in the bins labeled with outrageously high prices. A native woman must have noticed my look of dismay.

"You're a day early. The new freight comes in tomorrow. There'll be lots of good stuff comin' in. Gotta shop on the freight days. Day before freight day's always bad."

"Oh. Thanks for telling me. That's good to know." So there was hope for getting better groceries next time. But for now, I was glad we had picked up most of our groceries in Prince Rupert and only needed a few things to top up our supplies. Robert wanted pancake mix. While I checked the list for anything else I might need, I turned into the cereals aisle and crashed into another cart.

"Oh, I'm sorry. I wasn't wa—Jim!"

"Well, well. I was hoping I'd run into you. Not like this, but—"

"I'm so glad to see you." I looked all around and over my shoulder.

"Jeez, Andrea, you look like a hunted animal. Relax. It'll be all right."

I wasn't so sure about that. "It's going to be such a long summer." The weeks ahead loomed like a dark cloud. Weeks of trying to manage Robert's mood swings.

"I know. I know. I've racked my brain for a way to get you away from him sooner," he said in a hushed tone, "but if I can get a few trips in first, we'd have more to live on this winter."

"And anyway," I pointed out, "it's impossible for me to go with you now and keep fishing. Robert would ram your boat or shoot us."

"Naw, he wouldn't do that. He's a bit strange, but he wouldn't do that."

I shuddered remembering how he threw a chair across the room last time he had a tantrum in the cabin. "Oh, yes! He would! You don't know what he's capable of. The things I've seen him do. He has a terrible temper."

Jim gritted his teeth. "So I saw—and heard—at Squatteree. Has he touched you since then?"

"No. I'm trying really hard to be nice to him just so he doesn't hurt me. It seems to be working. He even let me come get groceries by myself." I feel like I'm walking a tightrope.

Jim shook his head sadly. "If you could hear yourself. 'He lets you get groceries by yourself.'"

"You don't understand. Since last November when he got kicked out of Hope Bay—"

Jim's mouth dropped open. "He what?! He got kicked out? That's not how he tells it."

"He shot a neighbour's dog. A nice lab that never hurt anyone."

"Jeezus! He really is going off the deep end."

"Yeah, that's for sure. Anyway, since then I've been to Squirrel Cove twice, and other than that he hasn't let me away from the cabin until now. And the only reason I'm here is because he's afraid I'd run away if he left me behind."

"You're a bloody prisoner."

"I know! I know! That's exactly how I feel. A prisoner he can beat on." I bit my lip, and stifled a sob. I took a deep quavery breath and pulled myself together. I couldn't fall apart now, in the middle of the grocery store.

Jim started to reach for me but pulled his hand back as another shopper came around the corner. "Small town," he said. "We'd better be careful."

My vision blurred. "Or I'll pay for it." Robert's fist loomed in front of my face. I winced.

"When spring fishing is closed, in a few weeks, I'll do one trip for coho. When we come into town, we'll watch for our chance and take off. Sound okay?" He looked worried and squeezed my hand. "I wish it could be sooner."

"How can we get away from Robert when the time comes?" I couldn't imagine him letting his guard down. "He'll just chase us in the Hawkeye."

"I've been thinking about that. I'll tell him I'm leaving a day early to get another crack at the coho so I can bring a few home. You'll go uptown to get groceries, supposedly. I'll leave from the government wharf and pull in at the fuel dock. You'll meet me there and jump aboard. We'll be gone before he thinks to look for you. He won't suspect you're on the Serenity."

I put my hand on Jim's arm and whispered, "Thank you, thank you, thank you." I wanted to throw myself into his arms and press him tightly to me and never let him go, but I was in the Co-op with shoppers all around. I didn't know who might know Robert or what they might tell him if I did anything to attract attention to myself.

We finished our shopping and shared a taxi to bring our groceries back. About a block from the wharf, Jim tapped the driver on the shoulder. "Pull over for a minute. Keep the meter running and wait for us."

We got out by a large panel van that had pulled into an empty gravel area beside the road. A sign read Foissy's Chipmobile. The aromas wafting from it were irresistible.

"Want a burger and fries?" He looked at me pleadingly. "Come on, we can spare a few minutes. And anyway I want you to meet Foissy. I've known her for years. If you ever need a good friend, go to her. You can trust her completely."

"I don't know, Jim. Robert's pretty tight with his money. He'd be mad if I spent it on a burger."

"My treat." He turned to the smiling woman in the chipmobile. "How are you Foissy?"

"Hi, Jimmy!" she said. She threw off her apron, jumped out of the van, and hugged him. "Is that your taxi? Pay him and tell him to go away. Use my car. That way you can take your time."

"Thanks, Foissy. Be right back."

"That's very nice of you," I said to her while Jim was moving the bags. "Have you known Jim long?"

"Oh, for years. He's the sweetest man. I just love him."

"Me too." I stopped talking and clamped a hand over my mouth.

"Are you his girlfriend then?" she asked. "Lucky you!"

"No," I said quietly. "My name's Andrea. I'm married to Robert. You know him? On the Hawkeye?"

"Oh-h-h yes. I know him." She nodded. "Oh-h-h yes. We've had a few run-ins." She shuddered. "And how is Robert?"

"He's ... he's ..." I swallowed hard. "A bastard," I whispered. I wondered if I should have said that, but it just slipped out. Jim had said I could trust her but still, I should have been more careful.

Foissy put an arm around me. "Listen. I've known Jim for many years. He's a good man. If I wasn't married, I'd be after him myself." She seemed lost in thought for a moment, looked at her hand and turned her wedding band around and around her finger. Then her head snapped up, as if she had just remembered that I was here. "Have I misread this situation? You and Jim?"

I felt instinctively that I could trust this woman. "I married the wrong man and I'm trying to fix it. But please don't say a word to anyone. Please."

"You can count on me." She gave me a hug. "And if you ever need help, you can always come to me."

"Thank you so much. That means a lot to me. I don't know anyone here." I felt tears welling and smiled, quickly wiping them away. It seemed that over the past year I was often wiping away tears.

Jim came back and Foissy stepped back into the van. "Good grief! I almost burned the burgers and the chips are well done! I hope you like them light black."

Jim handed a twenty through the van window. Foissy said, "For you, Jimmy, it's on the house."

But Jim insisted, and he pressed the money into her hands. "For you, Foissy. This isn't enough. Thanks so much. You've always been a good friend to me."

On the way to the wharf, I said, "Those chips and burgers were the best I've ever had."

"Yup. The best. And so is she," Jim said. "Very nice lady."

"I liked her right away. She wasn't impressed when I mentioned Robert's name."

"Not surprising. He owes her money. He's such a...."
He sighed. "Let's not talk about him. We'll be leaving
tomorrow. I won't see much of you for about a week." Jim
stopped Foissy's car at the side of the road and looked at
me for a few seconds without saying anything. Suddenly,
he drove on, turned left past the government wharf and
headed for the causeway, out of town. It took less than
five minutes to leave the houses behind. I thought of
protesting, but the irrational side of my brain won out
over the rational side.

"What if someone sees us and tells Robert?"

"No one is expecting us to be in Foissy's car. And
anyway, do you see any people?" He pulled onto a deserted
side road, stopped the engine and reached for me.

His kiss was so gentle I thought I would melt. I was
used to being handled roughly and this was a complete
change for me. I relaxed my lips and Jim's tongue played
with mine. Tingles rushed from my head to my most
private parts. I thought I'd explode.

Jim took my hand and pressed it to his crotch.

I could only moan, "Oh Jim." I pulled away and
whispered, "How am I going to wait so long for you?"

"You don't have to." He jumped out of the car and
came around to my side and opened the door. He pulled
me out and ran with me into the thick trees and bushes.
He threw his jacket on the ground. "Sir Walter Raleigh at
your service." Then he pulled me down onto it, kissing
and undressing me at the same time.

I wanted him inside me so badly. I didn't know I could
still want sex so much. "I feel like I'm on fire—all over."
Forget about preliminaries. I put my hands on Jim's bare
buns and my legs around his. I needed him desperately. As
we became one, I became aware of the give and take that
I'd been missing. I felt alive and ecstatic beyond anything
I could have imagined. So this is what it's supposed to

feel like. Then without warning, my body tensed up. My grip around Jim's back tightened and I sobbed into his neck.

"There, there, sweetheart." Jim's voice was so mellow and tender. He stroked my hair and kissed my ears, my eyes, my lips. "Everything's going to be all right."

"Oh, Jim. I'd forgotten that this is how it should feel." I pressed my cheek into his neck.

"Andrea, I love you so much," he breathed and hugged me tighter. I made a point of remembering that moment to draw on later if I should need it, and I knew I would.

"I love you too, Jim. I think I loved you the first day in Lund when I fell in the water."

He smiled at the memory. "That's a story we'll tell our grandchildren."

"I'm going to hang onto that thought until we can be together for good."

We pulled our clothes on hurriedly, like a couple of teenagers making out, in danger of being discovered.

"Take care of yourself. Use the radio if there's a problem. Heck, use the radio anyway and talk to me about ordinary things."

"Maybe I can do that once in a while without Robert getting suspicious."

"Sure. People chat on the radio all the time out there. And before you know it the time will have gone by. We'll be together soon. Now let's get you back. You can say I had to run a quick errand while I was bringing you and the groceries home, saving you the price of the taxi."

"He should be glad of that. He's always counting his money."

But as I brought the groceries down to the Hawkeye I saw Robert, hands on hips, glowering at me.

I kept my head down and busied myself with putting groceries away. Robert stared for a while, until I said, "You could help put things away if you aren't busy."

"I'm just wondering why you arrived in a red car. Thought I told you to take a taxi." He watched for my reaction, but I held the pancake mix in front of my face to show him that I got what he wanted, and turned away to put it in the cupboard.

"That was Jim's friend's car and he offered me a ride to save us the taxi money. I thought you'd be glad. Here's your change from the groceries."

He half closed one eye and looked at me suspiciously, then turned to go back down into the engine room. "Keep it. You'll need it for the laundry."

I was glad to get away with the laundry. I loaded the washer and had a shower while I waited. I needed to check myself over for twigs and bits of moss that might have betrayed me.

Chapter 57

The next day was overcast, but the wind had died down. We left Masset Inlet and turned west towards Langara Island.

"We should be there in about five hours," Robert said. "You'll be surprised at all the charter boats hanging around there. Sporties!" He snorted in disgust.

My brow furrowed as I tried to understand. "Thought you liked sport fishing."

"Sure, but we used to be able to fish all around the beaches. Now we have to stay a mile off shore so these guys can play. Whatever happened to 'first the work, then the play'?"

"They probably do work and then this is their play."

"Yeah, but it's my work! Why should I give it up so they can play?" A vein on Robert's temple bulged out and I could see it pulsing. "What? Are you defending them now?" His grip tightened on the helm. "Figures that's how a stupid woman would think."

I swallowed my anger. Stay calm. Stay calm and just ignore the insult. "No, of course I'm not defending them. But why can't everyone share the fish grounds?"

"Because! Most of these assholes don't know how to run a boat and the rest don't pay attention to what's going on around them. We can't get out of their way with our trolling lines out so far. They could easily move for us. But no! We're the ones who have to get cut out so the fishing lodges can make their money." He looked at me for understanding and sympathy.

"I don't understand why this was allowed to happen."

"Ha! They suckered the locals. Told them it would be good for their economy. That's the spin they put on it anyway. 'Look at all the business it will bring to small towns like Masset.' But what happened? They fly the guests in by chopper and bypass Masset completely. The lodges are completely self-contained. Masset gets nothing."

"That doesn't seem fair." I agreed with him, but what I really wanted was to calm him down. "But Masset benefits from the commercial fleet," I said. "Fishboats go in after each trip and you buy groceries, fuel, hardware—everything you need. And look at all the people who find work at the dock and the fish plants because of commercial fishing."

"People say how greedy commercial fishermen are, catching all those fish. Do they think we eat them all ourselves? Who do they think provides the fish for the stores so everyone can buy it? Some old woman can't go sport fishing to catch her own fish. So we do it for her." Robert was getting himself all worked up again. "Ah! Crap! Those government weenies don't have a clue what's going on and they don't give a flying fuck either." His eyes narrowed and his nostrils flared.

"Well, there's nothing we can do about it right now. Let's try to work around it." If I couldn't get him off this topic, I'd pay for it. "Why don't you tell me about how the trolling works. You know, how to put the gear on the lines, and how to put the lines out."

"Too complicated. Tomorrow morning I'll get us started and then when it's a slow time I'll show you bit by bit."

"Sounds good." Whew! He seemed to be calmer. "How about some pancakes?"

Okay," Robert said the next morning, "I've got three sets of steel trolling wire fishing each side of the boat. He pointed at the three spools of wire on the gurdies. The bow line fishes up front, the main line in the middle of the boat, and the pig line at the back. Got that? Bow, main, pig. Every couple of fathoms, I hooked short leaders of perlon fishing line onto the trolling wires. There's a spoon—a lure—with a hook at the end of each of those perlon lines, so don't go getting a hook in your hand when we bring them in to check the lines."

The gurdies were for winding the heavy steel wires up or down. It would be impossible to do it by hand. I pushed a lever on whichever spool of trolling wire I wanted to wind. Then I turned the handle that allowed the hydraulic power to flow and start winding the spool. I managed to get the hang of it after a few tries.

"Check your pig line," Robert called from the wheelhouse. "Seems to be dragging over to the side too far. Might've picked up some seaweed."

I stayed in the stern as much as possible and kept out of Robert's way. Standing in the cockpit at the very back of the boat, my waist was level with the deck. It was designed to be a safe place to stand for checking the lines and bringing in fish.

"Why do they call it the pig line?" I asked as I brought in the line that fished farthest back from the boat.

"That Styrofoam float you're bringing in used to be made of pigskin in the old days. That's why it's called the pig and that's the pig line. It needs that extra float to keep it far enough back so it doesn't tangle with the other lines."

I unclipped the float. "It looks like a skinny foam suitcase." The perlon lines with the lures came up next and I unhooked them from the trolling wire. As I took each one off, it had to be tidily coiled in the small workspace in front of me so it wouldn't get tangled when I had to hook it back onto the trolling wire to put the line out again.

"You were right," I said, as the last spoon came near the surface. "It's dragging a big hunk of kelp."

"Take the knife and cut it away. Just don't cut the perlon." Robert had come out on deck to stand over me. "And don't have so much tension on the line or that hook will come up and jump into your face once it's free of kelp. Let that line down a bit. Use the gaff to grab the seaweed."

I cleared the line and started putting it back. Robert jumped into the cockpit and brought the bow line up on his side. "Might as well check all the lines," he said. "Hurry up and get that pig line out again. It can't catch fish if it's not in the water."

I worked as quickly as I could, but Robert had the bow line on his side up, landed two spring salmon, and lowered it again, before I finished putting the pig line out.

"Hurry up and do your main next." He was hyped from landing the two springs that still thumped sporadically in the checkers, the enclosed deck space in front of the cockpit where we stood. The salmon were a good size and he should have been happy, but it seemed to make him all the more stressed and eager to get the rest of the lines checked.

"Lean out and take a look to the front for boats now and then."

"Are we going in the right direction with no one steering?" I asked.

"It's on auto right now, but I can steer it from back here." He pointed to a lever under the deck near our knees. "Hurry up with that main," he snapped.

"All right, all right. I'm going as fast as I can." I called him names in my mind. I turned the handle on the gurdies to go faster and immediately heard a sound that wasn't right. Robert reached across and slapped the lever out of gear.

"God dammit. Move over." I backed up in the cramped space. Robert squeezed in front of me and stood on my feet. He gave me a shove. "Get outta the way."

With him standing on my feet, of course I fell down. He didn't even notice; just moved his feet slightly and kicked backwards at me like I was a piece of clutter in his way. He moved the control handle to lower the trolling wire. I had missed taking one of the fishing lines off in time and it got jammed in a gadget that looked like an empty spool of thread, only slightly bigger. It was there to prevent anything from passing through it except trolling wire so nothing else would get wound onto the big wire spool.

I had screwed up. I was sorry, yet I could forgive myself for not knowing how to do everything right on a fishboat. But Robert's treatment of me was inexcusable, and I was angry and hurt and scared of him. I didn't like being pushed around and yelled at.

"Fucking mess!"

"Sorry." I had my arm ready to protect my face in case he hit me, but this time, he didn't. "I was trying to hurry." I simply couldn't go as fast as Robert. Why didn't he understand that this was all new to me?

Robert went back to his side of the boat with a scowl on his face. I continued to bring in the main line. "I've got a fish on," I said.

"So take the gaff and bring it in. Just don't knock it off the spoon," he growled.

I had watched Robert club a fish on the head with the back of the gaff and then drive the sharp spike of the gaff into its head and lift it aboard. It had looked so easy. I lifted the gaff, but the fish reacted to the movement and thrashed to get out of the way. I whacked the water with the gaff. Almost lost the gaff! Oh Jeez! That would have been a bad mistake. That would have really set him off. And what if I couldn't get that fish aboard? He'd fly off the handle again just like when I lost the snapper at Squatteree.

A nervous trembling started from my stomach and radiated to all parts of my body. My hands shook so hard that I almost dropped the gaff again. I couldn't mess this up. I took hold of the line again with my left hand and pulled it closer. This time I had the gaff high before the fish surfaced. I hit him on the head.

"Gaff him quick now." Robert hovered behind me. I drove the gaff into the fish and tried to pull it aboard. It was heavier than I thought and fighting to escape. I struggled with its weight. "Two hands," Robert shouted.

I let go of the line and used two hands on the gaff to lift the fish aboard. I leaned back and the salmon slithered against me. I gave the gaff a flick of the wrist and barely managed to slap that fish into the checkers.

"Whew!" I could feel my heart pumping extra hard from the exertion, and a rush buzzed through me. I had managed to take a big fish out of the ocean almost with my bare hands. The large spring salmon was nearly all muscle. It thrashed around in the checkers in front of me, slapping the deck again and again squirting blood everywhere. Is this how a killer feels? This incredible adrenaline rush? I shuddered, horrified to think that a part of me could enjoy violence like this. But there was no denying it. Is this what Robert feels when he beats on me? He leaned over to kiss me on the cheek. "Your face is splattered with blood," I said.

"So is yours. I like it like that."

Chapter 58

We were tied to the dock in Masset after selling a load of fish when Jim appeared on the deck of the Hawkeye.

"Where's Robert?"

"He went up to the hardware store. Had to get some hose clamps."

"Good timing." Jim smiled. "So how did it go this trip?"

"Not too bad. Better than the first trip. That time, I think did everything wrong, so this time was better."

He nodded, but then frowned. "I thought you were going to talk to me on the radio? What happened to that?"

"I know. I hear people chit chatting on the radio all the time. But Robert wouldn't let me touch the radio. Probably afraid of what I'll say. I don't know. He's so paranoid. Getting worse all the time."

Jim shook his head. "I'll see if I can get him to let you talk on the radio. I'll tell him you should know how to use it in an emergency, and anyway, if he's busy in the stern, and someone calls, he shouldn't have to leave what he's doing."

"Maybe. That might help. It sure would be nice to hear your voice—I mean I hear it when you're talking to Robert—but it would be nice to hear you talking to me." *Right now the only voice that talks to me is Robert's. All week long.*

Jim laughed. "Just remember they're public airways. There was a couple a few years ago who had a secret thing going on. He had his own boat, and she was the girlfriend-deckhand of a guy on another boat. She called up the new boyfriend on the VHF and said in a hushed voice, 'We can talk now. He's in the stern.' She forgot all about the loudspeaker outside the wheelhouse. Her skipper heard every word she whispered into the radio, loud and clear. So did the whole fleet. It was very entertaining."

"How embarrassing. But so dumb." I had to chuckle as I imagined it. "Don't worry. I won't do anything that stupid."

"Of course not." He started to reach for me but dropped his hand. The dock was a busy place. "I only meant it was a funny story."

"I know." I gave him a quick smile. "How much longer do you think it'll be?" I didn't want to sound like I was whining, but I found the waiting so hard. I hoped Robert didn't kill me before the fishing season was over. He was getting more and more stressed and harder to keep happy.

"Maybe another two weeks? The trip after the next one, we can see about you jumping ship." He looked over his shoulder. "I'd better go now. You hang in there. We'll be together soon. It won't be long."

Yes, it will. Another day is too long. Another minute is too long. I sighed.

"I wish it could be now, but we have to do this right." He stepped off the boat onto the dock, turned and whispered, "Love you." Those two little words meant everything to me.

"Okay. Take care." *Love you too.*

Call up Jim and ask where he wants to anchor tonight." Jim's talk with Robert had apparently worked.

"He says he's going in to Pillar Bay. Wants to know if you're going there too."

"Tell him I was going to go to Egeria Bay."

"Okay." I didn't know why he couldn't go to Pillar Bay too. We were close to it.

I called Jim back. It was so comforting to hear his voice. I didn't care much about the words. I just loved the sound. "He says he has a bit of a leak in his water pump," I reported back to Robert. "He has to fix it tonight. Wondered if you had any gasket sealing goop."

Robert pulled himself up onto the deck by a rope hung in front of the cockpit. He took the microphone. "Jim. What's up?"

Jim explained everything again.

"I have an extra tube of that Permatex gasket maker. I'll see you tonight then. I'll back up my stern to yours and toss it to you."

"Why stern to stern?" I asked after they had signed off.

"Well, use your head, girl. What would happen if we came up alongside of him?"

"I don't know. What?" I didn't know what the big mystery was.

"Jeezus you've got no brains. The trolling poles are down, aren't they? Ours are down. His are down. Crash? Splinter? Tangle? Duh!" He went back out on deck shaking his head and muttering something about stupid broads. I wished I hadn't asked and I did feel stupid. But how else would I know these things?

The Serenity was already anchored when we came in to Pillar Bay and Robert maneuvered the Hawkeye's stern up to hers.

"Go out on the stern and get ready to toss that tube of stuff to Jim. And don't drop it into the water." Robert was busy with the controls, getting us lined up with the Serenity. I took the tube and stood on the cap railing at the back of the Hawkeye. With one hand, Jim held onto a rope on his boat and with the other he reached out to me. I passed the tube to him and his hand touched mine. I could feel the tenderness in that touch flow through my whole body. How sad that I craved gentle touching so much. His eyes met mine, and I saw love there. *Or did I only see what I wanted to see?* At this point, I didn't care. I needed to believe in Jim. He was my only hope. He was all I wanted. I would make sure he was happy with me if only we could be together.

"I hope you get it fixed."

"There's nothing wrong with the water pump," he said. "I just wanted to see you."

I grinned broadly. Joy flooded through me, leaving every part of me tingling.

"Stop smiling or you'll be in deep shit."

"Deeper than I already am?" But I did take a quick breath and sober up. "Okay, good luck," I said in a louder voice, and clambered back onto the main deck.

Jim lifted his hand in a wave to us, as Robert pulled away to find a spot to anchor. I was glad he had to mind the wheel. I stayed on deck to compose myself. I had to stop smiling so hard or Robert would give me good reason to stop.

Chapter 59

"We have a nice load of coho. With the springs we caught earlier, that makes a good season." Robert sounded smug. "I think we can call it quits after we sell this trip. We'll tidy the boat up and get fresh grub for the trip home. I'll do an oil change, take on fuel and water, and we'll be all set."

"It'll be good to get back and do land things again." I tried to sound cheerful but the thought of going back to that cabin.... I shuddered involuntarily. Somewhere between Masset and our cabin, I had to make my escape. I couldn't go through another winter in isolation with Robert.

"Jim's had enough too. He said he might leave a day or two ahead of us and get a few coho outside of Masset. He'll stay at Seven Mile in the evenings rather than come back into Masset. Then he'll catch up to us when we leave and we can travel back home together."

"Sounds fine to me." I shrugged and looked away. I couldn't meet Robert's eyes, afraid my guilt would show. "Whatever." I pretended not to care what Jim did. I knew that the Serenity was tied to the floats at the very end. Looked to me like he was ready for a fast getaway.

"Hey, Robert! Andrea!" Jim called from farther down the dock. I perked up at the sound of his voice. He hustled over to the Hawkeye. "I'm going to pull out now. I'll stop for fuel on the way out of town. See you in a couple of days, right?"

"Sure thing," Robert said. "Talk to you later." When he turned to go back into the wheelhouse, Jim mouthed to me. "See you at the fuel dock."

"See you," I called after him.

I tidied up the wheelhouse, making the bed and washing the breakfast dishes. Out on deck, I pretended to be busy cleaning and watched for the Serenity to leave the dock. Seeing that she was gone, I stuck my head in the wheelhouse door. "Guess I could go get those groceries before they get picked over."

"Yeah, okay. Take some money out of my wallet."

I felt guilty taking any money from him this time. I knew I wouldn't be spending it on groceries. But then I thought, how much is a black eye worth? And I helped myself to "grocery money." I didn't dare take anything extra that might make Robert suspicious. $100 should be a reasonable amount. I'd have to get by with the clothes on my back. Somehow none of that mattered now. It was all about getting away.

He'd have to do an oil change, and maybe get some parts before we left, so I figured I had a good hour or two before he wondered where I was.

"See you later," I called. *Much, much later. Maybe in hell.* I had to stop myself from skipping up the ramp to the top of the wharf. *Walk normally,* I told myself. *Time for skipping later.*

Not far from the wharf, directly ahead of me I saw Foissy's Chipmobile. As I approached, I couldn't keep the smile off my face.

"What are you so happy about today?" Foissy asked. I looked around at her customers and shrugged.

"Hi Andrea." Jack, one of the fishermen I recognized from the wharf, stood at the front of the line. "All done for the season?" He picked up the burger and fries that Foissy handed him and gave her a ten dollar bill. "Keep the change, dear," he said.

"Yup! We're all done. Just going up to get a few groceries for the trip home. Isn't it great to be finished?" I allowed myself a smile.

"It will be. I still gots a few days of fishin' to do. Kind of a cleanup fishery. Git some to take home to the ole blister. She'll be mighty pissed if I don't bring her some fish. Well, see ya later." He headed back to the wharf eating his burger.

"Good luck," I called after him.

"Come on inside and talk to me for a while," Foissy said. She opened her door and pointed to a small stool in the corner. "Just a sec while I finish up here." She had two more customers and I was a bit anxious to get going, but I figured I could spare a couple of minutes. I wondered if Jack would mention that he'd seen me. I stood up and looked towards the wharf. He was already at the top of the ramp. I should be going, but I wanted to tell Foissy my plan. It seemed to take forever for her to serve the last two people. I couldn't stop the nervous bouncing of my leg. At last she was done and sat down. "Well, what's the good news?"

"I'm leaving with Jim today!" I blurted out. "He's waiting for me at the fuel dock. Robert thinks I've gone for groceries."

Foissy stood up to hug me. "Wonderful! I'm so happy for you. Jim's a good person. I—"

"What's wrong?"

Foissy had a shocked look on her face. "It's Robert coming up the road," she hissed. "His face is black as a thundercloud."

"Oh no! Oh shit, shit, shit. Not now. Why now?" I could see my happy life crumbling.

"Stay down. He doesn't have to know you're here. Stay in the corner and keep low. He can't see in."

"Foissy, where's Andrea?" Robert sounded pissed off, although I couldn't imagine why. He didn't know anything. He couldn't.

"How would I know where she is?" Foissy stood her ground. She didn't sound intimidated at all.

"Jack was just here and he said he saw her."

"So?"

"So. Why are you lying about it?"

"Who says I'm lying? What do you need her for anyway?"

"She said she was going for groceries. She had no business stopping here and gallivanting around town, dammit. She knows better. Now where is she? Is she in there?" He headed for the door to the van, but Foissy was quicker. She slammed it shut and locked it. Robert banged on the door with his fist and yelled, "I know she's in there. You bitch! Andrea!" He pounded hard on the door. "When I get my hands on you, you'll be sorry."

"Robert!" Foissy yelled. "You're going to wreck my van. Back off or I'll throw a pot of boiling oil out the window at you, and don't think I won't do it, you lunatic."

Robert must have backed off. In a second, Foissy had slapped the lids on the deep fryers and turned off the propane. She jumped into the driver's seat and started the engine. She drove the van slowly at first because of the potholes in the off-road area.

"Where are you meeting Jim? The fuel dock, did you say?" she called back to me.

"Yes, the fuel dock. He said he'd be tied there waiting for me."

"I'll drive you down there and you can jump out." Foissy went as fast as she dared with the deep fryers sloshing oil. "Come up front and get ready to jump out and make a run for it." She glanced in the mirror. "Oh shit!"

"What's wrong?" I felt panic creeping up on me.

"Robert is chasing us." She laughed without mirth and immediately became serious again. "Like a dog chasing a car. You're going to have to be quick."

She slowed the van to make the turn onto the street that led to the fuel dock and then sped up as much as she dared.

"I think we've left him behind. Make a run for it."

"If I don't make it, would you go down to the fuel dock and tell Jim to go on without me. We'll meet up someplace else somehow. Thanks for everything, Foissy." I jumped out as she called out good luck and drove off slowly.

Robert must have been right behind the van, keeping out of sight of the mirrors. I barely had time to look around when his strong hand grasped my upper arm so tightly I cried out. The quiet side street was empty, so no one saw him slap my face. My nose started to bleed and I had no tissue. I wiped the blood on my sleeve. At the sight of the blood, his eyes seemed to get glassy. His hold on my arm was like a vise grip.

Up ahead, Foissy had pulled over and jumped out of the chipmobile.

"What the hell kind of bully treats a woman like that?" she shouted. "You despicable piece of shit! Let go of her."

"You mind your own fuckin' business, you lying bitch. Now get the fuck out of my way or I'll deck you too."

"I'm getting the police down to the wharf!" Foissy yelled. I didn't have time to give her more than a quick glance as she got back in her van. I knew there'd be no police coming to the wharf. In a small town like this there was probably an answering machine in a little RCMP office and that would be it for police presence. Or they'd be out dealing with other more important issues. Anyway, what could she tell them that Robert wouldn't deny?

Sobbing and swiping at my bleeding nose, I tried to keep up with Robert's long, angry strides to avoid falling. When I did trip, he jerked me upright. He didn't relax his grip until we came back to the wharf via the back roads. At the top of the wharf he said, through gritted teeth, "I'm going to let go of your arm, and you're going to walk down to the boat beside me. If you do anything to draw attention to yourself or make any move to run, I'll beat the snot out of you when we get back to the boat. I can wait till we get away from the nosy people on the dock." He let go so abruptly I staggered. "Walk with me," he growled.

I wanted to die.

When we got back to the Hawkeye, Robert gave me a shove into the wheelhouse. I tried to catch myself and seared my hand on the stove. I yanked my hand back and had no time to check the burn.

"Get downstairs," he snapped. He gave me another shove that had me tripping down the three steps to the fo'c'sle. "Can't trust you."

I jumped up to climb out. "Robert I—" He shoved me harder this time. I hit my head on the bunk frame and landed, sobbing and bleeding in a heap on the fo'c'sle floor. The door slammed shut. I heard him wedging something in the lever that kept the door closed, effectively locking me in. "Don't do this to me," I wailed.

Then I heard him drop into his bunk upstairs. He took a few deep breaths, then let out a big sigh and whispered, "Fuck!"

I peeked up through the crack at the side of the door and saw him sitting on the edge of the bunk holding his head in his hands, moaning. He rubbed his temples and made little whimpering noises. He pulled the curtains shut, darkening the wheelhouse, and lay down in the bunk with a long drawn out groan.

In my bunk below, I turned my face to the wall. I had no desire to get up ever again. I thought about looking for pills in the medicine bin. It was handy in the closet opposite my bunk. I could have tried to end it then, but my mother would have been disappointed in me if I gave up without more of a fight. I tried to hold the image of my parents in my mind and that gave me the strength I needed. I licked the burn on my hand carefully, just to wet it, then pulled the pillow over my head and sobbed until I fell asleep.

Sometime later, I heard the engine start up. The gentle rocking motion of the boat told me we had left the dock. Looking up through the skylight, I judged it was around noon. The rocking was soon accompanied by rolling which meant we had to be in the open water outside Masset Inlet. I had no way of knowing which way Robert turned at the mouth of the inlet, but I assumed he would be heading towards Prince Rupert and home. It would be dark before we got across Hecate Strait to the mainland side. If he fell asleep at the wheel during the long run, we could be in trouble, but I was beyond caring whether I died now at sea or later from a beating at the cabin.

I lay there staring at the ceiling, too miserable and defeated to dream about the life I would never have with Jim. He must have wondered why I didn't show up. He would have been waiting in his boat so no one would see us together and be able to tell Robert where I was. Foissy would probably tell him what happened. It was all too painful to think about. I drifted into some dark recess of my mind until the waves rocked me to sleep again.

The anchor chain rattling over the bow woke me. Then the engine stopped. The alarm bell rang to signify the drop in oil pressure, as it did whenever the engine shut down.

I heard Robert push the button to stop the alarm. And then, nothing. Quiet. Above the skylight, stars twinkled in the dark night sky. Stupidly, uselessly, I chose a big star and made a wish. I wondered if Jim was looking at these same stars. Probably not, but it made me feel better to think he might be.

I heard Robert get into his bunk. I'm sure he must have thought I was asleep or he would never have let those sobs escape. His soft crying made me feel sorry for him. I wondered what torment he must be going through, to have to keep me prisoner now for fear of losing me. Yes, I wanted to get away from him—so badly—but he couldn't help himself when he had those outbursts and I knew he felt terrible about them.

"Robert?" I called out softly. "Robert, can you hear me?"

"Mmm?" His answer was muffled and I heard a sniff. "What?"

"Could you let me out now? Please?"

I heard the covers being thrown back; heard his weight on the floor. He fiddled with the wedge in the lever of my door.

I stepped up onto the main deck level and Robert put his arms around me. He hugged me tightly and sobbed.

"Sh-sh-shhh," I said. "Don't worry. Sh-sh. It'll be okay."

"I hate myself," he choked out. "It's as if someone else takes over my mind and I can't control it. I hate myself." He caressed the back of my head tenderly. "Andrea, I don't know what comes over me. You say it scares you. It scares me too." He sobbed softly into my hair. "I love you so much, and now I can never make you love me again."

"Hush now," I said. "Let's not worry about forever right now. How about a cup of tea?" The good old cup of tea. Seemed that was the only cure I knew for disaster.

Robert had black circles around his eyes from the strain of staying awake for the long crossing to Squatteree. I probably had a black ring under one of my eyes too, though it wasn't from lack of sleep.

I poured the tea with my left hand, holding my right hand protectively close to my body.

"What happened to your hand?" Robert reached for it but I pulled away.

Slowly I opened my palm to show him the burn. "When you pushed me into the wheelhouse, I fell against the stove."

"Oh, Jesus. I'm sorry." Tears welled in his eyes. He turned his head away and sniffed. "I need to go see that shrink again. This can't go on."

We sat sipping tea in silence. "Andrea?" Robert chewed his lip and seemed to be searching for words. "If I didn't have this problem ... do you think we could be happy together?"

But you do, and that will never change. I had to fight the impulse to laugh out loud, but I knew he was being sincere. Naïve, but sincere. I nodded. "Yup. I think so."

"We haven't had sex for a long time." He must have sensed me tensing up. "Don't worry, I won't bother you."

"It's not a bother. It's just that I have a sore face and a burnt hand." *And I'm wishing I were anywhere but here.*

"I know," he whispered. "I'm really sorry." He let out a big sigh. "I know I keep saying I'm going to do better, but this time I mean it."

"You meant it before too. You always have good intentions. But then it happens anyway." I was beyond caring if that kind of talk provoked him, but I didn't want him to play games with my head anymore. "Is there anything we can do that will help?"

"I don't know. I know it makes me mad when you don't do what I want."

"But—"

He put his hand up to stop me from saying more. "I know, I know. That's not fair. But I can't control it once I start to get mad and that seems to be one of the things that sets me off."

"Well...." It was my turn to let out a big sigh. "I guess if that's what it takes, I'll try to remember to do what you say." He relaxed then and I added quickly, "But you have to try not to boss me around so much too."

"Yes, okay. I'll try." He reached for my good hand and patted it.

"What about Jim?" I asked.

He jerked his hand away and his eyes narrowed ever so slightly. "What about him?"

"Didn't you arrange to make the trip home with him?" *I was walking on eggs here but I wanted to know Jim was near.* And maybe I wouldn't have to think about dying yet. Maybe someday I could still escape this misery.

"I've decided to do this trip home by ourselves. I want to get home as fast as we can."

"But wouldn't it be safer to travel with someone?"

"Maybe. But I don't like the way he looks at you." His jaw muscles worked as he clenched his teeth. It was time to leave the topic alone.

"Okay," I nodded. "No problem."

"We'd best get to bed," he said. "We'll be making long runs and maybe running at night too. We can take turns at the wheel."

I could only pray that Jim would stop at the cabin on his way home. If he did, come hell or high water, I was hitching a ride.

Chapter 60

One look at Foissy's face and I knew something had gone wrong.

"Jimmy," she said through a tight throat, "he got her." A sniffle escaped her. "That monster! He got her." Foissy's face contorted as she struggled not to cry.

"What happened? Where is she? Does he know she was coming to meet me?"

She shook her head. "I don't think so. He was mad at her for stopping to talk to me. I told her to keep down so he wouldn't know she was in the van, but that was a mistake. Then I drove away with her, and he chased us. Chased us like a dog! I thought I'd lost him, but he must have been right behind the van where I couldn't see him. He got her as soon as she stepped out of the van. And she's paying for it now." Foissy dropped her face into her hands and cried.

I rubbed her back till the crying eased. "It's okay. You did your best."

"Oh Jimmy, I saw him smack her in the face. There was blood." Foissy's voice closed up. She dropped her head and rubbed her eyes with the heel of her hands. "I stopped and got out to try to make him let her go but he yelled at me like a madman. Said he'd deck me too. I told him I'd call the cops." She laughed mirthlessly. "Not enough cops here to deal with everything. Never get there in time anyway. B'sides, not much they can do. I was no help to her at all. He was marching her down to the wharf, holding onto her really tight."

"That goddamned bastard! I'm going down there and ... well, whatever happens, happens." Bloody bastard. Fucking coward. Hitting a woman. "Thanks for trying to help, Foissy. I'll go down there and at least make sure she's okay."

"Okay. I'm so sorry." She pulled out a Kleenex and dabbed her eyes. She blew her nose and took a big breath. "Good luck, Jimmy."

I gave her a hug and a kiss on the cheek. "Thanks. And don't worry."

I made sure Serenity was tied securely to the fuel dock and told them I wouldn't be in their way much longer. I walked across town to the government wharf and scanned the floats for the Hawkeye as I came down the ramp. The dock was crammed with fishboats waiting to unload their spring salmon now that the season for them had just closed. Hawkeye wasn't tied to the place where she was when I left late this morning. I went right to the end of the float and looked on both sides. No Hawkeye.

"Jack," I called to the skipper of the Sea Maid, "do you know where the Hawkeye's tied up?"

"She's not. They just left." He pointed to the end of the float and out into the inlet. I could just see her disappearing around the point of land.

"Damn! I needed to talk to him," I said, half to myself.

"Who? Robert? He wasn't fit to talk to anybody today. Never seen a buddy get in such a flap. All's I said to him this mornin' was I seen Andrea talkin' to Foissy and she looked right happy. Next thing I knows he's stormin' up the ramp. Going to look for her, I guess. Cuz he found her all right. Brought her back with a bloody nose. 'F I'd 'a known he was gonna do that to her, I'd 'a kep' my mouth shut."

"Well, thanks," I mumbled. Shit! Shit! Shit! I didn't know what to do then. Go back to my boat. Go home. Alone. I pounded my fist into my palm. I should have grabbed her the first day when I had a chance and just said to hell with the fishing season. I had kept telling myself it doesn't matter if you love her. She's his wife. You have no business interfering. But I should have seen how badly she needed help. How could I have missed that?

I'd have to follow them. I wasn't sure if the jig was up or not. Had Andrea confessed? In that case what might Robert do to her if he saw me following them? I had to hope that she hadn't said anything about us.

"Hawkeye, Hawkeye. Are you on here Robert?" I tried several of the usual VHF channels and the sideband frequency we had agreed to use. No answer.

"Hawkeye, Serenity. Do you pick me up, Robert?" No answer.

Could be he's too mad to speak to me. Probably got his radios turned off. I have to catch up to him.

A week later, I pulled into Robert's bay. Even though I put in long days, I didn't have the luxury of having someone to spell me at the wheel. Robert would have made Andrea take shifts at the helm while he slept and so could cover the distance in fewer days. Probably ran at night too. Sure enough, the Hawkeye was tied to the float. I looked for the cabin, but saw nothing until I got closer. Holy shit! What the hell happened? As I pulled up to the float, Robert came out of the Hawkeye and grabbed my tie up line.

"What's going on?" I stepped out onto the dock. "What happened to the cabin?"

"I guess somebody vandalized it over the summer." Robert's chin went up slightly in challenge.

"Where's Andrea?" I hoped the disappointment didn't show on my face. She would have been here to see me if she could. I wondered if he'd told her to stay out of sight in the Hawkeye's wheelhouse and craned my neck to look in that direction. If he hurt her again.... My body tensed.

"She's in Powell River. When she saw the cabin all burnt down she said she'd had enough. We weren't getting along all that well anyway, if you must know." He let out a big sigh. "So I didn't even let the engine cool down. I took her to Powell River and dropped her off. Gave her enough money for a plane ticket home and that's the end of that story."

I walked towards the pile of ashes. If it was true that she got away, then I'd find her. I relaxed a bit. "What are you going to do now?"

"Sleep on the boat. Rebuild the cabin. Little bit bigger. Better." Robert stayed on the float as I walked towards the burn site. I could feel warmth coming from the ashes.

"This must have just happened before you arrived. It's still warm."

"Could be. I didn't really come ashore to check it out because Andrea wanted to keep going to Powell River. Don't go too close if it's still warm. Come on aboard and I'll get us a beer."

He sure didn't want me to get near the ashes. A gasoline can lay on its side a few feet away, not burned. And the way the whole cabin was gone made me think the fire had some help. You'd think there would be a few charred boards left standing, but there was nothing but ash. And of course the wood stove in the middle, and some other metal thing in one corner—looked like a burnt out sewing machine.

What about Monique in Lund? She wouldn't go to Powell River when she could first go to Lund. "Are you sure you took Andrea to Powell River?"

"Of course I'm sure. That's where she wanted to go. What? You don't believe me?"

"Sure, sure. Just seems odd she wouldn't want to go to Lund." *Something's not right here.*

"Well, she might have gone to Lund from Powell River. I really don't give a shit. But she said she was flying back home."

"I think I'll pass on that beer, Robert. I still have a way to go before I get home. Don't want to fall asleep at the helm. Sorry about you and Andrea. Stop in if you're over my way."

"Sure thing."

I couldn't wait to get out of there. I had to get to Powell River and find Andrea. First I'd stop at Lund and see Monique. But as I walked past the Hawkeye, I saw the leather thong holding Andrea's lapis lazuli amulet draped over the compass light on the dash. She always wore it for good luck. Said it had been a gift from her mother. She would never leave without it.

Chapter 61

I hardly noticed the beauty of the coast on the way home. Home! Ha! Prison was a more fitting word. Robert had insisted on making long runs, from dawn till well after dark. Rather than a week, the trip home took us barely four days.

"There she is. Home sweet home." He lifted the binoculars to get a better look. Under them I could see that his smile was huge. Funny that he could feel so happy about arriving while I could barely hold back tears of despair. I swallowed hard and tried to think of a happy thought. Any happy thought. But none came. Instead I turned my face away so I wouldn't ruin Robert's good mood. As always, it was important for me to keep him happy, but my stomach was a burning knot.

I jumped out onto the little dock and tied the Hawkeye's lines. Robert shut the engine down and we went ashore to check the cabin. The crowbar lay in the kindling box on the porch. Robert used it to pry off the board he had nailed across the door.

"Might as well do the windows too while I'm at it." He came back moments later. "All done."

Inside, everything looked bare. "Don't worry," I said. "I'll get it looking lived in again as soon as we get a few things unloaded from the Hawkeye." If I hurried to get the place looking cozy, things would go easier for me. I opened a cupboard door. "Hmm. Looks like we have new tenants."

"Mouse shit." Robert scowled. "Damn things! I have a mouse trap somewhere."

I found a pail of water, soap, and a rag to clean out the cupboards while Robert went to look for the trap. Then, I went to the boat to bring in some of the basic necessities. In the fo'c'sle I packed up my toiletries. As I rolled up my sleeping bag, I remembered the fanny pack stashed in the cubbyhole at the foot of the bunk. Might as well get that into the house. You never knew what animals had moved closer since we were gone. Maybe something larger than a mouse.

I put boxes of dry goods on the table and plastic bags of laundry on the floor and went back for several more loads, stashing them wherever I could find a space in the cabin.

"What's for supper?" Robert growled.

"I don't know. I hadn't even thought about it yet. Just been moving bags of stuff from the boat." I had no appetite for eating anyway.

"Don't you think you should put some of the things away before you bring more in? We can't even use the table till you deal with that."

"I was waiting till you were finished with the cupboard and got that mouse trap set." I'd been working as hard as I could and still he was dangerously close to losing his temper. My nerves jangled.

"So it's my fault the kitchen's a mess?" His tone rose.

"Of course not. I was only explaining." *Oh God, please, please don't let him get mad.*

"Well, I'm done, so you can get to work." He put the mouse trap down and it jumped up with a sharp thwack. "Ouch! Jeezus. Fuckin' thing." He hopped around the room with the mouse trap on his thumb.

I giggled at the sight and then clapped my hand over my mouth. How could I have let my guard down like that?

Robert's eyes narrowed dangerously and his jaws clamped shut. He pulled the trap off his thumb and smashed me in the face with the same hand. My ears roared with the force of the blow and my eyes momentarily couldn't focus. "You bitch. How dare you laugh at me?" I staggered backwards and fell on top of my fanny pack. While Robert took the time to nurse his thumb, I unzipped the pack and pulled out the revolver, keeping it hidden behind me as I sat leaning against the wall. I felt empowered by the hard steel. I could point it at him now and blow him away. It would be so easy. But then I'd be as nuts as he was.

Perhaps it was the sight of blood trickling down from my nose or the terror in my eyes; whatever it was, something triggered the next phase of his rage. He bunched up his fist and took a step towards me. Teeth gritted, eyes glassy and staring in concentration, lips curled into a sneer; every muscle was wound up tightly ready to do battle. Fear washed over me. This time he was going to hurt me—badly.

I pulled the revolver out from behind my back and yelled, "Stop right there, Robert. I swear I'll shoot you if you come near me." Oh, I wanted to shoot. Whether he came at me or not, I wanted to stop him forever.

He straightened up and hesitated, his mouth open slightly in shock. My burned hand began to shake. I put a second hand on the gun for support, but now both hands shook. "Believe me, I'll shoot if you don't back off."

Gradually a smile spread across his face. "All right," he drawled. "If that's the way you want to play it." He strode out the door. I heard his determined steps beside the cabin and jumped to the window to look for him. He had picked up a shovel. Was he coming back to beat me with a shovel? No. He wouldn't do that. I had the gun.

Stretching over the counter to look out the kitchen window, I saw him go to the far side of the property. He was digging. What on earth is he doing? Digging a grave to bury me? He flung several shovelfuls of dirt aside, and stopped. He stepped to the right and dug again. Again he stopped after a few shovelfuls. *Oh my God! He's digging up the rifles!* I shook so badly I was afraid I might drop the revolver.

"Son of a bitch!" I heard him swear. "Where are you, you mother fucker?" Abruptly he stood up tall and still, almost as if he heard something or had an idea. He tossed the shovel on the ground and stomped to the porch.

I raised the revolver and stood, aiming it at the door.

"Andrea?" he said in what sounded almost like a normal voice.

"What?" I didn't trust him one bit.

"Do you love me?"

What? He really was crazy. But what could I say? "Robert, I do love you, but I know you have a problem with anger." I hoped that would satisfy him.

"So you really do love me?"

"Y-yes, yes I do." What was he getting at?

"I want you to prove you love me." It was quiet outside the door as he waited for my answer.

"Okay? What do you want?" If he wanted me to prove it and if it would calm him down, I'd go along with whatever it was. What choice did I have? Other than killing him?

I heard the sound of something heavy slamming up against the door and then hammering. I pushed on the door. It didn't budge.

"What are you doing? Robert? Why are you barring the door?" I banged on it with my fist. My mouth felt dry and my chest tightened until I could hardly breathe.

"You said you loved me." I heard splashes like water being spilled. "You can prove it by walking through that door."

A liquid seeped under the door. The splashing sounds continued outside. I sniffed. Gasoline!

"Robert!" I shrieked. "Open the door!" I pounded on the door with my fists as hard as I could. "Rober-r-r-t! Robert don't do this! Ple-e-e-ease! Rober-r-r-t!" My throat was raw from screaming.

"If you love me, you'll walk through fire for me," he said calmly. Then the gasoline ignited with a loud whoosh. Smoke poured in through the doorframe.

I spun around looking for a way out. Only one door and I knew that whole side of the house was a wall of fire. Smoke filled the upper part of the room as the flames licked at the roof shingles. I coughed and threw an arm over my stinging eyes.

The windows. No. The kitchen window was already engulfed in flames. The intense heat forced me back. I had to get out of here. But how? Only the bedroom was yet untouched by fire. I grabbed the revolver and jammed it into the fanny pack. Then staying below the smoke cloud in the room I crawled through the bedroom doorway to the window behind the bed. I slid it open and slipped out the back. With a firm grip on the pack, I ran on wobbly legs towards the woods. The sun was going down and soon I would have the blessed cover of darkness to hide in.

At the top of the slight incline behind the house, I crouched behind thick bushes and watched the scene below me. Robert stood several feet away from the cabin. The front of his body glowed in the light of the flames. He was grinning broadly. Then he threw back his head, clapped his hands, and roared and laughed hysterically.

Chapter 62

I ran along the path quickly to take advantage of the last bit of twilight. All those walks I had taken last fall and winter, farther and farther each time, paid off for me now. I knew where I was going—at least for the first few miles.

At a bend in the creek that supplied the cabin's water, I filled the empty water bottle in my fanny pack. I had a good drink of water from the creek. Who knew when I might have access to fresh water again?

I worried at first that Robert might notice I was gone, but the expression on his face had told me he was enthralled by the fire. He hadn't made any move to look for me: must have assumed I went up in smoke with the cabin. The roaring and crackling of the fire would have masked any sound my dash through the bushes might have made.

On my many walks in the woods beyond the cabin, I had chosen some likely places for shelter. I didn't want to stumble around in the pitch dark tonight, nor did I want to use the flashlight so close to the cabin. When I came to the first of the shelters, I took out one of my garbage bags and cut a hole for my head in the middle of the sealed bottom end, and a small armhole on each side. I unwrapped, for the first time, the space blanket folded into a tiny package that Mary had given me when we were mushroom picking. I put it down for a ground sheet. Thank you, Mary. Huddled on it, wearing my plastic garbage bag like a tunic, I leaned into the undercut bank to rest and used the fanny pack as a pillow. I listened to the night noises. The possibility of wild animals nearby worried me, but not nearly as much the thought of Robert finding me. With my revolver beside me and the bear spray in my lap, I eventually fell asleep.

At first light, I was up and on my way. My garbage bag and space blanket had been adequate protection. It was late August and although the days were still warm, nights were quite cool. I packed the precious plastic away carefully, knowing I'd need it again.

My plan was to get to Hope Bay. I'd follow the shoreline, only going inland when the terrain forced me to detour. I took careful compass readings whenever I had to move inland so I would always find the water again.

At some points the salal was so thick I could barely make any headway. Salal! I could eat these berries. I didn't want to waste too much time but I hadn't eaten since lunch the previous day. I filled up on berries as quickly as I could and continued to thrash my way through the waist-high bushes. At last the going was easier and I made good time.

By the late afternoon, I was beginning to think about water and was glad to see another creek mouth. I could refill my water bottle but I'd have to go farther upstream. It was sure to be salty here near the ocean. I hadn't counted on the creek being so wide or so deep. Looking for a better place to ford it, I must have added half a mile to my journey and still the creek was deep and swift as far as I could see upstream. I decided I would have to try crossing it and I would probably get wet.

The water was like ice, most likely straight off one of those distant snow-capped mountains. It seeped into my runners like liquid ice cubes. I tried to ignore the pain in my arches and get across as fast as I could. The slippery rocks made it difficult to get a good footing and several times I had both hands in the water to catch myself. Fortunately the fanny pack was on my back and stayed dry. I was three feet from the far side when I stepped into a hole and twisted my ankle. It didn't feel too bad though and I hopped out on the other side. I sat down to take off my runners and dump out the water. About a cup of water poured out of my socks as I wrung them out. Why hadn't I thought to take them off and carry them? Stupid, stupid, stupid! But now to put them back on. I managed the first one, but the second didn't want to go over the ankle that was already swelling. *Oh damn! How am I going to walk on that? I have to! That's all there is to it.* I hadn't felt it at first because of the icy water, but now it was like sharp tacks piercing my ankle. I had to shut out the pain, shut out my fears, and keep going. I couldn't give up now. There was no one to help me except myself. I had to get to Hope Bay, one step at a time.

I stuck my wet runners on and stood up with my weight on my good leg. Limping along was going to be difficult, but I had to keep going or die out here. At the edge of the creek, young alders grew thick. I took my heavy knife and cut a stick for a crutch. That would have to do. My foot was on fire but I hobbled along, leaning heavily on the stick. Eventually I worked my way back down the other side of the creek to the salt water again, and continued along the beach. I was around the point and out of sight of the cabin, so I didn't worry about being spotted by Robert. Walking along the beach was much easier than going through the bush.

As evening fell, I stopped in a place where the beach was not too steep and I could safely make a fire in the rocks above the high tide mark. I needed to dry out my clothes as much as possible and try to keep warm. I didn't think the garbage bags were going to be enough to do the trick tonight with the bottoms of my jeans wet and my sweat shirt sleeves soaked.

I had a can of sterno and a flint, all thanks to Mary's store supplies. I'd thrown in an extra candle stub from home when we still lived in Hope Bay. Shavings from the candle could help get a fire going when dry wood was hard to find. Thank you, Robert, I thought. If only he knew how handy the heavy knife he'd brought me from Powell River turned out to be. I used it to chop at the base of an old cedar tree, as Mary had shown me, and cut bits of kindling from inside the bark. Once the sterno had done its job of getting the fire started, I fished the can out of the flames and put the lid on it, snuffing it. If I looked after it, the sterno would be good for starting several more fires. I stood back proudly and admired my accomplishment. A few dry pieces of driftwood from high up the beach helped get the fire going nicely.

I toasted my socks like wieners on a stick. Oh how I wished that's what they were! I was so hungry. But at least I had plenty of water since crossing the creek. I got the fire burning steadily and made sure I had lots of extra sticks to feed it through the night. I knew I wouldn't be sleeping much with my ankle paining, but with the fire I felt safer in case of prowling animals. I kept my bear spray handy just in case.

Sometime during the night I was sure Robert had found me. With a gasp, I jolted awake. My heart pounded. *Where am I?* I whipped my head left and right searching the dark shadows for Robert. I listened for footsteps. Nothing. Just a dream. The fire was nearly out so I threw more wood on. I needed its reassuring light and warmth.

My runners were much drier by morning and the socks smelled like the inside of a chimney but they were dry. It was a killer getting the sock on the sprained foot, but I didn't want to add blisters to the problem. Blisters, band-aids, mini first aid kit! Where are my brains? I have a roll of tensor tape in my fanny pack. Oh bless you Mary and Samantha and all those mushrooming trips. I found the roll and wrapped my ankle tightly, put the sock on and stuffed it into my runner. *Ah! That's so much better! Why didn't I think of that yesterday?*

I picked up the makeshift alder crutch and set out. I found some chanterelles that I put in my pack. I could toast them over the fire tonight. Huckleberries, Oregon grape, and salal berries kept me nourished through the day.

I knew my progress was slow, every step a painful one. I played mind games with myself to keep going. I compared the pain in my ankle to the pain of my arm being wrenched, or my nose being punched. With each step on my hurt foot, I substituted an injury inflicted by Robert—slapped face, punched nose, black eye, twisted wrist, kicked hip, head knocked against the wall. They made the pain of my sprained ankle feel like a flea bite. Each hobbling step was taking me farther away from that other greater pain, and the humiliation that came with it. Every searing stab of pain was worth it. I was going to make my escape good this time or die trying. Nothing would make me give up. Nothing!

Chapter 63

When I first saw her lying there, I was sure she was dead; hair a dirty mess of tangles and her bruised face scraped and scratched, as if she had fallen down a rocky embankment. Blood had pooled into a crusty cake at her hairline from a cut on the side of her head. Battered as she was, I could see that she must have been pretty once.

Her shredded jeans had offered little protection. Like the heels of her hands, her knees had tiny pieces of gravel embedded in them. One ankle was hugely swollen; a filthy tensor bandage trailed from it half unraveled. Her skin was almost translucent pale bluish gray. I knew it was futile, but I searched for a pulse. Adrenaline rushed through me as I felt the faint blip, blip of her neck artery.

I had a satellite phone. But when would I get a signal? I glanced at my watch. Should be one within the hour. Pray it wouldn't be too late. And that I could reach someone—the Coast Guard would be best. My GPS would help pinpoint our location. Yes! I could do this.

"Hang on, girl. Hang on." I squeezed her shoulder and pushed a strand of hair back from her face. She didn't look like she had much longer. I had to get help for her, and fast.

I ran for my phone and a blanket, leaping over boulders and logs strewn along the rugged beach. Thick brush close to the water's edge slowed me down, but I sprinted the last stretch to my kayak along the gravelly shore.

With so much of the shorefront dropping steeply into the water, I'd felt lucky to find a relatively flat spot to come ashore and camp. It made sense that a kayaker like me would come here, but that girl? What the hell was she doing there? Where could she possibly have come from? I looked for remnants of a kayak or canoe. Nothing.

While I waited for the Coast Guard's chopper to arrive, I opened the girl's fanny pack. Maybe she had some I.D. in there. Whoa! What's this? A revolver? Loaded too. I looked around, at a loss for what to do. If she were found with the revolver she could be charged with possession of a restricted weapon. You could own these things but not carry them around with you. I could hide the gun and possibly save her some trouble. But what if it was important for the police to know about it? Maybe she had a good reason to be carrying it and would be looking for it when she woke up—if she lived, that is—and then they'd wonder if I had kept it for myself. Probably better not to tamper with evidence.

I continued my cursory search of her fanny pack and found her picture I.D. Andrea Parker Bolton. On the photo she was a looker all right. You'd hardly think it was the same person. I patted her shoulder. You poor dear. You look like you've been through hell. In a side pocket of the fanny pack, tucked out of sight, I found a worn business card. Jim McIntyre, Serenity, 250-339-1212, with the name Monique Fournier and a phone number written on the back.

The wind from the chopper blades sent debris flying everywhere. I held the blanket over Andrea and tried to shield her from the blowing sand and grit. Two medics jumped out with a stretcher and loaded her onto the chopper.

"Here!" I shouted over the noise of the engine. "I.D. and contact info in here. Careful, there's a loaded revolver in the pack too." I ducked and kept my head down as the chopper lifted off. *Good luck, pretty Andrea. I hope you make it.*

Chapter 64

Sticky sweet cotton batten taste in my mouth, an IV tube in the back of my hand, a sea of pale green all around me. I struggled to open my eyes wider and let them take me on a visual tour of the room. A window with metal blinds slanted to keep out the full sun. White curtain beside my bed. A stranger's friendly face above me—smiling.

"How are you doing, Andrea?" The woman held my hand.

"Where am I?" My head felt fuzzy. "Why do I feel like I'm dreaming?"

"Could be the sedatives wearing off." The woman picked up a facecloth and patted my forehead with it. "Feel better?"

"Yes, but where am I?" I repeated.

"You're in St. Paul's Hospital." So she's a nurse.

"Where's that?"

"Vancouver."

"Vancouver?! Are you sure? How did I get to Vancouver?" I must be dreaming. "And how did you know my name?"

"A kayaker found you on the beach near Hope Bay four days ago. You had contact information on your I.D. card and a business card. We've called them. Actually, someone has been waiting to see you.

"As long as it's not my husband...."

"It's a woman. I'll tell her you're awake if you'd like to see her. I think you'll be cleared to go home tomorrow. You might want to make some arrangements." She patted my hand and left the room.

Home? I didn't have a home to go to. I chewed on my lip as tears started to prickle my eyes.

"Andrea! 'Ow are you doing?" Monique rushed into the room and threw her arms around me. She kissed my cheek.

"Monique!" I clung to her tightly. "It's so good to see you. You just can't imagine."

"Mon Dieu, ma pauvre!" She held me at arm's length. "Look at you, all bruised. Does it 'urt?" She hugged me again. "What 'appened to you?"

As I told Monique my story, her fingers gently touched my face checking me over for bruises and cuts.

"Dat Robert! Animale! If I get my 'ands on 'im ..."

"Oh no you don't. I want first crack at him. He's hit me for the last time. I was so stupid to let it happen. I should have listened to you. But don't worry. No one will hit me ever again."

"Dat's good." Monique sat on the chair beside the bed. "And now?" She hesitated. "Will you come 'ome wit' me?"

"I don't know. I could go home to Ontario." But maybe I wasn't ready to explain everything to my parents until I had a plan in place. I knew they would say come home and I wasn't ready to do that yet. "Um, Monique, have you ... um ... I was wondering about Jim?" Monique's face dropped. I knew how much I was hurting her, but I had to ask. "Have you heard from him?"

She pressed her lips together and turned her face away. *"Eh bien,"* she said. "Yes, I talked to 'im last night. 'E is on 'is way 'ere today, but you know it take time to get 'ere on de ferry." She swallowed hard. "I 'oped you will come to live wit' me."

"Oh, Monique. I'm sorry." I reached for her hand.

Monique's chin dropped to her chest and she let out a long sigh.

"I'm sorry, Monique. I'm so sorry, but I don't know what will happen when Jim comes. Maybe he'll want me, maybe not. Either way, I'll be okay. I can handle it now."

Monique hugged me to herself and we both struggled not to cry. "And I promise I'll visit you again in Lund, sometime soon."

Monique kissed me on the mouth. "You take care of yourself. You know you can always call me if you need me, or even if you don't need me and just want me." She swiped at her tears. "Okay, I know Jim is coming and 'e will take care of you. I will go now."

My throat was knotted up. "Thank you, Monique. Thank you."

Her chin quivered and she nodded. "Bye." At the door she turned, blew me a kiss and whispered, *"Je t'aime."*

"Love you too," I whispered.

I must have drifted off to sleep. Sometime later, I woke and saw the nurse at my bedside.

"A young man is here for you." she said. "And he's brought you a huge bouquet of orchids."

The End